More praise for *Funeral for a Dog*

"[A] complex story about how people deal with love and loss. . . . Pletzinger does an admirable job of revealing intriguing characters without being heavy-handed or coy, and the story he tells is smart and well paved, no small feat considering the large scope and the messiness of the lives chronicled. . . . [*Funeral for a Dog*] is marked by accomplished writing, a slick translation, and intelligent takes on the absurdities of contemporary life."

—*Publishers Weekly*, starred review

"Like Etgar Keret or Haruki Murakami, Pletzinger has found a translator who bridges the distance between two languages and almost makes it disappear. He should win a large, and devoted, American readership."   —Jess Row, author of *The Train to Lo Wu*

"If Thomas Pletzinger's ballsy novel is any indication, things are happening in German fiction right now that we owe it to ourselves to pay attention to."   —John Wray, author of *Lowboy*

"A love triangle. A three-legged dog. Journalism. Sex. More sex. Sex in Hamburg, sex in Finland, sex next door to Moby—Thomas Pletzinger's book has it all. A magnificent, emotional, haptic book. Actually, this is not a book, this is a rocket ship."

—Saša Stanišić, author of *How the Soldier Repairs the Gramophone*

"[*Funeral for a Dog*] employs a surprisingly unique style to advance its unusual tale of storytellers and their self-deceptions. . . . [An] undeniably uncommon journey. Pletzinger is a unique young voice emerging from the hotbed of the German literary scene."

—*Kirkus Reviews*

"We are looking at a young novelist who is going to make an amazing mark not only on German literature, but on world literature." —Gerald Stern, National Book Award–winning poet

"*Funeral for a Dog* reminds me of nothing so much as D. M. Thomas's *The White Hotel*—the same astounding and precise imagination, the unflinching eye for human misery and perseverance, the lush sensual detail and nearly fantastic sense of moving through space and time."
—Kim Barnes, author of *A Country Called Home*

"The kind of writing that makes us want to read the whole book as soon as possible." —David Varno, *Words without Borders*

"[*Funeral for a Dog* is] the rare experimental novel that, astonishingly, does not have its head up its own ass. Pletzinger has looked at the United States just as hard as he's looked at everything else, and allowed me to see my own country in a new way."
—Tom Bissell, author of *Extra Lives*

"Pletzinger's debut is a real smash hit. It's been a long time since a young German writer has thrown himself into the hurly-burly of life and literature with so much intelligence and bravado."
—Wolfgang Höbel, *Der Spiegel*

"A love triangle story, a tale of self-discovery and a mystery, drastic and hip as well as structurally sophisticated and elegantly written."
—Kirsten Riesselmann, *Der Tagesspiegel*

"Pletzinger writes a fast-paced story about cockfights, chainsaws, sex, air guitars, models, but always about love, life, happiness."
—Matthias Kalle, *Zitty Berlin*

Funeral for a Dog

A NOVEL

Thomas Pletzinger

TRANSLATED BY ROSS BENJAMIN

W. W. NORTON & COMPANY

NEW YORK   LONDON

Copyright © 2008 by Verlag Kiepenheuer & Witsch, Köln

GOETHE-INSTITUT The translation of this work was supported by a
grant from the Goethe-Institut which is funded by
the German Ministry of Foreign Affairs.

English translation copyright © 2011 by Ross Benjamin

Originally published in German under the title *Bestattung eines Hundes*.

For information about permission to reproduce selections from this book,
write to Permissions, W. W. Norton & Company, Inc.,
500 Fifth Avenue, New York, NY 10110

For information about special discounts for bulk purchases,
please contact W. W. Norton Special Sales at
specialsales@wwnorton.com or 800-233-4830

Manufacturing by Courier Westford
Book design by Lovedog Studio
Production manager: Devon Zahn

Library of Congress Cataloging-in-Publication Data

Pletzinger, Thomas, 1975–
[Bestattung eines Hundes. English]
Funeral for a dog : a novel / Thomas Pletzinger ; translated by
Ross Benjamin.
p. cm.
ISBN 978-0-393-33725-9 (pbk.)
I. Benjamin, Ross. II. Title.
PT2716.L47B4713 2011
833'.92—dc22

2010039784

W. W. Norton & Company, Inc.
500 Fifth Avenue, New York, N.Y. 10110
www.wwnorton.com

W. W. Norton & Company Ltd.
Castle House, 75/76 Wells Street, London W1T 3QT

1 2 3 4 5 6 7 8 9 0

For Carol Houck Smith

Funeral for a Dog

(On love as a relationship between the sexes there is nothing new to report, literature has depicted it in all its variations, once and for all, it is no longer a subject for literature that is worthy of the name—such pronouncements are being made; they fail to recognize that the relation between the sexes changes, that other love stories will take place.)

– Max Frisch –

hardly art, hardly garbage

– The Thermals –

Lugano, August 10, 2005

(I)

My dear Elisabeth,

You want to know where I've been? I'm sending you seven postcards and a stack of paper, 322 pages. This stack is about me. And about memory and the future. I've been reading and sorting all afternoon. You were right, Elisabeth: Svensson is a strange man, and: yes, there is a story here. Svensson's children's book is only the last chapter. He's been carrying a whole suitcase of stories around with him, a suitcase full of . . .

[Image: *Hamburg Volkspark Stadium*, aerial view, 1999]

. . . .

(II)

. . . tales told and secrets kept, full of stones and flowers. I've saved what I could. This stack of paper is my days with Svensson, my notes and interviews, Svensson's desert and his rain forest, beer cans and streamers, dogs, rats, pigeons, gulls, horses, ravens, swans, snakes, butterflies, fish, the downtrodden animals of creation (black), Svensson's dead, his Seraverde and his Williamsburg. Sometimes I feel like I'm Svensson, I've . . .

[Image: *Monte Brè at Evening*, poster by Daniele Buzzi, 1950]

(III)

. . . mixed up our stories. I asked the waiter with the sweaty mustache. *Prego,* he said, it's Wednesday. My reply: *Mille grazie e un altro bicchiere di vino per favore.* So I've fallen out of time, but now I'm back in Lugano, today is Wednesday. Black plastic ducks are floating in the pool at the Lido Seegarten, a rat . . .

[Image: *Vaccatione en Svizzera,* illustrator unknown, 1925]

. . . .

(IV)

. . . is waiting at the poolside, on the floating dock in the lake a heron is standing on green Astroturf. Time is a lake and memory a sad dog. Herons can fly extremely slowly when they want to. I've learned to observe such things again. You were right, Elisabeth: this Svensson is a strange man, but he's no stranger than the rest of us. Our stories don't fit on a newspaper page. I'm tired of newspaper pages, Elisabeth. Life is a spiral, not a line.

[Image: *Ticino Village Scene,* poster by Daniele Buzzi, 1943]

(V)

I'm eating peanuts and have been feeding them to the rat. You were right, Elisabeth: the hotel is beautiful, but it's decaying, as all beautiful things decay (roses, geraniums, plastic deck chairs). On the lakeside an old married couple is eating fish under strings of lights while Chopin plays from a tape, next to me is a freezer (the cords yanked out). The sun is setting.

[Image: *Caffè del Porto,* b/w, "Invierno 1939/40"]

. . . .

(VI)

I'm sending you our story, Elisabeth. The rest is history and blind obedience (*obbedienza cieca*), and it's rotting away with a three-legged German shepherd (Lua) at what is probably the deepest point in Lake Lugano (288 meters). No light penetrates down there, Svensson said, down there the fish are white and insanely beautiful.

[Image: *Monte Brè at Morning,* poster by Daniele Buzzi, 1950]

(VII)

Dear Elisabeth, I've learned: we don't have to make such a big deal out of everything. I'm staying a few more days. You were right: there is a good Barbaresco in this region (Taleggio & Quartirolo). No cigarettes. I kissed a small, pretty woman and meant you. I'm tired. I'm taking the train back. I've thought about it.

Minä tulen sinne, rakkain terveisin,

~~Mandelkern~~

Daniel

[Image: *Porlezza*, 2001]

August 6, 2005

(And who exactly is Daniel Mandelkern?)

Elisabeth demanded a decision, and I left our apartment without making one. It can't go on like this. My flight to Milan doesn't leave Hamburg for an hour. I'm sitting alone and completely exhausted in the waiting area at Gate 8 (on the other side of the airfield, the pines on the edge of Niendorf). At Gate 7 two Italian businesswomen are joking around. I get up, I have to move so I don't fall asleep. Somewhat farther down the corridor a newsstand: I buy a newspaper (*Süddeutsche Zeitung*), I buy a postcard (image: *Hamburg Volkspark Stadium*, aerial view, 1999), I see Semikolon brand notebooks. The only other place that carries them is a stationery store next to the Academy of Fine Arts on Lerchenfeld, which is always an all-day trip, so I buy three of them. I buy cigarettes. I'm starting to smoke again now, because smoking reduces fertility, smokers' sperm don't hold out as long (eventually their sperm give up). Cigarettes have gotten more expensive since my last pack. I buy coffee at a vending machine and go back to the gate, I tear the cellophane off the notebook and make a note of my fatigue and my headache. Then I make a note of the headlines in the *Süddeutsche Zeitung* of August 6–7, 2005:

Caesarean Risk
Craze for the Mobile Lifestyle
Air in Sunken Mini-Submarine Running Out

I'm writing because I always write when things get complicated. I'm alone, I could smoke. I could throw the notebooks into the garbage cans next to me (one red, one green, one blue, color-coded for trash separation). I should get up and go back, back to my wife.

Samsonite

How I got here: Elisabeth and I didn't raise our voices, I left our apartment in the middle of the night and without closure (we fight in our indoor voices). Took the Svensson file from the kitchen table and carried my half-packed suitcase through the hallway, but then slammed the apartment door behind me much too hard and almost ran down the street in the light drizzle. Away from Elisabeth, the sound of the ridiculous rolling suitcase on the slabs of the sidewalk behind me is louder than expected (for your reporting trips, Elisabeth had said, putting the suitcase in my office). I turned off my phone so I could ignore her calls (she'll want to have the last word, as always). Gave the taxi driver who took me from the Hoheluft Bridge to the airport an absurdly high tip (ransom). At the only staffed counter in the otherwise empty terminal, I opened my suitcase and buried my phone between suit and shirts (between recording device and shaver). I stuck my toothbrush in my shirt pocket. The ground personnel seemed to have been waiting for me. Milan? Yes. Identification? Herr Mandelkern? Yes. As I began to explain myself and my more-than-punctual arrival, the Lufthansa agent gave a routine laugh: as far as she was concerned, I could fold my whole life into my luggage as long as it stayed below the allowable weight limit (the scale showed 12.7 kilos). There was still a seat available on the earlier, direct flight, did I want it? Okay. At dawn I was the only passenger at the security checkpoint, I put the two folders full of research on Svensson next to my belt in the gray plastic tub. No, I said, I had nothing else with me (I had surrendered everything at check-in). The ring on my finger didn't set off any alarm. Now I'm sitting here at six-thirty in the Hamburg Airport in the nearly empty waiting area at Gate 8, much too early, because I left our apartment in the middle of the night and without a word. I simply left.

Dirk Svensson?

I asked last Wednesday at the weekly editorial meeting, which Elisabeth leads, because the travel assignment was listed as "Dirk Svensson" on her updated monthly schedule and followed by my name. The passing thought of getting up immediately and leaving, of refusing the assignment outright.

Dirk Svensson: Interview and Profile (*Mandelkern*)

Elisabeth and I haven't exchanged a personal word for days, and professionally she's met me with stubborn resolve for weeks. She gave me the assignment as I returned her gaze aloofly and angrily (her urgent mouth). "Dirk Svensson: Interview and Profile" means a weekend's less time for what I'd like to say privately to Elisabeth. I've heard of Svensson. You can't escape his name these days, he's written one children's book and is probably on the verge of making a fortune. I'm not interested in children's books or their authors, I don't want to write a story about this Svensson, I could have said at the editorial meeting, I want to talk to you. But I remained seated and looked first at Elisabeth (red hair tied back off her neck) and then at my feet (green flip-flops). Why now? I asked, and Elisabeth gave a completely professional answer: If the piece couldn't appear next week, she said, or the week after at the latest, then another newspaper would do the story. The appointment had presented itself today, Svensson had called and actually agreed to a meeting (the connection had been really bad). Svensson the man, Elisabeth said at the editorial meeting, the man remains hidden behind this one children's book and its sales figures. I'd started the research, but then I passed the job on to her intern, because I've never been interested in children's books. For weeks the editorial department has been abuzz with talk about him, and for weeks the story has been postponed. Svensson doesn't want to travel, he cancels all his appointments, he lives alone with his dog, and apparently this dog is everything to him (a black German shepherd with three legs). Svensson's exact place of residence is unknown to us: northeast of Milan, somewhere on Lago di Lugano. Elisabeth pushed the two black folders across the table to me. Mandelkern is the perfect man for this story, she explained at the editorial meeting, this assignment suited me better than anyone else. The trip to the anti-doping laboratory in Châtenay-Malabry would be reassigned to Harnisch, since he's a former sportswriter (Harnisch is as athletic as a pencil). I'm an ethnologist and get the strange assignments from Elisabeth: Mandelkern writes about anthropological concepts like matrilineality and male childbed, so Mandelkern meets children's book authors and their dogs. On Saturday (today) I would fly to Milan and return on Sunday (at four). Svensson is peculiar, said Elisabeth with a laugh, but profiles and strangeness are your specialties, Mandelkern.

Taleggio & Quartirolo

It's Elisabeth's diplomacy in front of our colleagues that I can't bear, her defiant diplomacy, which, to appear fair, has to be unfair (the evenly distributed green of her eyes). Her intern had done the research, printed it out, and bound it, Elisabeth said later in the hallway outside the conference room, now it was my turn. She pointed to the black folders in my hand, then her telephone interrupted us. Elisabeth answered with her first name. You'll definitely find Taleggio and Quartirolo down there, she whispered to me, as if I were running out to the Swiss gourmet deli on Grindelallee to pick up a few things (Christl's Comestibles). And Barbaresco! That was on Wednesday: she wanted to get personal, I turned around and left. On Thursday we lived alongside and past each other: Elisabeth was asleep when I got home, I was asleep when she headed out (since I started working for Elisabeth's department, our marriage has become more professional). On Friday morning we happened to meet in the kitchen. We should go out to eat tonight, I said, we can talk rationally on neutral terrain (Elisabeth's red hair in the backlight like a halo, Elisabeth is a holy witch). Elisabeth's reply: We drink too much. We don't have to drink, I said, we have to talk.

Black Dogs

We arranged to meet in an extremely loud restaurant on Paulinenplatz (mandolin music and Italian stage noise). At least it's from Italy, I said, meaning the wine. I wanted to begin the conversation with all due caution. Elisabeth's reply: Svensson doesn't have children either, even though he's a children's book author, he seems to be a strange man, maybe the two of you will get along. I noticed Elisabeth wasn't smoking. I don't think so, I shouted back, straining to laugh, he has a black dog with three legs, I'm averse to black dogs, starting with the color, black dogs stand guard at the gates of hell and wait. Elisabeth gulped her wine down quickly and refilled our glasses. I'd like to have your problems, she said, maybe there's a good story there. We ordered and gazed into our glasses (Elisabeth's slender neck when she swallows like a swan). When I asked later why it had to be this weekend, Elisabeth answered: Staff availability. Or would you have preferred to go to Châtenay-Malabry and test the moral content of Lance Armstrong's frozen urine samples?

But Elisabeth doesn't have my problems.

She ordered another wine, the same grape variety, this time a glass (Barbaresco). We still had some bottles in our apartment, Elisabeth said, and I replied only reluctantly: Okay. Not much later I opened one of those bottles and we started drinking in the kitchen (our kitchen), and didn't speak much there either (she on the glass stovetop, I on the floor next to the cases of wine). I ignored the two black folders full of research on Svensson lying on the kitchen table. She informed me she was giving up smoking, like this and that female editor, she talked about yoga and her thirty-eighth birthday. I knew all these things already, I began, these days we only spoke on this surface level, I really needed to talk again sometime to the woman I'd married, we should have an actual conversation again sometime (we're circling a child). Elisabeth stood up, put down her wine glass and took a breath:

You should actually write something good again sometime, Mandelkern!

So that she wouldn't keep talking, I stood up and tried to kiss her. We wrestled, we looked resolutely past each other, then she caught me on the upper lip with her elbow, reflexively I grabbed her wrist a bit too tightly. Her incredulous laugh as I let go of her and felt my upper lip for blood (our work is coming between our lives). Somewhat later, and finally drunk, we ended up in bed after all, for the last few weeks sex for Elisabeth and me has been a question of drunkenness, and maybe we had to ignore the condoms next to the bed (her pills in the old pencil box from school, three names carved into the back, I couldn't find much else from her life before me). As we rolled over each other and I slipped out of her for a moment, Elisabeth said: Nothing is going to grow in me today, now hold still, Mandelkern! Elisabeth suspects my plans for the childless months and years to come (up to now I haven't been able to say anything to her; I can't manage to do it). Elisabeth knows: sometimes one wrong word is all it takes, and I shrink and dwindle and get up and go to the window, only to look out at the darker end of Bismarckstrasse and say it can't go on like this (in summer you can't see the streetlights through the leaves of the chestnut trees). So I held still (so I decided to take the plane).

Daniel Daniel

Elisabeth and I live in a prewar apartment that is too large and too expensive for my means on the corner of Bismarckstrasse and Mansteinstrasse. Bedroom, living room, study. We got married in the summer of 2003. I love Elisabeth. I'm educated as an ethnologist and work as a freelance journalist writing for the culture pages. I struggle as everyone struggles. We have an empty room that we call a guest room. Elisabeth is a beautiful woman. I drive a twenty-year-old Renault 4. Maybe another life is a better life. With our salaries the only sensible thing, says Elisabeth, is for me to pay the rent and you the telephone bill. Elisabeth is the most beautiful woman I've ever lived in a prewar apartment with. For me, ethnology has nothing to do with Papua New Guinea. I wear a wedding ring on my left hand (brushed silver). Elisabeth has stopped taking the pill, now she wants a child. Elisabeth is a sober woman. She had a child, she lost it, she wants to risk it again. Nothing is going to grow in here, said Elisabeth. So I held still. Then Elisabeth cried Daniel Daniel, she cried Daniel right in my face, she must have really meant me.

Barbaresco

Stood in the hallway in front of the floor-length mirror and finished off the wine. Looked at the blood on me, the streaks next to my belly button, and from behind me Elisabeth reached into the dried blood on my cock, into her own dried blood on my cock and in my pubic hair, and said, Tomorrow in the battle think on me (my cock a blunt sword; Elisabeth and I warlike: we grind ourselves dull against each other, we strike our blades jagged). As I was about to wash off the blood in the bathroom, Elisabeth was sitting on the toilet and said, you know, Daniel Mandelkern, I'm waiting for you to decide (the bluntness of pissing women).

Yes / No / Maybe

Elisabeth was waiting for a decision, I was standing all sticky in front of the sink. She brushed her hair back behind her ears and reached for the toilet paper. Mandelkern? I must have been staring at her. Daniel? She wiped herself clean and flushed. Suddenly Elisabeth was everywhere: I saw and heard and smelled and tasted her, her blood on me, her wine in my mouth, I felt for my swollen lip, my tongue ran over the fine cut on the inside, which was still bleeding (her accidental elbow). You look like an idiot staring at a math test, said Elisabeth. Did I understand what she'd said? Yes, I said, and kept staring, no, I said, maybe (dashboardgearshift-Italy-university-Mandelkern-Hamburg-Berkeley-blood-almond-ethnology-time-Barolo-Breton-child-Renault-Anne-Laura-Eva-Hornberg-CarolinaOne-PetShopBoys-Katrin-Britta-paternoster-Kolberg-matrilineality-Geertz-Svensson-octahedron-aquarium-aquarium-couvade-Venasque-Malinowski-nostalgiatourists). One minute, I said, and spit in the bathtub. I turned my back on Elisabeth and shut the bathroom door behind me, I gathered up my scattered clothes and got the folders from the dark kitchen. Then I took the suitcase and left.

my headings, my categories

I'm actually an ethnologist. In America I'm a cultural anthropologist. I observe people, I collect conversations, I probe hierarchies, I take pictures, I sort texts, I catalogue materials, I assemble my ideas. In England I'm a social anthropologist. For almost two years I've been writing for Elisabeth's editorial department. I've questioned and profiled people for her, I've taken down life stories in shorthand and summarized worldviews, I've fulfilled her requests. I conduct interviews and write portraits, framed by days of silence in airplanes, hotels, and bus stations. I take notes because I want to put things in order (I want to sort myself out).

Why take notes instead of going back?

I hold the pen in my hand and write, I make a note of myself
(Daniel Mandelkern). I don't let much pass without remark, I
make a note of almost everything (airport terminals, newspapers, cigarette prices, black German shepherds with three legs). I
write my body: diarrhea, three-and-a-half liters of wine last night,
the two of us. I'm still waiting alone at the gate. The red wine
didn't agree with me (headache). Later I want to write Elisabeth's
hair, her blood on me, still later the chatter a few seats down, the
two Italian women are still sitting there, my Italian is miserable,
hence the word "chatter." I make a note of my anxiety, my happiness and hesitation, I write:

Elisabeth Elisabeth Elisabeth,

the third time with distinct reproach in my handwriting. I make
a note that it doesn't do you any good to be married to your
boss, that it's wrong to work for your wife, that a child won't
solve our problem. That it can't go on like this, Elisabeth! With
a paper cup of coffee and my first cigarette in months, I'm sitting
in the nonsmoking waiting area of the Hamburg Airport. I write
"nonsmoking waiting area" even though I'm now smoking, even
though no one besides me is waiting (so much for truth).

my thin skin

Why a bus now, of all things? But I can't get off and walk the
few meters to the airplane (departure begins with the hiss of the
hydraulic doors). The accordion bus only half full, with colorful
summer shirts, a few carry-on travelers and frequent fliers, most

of them on the phone. I have to put up with the rocking (in the mirror over the bus door: red wine residue on my lips). The wine didn't agree with me, the wine was just too much wine. I wonder if I should call Elisabeth. I'd wake her, and then I wouldn't be the only one feeling wretched. She'll want to go on sleeping despite her headache (our last, half-empty bottle next to the red digits of the alarm clock). I'd have to explain to her why I left. I'd have to talk about decisions and wanting a child and life plans. I'd have to tell Elisabeth I'm having doubts about marriage (about our marriage). I might utter the word "divorce," I might quote my mother: it's not what you say but how you say it. I don't call, I buried my telephone in the suitcase (such thoughts, such strategies, such cruelties).

Suomi

A few seats in front of me on the bus, a woman with a child. It's not the green of her tank top that makes me notice her. She lights a cigarette. The woman is very small, her back slightly bent, the vertebrae on the nape of her neck clearly visible, short blonde hair held back by a tacky hair band (pink roses on a black background), her flowered skirt a little too short (her feet are resting on the wheel hump). I see her from behind, I have a hard time imagining a face to go with this back and this hair band. She has no baggage, in her small hand she's holding only a pack of cigarettes and a passport (Suomi—Finland). She's smoking even though it's prohibited (like me). The boy clutches a small, light-blue backpack on his lap. Three, maybe five years old, I can't tell the ages of children (his light hair—her light hair). Hard to imagine: her body as the body of a mother. Elisabeth is longer-limbed than this woman (Elisabeth with the skin of a redhead, her age is visible only in the corners of her eyes and around the caesarean scar below her belly button). Nonsmoking bus! cries a man, but the woman ignores him and turns around to me as if I were the one who had admonished her. She smiles at me (obstinate and condescending, Elisabeth is a master of this exact same expression). The boy whispers something in her ear. The Nordic sky outside the windows hangs over the pines (airfield, Niendorf), the bright asphalt, and the engines. The woman turns back around and strokes the boy's hair, gives him the passport and the pack of cigarettes, he stows them in his backpack (she's careful not to blow smoke in his direction). The bus leans into one last turn and stops by a small plane. I'm going to take a walk around the airplane now, Mama, says the boy. He takes the backpack and climbs carefully off the bus. His eyes scrutinize his mother behind the bus window.

She stays where she is

until the driver finally asks her to get off, and she stamps out the cigarette on the airfield with her heel as pointedly as if the driver were the one in the wrong (dark-green Converse). The boy carries his small backpack up the stairs (one step at a time, his legs are too short), stops for a moment in front of the oval door and takes a big step over the threshold without looking back. Only then does she follow him, and I her.

Flight LH 3920

I ended up getting a window seat, and the airplane turns me away from the terminal. I notice a gray heron standing on the other side of the airfield, it soars into the air and disappears in the bright fog. The business travelers around me are talking on their phones, a crash caused by the use of electronic devices on board is now briefly my only worry. I don't have to be warned, even though I don't understand what telephones and computers have to do with the navigation of an airplane (I buried my telephone in my luggage). In the row in front of me, the woman in the green tank top, next to her the blond boy is standing on the seat and looking at me (light blue eyes, no resemblance in their faces). The woman climbs up on the seat too and takes a book out of the backpack in the overhead compartment (her somewhat too-round face and her tired eyes).

my own STORY

I'm preparing myself. The meticulous intern has compiled 90 pages of material, catalogues and reviews, as well as this children's book (title: *The Story of Leo and the Notmuch*). She even printed out a city map of Lugano. There's not one interview, no real profile, there are only brief bios and conjectures about Dirk Svensson. His book has so far sold more than 100,000 copies as of July 31, the publisher optimistically anticipates double that. The book is to be translated into at least 17 languages, despite the rhymes, even into Icelandic, an American edition is already available. It's already a huge success. My colleague Jagla speaks of "a relevance that is rare in children's books," the *New York Times* of "fundamental accuracy of statement, rarely found in children's literature." Who copied whom here? On top of the stack lies a message from Elisabeth: "My Mandelkern, the story of Leo and the Notmuch. You're meeting on Saturday in Lugano at the Riva Albertolli pier, right by the green pedal boats. The Hotel Lido Seegarten is beautiful. This is your story now. Think about it! Elisabeth."

Think about it, Mandelkern!

She must have added the note before our fight. My Mandelkern! Think about it! 90 pages of children's book reviews, Elisabeth's enclosed commanding tone, an ambiguous assignment, my relegation to the countryside. Elisabeth demanded a decision, I resisted (my spitting, turning around, closing the doors). On instructions from my wife and superior, with a printed-out city map on a plane to Milan, on the way to a boat dock in Lugano, below us Niendorf and farther down Eimsbüttel and the Alster (my window and the ducking pines on the edge of the airfield, the howling takeoff, no complications). Elisabeth will be waking up now and vomiting the wine; she drinks so she can listen without correcting me. I drink so I can talk and not just have to listen; yesterday she drank more than I did. Then the clouds between us and the earth, the disappearance of the Fasten Seatbelts sign, a stewardess who's at least sixty years old, two mineral waters for the headache. I read in the research folders: Lake Lugano is a lake in the south of the canton of Ticino, half in Switzerland and half in Italy, named after the city of Lugano, also known as Lago Ceresio, deepest point 288 meters. Hermann Hesse lived in Montagnola in the hills overlooking the lake (and who exactly is this Svensson? my wife's large handwriting quotes me on a photocopied page). Elisabeth's professional instructions: a profile of 3,000 words. In the roar of the airplane the small woman in front of me reads to the small boy from a book: *The Story of Leo and the Notmuch*, she reads, begins like this.

Who exactly is Daniel Mande

A journalist on a business trip in an airpl

dried blood on his hands (Elisabeth, I think, E

me that the small woman is reading Svensson's o

of all things, to the boy. I stand ducking in front of

and scrutinize myself: I look tired, unshaven, and hungover

wine stain on my white shirtsleeve, flip-flops on my feet, my su

pants open. I ask myself in the mirror—I ask you, Elisabeth—how

it could have gone this far. In the much too low-ceilinged airplane

bathroom of flight LH 3920, bent over and with a forced smile, I

wonder when we lost our first names. We were once able to talk

to each other, we were once the same age, we once knew who we

were (we were once: us).

We once knew each other, Elisabeth!

I hold my shirt up under my chin and try to get the blood off my

belly and out of my pubic hair with paper towels, but the towels

come apart and crumble. Your blood won't go away. I feel the fine

cut in my upper lip, the plane must already be in the airspace over

Frankfurt, but the word "divorce" hangs persistently in the air

(the possibility of another life). When someone knocks a second

time on the bathroom door, I pull my ring off my finger and stick

it in my pants pocket (E. E. E.). I roll up my shirtsleeves and brush

my teeth with water (the small, pretty mother shouldn't see the

red wine).

DOG

lkern?
ne bathroom, his wife's
isabeth). It confuses
hildren's book,
he mirror
a red

ay makes an old

in the moonlight),

a family album. A

d much too real for

been a thick blanket of

man looks at me a bit too

long as she passes ... bathroom (she's changed
her hair band). I'm only on this pl... , I think, because my boss
has given me this annoying assignment. Instead of talking to my
wife, I'm on the way to Lugano. My wedding ring is in my pants
pocket, but Elisabeth's blood couldn't be washed off. The small
woman smiles, I smile back. The pilot's announcement interrupts
our look: we're flying over the St. Gotthard Pass, he says, below
us the north-south weather divide. I look out the window, the
blanket of clouds breaks over the rugged mountains. Behind us I
can still make out veils of rain, toward the south the mountains
are in sunlight, deserted, the roads and paths hard to distinguish
(scattered houses). If she and I lived down there, I think, no one
would know us (another life).

Caesarean Risk

is printed on the front page of the *Süddeutsche*. On my right a man
stirring salt into his tomato juice, then vodka. An article on birth
rates and caesarean statistics. After the first operation women are

less likely to get pregnant again, it reads. It's possible that women intentionally avoid another pregnancy because the caesarean was such a negative experience, says Siładitya Bhattacharya, of the University of Aberdeen. Due to pains and inflammations that occur after the operation, women often don't wish to give birth again. Elisabeth wants to risk it again (drinking on flights, headaches). I ask for another water with the cheese sandwich (the habit of taking an interest in the local cuisine when traveling; Taleggio and Quartirolo, Elisabeth loves cheese). Once Elisabeth ordered eight cases of Barbaresco at Christl's Comestibles on Grindelallee, and I felt like a child signing for the delivery.

(making connections where there are no connections)

While the pretty mother reads to the boy, I leaf through the book and look at the pictures. At one point her reading voice breaks off and the boy starts over from the beginning. I read on. *Leo and the Notmuch*, the five-year-old Leo loses his best friend (is death for children like moving away?). For a whole summer he sits in his room and makes up stories. When his mother knocks and asks what he's doing in his room, he answers: not much. Does he miss his friend? Not much, always: not much. Leo's stories are the Notmuch (what kind of an idea is a Notmuch? It's not nothing, at least).

Daniel & Mandelkern

Before my eyes this image remains: a man named Mandelkern lies still on his back (me), a woman named Elisabeth comes, straddling him, staring into the emptiness of her head, clasps her ankles with her hands (you). Several times she screams his first name into the air between them, and when he later asks the reason why (why Daniel Daniel), she answers that she always thinks that when he doesn't talk back to her. Elisabeth laughs, Mandelkern doesn't.

Lost & Found

My baggage has not arrived in Milan, I'm informed by the woman working at the Lost & Found, at least that's what the system says. The suitcase is probably in Frankfurt, most likely due to the last minute rebooking, I arrived earlier than my baggage. There is no sense in cursing now. I leave the address of the hotel: *Hotel Lido Seegarten, Viale Castagnola 24, CH-6906 Lugano* (I'll have to record the interview with pen and paper).

Aeroporti Milano Malpensa

With my plastic bag on a bench next to the bus stop (the airport building dull green, fields of light and glass facades). "The best Malpensa-Lugano connection is the Airport Express!" reads the itinerary that Elisabeth's intern wrote (a greasy person with a telephone voice and an absurd talent for data banks and time-tables). Not far away the small woman in the tank top again, now holding the sleepy boy's hand. She brushes a damp strand of hair from his forehead with her index finger and looks into the emptiness beyond the buses; she is his mother (but above all she has an inscrutable beauty, a slender beauty). Her legs are short, but much too delicate to seem ungraceful. She looks over at me briefly, then she disappears behind a bus (www.airportbus.ch). I could carry her suitcase (I could offer her my life), but she's apparently traveling without baggage.

Biglietto di andata no 133567

Il biglietto di corsa semplice è valido per il giorno cui è stato rilasciato. La mancata effettuazione del viaggio per causa di forza maggiore o per fatto proprio del passagero non dà diritto ad alcun rimborso, né alla proroga di validità.

Malpensa—Chiasso—Lugano

Sometimes people find themselves on a journey together. To my surprise, the small, pretty woman with the boy gets on the bus to Lugano too, this time she's sitting a few rows behind me. The bus follows entrance ramps onto the highway, traveling at first over flat land (prefab warehouses, Parmalat and Danone factories, palm trees), at one point through a residential area (the backs of five-story houses, laundry between the windows, lots of pink). I read on in the Svensson file: Dirk Svensson, born in 1973 in the Ruhr area and grew up there, the photo in the publisher's catalogue shows him smiling in front of a stone house, he's wearing a shirt with rolled-up sleeves and suit pants. He's kneeling next to a black dog (you can't tell if it has only three legs: Svensson is blocking the view). His biography sounds like mine (his shirt rolled up like mine). At Chiasso on the Swiss border, the boy stands on the seat and takes the passports out of his backpack, his mother is asleep now (years ago I learned a smattering of Finnish). I hold up Svensson's book and wink at him, the boy raises his hand (then the bus station on the mountain over the city, the water is shining in the sun like metal, the boats on it like scratches). When we get off the bus and the boy actually waves good-bye to me, I could go over and speak to the two of them, I could offer the small, pretty mother a cigarette, but she pulls the boy across the plaza toward the city and disappears into a gray concrete entrance (Funicolare, pigeons). I take a taxi to Piazza Manzoni and sit down in a café (three mineral waters, the possibility of another life).

Piazza Manzoni, Lugano, 2:30 PM

I'm waiting for Svensson. I'll have two hours to ask my questions. Actually, I should skim through the file one more time, but in my fatigue the letters blur (headache). I wait with a view of the fountain. Lugano is a city that is aware of its beauty: through a gap between the houses shimmers the lake, at times a blindingly white sail, chestnuts, ginkgos and palm trees in the early afternoon light. I could get up and leave the folders here, I could wait in the hotel for the return journey (I could refuse). The sun slants steeply on the cobblestones, children and pigeons under the tables, the sparrows on the breadbaskets of the cafés are casually waved away (friendly sparrows are compliments). The light green of the branches hanging toward the water, a boy is feeding swans (8) hamburger buns from a McDonald's bag, couples have their photos taken in front of the fountain (their faces happy for the duration of the picture). I'm much too early here too. I think of Elisabeth and the numbness that my departure has left behind. Then, despite everything: that I'm not appropriately dressed for an interview (flip-flops and red wine stains). In the Manor department store I buy a clean shirt, I buy another pack of cigarettes (Muratti 2000), I buy postcards (image 1: *Monte Brè at Evening*, image 2: *Vacation in Switzerland*, image 3: *Ticino Village Scene*— all three: Museum of Design, Zurich). I walk along the shore in the direction of the casino, at the Riva Albertolli I sit down on a bench by the water (red; the last surge of pain directly above my

nose). The green pedal boats lie waiting in the water, reluctantly
I write down

—Who exactly is Dirk Svensson?
—Why should I be the one to ask him this question?
—Where does he live and why there?
—How does he live?
—Why a children's book?
—Is Svensson first and foremost an author or illustrator?
—Can you be two things at the same time?

and suddenly there's the small, pretty woman with the boy (ice
cream on his T-shirt) sitting two benches down. She wipes his
mouth clean and then licks his ice cream off her finger, she takes a
cigarette out of his backpack. She looks over at me, and this time
she laughs. In front of her stands a small suitcase. Up to this point
we've taken the same path, but soon I'll meet Svensson. We'll go
our separate ways, we'll have to part. I concentrate and write

—Can you want two things at the same time?
—Does the black dog really exist? And if so:
—Where is its fourth leg?
—Who exactly is Daniel Mandelkern?

Lua

I'm early, Svensson is early. There really is a black dog with
three legs standing on the deck and coughing as the boat docks
(*Macumba* in blue writing on the pale wood). Dirk Svensson
pushes the gearshift into neutral with the ball of his thumb and

throws the line to me (the children's book author in a purple T-shirt and taller and heavier than in the pictures). Hello, I say, it's very nice to meet you. Svensson shuts off the outboard and doesn't reply, he's wearing a cap (Los Angeles Lakers, the purple faded, but not the gold). Daniel Mandelkern, I say, but Svensson is looking past me. *Macumba* scrapes along the green pedal boats. Svensson suddenly ignores his boat, he gives me a nod, me and my tugging at the rope, he climbs across a few pedal boats to the shore. The small, pretty woman with the boy is still sitting two benches down, she's sitting there in her green, in her beauty, and waiting with the boy in the shade of a linden tree. Svensson leaves me standing there and goes to her (remain polite and get all this over with). Tuuli, he says, and reaches for her wrist and the nape of her neck. The woman gets up, Svensson pulls her up, her back bolt upright, the dog coughs, the dirty swans of Lugano hiss, yellowed as if from cigarettes, the dog barks. Quiet, Lua, says Svensson, quiet.

Shut up and play

THE CITY IS FUNCTIONING AGAIN, THE GARBAGE IS GETTING collected, the Brooklyn-Queens Expressway is drivable again, and there are cars on it. The wreckage is being removed, they've stopped searching for survivors. My goal tonight is to remove the last splinters of the past few weeks, so I close the door from outside and buy another beer at Giacomo's. Eventually I've had as much as I can take, so I hail a taxi at the entrance ramp and say, Enid's, at which point the driver turns around and asks why I want to visit his mother, and when I look at him blankly, he says it was only a joke. Great joke, taxi driver with cowboy hat, I think, today I'm in no mood for jokes, today I'm in the mood for a tabula rasa. Lua is black, at night he can hide unnoticed in the taxi's footwell despite his size, he waits on the roadside and jumps into the car when I open the door. I say, Enid's, the bar, please, Manhattan Avenue, next exit, and so that he doesn't ask any more questions but instead keeps listening to country as if I weren't there at all, I say that I stepped on a nail, inflamed wound, that makes even the shortest distance too far. I understand, says the taxi driver, my mother, God bless her, was named Enid, that's why. Seventeen years ago she was run over with seven shopping bags in her arms in front of Zabar's on the Upper West Side, on my birthday. By a Pakistani taxi driver. The shopping bags were for my birthday party. Really? I ask. Really, he says, that's why I became a taxi driver, the Pakistanis and Indians and blacks drive

like Italians. I'm out here to keep the streets clean. Really? I ask.
Really, he says, and after his mother's death he just stopped going
to school, good Lord, maybe it's a coincidence, on his birthday
and the anniversary of his mother's death someone wants a ride
to a bar named Enid's. Would he mind not talking so much, I ask,
I have my own problems. The taxi driver takes off his cowboy
hat and looks in the rearview mirror, he's not much older than
I, in New York there's usually a language barrier between driver
and passenger, for the safety of both. But today the taxi driver,
according to his ID card, is one Jack Vonderlippe, stuck to his
Plexiglas window are stars and stripes and pictures of the New
York fire department and police, New York's Finest. A New York
taxi driver named Vonderlippe, and there's even a little flag
dangling from the mirror with the inscription "Don't mess with
Texas—not even in NYC!"

I take a sip from my beer can, Vonderlippe looks at me in the
rearview mirror. No open containers in the car, he quotes in a
dull voice, no open containers, no animals, no weapons, says
Vonderlippe with the law behind him. Laws are in vogue these
days, Lua barks. I can't close the beer can, I say, at which point
Vonderlippe says that he has to expel me from the vehicle anyway
because of the dog. Okay, I say, nothing can be done about it,
sometimes there's no way back, once something's open it's open,
at least when it comes to beer cans. In the middle of the BQE
Vonderlippe puts on his hazard lights and pulls over. Couldn't
you at least let me out at the next exit? I ask, but Vonderlippe
just shakes his head, this is no time or place for compromises, so
Lua and I get out. Vonderlippe immediately drives off and leaves
us with my beer can in the middle of a bridge over the roofs of
Brooklyn, good luck with your foot, he yells out the window.
Happy birthday, asshole, I shout, and want to throw the beer

can after him, but these days overreactions lead to nothing but trouble. And I don't have a nail in my foot anyway, I think, I have a splinter in my heart, my God, I'll just walk.

Lately I've been avoiding walking to Enid's, the way there leads past too much. On the bridge there's no shoulder to speak of, the cars honk, a helicopter with a searchlight flies over me, but they're not searching for people with beer cans, they're searching for terrorists. My telephone rings, it's Tuuli or Felix, I don't answer. Since Monday I've stopped answering when Tuuli or Felix calls. Today is Saturday, on Monday I moved out. Because of Tuuli and Felix I've stopped walking to Enid's, my old apartment on Lorimer Street stands in the way, the two of them are living there for now. They lugged his old leather suitcase up the stairs, his cameras and Tuuli's books, Tuuli her pregnant belly. I liked the apartment, the three rooms and the leaky roof, the smell of the bakery, but eventually there's only so much you can take. I left on friendly terms, at least it looks that way, the lease is still in my name, the telephone too. Now I live with Lua on a sofa owned by a sculptor who's in Holland welding scrap metal into art in public space. When Tuuli or Felix calls, *Svensson Home* comes up on the display, but I don't want to talk to Tuuli or Felix. We're not alone, we're three, we said, but we miscalculated.

Pressed against the plastic guardrail, Lua and I slowly make our way across the bridge and jump down the slope on the other side. In a few weeks the three of us will be four. The telephone rings again, I trip over some black plastic bags and spill beer on my pants, but I don't answer. When I find a hole in the barbed wire for Lua, I cut my hand, and when I myself land on the sidewalk, I twist my ankle. I curse and Lua barks. Apparently I'm in Greenpoint. That's good, that's where I wanted to be. Under a streetlight two old men are sitting in wheelchairs and smoking,

I ask them for the time and for cigarettes. The younger one says, almost midnight. I don't smoke, but for weeks I've been pocketing one cigarette after another. I collect cigarettes. First you're a nonsmoker, and then suddenly you're collecting cigarettes. Tuuli will eventually want to start smoking again, and then I'll be able to offer her some. I ask where Manhattan Avenue is and the older of the two old men says, the hospital's that way, as he gives me the cigarette. Are you okay, young man? The other old man gives me a light. My hand is bleeding on the cigarette and on my shirt, Lua and I are limping, I have a beer can in my hand and a cigarette in my mouth, I inhale and inadvertently cough smoke into the face of the man in the wheelchair. No time for the hospital, I cough, we still have something to take care of.

By the time we get to Enid's the beer can is empty, and I buy a Rolling Rock at the bar. What happened to you, asks the bartender. Nothing, I say, and as a matter of fact for a few weeks not much has been happening. Tuuli, who may be the love of my life, and my friend Felix are making phone calls on my dime, they're probably fucking between calls, Felix is probably fucking Tuuli surrounded by my furniture, my books. Tuuli is seven months pregnant, Felix is taking care of Tuuli, I now take care of the dog. They always call me when they've finished fucking, *Svensson Home* appears on my display. But because eventually there's only so much grieving you can take, tonight I'm wearing Tuuli's purple T-shirt, that's a first step away from the widower I am. I have to give things new meaning, I think, on the purple you can scarcely see the blood-stains. Can I quickly wash the blood off myself in the back? I ask, and the bartender says, sure, honey, but it actually looks really good on the purple. Of course, I think, wounds and scars make a man interesting, my blood is a fashion statement. The bartender is probably a fashion designer, and fashion is going crazy, so the bartender is going crazy. In the Enid's storeroom I wash the blood off my fingers. What madness, I think, and watch myself in the fluorescent light over the mirror as I down the new beer in one swig. My telephone rings, *Svensson Home*. I don't answer, I take another bottle of Rolling Rock out of a case. Tomorrow I'll get a haircut, I think, holding my hand next to my face, the blood from the cut mingles with the water. I look myself in the eyes and ask myself how it could have gone this far. From the hole in my hand blood is running down my arm and dripping into the sink. Nena is playing in the bar, here in Enid's they're at the forefront of retro, time is passing much too quickly for me too, and as I watch myself burping and crying, there's a woman with a camera standing behind me, she brushes my hair from my forehead, just a second, please, she says, can you stay like that?

Two hours later Lua and I are sitting on a stoop next to Enid's. The woman with the camera is taking pictures, I open another beer. She's wearing black pants and a black blouse, she has black curly hair and dark eyes, her laughter flashes in the darkness. My hand has stopped bleeding. Lua gets up, hobbles across the street and through an open steel door into the Polish bakery and comes back with a loaf of bread. A baker chases him into the street, fucking dog, he shouts, and stops when he sees the woman with the camera. She takes pictures. It's all just a fashion statement, absolutely, I say to Lua. We share the bread and the beer, and maybe the dog says, strange times. At which point I raise my drink to him and he takes another bite. Lua reserves his wisdom for the decisive moments, I'm drunk and full of resolutions. Things have to be different from now on, I say to Lua, and kiss him on his scruff, but how's Tuuli doing? No idea, says Lua, why don't you ask her. And how am I supposed to do that? Call, says Lua, or even simpler: pick up the phone! But it's not that simple,

I think, don't pick up under any circumstances, I resolve, today
the splinter is getting removed. Lua puts his foreleg on my knee
and looks into the camera. Stay like that, says the woman with
the camera, you two look good. Can you give the dog some more
beer? she asks, and takes pictures. When the dog is drunk, I say,
we have good conversations. A dog isn't a parrot, says the woman.
Lua got some bread, I say, petting the dog between the ears. You
know, Lua, I say, lately I haven't been getting enough sleep, lately
I haven't really been myself. Come with me, the woman with the
camera says, and walks to a Polish corner store two blocks down,
you can't go to a party empty-handed. So we buy two six-packs.

A GIRL WITH RED hair and a birdcage without a bird is climbing
the stairs behind us and says, I've lost hope. What? asks a short
Mexican guy with a pink water gun in his hand. On the top floor
it's loud, everywhere people are raising their arms to the music,
everyone's wearing white. I've lost hope, repeats the girl with the
birdcage. Let's hope I get the bastard, says the Mexican, hiding
behind a sofa on which some people in white are balancing with
their arms in the air. Kiki Kaufman, says the host to the woman
with the camera, kissing her on the neck. He apparently knows
Lua too, good evening, Mr. Dog, he says. Lua doesn't say anything,
but instead lies down in the middle of the loft under a gigantic,
dust-brown Christmas tree with purple glass ball ornaments.
Behind a cardboard Dolph Lundgren, a tall black guy in a white
shirt is kneeling on the floor, he leaps over Lua in a single bound
and aims his Super Soaker full of red wine at the Mexican guy,
who defends himself. Showdown, he yells, die, motherfucker,
die! They both empty their magazines, boom, boom, bye-bye,
shouts the black guy, cha-cha-cha, yells the Latino. White is inno-
cence and red is war, says the host, with red wine you see the hits

better, there's beer in the bathtub, and yes, there's a truckload of plastic toys hanging on the walls, salvage items, there's liquor on the roof, don't ash on the Christmas tree, it's four years old, fire-extinguishing water is in the buckets by the window, piss from the roof into the neighbor's garden in the back. I'm Pierre, says the host, make yourself at home. Take care of yourself, says Kiki Kaufman. Pierre grabs her hand and pulls her along behind him onto the roof. I'm Svensson, I say. I've lost hope, sings the girl with the birdcage. Want a beer anyway? I ask, but she dances through the room and isn't listening to me anymore. On the edge of the bathtub a gorgeous Chinese girl in a snow-white suede coat is sitting and cooling her feet in the beer bottles. My shoes are too small, she says. You can have mine, I say.

From the roof you can see the island behind the bridges and the smokestacks of the empty factories on the riverbank. We're sitting on the edge, behind us two Russians are playing Ping-Pong. We're drinking gimlets, and the girl with the red hair puts down the rusty birdcage on the tar paper, fuck off, will you, says one of the Russians, her search for hope is interfering with his serve. Lawyer, says a long-haired guy in a white suit and metal tie, Morgan Stanley. Illustrator, says a guy named Christoph, and the ice cubes clink in the vase he's drinking from, *New Yorker* and *New York Times* and this and that, he says. The Mexican guy pees off the roof, the red wine stains on his shirt look like my fashion statement. The guy with the Super Soaker gives him a whack in the face, order must be maintained, he yells, cha-cha-cha, shouts the Mexican, and the two of them dance over the abyss. The roof trembles, Pierre weaves a wreath for Kiki out of hanging gera-niums and says, Morgan Stanley has been flattened, they were in the South Tower, at which point the long-haired guy in the white suit loosens his metal tie and says, everything's going to be okay. My telephone vibrates, *Svensson Home,* to answer would be too simple, it would be too easy. I sit on the edge and think about what the metal-tie man said. What exactly is going to be okay? I think, and how, I wonder, and where is Tuuli right now, I'm always wondering where Tuuli is. Kiki gives me a book, writes "646-299-1036 Kiki Kaufman!" in it, and I put it in my jacket pocket.

I drink another glass and lie down on my back, I look into the sky, into the clouds, I haven't been this drunk in a long time, I'm smoking one of Tuuli's cigarettes, I notice that I feel my feet less and less. Why does Tuuli always have to call when they've finished fucking surrounded by my books, I wonder, can someone that pregnant still fuck, or is it only Felix on the phone, wanting to know what Tuuli's favorite breakfast is? Tuuli eats cold pizza with capers for breakfast, she drinks her coffee with milk and no sugar, she hates nail scissors but tolerates nail clippers. She feels at home when she eats snails. Her father has a snail farm in Lapland. I know how she folds sheets and that she sings the Finnish national anthem when the weather's bad and seriously believes that will make it better. I know that she thinks Felix kisses like a rock and I like a cup of tea. She told me that, definitely didn't tell him. I know all this and also that we miscalculated, we're three, we said, we're not alone. A hand gives me a light. If Felix only knew that he kisses like a rock, but I won't tell him.

It smells like autumn, it is autumn, I hear people talking, I see people dancing, the music is playing far away, Kiki with the geranium wreath and the camera is holding my hand, I close my eyes. How long it's been since everything has spun like this! Kiki lets go of my hand, the dog lies down between us, I plant a foot to stop the spinning. Take it easy, says the dog, everything all right? Yup, I say, today the thorn is getting taken out. Do you like pizza? asks the dog. Yes, please, I say, with capers, then I can save a piece for Tuuli. The dog licks my ear. Mr. Dog, I say, how I'd like a slice of pizza right now, how I'd like to be somewhere else right now. Then let's go, says Lua, licking my face, the taxi's waiting below, he says, and when he takes my hand and the telephone vibrates and I open my eyes, when the Chinese girl in the suede coat suddenly flicks her tongue in my ear, nothing is spinning anymore. I'm Svensson, by the way, I say. Grace, says Grace. I'm going to get some pizza, I say to Kiki and Lua, but Kiki and her geranium wreath are nowhere to be seen, and Lua under the Christmas tree doesn't wake up until I'm climbing in my socks down the fire escape behind Grace and getting into the back of a taxi. West Eleventh and Greenwich, Grace says to the driver, Lua performs his taxi trick, Grace kisses me, and the girl with the red hair buckles up the birdcage next to us as if it were a person. Okay, I think. The taxi is crossing a bridge to Manhattan, I'm hungry, the telephone is ringing, and I don't answer, have you found hope? I ask. In the front the girl with the red hair sings her reply, and Grace tastes like smoke.

My pizza is called Earth Mother, and I take it to go. The girl with the red hair and her cage got out along the way. I was asleep on the edge of the roof longer than I thought. I have to piss. In the bathroom of Two Boots in the West Village, I put my shoes back on, check my teeth in the mirror and tense my abs. I hold my telephone over the toilet bowl, but then just turn it off. Grace and Lua are waiting outside with the pizza. We turn the corner onto Waverly Place, it looks like something out of an American film set in Paris. Small trees are growing out of the sidewalk, the street is a miniature boulevard, the garbage truck is blinking orange and collecting the black bags from the sidewalk in front of the cafés. Under a streetlight Grace stops and asks, my place or yours, and I ask, where do you live? Here, she says, and points to number seven, and I'm not wearing anything underneath. Grace puts down the pizza box, lifts her suede skirt and takes my hands. She really doesn't have anything on. Grace kisses me, she bites my neck, she pushes me past the streetlight and against the glass door. I'm hungry, I say, the pizza's getting cold, but as Grace breathes heavily in my ear I notice I'm getting hard. She breathes directly into my ear, makes soft squealing sounds and fumbles with my pants button. Lua is standing under a streetlight, the garbage men are watching us, I say. I just wanna fuck you right here, Grace says, and sounds like an actress. From an upstairs window comes "Downtown Train," Tom Waits's voice and the French scenery get mixed up, I take my hands off Grace's naked ass under the suede skirt and her hands off me, let's go upstairs, I say, and Grace jiggles the key in the lock.

In the hallway she briefly lifts her skirt again and looks me directly in the eyes, I have to decide and vacillate as quickly as possible between eyes and shaved patch, which is narrower than Tuuli's. I come to rest on her mouth and kiss Grace against the elevator door, this time longer and deeper. My hand searches for her narrow butt, finds it and conforms to it. The elevator's out of order, says Grace, her fingers above us clawing into the elevator grate. Okay, race you, I say, okay, carry me up, says Grace, and Grace is calling the shots here. She bites and then clings to my neck, until on the fourth floor I can no longer breathe. I put her down. Lua is already there, yawning. Grace points to a door and says, that's where Moby lives. Who's Moby? The singing vegetarian, she says. Does Moby want my cold pizza? I ask, and take the box from Grace's hand, or does he only eat plankton? Plankton? Grace takes back the box, that's the sort of thing you find funny, is it? Yup, I say, and pound the artichoke-shaped doorknocker against

Moby's door. *Ist Moby dick?* I ask, and bound up the stairs, Grace runs after me, but no one opens Moby's door. Moby is on tour, says Grace, and tries to take off my T-shirt. Then we can listen to loud music, I say, opening the pizza box. In it there are a garlic shaker and a very small pair of orange underpants. I hold the underpants in the air. When did you take these off? I ask. Outside the pizzeria, says Grace. And no one saw? I unlock Grace's door. Maybe, she says, there's something to drink in the fridge.

When I enter the bedroom with a container of milk, Grace is standing in the middle of the room between her suede skirt and her white shirt. In the corner stands a giant porcelain greyhound, Lua is lying next to it and sleeping, Grace is posing like a ring card girl. I meant the vodka, she says. Milk is good for you, I say, and give her the container. She sits down on the bed and as she drinks the milk, her nipples get erect. She's taller than Tuuli, I think, but just as thin. She sits cross-legged on the bed, her labia are unexpectedly dark, three stars are tattooed under Grace's left breast, one red, one yellow, one green.

I stand with the pizza box in the room, and Grace says, get undressed, you idiot! She puts the milk on the floor and ties her hair back with a rubber band. Nice stars, I say, standing on one leg, and kick my pants over to her clothes. One for each love, says Grace. Where are they now? I ask. Not here, says Grace, pulling me onto the bed and between her legs. She does that much too soon, the pulling me between her legs, she kisses me, she almost devours me, she swallows me, she clings to my shoulder, and I can't stop it or help it. I kiss back, but I don't kiss big enough for her, things aren't moving fast enough for her, fuck, let's get this going, she says, pushes me off her and turns me on my back, she lets down her hair. Faster than I can think she has my cock in her mouth, her hair brushes against my belly. Grace, I say, putting my hand on her forehead to stop her brushing and breathing and squealing and her up and down, even though I'm not supposed to object to it, even though it should sound good. Grace, I say, but that doesn't sound right either. Bullshit, says Grace with my cock in her mouth, and keeps going. Stop, I say, but she doesn't stop until I take her head in both hands and stare into her eyes, maybe a bit too dramatically. My wet cock lies cold on my belly. The pizza, I say. I hear myself talking and don't like what I hear. Grace ties her hair back again. You're weird, she says. The pizza, I say, all words fail me except "pizza," and so we share her slice, then Grace goes into the bathroom and gets an Advil. Want one too? she calls out, and once again she's faster than I. She comes back, draws the curtains, turns around, and strokes herself between her legs, I'm still wet, she smiles. No, thanks, I say, meaning the headache pills, and Grace turns away and washes down her Advil with milk, before long she's asleep, her mouth slightly open, her stars in the dawn.

I OPEN MY EYES and for a few seconds don't know where I am. Grace turns her back to me, from the nape of her neck to her tailbone seventeen Chinese characters. Get out of here, I think, just get out, because I want to think this thought, and I take the milk and what's left of the Earth Mother, take my T-shirt and shoes and run into the porcelain dog in the dark. I close the door softly and get dressed only once I'm in the stairwell. It says *Grace Chan* on the door of apartment 4F. I feel my pulse in my hand again, my ankle hurts, I have a headache. I walk along Waverly Place and want to hail a taxi, want to go home, but where is my home? I think. It should be with Tuuli and Felix, that's what we said, but it's not there anymore, and no taxis are stopping. Fucking cabbie bastards, I shout. That's right, says a woman in high heels standing outside the pizzeria, and I walk uptown toward Chelsea.

In front of a French bakery a Chihuahua barks at me as if I were a bum. Someone has tied him to a streetlight. I talk to dogs now, I remember, and say politely, *bonjour, Monsieur Dog*, but the Chihuahua doesn't reply, he just barks. Nothing is simple, I say, just look at all this shit: things can't go on like this, you should have seen this woman, she takes off her panties in the pizzeria, and I make stupid jokes and forget Lua in her living room. I kneel down on the ground next to the Chihuahua, he looks at me and growls. You know, I say, Tuuli and Felix are fucking their brains out in my apartment, even though they're expecting a child, and I'm accomplishing nothing here, nothing at all. The dog tilts his head, he's wearing a green collar. Things can't go on like this, can they? I ask, and feel my tears coming. Nice collar, by the way, I say to the Chihuahua, offering him some of the milk, he doesn't drink. You know, I say, I want to get rid of this feeling, I want nothing more to do with the two of them, I don't want to always remember them, I don't want to think of Tuuli every fucking minute and of Felix every other one, I want, I want, oh, I have no idea. I'm kneeling in a blood-smeared T-shirt next to a streetlight in the West Village, talking to a Chihuahua and wiping away my tears when a little girl holding two baguettes comes out of the bakery and says, you talking to my dog, mister? and the ring of the bell when she opens the door feels like a slap in the face.

ON A PLAYGROUND at the edge of the West Village, I'm sitting on the end of a metal slide and finally eating the pizza when two guys climb through the hole in the fence, hey, Yo-Yo, what do you think of Bird? says the first one, a short, stout Mexican guy. Yo-Yo snatches the basketball from his hands and bounces it twice through his legs. He looks me in the eyes, I chew the pizza. Hey, Yo-Yo, says the Mexican guy, what do you think of Larry Bird? Yo-Yo dribbles two more times and says, he got nothin', Eduardo. Yo-Yo shoots and scores, and Eduardo in baggy pants comes over to me. Hey, white boy, what do you think of Larry Bird? He doesn't look at me, he looks past my eyes at my left ear. Larry Bird is the best player of his generation, I say with my mouth full. What? asks the Mexican guy. Yo-Yo is standing behind him, spinning the ball in his hands. You've got to be kidding, I think, drinking the rest of the milk, you've got to be kidding, the short, stout one is talking, and the tall one is waiting and playing, and in a moment the short, stout one will threaten me, and the tall one will want to play me for honor or my nuts, I think, putting the milk down between my feet. Afterward I'll be told never to show my face on this playground again, because this is their turf, those are the rules in the ghetto, those are the rules on television. What? asks the Mexican guy again, what did you just say? and his voice makes a small leap. Listen, kid, I say, not meaning Eduardo or Yo-Yo, but rather myself and that I'm sitting on a metal slide and eating pizza while Grace is asleep upstairs. Okay, I think, I have a headache and blood stains on my T-shirt, I'm drunk, and Tuuli and Felix are playing by their own rules in my apartment, under my roof, and if this is all a game, then I'm up for it, I'll play along. I say, Larry Bird was the most complete player of his generation, and your mother saw it on television and cried with joy, I say, since she definitely can't read, so shut up and play. Eduardo laughs and spits on the pavement. Yo-Yo stares at me, now he's spinning the ball on his finger. What are you doing here, white boy? asks Eduardo, as if he didn't hear me, he's not talking to me, he's just talking, wasn't that your mother calling you a minute ago to come home and fuck her? Is your father shitfaced again?

Shut up and play, I say, taking fifteen dollars out of my pants pocket, your mother, your father, your sister, if I win, the money stays here along with yours, and you do a job for me tonight. I put the money on the ground between my feet and place the milk container on top of the bills. To eleven, says Eduardo, throwing fifteen dollars in the pot. Rule one: whoever scores keeps the ball, two: it's a foul when I say so, and three: if you lose, you fuck off. Got it, I say, and Yo-Yo asks, you drinking milk, pansy ass?

Yo-Yo and I play in jeans, Eduardo sits on the slide and smokes, foul, he says. Yo-Yo has a good inside game, Yo-Yo can jump, but Yo-Yo has no outside shot. I have the ball and fake Yo-Yo out with a crossover, the first shot goes in from the free-throw line, a moment later one from outside, two points, then I score again from the left, I'm winning three nothing, crybaby, I say, wimp, pussy, come on! I say to Yo-Yo, come on. I drive past Yo-Yo with the ball through my legs, seven nothing. Yo-Yo grins at me and throws the ball at my knees. I catch it and am about to drive past him on the right, I think, today the thorn is coming out, tonight these two will carry my sofa out of the Lorimer Street apartment, they don't look like movers for nothing. I see them carrying the boxes of books, the records, and for a brief moment I know I'm going to win, but on the very next offensive possession Yo-Yo's hand comes down past the ball on my arm. I miss my shot, I shout, that's a foul, asshole, and Yo-Yo snags the ball from the backboard. Ref didn't see it, says referee Eduardo, and Yo-Yo keeps the ball, streetball, white boy. Yo-Yo can jump, Yo-Yo weighs ten kilos more than I do, all in the upper arms. At nine in the morning Yo-Yo throws his T-shirt on the ground and boxes me out so I tear my pants and my knee on the asphalt. Eduardo calls fouls that aren't fouls, Eduardo rolls a joint and smokes, traveling, he says, as I make a clean drive past Yo-Yo. Yo-Yo has a good inside game and pushes me under the basket with his broad back, Yo-Yo dunks on me, Yo-Yo is fast, Yo-Yo makes a midrange shot, and now Eduardo is shouting "in your face" and "pussy" and "yo mama." Seven to five, then seven to nine. I roll up my sleeves, I gasp for breath, I've used up my vocabulary and my strength, because for weeks I've been preoccupied with other things. I feel my twisted ankle, there's a hole in my shooting hand, and when two other people are making the rules, you're outnumbered. Once again the calculation is off. Good work, Svensson, I think, as Yo-Yo leaves me in the dust and the ball rattles through the chain net, seven to eleven, it's over. Larry Bird's a bitch, shouts Eduardo, your girl is a bitch. She is not, little man, I say, I don't care about Larry Bird and I don't care about basketball, but don't talk about Tuuli, man, don't talk about Tuuli! My knee is bleeding, Yo-Yo puts his T-shirt back on, and Eduardo takes the money from under the milk container. I take one of Tuuli's cigarettes out of my jacket and offer one to Eduardo and Yo-Yo. Eduardo gives me a light and my money. Keep it, white boy, he says, you look like you need it. And what now? What now? I limp to the hole in the fence, nothing can come of this, I think, enough is enough, and Eduardo calls after me, the rules of streetball, brother.

Because I forgot Lua, I go back to Grace's apartment. At the bakery where I was kneeling a short while ago, I buy coffee and croissants, and because in the West Village there are convenience stores everywhere and Grace meant the vodka and not the milk, I buy a bag of ice cubes and walk up to the fourth floor. Breakfast, I say when Grace opens the door, and give her the coffee and croissants. Lua wakes up and barks, I stand soaked with sweat and still covered in blood in front of Grace. I hold the dripping bag of ice cubes behind my back. You're weird, she says, and climbs back into bed. I hop in the shower, that's enough, I think under the cold water, things can't go on like this, and because I'm now faster than I was two hours ago, I mix two martinis in water glasses and, wearing Grace's purple bathrobe, go back to the bedroom, where she's still lying on her side. I can pick up where I left off. I let a drop of condensation drip from the glass onto Grace's hip and kiss her on all seventeen characters one after another. At the thirteenth she wakes up, or at the thirteenth she reveals that she's already awake, and when she takes the glass and drinks, a shiver runs over her skin, as if we'd stopped and turned back time. Grace puts her glass on the windowsill next to the bed, then mine too, forces me directly onto my back, or I let her force me. And because we're playing by other rules here and now, she at first keeps her mouth off my cock and takes a big bite into my face again like last night by the elevator. Then takes the cue "breakfast" and has me for breakfast, I think, and the word "cue" is right on cue, because between kisses Grace immediately breathes in my ear again, directly in my ear, and reels off her squealing sounds like the actress she is. She lets down her hair and brushes it across my face, and I reach around her narrow waist with my left hand, grab her ass too far down and too far in, pull it too far apart to be going for her ass and end up with index finger and middle finger directly on her pussy. But she can't be that fast, and she isn't, so I bring both hands up to her head, and with my hands on her ears I tell her without many words that this is the time and place for kissing and drinking martinis. I take a glass and a sip and warm the vodka, then I turn her over and plunge between her legs and spit her full to have something to lick, and lick her empty. Does vodka burn? I ask myself and her, but Grace is caught up in the wordless script she's still rehearsing. I come up and now she drinks from the glass and disinfects our tongues, because pussies are the dirtiest places in the world, she's read, she doesn't like her own taste, so it's a good thing the vodka's there. Grace's tongue dipped in vodka, and still, to my amazement, she kisses and breathes in my ear at the same time. She does that for a long time, her hand holding my cock. Eventually she straddles me and leans her head back, she does what she has to, she goes berserk and tosses her head back and forth, her hips roll, her bed on rollers moves through the room, and I think about Vonderlippe, about Lua, and watch my hands, see how they do most things right, how Grace and I go through the motions, how she loudly and ardently comes and scratches and claws and notices that I'm not coming, and then keeps going and going and getting louder. How she fulfills her expectations and I don't stop her, how I close my eyes and concentrate. And suddenly Tuuli is there, not only the thought of her body, but also how she sounds, and it's her name that fills my head. As I explode behind my closed eyelids and then open my eyes again, I'm surprised to be in Grace's apartment, in Grace, at the end of the night on which I wanted to remove the splinter. The porcelain dog and Lua look at me.

Grace's breast moves in my hand as I dial Tuuli's number, *Svensson Home.* Grace is asleep or pretending to be asleep. If Felix answers, I'll hang up, I decide, and with each ring in the receiver, with each inhalation, with each exhalation, I say to myself what I'll say to Tuuli: the two of you stop calling me, get your own telephone number, do whatever you want, but give me my books back, give me my plants back, and what about the plates and cups, what am I supposed to eat off and drink from? If the two of you could see me now, you'd be surprised how thin I am, Svensson's all skin and bones, the old Svensson has almost disappeared. Fuck and live wherever you want, but if you could see me now, Tuuli, if you could see me now, you'd be worried. Grace wakes up, I trace my finger around her nipple, the sunlight is pouring into the room and I'm in the middle of it, on the fire escape sits a crow, the porcelain dog is still staring, Grace's nipple is so much darker, it contracts so much more than Tuuli's. Do you know any German? I ask. You're my first one, says Grace. She turns on her side, she's not interested in the telephone either. I count the tattoos just to the left of her spine, down her whole back, the characters I can't read. I lay my other ear on Grace's hip, look directly into the sun and grab her from behind between the legs, maybe because I have to, when someone picks up the phone. I say, I just want to see your face, Tuuli, that's all. But then it's Felix who answers and says the boy was born on Saturday.

August 6, 2005

(Master of chairs, master of chickens)

In my head this image remains: Elisabeth in late summer under a village linden between Fischland and Darss, leaning on the hood of my R4, her red dress (second wedding not in white!) and the dahlias in her left hand, singing "The Linden Tree," *Am Brunnen vor dem Tore, / Da steht ein Lindenbaum*, at her side children wrapped in towels on the way back from the beach. How she then goes down on her knees next to a little girl and points at me, that man over there is named Mandelkern and is now my husband (the red of the dress and the towel's green fight). Elisabeth laughs, I laugh too.

Lua

Now the small, pretty mother is laughing and the dog is coughing. I'm standing with the rope in my hand under an alley of lindens on the shore of Lake Lugano and observing Svensson (in the sunlight the fine drops of the linden flowers, which will now be sticking to our windshield in Hamburg). Svensson lets go of the small woman's hand, the boy stands next to his mother and observes the three-legged dog on the boat. The animal is a kind of German shepherd, black and old, he has a light spot on his chest and stands on his foreleg coughing on the boat's bench, or maybe he's barking, I can't tell the difference (fatigue). The dirty swans turn away. I don't understand what Svensson is saying, he's gesturing at the boat and the dog, he's pointing at me, then out at the lake. Finally he holds out his cap to the boy, but the boy doesn't take the cap. When Svensson then tries to shake his hand, the boy evades him and starts to climb across two or three pedal boats toward the boat (Svensson awkwardly following). The boy looks past Svensson to his mother. The sun has now sunk lower over the smooth water, occasionally a light breeze comes out of nowhere, and the dog stops his coughing (the lake suddenly like plastic wrap). The small, pretty woman (Tuuli) takes another two drags and again stamps out her cigarette with her heel.

Who exactly is Daniel Mandelkern?

I'm a journalist, I say, Daniel Mandelkern. Then I apologize to the small, pretty woman for not having introduced myself sooner, I'm here to conduct an interview with Svensson, I'm actually an ethnologist, but I'm currently working as a freelance cultural journalist. She smiles (she keeps her eye on the boy). So it's Mandelkern, *Manteli* in my language, she laughs, *Karvasmanteli* (*Manteli* must mean "almond" too). The success of Svensson's book is really remarkable, I say (awkwardly), of course I'm not the only one whose interest has been aroused, and: I find it equally remarkable that for the whole journey we had the same destination.

There are more important things,

she says, going around me and my outstretched hand, you're not going to get anywhere with your interview today, *Karvasmanteli*, just come along (she speaks slowly and clearly). Svensson jumps ashore again, and tries to help her across the pedal boats, but she too steers clear of Svensson. He holds his hands apologetically in the air. Svensson and I watch as she sits down on the deck between the dog and the boy. She talks to the boy, she seems to be explaining the dog's three legs (Finnish is a soft language). Finally Svensson asks: You're Mandelkern? In reply I repeat: yes, it's very nice to meet you, we have an appointment here this afternoon, Riva Albertolli, right? Svensson looks at me silently. I'm holding the plastic bag with my notebooks, postcards, and shirts in one hand and the small woman's suitcase in the other (in my head: Elisabeth in the bathroom; the drizzle on the chestnut trees as I ran off last night). I'm early, I say to Svensson, my baggage is still on its way, I'd be glad to wait here for you. In the sunlight between the lindens a few old men play chess, panama hats and bright summer shirts (I could join them). But Svensson shakes his head: Climb aboard and come along, he says, or stay here, it's completely up to you, Mandelkern. You decide (memory is bulky baggage).

hairpins and the deeper water

Here in Lugano there's no wind, the mountains on the right and left are wearing thin clouds, near the shore the lake is a translucent green, but after a few meters the bottom is already no longer visible. Svensson backs the boat between the pedal boats into the deeper water, then he shifts into forward, accelerating so suddenly that the boat rises steeply. The heavy dog loses his balance and, lying on his side, slides across the wet deck (his foreleg a frantic scratching on wood). Tuuli with the Finnish passport falls toward me, her head lies briefly on my shoulder (she clutches the boy immediately with both arms). From up close I don't smell any trace of her cigarettes, the light hair on the nape of her neck is sticky, I think of milk. Svensson apologizes, the boat slows down. The dog struggles to his feet, the boy closes his eyes, a hairpin falls on the deck and glimmers in the puddle (for blonde women there are golden hairpins, says Elisabeth, for dark-haired women there are black ones, but for redheads there are none. My reply: girls with freckles and red hair are honored guests in the devil's lair, followed by Elisabeth's laughter). I pick up the hairpin, dry it off, and give it back to Tuuli. The dog is coughing again, now the boy is crying after all, one of the yellow swans soars into the air and follows the boat.

Daniel Mandelkern?

In the afternoon Elisabeth will be going for a run along the canal, singing Celentano (Isekanal). The summer of 2003 was a summer of record-breaking heat. I know where my name comes from: my parents called themselves Mandler (they had to flee anyway). Elisabeth calls orgasms milky moments. I never liked telemarketing. Ethnology is a science, it's about the eye of a stranger on human groups. My grandfather is said to have gone bald too (on my mother's side). It's not up for discussion, Elisabeth said, I'm wearing red when we get married! Genealogically I'm not Jewish, but I am circumcised. Elisabeth is five years older than I, but doesn't look it, she says: I have a great metabolism. I'm not a practicing Catholic, but I remember my first confession. To write about art is art. In Hamburg I've moved four times: Dithmarscher Strasse, Schulterblatt, Marthastrasse, Bismarckstrasse, and I've always lived with women. My father's marriage to the youngest daughter of a member of the Quickborn Catholic youth movement in postwar Essen was problematic solely due to the age difference (he died in 1974, she in 1990). I've slept with twelve women. I speak German, English, a little bit of French, Swedish, Finnish, miserable Italian. To write about sports is art too. I manage as everyone manages. Elisabeth has stopped taking the pill, now she wants to have a child. I want you to decide, she says.

Why a children's book?

Svensson steers the boat slowly and in wide curves across the smooth lake. The dog lifts his foreleg onto the railing and barks at the water's surface (focused and dull as if something were there). Svensson puts his hand on the dog's head. When a gray motor-boat approaches, Svensson says customs, passports (Guardia di Finanza). He decelerates with a quick hand motion, the motor sputters, there's a smell of gas (multihued streaks on the smooth water). *Macumba* drifts on the lake. Here is the deepest point, Svensson says to the boy, 288 meters, no light penetrates down there, down there all the fish are white. The boy slowly makes his way to the middle of the boat (can children conceive of depth?). We have our passports ready, but the man at the steering wheel sees Svensson and the black dog, he shouts something Italian, Svensson shouts back. Both give a thumbs-up. The customs boat turns away with a deep roar of its motor, *Macumba* rocks alarmingly.

I had a fleeting acquaintance with Elisabeth

She entered the office, ABC Market and Opinion Polls, a tight Union Jack T-shirt over a pregnant belly (short hair, a dark henna red), and for a whole autumn sat two computers down from me every day, including Sundays. Sometimes I listened to her, she was efficient. We rarely talked (I smoked on the balcony during the break, she drank tea in the kitchen), and when it got too cold to smoke on the balcony, it must have been November 1996, overnight she became my superior for the first time (supervisor). One evening after work, as I walked through the snow a few meters behind her on the way to the Hamburger Strasse U-Bahn station, she sang softly to herself, "There are some who are in darkness / And the others are in light / And you see the ones in brightness / Those in darkness drop from sight." A few weeks later she was gone. Our colleagues assumed the child had been born. On the supermarket studies she'd been the best interviewer from the start, the manager said later in a training session, her voice had exactly the right register for market research, a frequency that sang resistance to pieces.

master of chairs, master of chickens

Svensson spreads his arms. This is where we live, he says (a children's book author and his three-legged dog). A narrow but tall stone house surrounded by cypresses, an oleander, and a gigantic sycamore. Svensson has moored Maçumba to the dock and helps us ashore one after another: first Tuuli, then the boy, then me, and finally the dog. In front of us there's a stone table and two stone benches covered with moss and pine needles (the benches shouldered by lions), next to them garden chairs with flaking white lacquer. Stainless garden chairs, an inflatable plastic armchair (blue, not much air). Also: wicker chairs, a few wooden chairs with warped and cracked plywood seats (on two of them large stones), next to them garden lounge chairs with mildewed cushions, also bare lounge chairs. And still more: a chair made of green lacquered metal (with canvas upholstery), folding chairs made of pale red wood, a granite table with two granite benches, white plastic chairs, blue plastic chairs, pink plastic chairs, four green children's chairs with a red children's table. There are terra-cotta pots, intact ones and broken ones, big ones and small ones, upright ones, overturned ones, empty ones and planted ones (tomatoes, herbs, kumquats). There's a circular saw and a stack of gray plastic pipes and rain gutters, next to them bags of cement. Behind and off to the side of the house a shed, next to the shed the garbage: a heap of black plastic bags, cardboard boxes, a boat's mast, a printer and a computer monitor with smashed screen (a surprised mouth, toothless). On a jutting branch of the gigantic sycamore hangs a child's wooden swing, a basketball hoop is screwed to the trunk. Under it a Ping-Pong table (I could challenge Svensson).

against the fox

Svensson leads us around the property. A small blue car with open driver's-side door is parked at the edge of the woods (FIAT 128 Sport L), covered in ivy and moss. Standing on the Fiat are two bored roosters (brown, white). Svensson introduces them: This is William Wordsworth, he says, and here we have Robby Naish. Under the oleander another chicken is pecking around in the wilted flowers on the ground. Daisy Duck, says Svensson, the hen. The white rooster crows, the boy laughs: cock-a-doodle-doo. Tuuli kneels next to him and, shaking her head, watches Svensson scatter seeds in the Fiat and slam the door. For a home, says Svensson, you need seventy-seven chairs, three chickens and a dog to guard against the fox.

Heiligengeistfeld

At first we didn't recognize each other. Because her hair was long and the T-shirt with the British flag long since discarded, five years later Elisabeth and I again worked for months in the same building without talking to each other (I never managed to find the T-shirt). Then it was she who rammed her tray into my back in the Gruner + Jahr cafeteria at noon and didn't apologize until early evening in the Baumwall U-Bahn station. She recited the prescribed salutation of the market and opinion polling company: Hello-my-name-is, I'm-calling-on-behalf-of, jogging my memory (her voice sings resistance to pieces). We talked about this and that, such as the port (the launches and cruise ships), her editorial department (*Brigitte* culture section) and my freelance work (*GEOkompakt*). Elisabeth seemed glad to see me, but when I asked her how long it had been since our sad interlude in market research (Esso, Wal-Mart), her child must already be five by now, between St. Pauli and Heiligengeistfeld Elisabeth suddenly said that she had to get off here, here was her home (she actually said: here is my home!), even though she'd previously mentioned the Generals' Quarter.

Yoko Mono

Elisabeth is a sober woman. She steered me through that evening and through the things that had to be clarified, places of residence, visions, and finally bodies. The whole time she looked me in the eyes (her voice a taxi). I'd jumped off the train behind her, and then she'd taken me along to a bar on Marktstrasse (Yoko Mono). She ordered wine, Barbera, she called out, with her right hand she bunched up her hair and tucked it behind her ears. I'd already gotten used to her face. When I quoted from an old book after the third glass (red hair, red hair, I tear it out, make a broom to fly about), she looked at me, lifted her glass to her mouth, and I noticed for the first time her swallow and her delicate neck. She undid one of her hairpins and took a calculable risk as she quoted the saying "rusty roof, damp cellar." Several blocks farther, she nonetheless said good-bye to me for now without a touch (at the corner of Bismarck-strasse and Scheideweg, of all places). We could see each other tomorrow afternoon in the cafeteria, she said.

little porno face

During the first few weeks, Elisabeth and I often saw each other in the cafeteria (the unpopular tables facing the courtyard) and quickly began to live off each other (her personal affairs and my personal affairs fused into one big affair). Elisabeth is a smart woman. The first time we slept together I was surprised by her porno face (her mouth an O, occasionally she bit her lips) and the speed with which she fucked me (that's how she talked, that's how it was), she by my soundlessness. She said: We don't fit. But we did fit after all. We met in the evening in bars we didn't know, we discussed how we could be (we imagined ourselves). As other people introduce their friends, we announced our bodies. She wanted: to be free when fucking. I wanted body and mind to be in step. Elisabeth said: some pain is natural. I said: theoretically. She said: exactly. She could come harder when she was squatting and had a finger lightly touching her asshole (words fail me). I said I like to watch women masturbate. That same week both of us suddenly got new job offers: I was given a regular freelance position at *GEO*, she became an editor (her still-husband would not have been uninvolved in that, but at that point she hadn't mentioned him yet). Our theory gave way to my euphoria. I'd already pictured her various faces beforehand (a vein on her forehead during sex as if she were carrying heavy suitcases). Your little porno face, said Elisabeth, as I came with less restraint than I was used to.

Santuario di Nostra Signora della Caravina

Now Svensson's talking. He explains the mountains: over there Monte dei Pizzoni, he says, and gestures upward at the shores to the right and left, here Monte Cecchi. Svensson throws pinecone after pinecone into the lake. He explains the villages: San Mamete on the opposite shore, Osteno over there behind the trees, Porlezza at the end of the lake. Svensson points to the opposite shore: Cima di Porlezza. Over there, under a rough, jagged mountain, is a village, in the middle of it a church is glowing yellow. Svensson says: Santuario di Nostra Signora della Caravina (a sleeping gecko, the left foreleg a rockslide). Below the church a grand villa (same yellow, in front of it palms, a dock with white posts). The boy examines the shattered monitor. At night the church tower is illuminated and looks like a gladiator, Svensson tells him, do you know what a gladiator is? But the boy looks up from the shards and asks,

Why does your dog have only three legs?

My notebook is still in the shopping bag as even the dog suddenly falls silent and looks at Svensson full of anticipation. Where the fourth leg of the dog is would have been one of my questions too. It took us an hour to cross the murkily reflective lake (long before the shore mosquitoes already swarming over the water), and now I'm sitting next to the small, pretty mother on a stone bench under the oleander (white and red flowers). She's smoking again. I'm here for my interview, and I have to go back to the city today (Lido Seegarten). I'll offer her one of my cigarettes. Well, Svensson begins, then he looks at the small woman and falters, he doesn't answer the question (the dog motionless as a photo, the fourth leg airbrushed out). The boy walks slowly toward his mother. Tuuli moves over and is suddenly close to me, she laughs smoke into my ear, don't write this, *Manteli*, she says, Svensson's stories are made up (I would only have to turn my head toward her).

Why does your dog have only three legs?

Lua was a professional night watchdog, he says in reply to the boy's almost-forgotten question, he wears the moon over his heart. Svensson lays his hand on the dog's black fur (dark gray from up close). I found him at full moon on the roadside, a car had hit him, he was lying in a pool of blood, right over there near the church. Svensson points to the other side of the lake. German shepherds are good night watchdogs. I brought him to the hospital in San Mamete, his leg had to be amputated, for a few weeks he couldn't move. Lua is a sad dog. Svensson goes back to the boat. The boy approaches the sad dog carefully and lifts his hand (hesitation). Svensson looks at Tuuli and says: but after some time dogs get used to any loss. Lua flops heavily on his side, over the shore lies a light mist, there's a smell of something burning. The boy withdraws his hand and asks, is Lua dangerous? Tuuli's reply: the dog is old, he's going to die soon.

Interview (first try)

MANDELKERN: Could you explain to me again what exactly I
    shouldn't write, Ms. . . .

TUULI: Call me Tuuli, *Karvasmanteli*, you can drop the formality,
    we're the same age.

M: I was born in 1972.

T: Exactly. You're in your early thirties and so are we. More or
    less. Svensson seems older and I younger. Right?

M: And how old is the dog?

T: Dog years? Human years?

M: Either way.

T: It must have been at least ten years ago when Felix Blaumeiser,
    the idiot, brought the dog back from Brazil.

M: May I ask who Felix is?

T: Felix is the reason we're here, *Manteli*.

black dogs

Come with me, says Svensson, taking my plastic bag from my
hand, it's my fault. He apologizes stiffly for the chaos, he'd be glad
if I stayed the night, we could talk tomorrow in peace ("please
forgive the mess"). Then I'll bring you back to the city in the
afternoon, he says, and because I was early this afternoon at the
arranged meeting place, because I burst into Svensson's private
life, at this point I answer unemphatically "okay" (otherwise I'd
return empty-handed). Svensson's house is a ruin: three stories of
natural stone and wood built at the foot of the cliff, on the side
facing the lake green window shutters (closed). The back section
of the roof a skeleton, ivy and vine are growing up the walls and
into the frame. The flat shed next to the house slants toward

the water (it must be a boat shed). Pigeons are fluttering everywhere, their droppings speckle the stone walls. Come with me,
Svensson repeats, and I follow him (I'm here to have my questions
answered). Lua trudges ahead, coughing, we walk between the
sycamore and the garbage heap around the house. A heavy door,
then a dark hallway with a terra-cotta floor, pictures all over the
walls and framed photographs with black centers (dogs maybe,
Lua maybe). We climb a dark staircase, closed doors on the right
and left. The dog breathes heavily in the dark, now the smell of
smoke is stronger. Svensson opens a door, then a window, and
stands in the backlight (Svensson is an opaque man).

crematorium

Over Svensson's property and over the lake in front of Svensson's
property lies an acrid stench. That's Claasen, says Svensson, in
answer to my question as to whether there isn't a smell of something burning (state the obvious and casually open the conversation). Clouds of smoke, stretching long and wide, hang over the
lake: burning leaves and underbrush, smoldering green wood,
burning paper. Svensson is standing with my bag in a room that
looks like a study (empty shelves, only a few books). This was my
study, he says. Lua flops down on a carpet in a corner of the room.
In the other corner lies a mattress with clean sheets. Claasen? I
ask, and Svensson nods as if I should be able to understand everything here, as if I had already been here for a long time. Every
day at four, says Svensson, Claasen burns another piece of his life.
Claasen is his own crematorium.

Can you elaborate on that?

Svensson's reply: Claasen is his neighbor, a former journalist from
Germany, his wife left him, the children are already grown up.
Now this pyromaniac in early retirement burns his possessions
every day at four, log after log, dry and damp wood, leaves, grass.
Svensson opens another window shutter. Furniture, pictures,
books. Clothing is the worst. Do you smell that? Melting seventies
synthetics: jackets, suits, shirts, dresses. Sometimes Claasen gazes
into a book for hours before he throws it into the fire. Depending
on the wind direction, a veil of the desire to forget hangs over
the shore, when no wind is blowing you sometimes can't see the
other side of the lake (Caravina). Svensson gives me back the bag
and turns to the door. Make yourself at home, Mandelkern, get
some rest, if you'd like. We'll call you down for dinner later, and
I again say "okay" (you look tired, Mandelkern, Elisabeth would
say, lie down).

my assignment, my profession

My assignment: get on the trail of Svensson the man. The true
personality of the artist, said Elisabeth after the editorial meeting
on Friday, always remains hidden behind success stories (this is
what interests Elisabeth). My assignment doesn't have much to do
with my vocation. My profession: I'm an ethnologist, even if my
dissertation has been shelved for two years ("Thick Participation
and Mediated Identity: A Method in Flux"). It deals with distance
and proximity (the ethnological dilemma). Sooner or later, everything I write has to do with me, I think, and of all thoughts it is
this one with which Svensson leaves me alone in his room (I find
myself in the middle of the group under investigation).

Optolyth

The room has very high ceilings. The shelves on the walls are nearly empty: a little bit of dust on them as if the books were only just removed, a few novels left behind. On the wall hang three large paintings (about 1 x 2 meters), opposite them under the three windows looking out on the lake stands a small, tidy desk, arranged on it along an invisible grid: two small yogurt jars (La Laitière), in the first a yellow pencil, some paper clips, loose change (Swiss francs, dollars, euros, *reais*), in the second a few crayons. Then a letter holder (without letters), an inkwell (without ink), in the middle a pair of binoculars (Optolyth). A hotel bill for 84.50 euros (Hotel Stella d'Italia, dated August 4, 2004). On the back of the desk a row of reference books (show me what you read, and I'll tell you who you are, Elisabeth once said to me, referring to my ethnographies, theoretical writings, lists, and notebooks). Next to the reference books a green plastic picture frame, in it a photo of Svensson and Tuuli. She's smiling, she looks tired, between them a blond man. Svensson is holding the camera. In the background a chimney, the three faces pale and red-eyed from the flash; the blond man is laughing exuberantly and holding a beer can up to the camera (Pabst Blue Ribbon). And finally, the outlines of a monitor and a keyboard in the dust on the desk. I put my bag on the desk and take out my notebook. It's now Saturday afternoon, Elisabeth will have gone to the office today despite everything. She'll drink water and write until her headache is gone. She'll try to call me at the Hotel Lido Seegarten, she'll dial my cell phone number. She'll realize that I've run off (I take notes to leave a trail, each word a pebble, each sentence a row of little stones). The smoke hangs low and thick and dense over the water.

Shoot the Freak

The paintings on Svensson's wall: 1. two old men in front of a wire fence, behind it shiny red lettering (Astroland); 2. a roller coaster and smoke (old dragon). The third and middle painting shows a very thin man in a purple T-shirt at the foot of a green children's slide. Behind him red tower blocks, snack stands, ocean waves, and hot dogs. The man is in the middle of all this, his eyes are ill at ease, they look straight ahead and seem to threaten the painter. His pants are pulled down and hang around his thin legs, his cock is sticking out from his body (erect, pale). All the paintings in thick oil on canvas, with bottle caps, sand, and beach grass pressed into them. The brushstrokes and colors are reminiscent of the pictures in Svensson's children's book. Between a hot dog stand and a lottery stand stretches a series of bright-colored pennants, on each pennant a letter: SHOOT*THE*FREAK. The man resembles Svensson (self-portrait). Svensson is a strange man.

Der Lindenbaum

In my head this image remains: Elisabeth moving into her new office in the spring of 2003. I put two moving boxes down on the carpet, she sits on her desk and watches me. Marry me, she says (the commanding green of her eyes). I laugh, I close the doors to the hallway and the other offices, but then the telephone rings, and Elisabeth says, wait here, Mandelkern, wait for me.

Who exactly is Dirk Svensson?

Sister Carrie by Theodore Dreiser

Onkel Tobi by Hans G. Lenzen

Water Supply Systems for Home Farming by Williams & Steynman

The Great Encyclopedia of Dog Breeds

The Encyclopedia of European Trees

Piccolo Mondo Antico by Giovanni Fogazzaro

Selected Poems by William Wordsworth

I lie down on the mattress in the corner of the room (headache) and fall asleep.

ATTENTION FRAGILE/ACHTUNG ZERBRECHLICH

At twilight I wake up and look around. Under the desk are an abandoned power strip and a huge brown leather suitcase with a heavy lock. On the ceiling a mobile that I didn't notice earlier dangles over me (small colorful airplanes). On the floor next to my head a cheap stuffed animal (a gray mouse in blue overalls, "Euromaus" on the bib). The dog must have forgotten it. I sit down at Svensson's desk and take Elisabeth's ring out of my pants pocket (E. E. E.). According to the intern's research, Svensson has no kids, even though he's a children's book author, and, Elisabeth added, that's exactly what makes him interesting. Outside the dog is coughing as if he really were going to die soon. I sit down at the desk and leaf through Svensson's books: the German shepherd, withers height 50–60 centimeters, weighs up to 40 kilos, thick undercoat, thick covering of fur, back straight and firm, life expectancy with good care and breeding fifteen years, even temperament, strong nerves, child-friendly, good-natured, and brave. My legs are too long, the desk is too low, the suitcase under the desk is too high (I'd have to sit with my legs askew). I try to move it, to pull it out, but the suitcase is defiant and drags only reluctantly across the wood, the sound must be audible in the whole house (its weight an invitation to open). I push it back into its place. Old leather, metal-reinforced corners, nicks and stickers, on the handle hangs a nametag: Felix Blaumeiser (this name for the second time already today, Tuuli called him an idiot). But Dirk Svensson is not Felix Blaumeiser, I think, unless it's a pseudonym (inquire at some point). I take a paper clip from the yogurt jar, bend it into a hook and try to open the suitcase, but the heavy lock refuses (copper is softer than people think). I sit back down at the desk, my legs aslant on the suitcase, and write down:

—What should I write about?
—What shouldn't I write about?
—Is the boy Svensson's son?
—Where will his pretty mother sleep?
—How do I get out of here?
—What's in the leather suitcase?
—Who exactly is Felix Blaumeiser?

stone smoke

No computer, no printer, no typewriter. I take the binoculars and look out the window across the lake. In Lugano and Cima the lights come on little by little. The smoke has dispersed. Tuuli and the boy are out of sight. Svensson is sitting on the dock, next to him lies the dog (shaking). I should call Svensson, I should conduct the interview immediately and get a ride to Lugano tomorrow morning at the latest if I don't want to miss my return flight.

Svensson kneels down next to Lua, and I'm not sure whether his hand is trembling. He strokes the dog and talks out over the water. Maybe he's talking to the lake, maybe to the other shore, maybe to the yellow light on the other side of the lake (Santuario di Nostra Signora della Caravina). No wind is blowing, cicadas can now be heard.

Animals, the Hearts of People

THE BOY WAS BORN, TWO MONTHS EARLY, AND I'M DRINKING milk and vodka out of Grace's belly button. Eventually the milk is gone, and Lua wakes up. Take it again from the top, I decide, and again close the door from outside and leave someone behind, but that can't matter to Grace and the porcelain greyhound, because when someone says good-bye to you by whispering "fuck you, weirdo, you and your dog," turns over and goes on sleeping, forgetting isn't far off. Today is Sunday or Monday, I take a walk through the West Village, along Houston Street, through SoHo. I should think and calm down, I should reflect. Lua and I walk past dogs with sunglasses and masters with sunglasses, it's autumn in New York, the leaves are yellow, the leaves are red, the flags flutter, and on the corners men are playing "America the Beautiful" on the fiddle. The tourists show their generosity, their coins jingle in the fiddlers' caps, in my pants pocket I have my credit card. I buy a suit and a shirt, I buy white sneakers, I buy Aspirin and Lysol, I buy a hundred-pack of vitamin C, I buy a toothbrush, I buy champagne for forty-seven dollars and ninety-nine cents. I buy Lua two cheeseburgers, Lua loves cheeseburgers, I buy him a green leather leash, exactly like the one the Chihuahua in front of the West Village bakery had. On Broadway we get into a taxi, at Times Square we get out, and I don't know why I'm here or where to go, but the sun is shining and the advertisements are glowing. I buy chicken soup, I buy chocolate, and in Bryant Park behind the New York Public Library women with sun hats sit on the steps between shopping bags, muffins, and coffee cups. Behind a pavilion I tie up Lua and give him the second cheeseburger. I'll be right back, I tell him, I have to calm down. I lean against a stone lion on its pedestal in front of the library and dip the chocolate in the chicken soup. A library is a good place to get to the bottom of things and figure out where to start. The security guard at the entrance searches my plastic bags for weapons, hi, how are you today? he asks, and I say, so-so.

In the bathroom I change my clothes. I try to flush my bloody T-shirt down the toilet, but the toilet gets clogged and overflows. So I'll have to throw my pants in the river, maybe in the Atlantic, my telephone and the calls and the hanging up right afterward, the waiting for Tuuli and Felix and for a boy whose name I don't know because I hung up too fast this morning. In the bathroom of the New York Public Library I raise the champagne for forty-seven ninety-nine toward the boy, toward Brooklyn, toward the towel dispenser. No drinks in the reading room, so I drink half the bottle of champagne here. The suit fits, I take an over-dose of vitamin C. Too much vitamin C gets excreted without consequences, unlike too much love. Too much love afflicts the stomach and the liver, it goes to the kidneys. I brush my teeth, I spray Lysol in the hole in my hand against tetanus, I spray Lysol on my cock against AIDS and against hepatitis and against gonor-rhea, it burns in my eyes, it would be too late anyway and the wrong method, it burns and burns and burns and I feel my way to the sink and hold my face under the cold water, I flush my eyes with it, splash some on the back of my neck. This is not a public washroom, sir, says a security guard, handing me my plastic bags, I have to ask you to leave.

In the reading room I take the book given to me by the woman with the camera out of my pants pocket and put it on a table, "646-299-1036 Kiki Kaufman!" The security guards don't bother people who are reading, so I'm glad to have the book. *Sister Carrie* by Theodore Dreiser. I leaf through it as the champagne hits me, I find champagne just the right thing for an afternoon. I skim the sentences marked in red and green, many are true, sometimes things are just simple and right and good, sometimes the world can be better understood in black and white, sometimes you need red and green markings. The book goes roughly like this: the not beautiful but unusual Carrie comes to Chicago from the countryside and doesn't find work, then she falls in love with the traveling salesman Drouet and ultimately with the bar manager Hurstwood. Carrie leaves Drouet and goes with Hurstwood to New York. Yes, that's where I am too right now, I think, and fall asleep on page seventy-six, New York, New York. When the library closes and the security guard shakes my shoulder, I wake up on page seventy-seven. Hurstwood is serving a bottle of sec, as he calls it. Alcohol is a good idea, I say to the security guard, and close the book. I put it in the bag, the guard asks, you all right, sir? and I say, so-so. Do you know the hotel with the best martinis in the city?

The SoHo Grand is on West Broadway and Canal Street, and if there was ever dust here, then the dust has been wiped away, because I can see Lua and myself in the windowpanes as we step out of the taxi. With suit and credit card and leather leash, we don't stand out here. I take the book out of the plastic bag and leave the bag at the cloakroom. I order a martini and ask for it to be brought to an armchair by the window. It's twilight, Lua gets water and falls asleep, I call "646-299-1036 Kiki Kaufman!" and ask whether she wants to meet again. Sure, she'll come by, she says, she's in the neighborhood. Down on the street a vendor is pushing home his hot dog stand, he looks like the security guard from the library. I put my new white sneakers on the armchair opposite me and open to page 207. The not beautiful but unusual Carrie is becoming an actress on Broadway, and Hurstwood is pouring drinks once again. So I get a refill too, outside the taxis and the rickshaws pass by. Carrie must look like Tuuli, not beautiful in the strict sense, but nonetheless the most beautiful. Hurstwood is sitting in a theater and watching her. I'm lying in the armchair by the window and reading, I'm observing Carrie and hearing Tuuli singing. In my head Tuuli is sitting on my roof in Brooklyn and singing, Felix and I are listening to her, we're so moved that we can't move and so in love that we can't speak, we drink silently, we lean our heads on the chimney and listen to each other breathing. I can't think and can't speak and can't even read in peace, all stories right now are Tuuli's and Felix's and mine. Of course these stories have to be told, I think, but who in them sings what and when, who can look how beautiful, who stands on whose stage and sings and stirs emotions, who speaks when and what can be said, I'd like to determine all that myself, I think, and I close the book and wait for Kiki Kaufman, the woman with the camera.

As I accept a glass of wine, Kiki Kaufman sits down in the armchair next to me and crosses her legs. Again she's wearing a plain black dress and black shoes, and is carrying a black bag, she has an empty glass in her hand and puts it down on the book. Could she have a sip of my wine? she asks, and takes one. She snaps a photo over her shoulder without looking and puts her camera on the table. Of course, I say, and Kiki Kaufman holds the wine up to the light. You look tired, Svensson, she says, isn't that right, aren't you tired? I know, I say. From a long period of time, she says, people remember the first day best. She pours my red wine in her white wine glass. Who are you actually? she asks, but I remember

how Lua came in first through the crack of the door, tilted his heavy head and climbed on the sofa like an old man; I remember how the door opened all the way and Felix said, fucking shit, Svensson! I remember how Felix took two bottles of Rolling Rock out of the bag and put the rest in the fridge. Beer makes you schmart, he said, in the corner of the apartment the television was on, "oh my God, oh my God" again and again, then the camera shook and the image blurred, again and again, like a mantra. Felix sat down next to me and watched, Lua lay down in front of the fridge and begged. Felix gave me the beer, we refrained from clinking bottles,

but at this point Kiki raises her glass and interrupts me. So it's that story, she says, for weeks I've been taking pictures of this city, pictures of this tragedy in many chapters. My 9/11 story isn't about this city, I say, not about that day and not about terrorism and colonialism and symbols and consequences. My story, I say to Kiki Kaufman, is about Tuuli and Felix and me:

Tuuli and Felix were staying in a hotel next to the World Trade Center, they were visiting New York for a few weeks and planned to return to Germany in mid-September. Felix's father was paying, Tuuli was seven months pregnant. We weren't alone, we were three, but on the tenth of September, of all days, Felix and I had talked the night away in a bar in Brooklyn, at first full of panic and later full of pride. Felix had slept on my sofa, Tuuli had stayed alone in her hotel. In the morning I'd gone to work as always. I remind myself and Kiki Kaufman that all I'd had to

drink after the World Trade Center collapsed that morning was
beer, and that it was already early evening when I arrived at my
apartment in Williamsburg. The sun was shining somewhat
more orange and the Brooklyn-Queens Expressway behind the
house roaring more softly than usual, but with more sirens. Felix
and I sat on the sofa and stared at the television. I must have called
the hotel a hundred times, said Felix. His voice was a bit too high.
At first the lines were jammed, and then no one picked up, not
even the receptionist. Felix drank without looking up from the
television, stiff as a pole he sat on his side of the sofa, he moved
only to lift his beer bottle. I knew that he was thinking about
Tuuli, I'd been thinking about her nonstop for hours, the question
of Tuuli had already been in the room with me long before Lua
and Felix arrived and it was waiting for someone to actually ask
it. But Felix didn't.

Our wine glasses are refilled. Kiki reaches for her camera and
takes a picture of me and the dog and herself in the mirror behind
us. I drink to that, for days I've been drinking milk and vodka and
champagne, and I tell Kiki that Felix too went to the fridge again
and twisted the caps off two more beer bottles. Felix had always
claimed to be a photographer himself, sometimes he'd managed
to sell one of his earlier pictures, but in early September he'd had
no luck and instead always had a beer in his hand. We had enough
to do with Tuuli and the child and the uncertainty. What uncertainty? asks Kiki with wide eyes. I lift my glass and start again
from the top. I explain that

the fall of the towers was visible from the window that morning
in the office of the literary agency where I worked, down on the
street dust-covered pedestrians on the way uptown and fire-truck

sirens on the way downtown. I'd been the first in the office on
the thirteenth floor overlooking Third Avenue. In the hallway
Jackson and Ismael from the mailroom were praying, there was
no television, the radio played solemn instrumental music. We
read Italian and German Web sites, we unscrewed the air condi-
tioners from the window frames. We suspected biological and
chemical agents in the airplanes and tried to seal the windows
with double-sided tape in order to survive. I tried to reach Tuuli in
the hotel. Nothing. When I called Felix in my apartment, the line
was also constantly busy. Then the phone lines died. Raffaella sat
in front of the fridge and cried hysterically, Mark worked out with
a pocket calculator how long our oxygen would last. We believed
there had been a complete closure of all bridges and tunnels out
of Manhattan. I wrote Tuuli and Felix a farewell e-mail, but I
couldn't send it because all the lines were overloaded. After half
an hour a German publisher was standing in the doorway and
offering us dried apricots from his hotel downtown. He was
unharmed, we would survive. On the street people streamed
northward, away from the smoke and dust. I walked directly
toward the towers to find Tuuli. Eventually I was stopped by a
policeman: Evacuation! I headed west and tried again and again,
it was Tuuli, please, they had to understand, but they shouted at
me: Go uptown! End of discussion! Eventually I turned around
and walked toward Brooklyn. Between LaGuardia and JFK the
sky was blue and empty, all airplanes were grounded, people
cringed when pigeons fluttered over their heads, on the way to
the bridge ramp on Fifty-ninth Street, among the hushed pedestrians on Second Avenue, later on the Queensboro Bridge over
the dirty East River, as the smoke turned from white to black. In
front of me two men were walking without shoes, their shoulders
covered in snow-white dust, the younger one said, this is what

Exodus must have been like, and the older one said, bullshit, this is like Genesis 3, verse 24, so he drove out the man and settled him east of the Garden of Eden. A thin, black woman asked for a cigarette, she heard the bridge was going to be blown up, she said, she quit smoking years ago, but "if I go down, I'm going down smoking," but I didn't have any cigarettes,

and on this cue Kiki Kaufman reaches into her bag. Those are the pictures that everyone knows, she says, and that she already photographed off a television in Chicago, in a salad bar on the Magnificent Mile. That afternoon she threw her things in the car and drove to New York. Since then I've been a camera, says Kiki Kaufman, elegantly rolling the tobacco in the paper, in front of the SoHo Grand smoking is still permitted, but that will probably change soon. Can she offer me one, she asks, but I say that I actually smoke only in exceptional situations, but she can roll me one. I collect cigarettes, it's hard to explain. Yes, says Kiki, this world is hard to explain. She rolls the cigarette, then hands it to me, and I repeat that

I walked all the way from the office back to Brooklyn, through Queens, then on the Pulaski Bridge, in Greenpoint and later through Williamsburg, past the shards and garbage bags by the river, through the smell of yeast dough from the Polish bakery on Manhattan Avenue. In front of Enid's the old Poles from the building were standing on the street and holding cans of beer in their hands. I tried calling Tuuli or Felix from a pay phone. Nothing. I didn't get through. Maybe Felix was searching for her, maybe he'd found her. What a fucked-up mess, said one of the Poles, and gave me a Pabst Blue Ribbon, he said, Joseph Barach, Bialystok, and because I didn't know how else to respond, I said my name and where I was from. Germany? asked Joseph Barach. He crushed his Pabst can and immediately opened another. Fuck, he said, four in the afternoon and I'm standing with a German in the middle of Manhattan Avenue and drinking beer? An old Polack like me! No way I would have done that yesterday, kiddo! What else should we have said? The Poles held out the beer cans to me like earthenware jugs in the Bohemian Hall, they looked down the street and across the river, the plume of smoke was turning in our direction, I waited awhile longer in front of Enid's, no police car forbade the drinking on the sidewalk, more and more people were standing around and drinking, but neither Felix nor Tuuli showed up. Around five the sun shone lower, around six we could smell the smoke, and Joseph Barach lifted his beer the way other people drop an anchor. The world and its beer brands are going downhill, he said. That whole warm September day all I had to drink was beer with the old men in front of Enid's, and then I at least sat with Felix and Rolling Rock on my sofa on Lorimer Street in Brooklyn and we waited together for Tuuli, for word from her. Around seven, I went to the fridge and gave Lua a cold cheeseburger to eat.

Lua likes cheeseburgers, says Kiki, she knew that already. Yesterday she had been photographing the half-naked bakers in front of their ovens before she found me and Lua, that direct rawness, that perceptible heat, the belly of the city. Lua and I seemed to her like the image of the amputated country. That's a different subject, I reply, but I still haven't gotten to my own, I'll stick to it, it's still about

Tuuli, seven months pregnant and still not there. We didn't know where she was, we were too anxious to talk nonsense. On the answering machine, there were twelve messages from Germany, we couldn't call back, we wanted to keep the phone line free for Tuuli. Felix, Lua, and I sat around and watched the airplanes on television, the fire, the running people, the dust clouds, the updates, eyewitness reports and amateur videos, the we-will-hunt-them-down-and-punish-those-responsible loop. When there was a knock at the door, we gave a start. In the doorway stood Tuuli, in jeans and a bright purple PricewaterhouseCoopers promotional T-shirt that was actually much too large. She'd rolled up her pants legs, the T-shirt stretched over her belly. She looked like she was in disguise, her pregnant belly seemed, like the clothes, not to belong to her body. In her hand she was holding Felix's huge leather suitcase. I'm sorry, she said, looking around the room. The light on the unwashed windowpanes was dark orange, almost red. In the morning she'd been standing on the roof terrace and observing the burning of the towers as if paralyzed, then the first one came down. The hotel was evacuated, she'd had to put on a gas mask. She'd gone down the stairs and out of the building, by boat to New Jersey, and came here over the bridges to the north. She hadn't been able to reach us. She was sorry. In the suitcase there was only a bathrobe. Felix fell back on the sofa, he let out air like an inflatable animal from which the plug has been pulled. Your pants are too big, he said weakly, the T-shirt color looks fantastic on you. I turned down the television, Mayor Giuliani at a press conference, they were now certain that there was no poison gas on board and that there were no biological agents. In the factories of New Jersey, Tuuli whispered, they wear clothes like these, then Felix put a hand on her dust-covered cheek. It's all right, he said, we were worried about you. There's still chocolate ice cream in the fridge, I said. Felix opened two more beers and we watched Tuuli as she very

intently and carefully spooned the whole cup of ice cream. Here
we were and we couldn't get away, no trains were leaving, no
buses were running, no airplane was permitted to take off, all the
bridges were closed. We expected the worst and had no idea what
the worst could be, but

Kiki interrupts me at this point. I can imagine the light, she says,
setting her glass on the knee-high table, not the worst. She wakes
Lua and positions his head on the arm of my chair, she takes a
picture of the two of us through her wine glass. You guys are
drunk again, says Lua, and I'm glad he's finally breaking his
silence, because he's been too quiet today, and Kiki Kaufman with
the camera doesn't object when I gesture for more wine, when
I decline to taste and approve, when the waiters in light of my
story and the camera finally replace Kiki's white wine glass with
a larger one. She presses the shutter release and raises her filled
glass first to me, then to the window and toward the sky, as if
she were saying thanks for the invitation. She nods as if she were
joining Tuuli and Felix and me, as if she were climbing with her
camera out the window and up the fire escape to us and sitting
down with us on the edge of the roof, as if she were watching

as Tuuli wiped the dust off the lens of her camera with her sleeve.
We were sitting on the roof over Lorimer Street. The answering
machine in the apartment clicked on, Lua howled with the sirens.
Felix and I took turns climbing down to get more beer. The lines
were jammed, we couldn't use the phone. Tuuli stared for a long
time at a blank billboard over the Brooklyn-Queens Expressway,
which obstructed the view of the place where that morning the
towers had still stood. She looked mellower now than she had at
the kitchen table. Felix was talking about the smoke cloud, how

strangely beautiful and aflame it was in the sunset, and Tuuli's tears smeared the ash on her face. Felix sat down next to her on the edge of the roof and said, your tears are smudging. He leaned toward her for a kiss. In one hand he was holding a beer can, the other was placed on the fine blonde hair on the back of Tuuli's neck. I kneeled down between the two of them, took the camera, and Felix lifted his beer into the picture at the right moment and asked

Can you look right over here? Kiki stops me, and I hold my glass up to her camera eye. Please don't interrupt me, I say, cameras don't talk. I'm drunk, I hold on to Lua's collar, I put down the wine, and Kiki photographs herself and me and Lua in the dark window and West Broadway in the rain on the other side. I remember

the sky like a soap bubble over the roof of 37 Lorimer Street, the sun behind the smoke and the billboard, the pale searchlights over lower Manhattan, familiar from operating rooms and film sets. I remember Felix and Tuuli sitting next to each other on the edge of the roof and more and more ambulances on the BQE. How Tuuli began to roll a joint for us, how she watched her fingers as she did so, how she sang softly to herself, how Felix and I listened to ourselves breathing, how Tuuli's song mingled with the singing of the Latino regulars in front of Oscar's corner store below, how Felix stood up after a while and claimed that Colombians were used to things like this: Colombians sang all the time, they had civil war and blown-up airplanes every day, they didn't even notice days like today anymore, that was a good solution. Anyway, said Felix, did we know that Bryan Adams and Keanu Reeves always shared a hotel room when they were in New York, at the Mark Hotel on Seventy-seventh Street and Madison Avenue.

Are they fucking? Kiki Kaufman laughs, and Lua is sleeping with a heavy head on his remaining front paw, he knows Felix's and my stories, he knows my questions and Felix's answers,

they're fucking, said Felix, yup. Couldn't Bryan Adams be Keanu Reeves's father? It didn't matter, the two of them were fucking. We laughed and clinked our beers, Tuuli sat on the edge of the roof and watched the ambulances on their way to Manhattan. People were jumping out, she said, a little boy next to me on the roof saw people falling onto the plaza, he asked, "Why are the birds burning, Mom?" Probably, said Tuuli, jumping is faster than burning, probably when it comes to dying, speed matters. She was done with the joint, Felix lit it and smoked between index finger and thumb, as if we were soldiers on watch, as if we had to conceal the burning tip, as if weapons were pointed at us, as if we were being observed, no open containers, no animals, no weapons. Then he leaned his head back and exhaled. Jumping is always better than burning or drowning, said Felix, he'd once fallen out a window himself, dislocated his shoulder and broken his tailbone, had he ever told us about that before? He'd told us, but when one of us is talking, the others can be silent, so we didn't interrupt him. Felix sat down on the edge of the roof, smoked and talked to himself. Down in the apartment the answering machine was recording messages again, someone wanted to know whether we were still alive. We lay on the roof as if in the beyond and listened to the voices from the other side of the world. We didn't answer, we couldn't move. Tuuli held her belly as if she had pains. I touched the back of her sweaty neck, her neck hairs were sticky. I thought you were dead, I said, and Tuuli bent over the edge. What are you guys talking about, she asked, and her voice sounded faded like the voices on the answering machine. Maybe that had to do with the fact that, a few seconds later, she puked very softly off the roof. Tuuli stood up and spat, we're done for, that was it, she said. I could have wiped the dust off Tuuli's face, given her clothes that fit her, declined the next beer and filled up Lua's bowl maybe, I could have offered her my toothbrush and my bed, myself too. I should have told her to get some sleep, tomorrow this world would definitely look different. But I waited too long. Nothing better occurs to you? Lua asked me. Tonight your words mean the exact same thing as your silence, he said. Felix brought a guitar up, he played something by Johnny Cash and pissed off the roof at the same time. In front of Corner Store Oscar's corner store the Colombians were drinking and singing their laments on Skillman Avenue, aah, more beer for the angels of Lorimer Street, said Corner Store Oscar, with his half-shot-off lower jaw, people are drinking today like there's no tomorrow. On the store's steps one of the Colombians was drumming on plastic paint buckets, the guy in the Argentinian soccer jersey was banging two beer bottles together, a Cuban regular was playing ukulele, Corner Store Oscar was shaking his keys. He was out of Rolling Rock, Budweiser, Coors Light. A six-pack of Pabst, I said, and Lua next to me ordered the same. Maybe so Corner Store Oscar wouldn't have to go for the beer twice, because in summer it's very warm even at night in New York. We and the beer brands are going downhill, said Lua, and when I returned to the roof, Tuuli looked up from Felix's mouth. We're not alone, she lied, we're three. I turned around and climbed back down to give word of our survival. The lines were finally free again.

Kiki is smiling, she knows those moments, the talking just to keep talking. What this or that person said when no one knew how things would go on at all. She strokes Lua's head. The rain is now running down the large windows of the SoHo Grand Hotel, Kiki puts her black shoes next to my white ones on the armchair and signals to the waiter for the bill. Stop? I ask, but Kiki says, keep going! Your story is a good story, still no flags or structures or morality, just uncertainty and clarity, it sounds like something out of a book. Lately, I say, I haven't been sleeping much, lately I've been waiting for the appropriate words. Then I finish my drink and pay the whole bill. I hold on to Lua's leash as we drift along Canal Street in the greasy Chinatown rain, from shop window to shop window, from awning to awning, plucked and smoked chickens on display, electrical appliances and videos, as we lean on garbage cans, as we look into Kiki's camera and then end up in Kiki's hotel room, where we take off our wet clothes and hang them on a few hooks. Where we don't touch each other as Kiki takes pictures of us under the fluorescent lights, the green paint of the walls behind our pale bodies, the light on her sad breasts, on my tired cock. And finally Kiki tells me that this hotel was once the flophouse on the Bowery where Hurstwood suffocated himself out of hopeless love in a gas stove at the end of *Sister Carrie*. Then she takes Lua's head in her hands and he closes his eyes. Animals are the hearts of people, I say, Lua is breathing heavily, and I can go to sleep.

August 7, 2005

(Ping-Pong)

Dawn lasts forever (the house drags itself into the day). On the narrow mattress in the corner of Svensson's study I'm trying to distinguish between sounds and thoughts: the wooden beams, the bedsprings (the ivy is growing). Actually my work could have been done a long time ago, but yesterday toward evening Svensson set plates and glasses and a candle on the kitchen table and between his words and his chewing left no room for questions. He talked about the village on the other side of the rock shelf (Osteno), about the water and about the mountains. He was busy with a knife in the candlelight, I sat at the table and searched for somewhere to start while Tuuli spoke Finnish with the boy. Svensson boiled water for noodles on a gas stove and explained that he'd had no electricity since Friday, a tree had fallen on a power line. There was only water and leftover wine, he wasn't prepared for guests, not for a personal visit and least of all for journalists (why am I here?). Svensson cooked a tomato and sage sauce, he served an earthenware bowl of radicchio and white beans (his laugh conciliatory). The boy grimaced and dropped his fork on the floor, under the table the dog panted. Svensson, said Tuuli, cutting the noodles into little pieces, no child can twirl spaghetti and no child eats radicchio (not conciliatory). Yes, he knew that. I ate silently and therefore too much, drank some red wine and tasted Elisabeth in it. Tuuli ate and smoked, the boy on her lap fell asleep (half a tomato in his hand dripped on her leg and fell to the floor). As Tuuli finally put the child with his smeared mouth to bed, I remained seated. For a few more minutes I tried to start a conversation with Svensson, but because he was speaking incessantly without talking about himself, I excused myself too (fatigue). Elisabeth's annoying assignment brought me as far as his kitchen, and I didn't manage even to ask the routine questions. For the interesting things there was no time (the owner of the suitcase, the boy, Svensson and Tuuli). Later I sat in Svensson's study and heard Tuuli's voice in another room singing a Finnish lullaby. I pictured her sitting on the edge of the bed and brushing the boy's hair from his forehead, I tried to write, but lost my image of her in my words. I fell asleep on Svensson's mattress and didn't wake up again until late at night. The cicadas were noisy. I didn't know where I was, I didn't know where the others were sleeping (I didn't know who I was).

Lugano–Chiasso–Malpensa

Now it's Sunday morning, a rooster is crowing, scattered birds and insects. I wait for the dog's coughing and the boy's crying. Nothing. I'm still in Svensson's house, but no one seems to be aware of me. On the Swiss side of the lake I could have woken up in my own hotel bed, a Sunday newspaper on the terrace, the first game day of the Bundesliga soccer season, etc. My return flight to Hamburg leaves today in the late afternoon, I have to go back to Milan (Lugano–Chiasso–Malpensa). Elisabeth would have tried to discuss my leaving with me, but I've made myself unreachable. I should notify the hotel, but I remain lying in the half-light of the study and don't touch anything (journalistic scrupulousness). I'm expecting Svensson's footsteps, I'm expecting his knock at the door. Apparently the only way to leave this place is with the boat.

Svensson is a mysterious man: he wouldn't live alone at the end
of the world and not want other people around him for no reason.
Svensson must not like people. I sit back down at his desk and take
notes, so as to retain the important things (the slosh of the water
against the dock).

Hotel Norge

In a dark, cheap double room in the Hotel Norge near the Chris-
tuskirche, I lay on my back and listened to the surge of the early
traffic. My 30th birthday, Elisabeth was already 36, a few weeks
earlier we'd met again. This evening we'd first eaten solemnly
(loup de mer) and then kept drinking so as to stop time, we drifted
through the night. When it began to rain toward morning, we
were standing outside the hotel's glass revolving door (time
refused and passed more swiftly). We could go to my place, said
Elisabeth. We could also stay here, I said (I don't know what held
me back). The hotel room was five hundred meters from her
apartment. At the reception desk I showed the night porter my
identification, and Elisabeth searched in her purse for her credit
card (our names on a bill together for the first time). The porter is
even younger than you, Daniel, she whispered, at least two years.
We were drunker than we thought. In the elevator she kissed me
as if I belonged to her. She wanted to fuck me right now, she said.
(Elisabeth has long talked straight. She has her reasons.) But then
she disappeared into the bathroom and stayed there for an unusu-
ally long time. I was torn about whether I should open the door,
whether we knew each other well enough. I turned the hotel
television on and off and wondered whether we could love each
other. Later Elisabeth's retching woke me. She was kneeling over
the toilet and vomiting. Would I stay with her anyway, she asked

between two regurgitations of fish and wine and bile (please, Daniel?).

my Renault 4

I want to retain the important things (our first hotel bill). Such as my first car, my first kiss, my first girlfriend, my first love, my first betrayal, my first abortion. My preferences and selection criteria, for example. Names with the vowel *a* in them, maybe, tallness under certain circumstances, maybe an unkitschy femininity, blonde hair possibly, more likely red. It's now Sunday morning, Elisabeth will have gone home late last night on my bike (the R4 parked on Bismarckstrasse, the windshields murky from the lindens). Now she's waking up in the bed. Before our wedding I slept with eleven women (I don't care about numbers, Daniel, said Elisabeth, you can almost count to eleven on two hands). I haven't yet told her everything about myself that seems important to me:

(1) Carolina. She came to Germany from Warsaw in 1989, at first she didn't speak much German and later she spoke it very well. Someone or other called her shoes cheap hooker boots, she was the prettiest girl I knew, she had seventy-centimeter-long blonde hair (I measured). We had no idea about sex, we were Catholic, I secretly accompanied her to her babysitting jobs. For a few months I forgot my age (we considered most things possible). We talked a lot, we wanted to take our time and be able to laugh even when having sex. But then it was a deeply serious matter with technical deficiencies (after a year she exchanged me for a boy with a red Toyota). I ran into her again in 2001 at Frankfurt Airport, she had a practical short haircut, she'd married someone from the

old days and since then had been living in Menden in the Sauerland. After Carolina I spent a while just listening when the other boys talked about girls. We called one another by our last names. Pfeifer recorded music tapes (U2), Debus always kissed right away, the rest comes naturally, he said, Hornberg had a girlfriend and joined her family on trips to the mini-golf course, Petrovic had a southeastern roll in his *r*, Issel a soulful gaze, Wilson was the shortest and relied on the cute little kid angle. Mandelkern just says too much weird stuff, they said, Mandelkern has Carolina in his bones. In the spring of 1991 I inherited the Renault in excellent condition from my mother (I rarely talk about her death). I picked up a smattering of French, left the *Süddeutsche* and an issue of *Spex* on the passenger seat (unread), and learned to search at the right moments for a slip of paper to make a note of a compelling sentence from one of my female passengers. We drove to local art-house cinemas. Within a few months, those who leaned over the dashboard gearshift were:

(2) Nadine,

(3) Tanja,

(4) Eva,

(5) Katrin. I stayed the night in their converted attics amid their application portfolios for art academies, their Janosch novels (*Polski Blues*), Tori Amos posters, and hammocks (in the end they studied art education). It was probably about proving our adulthood, we blurred our boundaries before we knew them (Tanja and Katrin kissed each other when I wasn't there).

(6) Hanna. With Hanna I developed the shrinking and dwindling and my it-can't-go-on-like-this (the discovery of fear). She lived with a biology student in a separate apartment in her parents' house, he bred geckos. Her mother was from Flensburg and was the examining physician at the district recruiting office

(my mother holds the balls of all the eighteen-year-old men in this town and makes them cough, she said). Hanna decided that I should stop with the newspaper thing (she meant the *Süddeutsche* on the passenger seat of the Renault). Hanna's father was an Indian engineer with an irritatingly single-minded fixation on the family honor. When Hanna was kneeling in front of me in the bushes behind the stadium one night, I could see her father and the biology student in the parking lot shining flashlights into the parked Renault (my cock in her mouth). I was declared unfit. They always did that when she came home later than arranged, said Hanna, and now cough (Hanna could do whatever she wanted, I wasn't functioning)!

(7) Britta. With Britta my first wrong turn. In 1994 Hornberg, Pfeifer, and I had left our town and driven the Renault to the university in Hamburg (all of us studying ethnology). For the first time it was about our whole life. Britta was older and beautiful, we talked on the phone for nights on end, I in my early twenties, she three years older. I was astonished by her complete and continuous interest in me. Then one of my friends (Wilson) called her a "stupid horse" in front of me, that made me absurdly insecure, we talked on the phone more rarely and slept together only one more time. And that wasn't until five years later, drunk and unnoticed, at that same undersized friend's wedding. I wanted to save us for later, I said, and she laughed at me. In the summer of 2004 she called me again: she was now living in Berlin, she was getting married next week, she was five months pregnant, she just wanted me to know that (I couldn't have been the father). I was, of all things, driving the R4 on the A24 from Berlin to Hamburg. I said I was sorry, I'd imagined things differently: the two of us and later. Britta's reply on the phone: but you're married too, Daniel! I said unnecessarily "yes, but" and the connection

broke immediately. Autobahn and life struck me as excessively straight (turning impossible and prohibited).

(8) Carolina. The second Carolina wore red shoes with her blonde hair and was the most honest person I knew. She stood in front of Hornberg, Pfeifer, and me in the lecture hall of the Museum of Ethnology and would mark our first academic papers ("Intensive Agriculture among the Kapauku in New Guinea"). Carolina was Professor Jansen's assistant and half Finnish, half Swedish. I'd never met a woman who could judge so clearly and run so fast (from her I learned to run, to write, to think). On her lower right leg a tattooed pack of foxes craved the grapes and rowanberries that climbed around her hip bones (the Fable of the Fox and the Grapes/*Fabeln om räven och rönnbären*). Carolina was twenty-five, she ran marathons and kickboxed (in a sparring session she once broke her opponent's nose with her fist). After three years I'd completed my studies and she her dissertation. Did I want to go for a doctorate, Professor Jansen asked me, and I said "yes." When the second Carolina then went back to the University of Helsinki, I brought her to the Hamburg Airport. The unattainable, she said at the security checkpoint, is something different for everyone (I got her assistantship in the witch archive).

(9) Eva. To this day Hornberg doesn't know anything about it (Eva taught me betrayal). Eva was Hornberg's second girlfriend and for two years mine at the same time (turn of the millennium on the Port of Hamburg; her tongue piercing rattled against my teeth while Hornberg peed off a landing pier). When he returned from Tanzania in July after three months of field research, Eva was pregnant (Hornberg was depressed from the malaria prophylaxis). I sat in the waiting room of the gynecologist and observed the colorful tropical fish in the octagonal tank (different perspectives through different plates of glass). Eva had decided against the

child without asking my opinion (she must have been thinking of Hornberg). She didn't want to deprive us of all other possibilities, she said. This time I would have been the father (I wanted to live up to the responsibility; I would have managed). When Eva awoke from the sedation, the doctor's assistant brought coffee and cinnamon buns and stroked her cheek (I didn't touch her, it struck me as inappropriate). When she called Hornberg in the afternoon and asked him not to contact her anymore, I was sitting on the floor of her room and felt the need to go far away. Hornberg later wrote to me in confidence that he'd wanted to have the child (he wrote "my child"). Then he got the Renault for a few years.

(10) Anne. Shortly thereafter, Professor Jansen's offer to me of the opportunity to go to Berkeley (winter semester 2000). I'm not eager to see you go, Mandelkern, said Jansen, putting his hand on my shoulder, but you have to get out of here! My dissertation fit the Berkeley department's profile (media-theory-oriented inquiries into the ethnographic film). There, Anne from Zurich sat in the office next to mine, we talked about documentary and feature films and strategies of direction and of authenticity and were silent at the decisive points (our bodies didn't mesh; we were nothing but words). Only after a few weeks did we sleep together in her small, shabby room near Ohlone Park (the smell of the seafood restaurant under her fire escape). Our dissertations progressed (our careers, our lives). In March 2001 we found an apartment to share on Delaware Street and San Pablo Avenue, we had a shared language that no one else in Berkeley seemed to speak (children were out of the question; we were academics). Shortly before an important lecture on Stéphane Breton's strategy of authenticity through the subjective camera, the two airplanes flew into the World Trade Center towers in New York. My lecture and the doctoral conference were postponed until further notice (I never

gave the talk). Anne and I fell into a panic. She decided to take the first flight back to Europe and immediately drove to the airport, either I would come with her to Switzerland or we would have to make do with e-mails. I stayed in Berkeley, grieved, and continued to tinker with my dissertation for a while (I wanted to wait and see). Anne discovered her interest in European ethnology. I read my paper again and again, gradually I found myself learning it by heart more than writing it. After a few weeks we broke up amicably and via e-mail (the affection had lost its tangibility).

(11) Laura. In early 2002 I had asked Jansen for permission to cut back on the dissertation for a few months due to financial difficulties. The scholarship had run out, I needed money and was compiling glossaries for *GEO* (but hurry, Mandelkern, said Jansen, in two years I'm leaving here!). On the way to work one morning someone threw himself in front of the train between Sternschanze and St. Pauli stations, Laura and I sat next to each other on the U-Bahn until the police and the forensic specialists had finished their work (a week before I met Elisabeth in the cafeteria). Laura had a vague resemblance to the second Carolina. We had a coffee in the Portuguese Quarter, she lived not far from there in Neustadt. This story was an attempt (it failed miserably).

(12) Elisabeth. You don't consider the number eleven an impressive tally, Elisabeth. You in the bathroom next to me, your blood on me. You sing "The Linden Tree" (the Renault in front of the house sticky and gray with linden blood). You and I in a parking lot on the Atlantic coast of Brittany, on Mont Ventoux, in a hotel room in Venasque. You and I on a traffic island in Lyon when the Renault gave up in the middle of the summer (we had to replace the engine). You on the bank of the Parsęta (our honeymoon). The scar under your belly button. Your red hair, the *a* in your

name, your athletic height, your long-limbed beauty (the green of your eyes).

Adho Mukha Svanasana

I got distracted. First, with the sun, the noise of the birds, the ledge outside Svensson's window is thickly crusted with pigeon droppings. Elisabeth is a consistent woman, she will now be jogging along the canal on the way to yoga, as she does every Sunday morning. After the wedding she kept her maiden name, I'm not you, she says, and you're not me, Mandelkern (Elisabeth Edda Emmerich). For the two of us a double name was out of the question. It's only logical that her spine is all but stiff despite years of practice, says Elisabeth. I practice and practice and practice, she says, and you bend like green wood in the slightest breeze. She's right: I can do the crow, I can do the crane, I can do the dog (Adho Mukha Svanasana). Later Elisabeth will have a cup of tea in the Schanzenviertel area. She stopped drinking coffee, she doesn't use her espresso pot anymore. Though caffeine in the months before pregnancy has no known harmful consequences, she says, there's no need to tempt fate (these days there's chai everywhere). I left the apartment without a word.

Method Section: Participant Observation

I know the first sentence of my dissertation by heart: "Since Malinowski's field studies on the Trobriand Islands, participant observation has been regarded as a standard method of ethnographic field research." Svensson has told me nothing of significance since yesterday afternoon. I should be patient (ethnological principle: "Silence is the older brother of the word"). I should observe the structure of the ethnos under investigation (the animals wake up first). I should find a main informant (Tuuli). I could work with the pitiful scientific methods I have at my disposal here, I could count (three chickens), I could measure (Tuuli's height), I could time (the minutes for the return journey to Lugano).

my pitiful methods

Now the wasps are buzzing in the undergrowth below the open window. Svensson and the dog are slowly walking toward the shore through a haze of dew and spiderwebs (Optolyth). I hear the chickens clucking. Lua's gait is heavy, only the missing leg puts some motion into the animal. Svensson, wearing blue shorts and sneakers, grabs Lua's ears and ruffles the fur on his head. Svensson is shirtless, he's much more robust than in the photo in his book, he stretches his thighs and calves, then he does sit-ups and push-ups. On the smooth lake two fishermen in a wooden boat are floating by incredibly slowly, one of the two catches a fish at this very instant, frees it from the hook, and throws it back in the water (the whistled melody of the other). Suddenly Svensson stands up, puts on the purple T-shirt, and disappears in the undergrowth behind the Fiat (the purple of a Mass vestment). With the binoculars I can see how the coughing shakes the dog's flanks (under "C" as in "cough" in the *Great Encyclopedia of Dog Breeds* various possibilities: canine distemper, for example; for dogs amputations are almost always accompanied by intense arthrosis of the compensating joint, in contrast to human beings, dogs do not perceive missing extremities as a psychic burden: "dogs live in the moment"). The suitcase is still under the desk, the paper clips still bend in the lock (an advertising sticker scrawled over with a felt-tip pen: Beer makes you schmart, it made ~~Thrifty~~ Felix wiser!).

my morbid idyll

The reader at the tower window, the vines are reclaiming the stones, an animal is dying, the chickens are strolling around the ruin (Romanticism). For a 3,000-word author profile, that won't be enough. I lack the starting point for a story (about the writer in the ivory tower there's nothing plausible left to be said), I think of Malinowski: "In this type of work, it is good for the ethnographer to put aside camera, notebook and pencil, and to join himself in what is going on." So I put aside the pen to finally speak with Svensson.

Lua's threat

So early in the morning the air is already warmer than yesterday in Hamburg. From a small balcony high above the ground, a much too narrow and much too steep wooden staircase leads down along the wall of the house (three steps are missing), swallows and pigeons are fluttering in the exposed gables, wasps are buzzing around my head. As I walk down to the dock, Lua lifts his head and looks at me. On the lake drift flowers, leaves, plastic bottles (the lake a stained mirror). It must be eight o'clock now, I think for a few unexpected seconds of Elisabeth (under the lindens in front of our house she's searching for her key; Svensson's ruin lies like a garbage bag ready for collection next to the Asian take-out place on the ground floor of 88 Bismarckstrasse). The noise of the wasps and the gurgle of the water are sounds that make you lonely, I would miss the breathing of the city here (the first buses, the first S-Bahn). Is anyone here? I ask. The two fishermen now row past me farther away from the shore, I raise my hand, but they don't return the greeting (I don't belong here). I walk very slowly and in a cautious curve back to the house, Lua's eyes follow me. Then the old dog suddenly sits up and barks at me threateningly and darkly, as if I were an intruder (as if I were getting too close to his secret). Tuuli? I ask, Svensson? Nothing. I'm alone with the three-legged dog.

museum

Svensson lives in the front and intact part of the narrow house, in the back wild vine and ivy are growing in through the windows and the cracked roof. The rusty door of the shed is locked, in front of it are the circular saw, the stack of plastic pipes, and a toolbox (green and yellow). The grass has grown high, even though there's a lawn mower resting in the middle of the meadow. The ground floor with a fireplace and floor-length windows facing the lake, stone steps are set in the wall on the left (without railing), a gallery runs along three sides of the room, above is the entrance to the sparse kitchen. Svensson's house is Svensson's museum. It's now light enough to view the pictures on the walls. I recognize the drawings from *The Story of Leo and the Notmuch* (I walk through Svensson's book). On the ground floor several portraits are hanging on the unplastered walls, oil on canvas, almost always showing Svensson in urban scenes, subway signs maybe, the Chrysler Building probably (New York). Settings and backgrounds fray at the edges, undercoats show through, sometimes the canvas too. On the other hand: Svensson's face is always clear and distinct, his eyes don't smile, his gaze bores directly into the viewer (can a painter look at himself this way?). I walk from painting to painting: Svensson in a suit in front of a take-out place in Chinatown (maybe), in the background hang chickens (naked and iodine-yellow, headfirst), Svensson naked on a bed against a splotchy green background without perspective, Svensson and Lua on steps. In the right lower corner of most of the paintings, two black letters (another pseudonym?):

k; k;

Finally, on the wall above the wooden table, a painting of Svensson on his Italian dock, some fleeting rings in the water, otherwise it's dark. Svensson is holding a hand in the air, in the darkness on the opposite shore a yellow light, on the lower edge in the same yellow

THE GREAT SVENSSON

(Can he be serious?)

She offered herself to me

An afternoon in August 2003: Elisabeth and I on our bikes on the way back from the Kaifu-Bad swimming pools. First we'd talked about this and that, then very theoretically about sex, about the individual body in a visual society, all day we'd lain side by side on a towel, the pool full of children's noise, piked somersaults, beer cans and cigarettes in the wet fingers of thin sixteen-year-old girls. Back in my apartment we left the bikes unlocked in front of the building (Marthastrasse), the clammy beach bag lay next to the dresser. Elisabeth held on to my pull-up bar with one hand, I buried my face in the scanty flesh of her stretched shoulder, reached for her surprisingly large breasts (in comparison) and Elisabeth threw her red bikini bottom on the living room floorboards. Dust hung in the room. I never told you that I'm married, said Elisabeth, arching her back (she offered herself to me).

Could she be serious?

I'm standing in the dark stairwell. Is no one here? The door to what seems to be Svensson's bedroom is wide open: a small room, a bed (white sheets, two pillows), next to it a blue and yellow baby changing table. In an open closet shirts wrapped in plastic, folded towels, suits, shorts, T-shirts (*Lavasecco Sole—Lavanderia & Stireria*). Some hangers with black dresses and skirts in bright colors, women's underwear and flip-flops. Then: a box of diapers (Pampers, Italian packaging). A baby changing table and diapers? The passing thought once again that Svensson must have been waiting for Tuuli and the boy, that he's the boy's father, that he got everything ready. An airplane mobile? A stuffed mouse?

What's all this about?

The kitchen window is open, the pots are neatly stacked, dappled sunlight on the floor, Lua's bowl in the corner (this museum is inhabited). At the head of the table a high chair for a toddler (the boy is too big for this chair). The walls are covered with framed photos, smaller canvases, thumbtacked sketches, here too sand, gravel, paper bags, admission tickets, and scraps of newspaper pressed into the paint. From up close concrete motifs, from a distance intentional errors of perspective and proportion. Svensson always too big or too small, standing out from the vanishing lines of the street, floating over steps, driving a taxi (someone who paints himself so often is a lonely man). I try to count the pictures and lose track (my empirical methods). I should call Elisabeth, I could take the boat and escape across the lake, but I remain in Svensson's kitchen (Svensson's museum). Above the sink hangs a mirrored cabinet as in bathrooms, but Svensson's house has no bath, only a yellow-tiled water closet (Svensson has only the lake). I have a story to write, I should do research, so I get my notebook from the room, so I open the cabinet (journalistic dubiousness).

counts and measurements

—Double-Tipped Cotton Q-Tips,
—a glass with toothbrushes (3), one of them a child's toothbrush,
—Crest toothpaste + Scope (stinks),
—Blendi toothpaste,
—40-pack of Tampax Regular Absorbency Tampons,
—month-pack of Ortho Tri-Cyclen Lo Birth Control Pills
—a Minnie Mouse hairbrush and
—a toiletry bag made of fake fur labeled KIKI (in it a receipt for $8.45 from the drugstore chain Duane Reade #345, 460 Eighth Avenue, New York, dated November 18, 2004).

I close the cabinet. Svensson doesn't live alone here (so much for truth).

Sampson

On a Sunday morning in the fall of 2004, stood naked in front of the bathroom cabinet and shaved off a week's growth of beard.

Elisabeth sat on the edge of the bathtub and watched me (we no longer knocked on bathroom doors). For Elisabeth body and word are in step. Hold still, she said, and took the electric shaver from my hand. When I asked what she was up to (why did I submit to this?), Elisabeth said, I'm going to shear you (my pubic hair on the tiles). The sex is more direct that way. Elisabeth knows what she's talking about when she talks about her body. So I held still.

research

On the refrigerator door hangs another Polaroid. I recognize Lua, I recognize Tuuli, her face on a white sheet, framed by her long hair (when did she cut it off?). On her right lies Svensson wearing a fur cap, on her left a blond man with a few days' growth of beard, he's holding the camera. On the lower edge of the picture the black Lua, forced into a blue hooded anorak. All three are looking into the camera (three mouths and a shared smile). I put down my notebook on the kitchen table and notice Tuuli's cool beauty, I wonder how her hair smells this morning. Is the second man next to her Felix Blaumeiser? On the white strip under the picture in thin handwriting with a ballpoint pen: Shitty Paradise City 2000.

my wet feet

Bring back whatever you can get, Mandelkern! Elisabeth ordered on Friday. We can't send a photographer, so you should handle that yourself. The passing thought of taking the picture from the fridge and pocketing it. Svensson wouldn't notice before my departure. The image tells a story: Svensson can laugh, Svensson wears funny fur caps, Svensson has good-looking friends, Svensson's success is justified (such assumptions, such connections, such ideas). Readers want to recognize themselves behind the facade of strangeness, says Elisabeth, and I recall a sentence from my dissertation: "It is of foremost importance that the methodological approach of participant observation seek a 'perception with all the senses.'" I actually hold Tuuli's picture under my nose and inhale deeply, but then she herself is standing there in the light in front of the window, holding the boy: Good morning, *Karvasmanteli*, she says,

Is this what your research looks like?

The peculiarity of this situation: I'm standing in a puddle of water on the floor in front of the fridge, a small, pretty woman in a short green nightshirt is making coffee, and I'm watching her. What order do these pictures belong in? I ask, as if Tuuli should know such things (her bare feet). The passing thought that I won't fulfill my assignment in such a naïve manner (the contents of medicine cabinets, the smell of Polaroids). Tuuli doesn't answer, instead she sets the boy on a chair, opens cabinet doors carefully and closes them loudly, until she finally finds an espresso pot. She cleans it, searches for coffee, opens the fridge (another flood of condensed water on the tiles), then she pours some spoiled milk into the sink and curses in Finnish. She lights the gas flame. I observe her without saying a word (I never gave Elisabeth an answer either). Tuuli's fingers are not at home in this kitchen and in this house, she keeps returning to the boy and reaching into his hair as if she doesn't want to leave him alone here. I'm fond of her delicate movements, her tentativeness, her care (she and the boy belong to each other). Only when the coffee is on the stove does she turn to me. On the table in front of Tuuli her cigarettes are still lying in the same spot where she was sitting yesterday evening (I'm still standing in the same spot where she found me a short while ago). She takes the picture from my hand and hangs it back on the fridge. She lights a cigarette and tosses me a dish towel (her breasts under the green nightshirt). Dry your feet, *Manteli*, she says, wet feet make you sick.

The Hotel Lido Seegarten is beautiful

It's the subtle condescensions of Elisabeth the successful journalist that I can't bear, her didactic interjections and motherly comments on consistency, discipline, and tallying expenses. Elisabeth will stand up from her seat at the conference table and say loudly and clearly that she is responsible for the department, including the budget for freelance writers. We shouldn't forget that (by which she means me). She will rebuke me professionally for the fact that the booked and prepaid stay in the Hotel Lido Seegarten has elapsed, and above all she will take it personally (then she'll later want to forgive me my transgression).

Interview (Tuuli & Manteli)

MANDELKERN: Do you like the pictures?

TUULI: I don't know these pictures, I'm seeing them for the first time.

M: You're in the Polaroids yourself.

T: Felix just snapped the shot when he thought the moment was perfect. It's not art.

M: I like them. Have you known each other long?

T: Yes. Have you said good morning yet?

THE BOY: —

T: Would you like to go out? You can play with Lua if you want. Lua is a good dog. I'll be right there, *annas kun keitän nopeasti kahvit.* Coffee, *Manteli?*

M: Yes, please.

B: I'm going to play with Lua now.

T: Yes, as long as you're careful.

B: And brave?

T: Yes, *älä pelkää.*

B: *Minä en pelkää, Äiti.*

T: And there's no reason to be, Samy. He says he's not afraid.

M: You just said his name for the first time. Samy.

my main informant

Tuuli's smoking and looking at her toes. We're standing barefoot by the large windows and watching the boy, we're drinking coffee. Tuuli's leaning casually against the pane, her toenail polish is chipped. The boy circles the dog, occasionally he shouts something I don't understand. Elisabeth polishes her nails only in spring, she'll be in the office now and will be asking whether I called. It must be about eleven in the morning, I have to leave in three hours at the latest, my questions are waiting, 3,000 words are waiting, my superior is waiting (the airplane won't wait). Tuuli is breathing directly on the glass door, on her right and left the cigarette smoke is shining in the sun. She comes much closer to me, her hair still unwashed, the imprint of the pillow still on her neck and left cheek. For participant observation, it's necessary to use all the senses. We observe the boy: he is now kneeling next to Lua in the grass. The dog has stopped coughing, he's twice as big as the boy (Samy). The child touches the animal with all due caution. Is the boy not afraid of dogs? I ask, are you not afraid for

Samy? Tuuli doesn't answer, the dog doesn't move. She stubs out her cigarette in the window putty. I'm sorry, *Manteli*, she says, turning to me. She looks up into my eyes and smiles (the last of the smoke in my face; it's impossible not to notice her nakedness under the nightshirt, her small breasts). She's sorry that she's interfering with my work. Tuuli puts her hand on my chest. The boy is now playing with the chairs by the shore, he's kneeling in front of the broken printer. No, I say, I'm sorry, if someone doesn't belong here, then it's definitely me, as a journalist and ethnologist in this private milieu I'm a foreign body. I just have a few brief questions for Svensson, as I've already mentioned, it's about Svensson the man against the background of the children's book (I'm talking too much). Tuuli's reply: Poppycock. She takes a step past me and sits down on the large table in the middle of the room (I could have moved). She crosses her legs, takes another cigarette out of the pack, and lights it with a match. Then she undoes a hairpin and puts it down next to her on the wood (golden for blonde hair). *Okei*, she says, what do you want to know, *Manteli*? Well, I say, but then words fail me. *Karvasmanteli*?

Manteli/Karvasmanteli

Tuuli's not the first. I've gotten used to comments and jokes about my name. My father was from Prague. My mother didn't choose the name Mandelkern until after his death (patrilineality, matrilineality), otherwise I would have been born and entered in the records as Daniel Mandler. I've looked myself up: To treat epileptics in the first half of the previous century neurologists removed the amygdala (the *Mandelkern*), the part of the brain responsible for emotional attachment to things, people, and situations, but also for fear and panic attacks. The amygdala is almond-shaped

(the Greek *amygdalē* means almond, just as my last name literally means "almond kernel"). My father was a lawyer in the
Ruhr area. When the first Carolina left me, Pfeifer laughed and
said: What a kick in the nuts for Mandelkern! The otherwise
unimaginative Hornberg insisted for years on my resemblance
to Marc Almond, he spoke of separation at birth (the idiot still
sings "Tainted Love" whenever we meet). My mother's mother
is named Röther, she was born Hülsmeier and is from Hamm,
in Westphalia. My pediatrician laughed as he diagnosed me with
inflammation of the amygdala when I was sent to him with my
first acne (*Mandelkernentzündung*). *Karvasmanteli* means bitter
almond. Elisabeth thinks that only characters in novels and journalists should be named Mandelkern. The name sounds like it
means something special, she says, your name leaves tracks (I
have to disappoint her).

Interview (author or illustrator?)

MANDELKERN: When are all these pictures from?

TUULI: We haven't seen each other for a long time.

M: So has Svensson always painted?

T: Svensson is a collector, *Manteli*, he's never painted a picture.

M: Then are the pictures in the book not by him at all?

T: He should tell you about that himself.

M: Are they by Felix Blaumeiser? Did Blaumeiser paint all these
   pictures?

T: The villa on the other side of the lake belongs to his family.
   Svensson's house too. Nothing else. Felix had nothing to do
   with art.

M: Had?

T: What has Svensson told you?

M: Nothing. Is there something to tell?

T: Everything Svensson says is made up, *Manteli*, you can write that. Svensson collects fragments and assembles them into a world he can bear.

Tears and Blood

Half an hour later Tuuli is cursing in Finnish. She carries the crying boy into the kitchen and opens the medicine cabinet. The boy is bleeding from a wound on his hand, his light blue T-shirt is stained, but he calms down quickly as Tuuli wipes the blood off his hands and the tears from his face. Was it the dog? I ask, but don't get an answer. I don't know how I can help. In her anger Tuuli's cheeks glow and her hands move faster (blood now on her nightshirt too). By the water the dog can be heard still coughing. No, Tuuli finally says, not the dog. It was Svensson. For years I wrote him e-mails, he read them and didn't reply, then I announced our visit and when he got that message, *idiootti*, he threw his computer out the window. No more computer, no mail, for days no power: Poppycock, she says, Svensson wants to be alone here. Lua forgot how to bite a long time ago.

Le silence est l'aîné de la parole

Around noon Svensson is standing in the doorway again, sweaty, an army rucksack full of groceries on his back, in his hand a yellow children's fishing rod wrapped in plastic. He ignores the blood and Tuuli's nimble fingers, he avoids the bandage on the child's hand. Here, he says, for tonight, to celebrate the occasion. Svensson bought bread, cheese, and wine (Taleggio & Barolo), he unpacks the groceries into the kitchen cabinets. Tomatoes,

onions, peppers. Tuuli and I watch him. Svensson unwraps three
fish from wax paper and lays them on the table, the eyes of the fish
stare in my direction. He holds the fishing rod out to the boy:

Here, for you!

But the boy doesn't take it, he leans on his mother's leg and looks
at Svensson. To celebrate the occasion? Tuuli asks Svensson, to
celebrate the occasion? She turns around, takes the boy's hand,
and leaves the room. I'm standing in the entrance to the terrace,
and want to focus on Svensson, on the questions I should ask
him, on his answers. Svensson arranges his purchases on the
table: fishing rod, cigarettes, three fish. What's the matter with
her? asks Svensson (the plastic-covered children's fishing rod next
to the fish, the bloody paper). Svensson lays an oleander flower in
front of his still life. Silence is the older brother of the word (the
fish is decomposing in the wax paper). Finally I ask: Are they self-
caught? As if I were in Svensson's house on the lake to talk about
delicacies (as if I wanted to get to know him from the ground
up). I don't know what's keeping me from asking my questions
or simply leaving. I should ask Svensson to bring me to Lugano
on the boat, I think, I could also set out on foot toward the village
on the other side of the woods (Osteno or Porlezza). There seems
to be a footpath, Svensson has just returned from shopping, and
from there I could hitchhike to Lugano. Yes, he says, self-caught.
In answer to my question as to whether we could talk now, time
is running out, Svensson looks at me. Then he pushes me through
the kitchen and out of the house. Come with me, Mandelkern,
he says.

against himself

Do you play basketball? he asks. He fetches the ball from under
the Ping-Pong table, looks at me, and turns to the sycamore. He
shoots. The ball flies in a high arc through the air, falls through
the hoop, bounces three times in the tall grass, and then comes
to rest. Svensson looks me directly in the eyes: he's stronger than
I am, he made the shot. I could pick up the ball, I could say: okay,
Svensson, here's the deal. I'd have to make a shot to get answers
to my questions (dramaturgy of sports). But Svensson nailed the
basket to the sycamore with his own hands, Svensson has the
home court advantage here (his house, his lake). I wouldn't win
here, my questions would remain unanswered. So I stand in the
knee-high grass, searching for an explanation for my "no," but
Svensson has apparently not reckoned with any resistance. He
pulls down the second half of the table (on it a swastika in red
spray-paint). Ping-Pong. He always plays only against himself
here, the Italians in the area aren't suited to it, says Svensson,
pointing to the swastika (the Italians must not like him). Svensson
tightens the net. And the dog is ultimately no use as an opponent
either, he says, brushing dry leaves off the table, the dog's missing
his paddle hand (my polite laugh). From the looks of you, it could
be an interesting game, Mandelkern. Svensson positions himself
at the table, under it two paddles and a yellow Ping-Pong ball
(Schöler + Micke). Okay, I say, Ping-Pong, but I have to leave
today, so it's really important to go through a few questions, that's
the reason I traveled here from Hamburg, after all. My return
flight is in a few hours. Best of three, Mandelkern, says Svensson.
If you win, I'll answer all your questions.

between the sets

It's been years since I've held a Ping-Pong paddle in my hand, but I can play (five years Eimsbüttel Sports Club). Svensson wasn't expecting that, and Elisabeth for her part used to take it as a joke (Mr. Mandelkern's Ping-Pong past, she said, an endless back-and-forth). Lua's now lying by the water again and coughing. I win the first set, we play silently and intently (the ticking of the ball a clock). Svensson plays close to the table and slams the yellow ball fiercely, in contrast I stand a few meters away from the table and return the ball slowly and with backspin. Svensson keeps track of the score. My shirt is soon sweaty (my luggage is waiting in Hamburg, Frankfurt, or Lugano). If Svensson mastered the drop shot, he'd have the advantage. I wonder if he can play against himself with such ferocity, alone against the raised half of the table. The 21–19—you–Mandelkern after the first set he states with pointed calm, sweeping a withered oleander flower off the table with a professional hand movement. He takes off his cap and wipes the sweat from his forehead, he suddenly looks distinctly older than his 32 or 33 years. This isn't going to get me any answers, I think, I should let him win. Tuuli and Samy are lying on a rusty deck chair under the oleander and watching us. Svensson gives me the blue and apparently worse paddle. Changing sides means changing paddles, Mandelkern! I nod and let him regroup (I let Svensson hit one past me). I'll give him the second set (be polite and get this over with). Svensson accepts my offer: he slams and slams. When I congratulate him on a successful point (14–7) and remind him once again of my questions (of his answers), he puts down the paddle and takes off his T-shirt.

Shut up and play, Mandelkern!

he says, and I reply to this inappropriate outburst with another friendly "okay." The situation is paradoxical: if I lose, Svensson will be silent, and if I win, he won't want to talk either. Between forceful strokes Svensson now announces the score increasingly loudly and clearly, 15–7, 16–7, 17–7, 18–7, 19–7, 20–7, 21–7. The boy and Tuuli clap their hands. One to one, says Svensson as we change sides again (but not paddles). Svensson takes a drink of water and doesn't offer me anything. He wants to win. Svensson has hung his T-shirt over a chair, zero to zero in the third and decisive set.

no winner/no loser

But then Svensson serves too low and opens the third set with a net ball. He doesn't know that he's playing in the decisive round not only against the sun, but also against my hands' memory (sharper slices, longer strokes, lower error rate). Ping-Pong is not a sport, said Elisabeth, seeming to doubt my masculinity, Ping-Pong is for school recess. Svensson and I stand opposite each other, our rallies get longer and fiercer. Now it's about the game and no longer about politeness and my story (decision: I'm not giving up the lead again). I shift into a defensive position and let Svensson go at me. He serves to my backhand, and I return the ball with a sharp slice close over the net. At 19–19, when I just barely return one of his smashes and slip (I land on my knees), Svensson, completely unchallenged, smacks the ball into the net (he wanted to make it too good). Svensson stands there, inhales through his nostrils and lays his paddle on the table. Then he walks to the dock, takes off his shoes, and jumps without comment into the water (drama-turgy of people). Did *Manteli* win? the boy asks, and Tuuli says,

Svensson can't win.

Shoot the Freak

THESE DAYS, WAKING UP IN A PANIC IS THE RULE. THE DOUBLE plank-bed is screwed to the walls, the room is the exact length of the bed and less than twice as wide. Yesterday I fell asleep naked and I have now woken up under a wool blanket, the time in between has escaped me. Lua is snoring under the bed, and if Lua is snoring, I think, things must be all right. My new suit is hanging on the wall, next to it the room key with a heavy wooden tag: 219. The door is secured from the inside with a padlock. Little by little most of the details come back to me. Kiki Kaufman is asleep next to me, her camera is lying between us on the bed. The Bowery Whitehouse Hotel is not a hotel but a large loft with dark masked windows and tin ceiling tiles. This is where Hurstwood killed himself. The rooms are not rooms but wooden boxes, open on top, with latticework to keep out thieves. In the murky semidarkness I don't know whether it's day or night, I don't have a watch, and I don't have a headache yet from vodka, champagne, and wine. I told Kiki Kaufman half of the story, now she's asleep. She's thin, she has wrapped herself up to her neck in a white sheet, her black curls are spread out around her head like a pillow. Kiki Kaufman's nose is covered with freckles. I remember West Broadway, China-town in the rain, the chickens on their hooks in the windows, the garbage cans, Kiki's camera, Lua next to the black plastic bags. This city never sleeps, I think, the neon lights never go out. In one of the boxes someone screams, Kiki wakes up, we're lying side by side. On the third floor of the Bowery Whitehouse Hotel we

listen to things: footsteps on the worn-down carpet, the opening
of beer cans, then a belch, the toilet at the end of the corridor, the
groans of sad people in their boxes. I haven't yet told Kiki that
Tuuli had a boy, or that his name is Samuli, that the two of them
are doing well, that I don't know who the father is, that I hung
up before Felix could say the name of the clinic. Samuli arrived
two months early, I say, he was actually supposed to be born in
Germany, now he's an American. Kiki asks whether I'm a sort of
uncle to him. After a while we hear a giggle outside our box, a
rattle of keys. From 218 first the sound of a door closing, then the
sound of greedy lips, two fast belt buckles, the squishing sound
of the washable mattress. Six o'clock, Kiki whispers, welcome to
the desert of the real. Then the tear of a wrapper and the snap
of rubber. At least they're using protection, says Kiki. A man is
breathing loudly and clearly, and a woman's voice directs, back,
back, baby. Good. Kiki and I lie on our backs and watch the fan
on the ceiling through the latticework. Next to our heads, the
panting and smacking goes on for a while, then the two voices
and bodies click into their unimaginative in-and-out automatism,
the man's voice sings a hymn, show me those tits, come on, show
me those tits, and the woman fills the gaps with the mantra of
these days, oh my God, oh my God, but her voice falters more
confidently and skillfully than in the television images. Kiki and
I don't move on the rubber mattress, we wait in the groaning of
the wooden walls, in the shaking of sleeping boxes 215 to 221, in
the New York round of the last days and weeks. We're not alone,
we're three, Tuuli said. We miscalculated. Kiki Kaufman, Lua,
and I listen to 215 breathing, 216 dying, 217 asking for quiet. 221
is cooking packet soup on a gas cooker. We hear a lubricant tube
and a lubricant squelch. When 218 then finishes loudly and clearly,
Kiki Kaufman grabs a towel from the hook on the washable wall,

takes a toothbrush out of a small bag, puts on underpants, a white T-shirt. Kiki walks barefoot out of the room, the last few days have to get washed off, she says. Lua sits up and asks me what we're going to do now. I don't know where to go, I answer, and a sign next to the door says *DO NOT leave valuables in room*, but Kiki has left us and the 219 key hanging here.

At ten, Lua, Kiki and I are leaning on the red fire-exit door and drinking vending machine coffee in the lobby. Today the sun is shining, Kiki is wearing a bright summer dress and taking pictures of the homeless people on the bench in front of the Whitehouse. A one-legged man is wearing the stars and stripes around his shoulders and playing a singing saw, he calls Lua his fellow veteran, he gives him a can of Yuengling Lager and puts down the saw on the linoleum when I can't give him any change. Lua drinks silently, Kiki has brushed and petted him, he has said enough for the moment, and because a minute of silence with George Bush is broadcast on television, for a few seconds it's unexpectedly quiet. The backpackers have disappeared, says the one-legged man, usually he lives off them. But then the first sirens are coming down the Bowery, the one-legged man picks up the saw again and plays "America the Beautiful," because Kiki has found another dollar and wants to take pictures. Lua lies at her feet. I get us another coffee, and Kiki says I have to tell her more.

The night from the eleventh to the twelfth of September we spent in my bed, Tuuli slept badly and Lua snored. Eventually I was woken up by the sun or the traffic on the BQE and climbed up to the roof. A little later, Tuuli came up the fire escape and gave me a blanket. I gathered the bottles and cans as she sat in the sun. She had on the purple PricewaterhouseCoopers T-shirt again, I see clearly before my eyes the material stretching across her belly and the cracked white lettering across her breasts. I lay down next to her. It was cold, the tar paper smelled of beer. Lua whimpered down in the apartment, I remember the answering machine coming on. Someone was stuck at some airport and playing pool for money in a hotel lobby. My mother called, then Tuuli's father, her mother, later the secretary of the Blaumeiser shipping company. In the first rays of sunlight we could see the gray houses of Williamsburg, farther away the brick buildings where the Latinos lived. Apart from the column of smoke, there wasn't a cloud in the sky, in the low sunbeams the sycamores along the street seemed to be shining from within. Was she thirsty too, I asked. I don't know, said Tuuli, and leaned toward me for a kiss. I taste like shit, I said to be safe, and she leaned back against the chimney. I closed my eyes and thought about nothing but the sun in my face, my headache, and Tuuli's hand in mine. Down on the street Corner Store Oscar pulled up the metal shutters, put out the garbage, and hung an American flag in the window. And now? asked Tuuli, when Felix later came up to the roof and sat down next to us. You have tar-paper imprints on your face, said Felix, and when I replied that he should stop talking for a few minutes, please, Tuuli removed her hand from mine. Someone had to make coffee.

The singing saw is singing again. There are more and more flags, Kiki interrupts me, and nods to the one-legged man, stars and stripes and rainbows, a time of fresh veterans and new one-legged people is approaching. Breakfast? she asks. Yes, I say, Lua too. When we step into the street from the lobby, the Bowery comes back to me. Right around the corner there are good Bloody Marys, I say, and take Kiki's hand. It's the first time I've touched her intentionally. Her hand in mine feels realer and warmer than

expected. Only now do I notice her eyes. Stop right there! she says
after two blocks and takes a picture of Lua and me in front of a
construction fence covered with missing-person posters. Burned-
out candles, Lua among dried roses and brownish lilies, *missing!*
missing! missing! like an aureole around our heads. Behind the
fence is the empty garden of the B Bar & Grill, this morning only
a fat cat is sitting here under the tree and its turned-off strings
of lights, the first leaves are falling. Lua lies down under the
table and immediately falls asleep. Here too a television is on.
Kiki orders coffee instead of Bloody Marys, as if we always ate
breakfast together, and on television Mayor Giuliani is talking
about how this city has to shop and live and have breakfast as if
everything were completely normal, good morning, New York!
Good morning!

Kiki pays and politely says thanks for Lua's water. That was the
last of my money, she says. Under a tree with Kiki, with the credit
card in my suit pocket and a coffee in my hand, the world looks
distinctly simpler, I think. But then, as Kiki puts her camera on
the table and laughs, as she looks at me with interest, as Lua sleeps
between our feet, I tell her about the cracked concrete slabs of the
Williamsburg piers around noon on September twelfth, the two
painters in the sunlight and their portable easels, the smoke over
the East River bridges in their oil paints. Everywhere people were
standing and staring and talking, the cloud was wafting south-
ward from the World Trade Center, we could smell it. Tuuli sat on
a plank, leaning back on her arms, stretching her pointy belly into
the sun. I threw stones in the water. A boy with horn-rimmed
glasses and a Pavement T-shirt sold Felix pieces of melon from
a cooler bag. Cars stopped, photographers took their pictures,
two camera crews searched for suitable perspectives, a journalist
asked us one by one whether we knew anyone down there, at

the site formerly known as the World Trade Center? He moved on without notes. The smoke smells like Seraverde, said Tuuli, throwing a melon rind into the river, like plastic, gasoline, fire, wet earth, and poverty. Lua jumped in after it. A photographer photographed him as he climbed out of the shallow water with the rind in his mouth and shook himself off, the column of smoke in the background.

Which must have been an interesting picture, Kiki Kaufman interrupts me. For two weeks now she's been taking pictures of the garbage collection and the piles of black garbage bags on the sidewalks, pictures of the police at roadblocks, of the heaps of flowers in front of fire stations, of starved cats and parakeets in evacuated apartments south of Canal Street, of the moral-support crowds lining the West Side Highway toward the south, the *USA! USA! USA!* posters, of bars and cafés and restaurants between Lafayette Street and the Bowery, of drunk people, of crying people, of the bakers in Brooklyn and of American flags in American windows, cars, and trains. Those seconds of this city, says Kiki, have not vanished as irretrievably as others before and after. On the morning of September twelfth, she set out toward New York from Chicago. After the long drive through Illinois, Indiana, Ohio, Pennsylvania, and New Jersey, she parked on the other side of the Hudson. As the only passenger heading toward Manhattan she made it on board an evacuation ship only after long discussion. She was inspected several times by police officers and private security services and finally made it through back alleys and restaurants into the restricted area south of Fourteenth Street, into the completely deserted "frozen zone." The city found itself in a sort of war, but she simply strolled through bars and between garden chairs. She had come too late and was only able to photograph the consequences, not the causes, but those ultimately couldn't be photographed anyway without a world journey. That was the first displacement of reality. She shot the cameras and camera vans and cameramen, who themselves filmed and photographed ruins and debris and dust, she took pictures of the cameras at Ground Zero, pictures of a German photographer in Brooklyn, an Italian camera crew in lower Manhattan, of French tourists with digital cameras, photojournalists with reflex cameras, children with disposable cameras and artists with Hasselblads. Kiki scratches Lua behind the ears and says that we should hit the road now. I want to show you something, she says, pulling Lua across the courtyard and out into the street, the two of them speak English with each other and walk side by side as if they've known each other for years. As we pass David's Kosher & Halal Meat on the way to Kiki's car, we buy Lua his breakfast. Kiki clears off the backseat of her green Honda, she puts three shoeboxes full of pictures in the trunk, takes out a blanket, and makes Lua a bed in the back. She gives me a bottle of water, I haven't drunk water for days, and as Manhattan gradually disappears in the rearview mirror, I unwrap Lua's first proper meal in days from the wax paper.

Along the way I tell her about Miguel and John and their duplex apartment overlooking Tompkins Square Park. John modeled for Tom Ford and Miguel was his agent. Miguel had invited us, so Tuuli, Felix, and I walked across the Williamsburg Bridge in the late afternoon. Tuuli was breathing heavily, and even Lua had a certain wariness in his dragging gait. Manhattan was quiet, the bridge spanned the river without cars on it. We sat down in front of Miguel's gigantic television, John was wearing a blue T-shirt with the red inscription *Super-Gay*, from the window we could see the smoke cloud hanging in the cold white light of Ground Zero. Everybody, this is Super-Gay, said Miguel, Super-Gay, this is everybody. The television was muted, in a glass display case were a few bottles of Bombay Sapphire, CNN flickered in our faces. The airplane loops had been dropped from the program, instead there were now images of the clean-up operation, the posters along the highways and green America Under Attack logos. Mayor Giuliani spoke in front of the first homemade missing-person posters on a lamppost. I already can't watch this shit anymore, said Miguel, America the Beautiful, Bush is hiding somewhere in the clouds over America and suddenly Zero Tolerance Giuliani is the city's savior, God bless New York, one nation under God, and Rudy will take care of everything, probably he'll want to be president soon. Miguel took his telephone from the table and pointed to the smoke, God bless America! Tuuli sat on the sofa and drank water, she rolled Felix a cigarette, occasionally she stood up and arched her back and stuck out her belly. On the terrace Miguel talked on the phone and gesticulated in a purple satin bathrobe, I heard Bach's *Goldberg Variations* from the living room and slowly got drunk again. Miguel yelled something Italian into his phone, took a running start, and slid on his Asian slippers across the marble or fake marble. I wanted to get up and climb down from the roof terrace, walk along Avenue B holding Tuuli's hand, go through one or two police checkpoints and get into a taxi to the airport. Lua could have stayed with Felix. They would let a pregnant woman through everywhere, Tuuli could have slept awhile at the airport, then we would have drunk Earl Grey and eaten oranges for breakfast. In an advanced stage of pregnancy she would have gotten special treatment and been put on the first flight out and back to Europe. In Helsinki or Berlin we would have already had to wear winter jackets, the child could have been born in the Charité. I could have been the official father. But I remained seated and drank, Tuuli closed her eyes, the moon stared over the rooftops, and eventually Felix poured his beer into Lua's bowl and we switched to gin.

The delivery's here, said Super-Gay. The deliveryman looked like a bike courier and brought coke with a receipt. We're first, said Miguel, so the two of them went into the bathroom. Why, no one knew, maybe it was due to a general, vague fear. Felix and I were coke partners, Tuuli watched us. For each round Miguel and John left us two very neat lines on the toilet lid. After the first round my tar-paper fatigue was gone, after the second I was praising Bret Easton Ellis. By the window Felix and John talked about the gin and how Bombay Sapphire had to be drunk straight no matter what, at the very most on the rocks, and so on, the cloud and the light, the visual sensation, the bright sound of Miguel's doorbell. Someone put on electronic music. A few people joined us in the kitchen, Felix switched to whisky, Miguel gave Lua still more beer and pulled him by the tail in a circle, Super-Gay ordered pizza, Felix sushi, Miguel: so what are we going to do now, foreign policy, all this is a reaction to fucked-up imperialism, this attack is only the beginning. Right, right. Lua vomited on the marble, the doorbell rang, people dropped by, deliverymen, messengers, couriers and DJs, writers, journalists, musicians.

The roller coaster is lying there like a slain dragon, Astroland is still empty. Kiki parks her Honda in the no-standing zone next to the Shore Hotel on Surf Avenue. At Nathan's we buy hot dogs with onions and sauerkraut, hot dogs with chili, cheeseburgers, french fries with ketchup, soda for two. I carry the bag, Kiki her camera, Lua drags his leash behind him. Even Coney Island is full of flags now, they're pinned to the padded coat of a Russian woman on Brighton Beach, they're painted on the clam and beer stands, on the wheels of a Korean War veteran's wheelchair, they billow over Astroland, they flutter blue and red and silvery over the boardwalk. Lua poses for Kiki next to the fishermen on the pier and in front of an army recruiting station. He looks boldly at the camera, we buy him cotton candy. A few more booths, then an empty, fenced-in lot with withered grass and paint stains, above it a garland of letters spelling *Shoot the Freak* shines into the sky. Painted in fairground-blue and carnival-yellow, the price is flaking off the walls, *3 for $1,* as is the announcement *Live Target! Paintball Freak! Moving Target! Shoot the Freak!* Kiki says that after the war rhetoric of the last two weeks what she'd like most of all is to shoot at someone herself, but around noon the shooting galleries are closed. Kiki takes pictures of Lua and me amid the bright colors. In the can toss I win a bottle of sugary sparkling wine, the good French stuff, says the woman at the counter, you know?—We do, says Kiki. She pops the cork, and Lua drinks the Coney Island champagne from the soda cup.

Later we sit on the beach next to a playground made of plastic: climbing cube, a few ladders, a slide. The Atlantic lies flat on its back, Astroland holds still. For the first time in weeks Lua gets to run free, for the first time I see the two warships on the horizon. Kiki takes only small sips, she has to get back on the road later, she says. She doesn't say where she's going. The September sun is now slanting steeply over the beach, two old men with metal detectors stroll slowly from right to left, occasionally one of them finds a syringe, bottle cap, or coin. Lua plods along the beach and toward us on his three legs, he flops down on the sand between us and says he's going to take his nap now. Kiki speaks of the beauty of this desolate area, of the decay that resides in places like this, she points to the apartment blocks of red brick behind the booths and carnival rides, one joyous sadness after another, she says, and photographs Lua and me at the bottom of the slide. Have you been together long? she asks, and I answer, yes, very long. And that I'll tell her about Lua's fourth leg and the Heckler & Koch that shot it off. There was still a lot to tell and explain, such as the blood on my T-shirt and my cigarettes. Such as why I'm here now and not with Tuuli and Felix, such as the child. When? Once I've put the last several days behind me, the good-bye first. Kiki packs up her camera and leans on me. Finish your story, Svensson!

Tuuli shut the bathroom door and turned the key. On the toilet lid there was only one line of cocaine. Last round, said Felix, as always. One of us gets the coke, one of us gets Tuuli. Things were what they were. I remember how Tuuli kneeled down between Felix and me on the tiles. Svensson? she asked me, and rummaged in the pockets of her too-large jeans. Yes, I said. She found a coin and showed it to us like a second in a duel. Felix? Tuuli nodded at Felix. I looked first into his face and then at myself in the mirror, our eyes were like dark winter puddles edged with ice. We raised our glasses. Eyes shut! said Tuuli, but I didn't obey. We sat down on the floor, I leaned my head against the wall and looked at Tuuli. Behind a massive block of frosted glass at her back shimmered fluorescent lights, from hidden speakers came the same music as in the apartment, even here in the bathroom a small television was on. I took a sip of my gin and put the heavy glass on the toilet lid. Then Tuuli ran her hand over my eyes as if I were dead. In Miguel's black-tiled bathroom I sat on the floor between the toilet and heated towel racks and suddenly no longer knew exactly who I was. For a few seconds I stopped being Dirk Svensson. I remember the clink of the tossed coin on the tiles and that I opened my eyes again even though it was prohibited. Tuuli put the coin back in her pocket and smiled at me. She swept up a few grains of coke with her index finger and stuck it in Felix's mouth as if he were a baby. He licked it off with his eyes closed. I'd lost, maybe I'd won, that night it couldn't be decided. I took the bill from the toilet lid and snorted the last line with my left nostril, then Tuuli leaned over the toilet and kissed me. Felix sat next to us with his eyes closed and drank his gin, smiling. Had he opened his eyes, maybe everything would have turned out differently. The bitter cocaine dripped into the back of my throat, and Tuuli's tongue tasted numbly of smoke and juniper berries. Okay, I said, and ran my fingers over Tuuli's pregnant belly under the PricewaterhouseCoopers T-shirt she was still wearing, my hands on her breasts, on the back of her neck, and suddenly the last several days and weeks and years and past and future contracted meaningfully and clearly in her lips. Tuuli took my hand, kissed it, and placed it back in my lap. Then someone pounded on the door, told us to open up, the taxi was here. Felix, still squeezing his eyes shut, let us guide him out of the apartment. On the way out I drained my gin and my nose began to bleed on Tuuli's T-shirt.

The taxi crossed the bridge back to Williamsburg, the lights of the Manhattan Bridge shimmered in the dawn of September 14, on the riverbank below us the factories were asleep. Felix gave the taxi driver a tip and bought a flask of whisky from Corner Store Oscar with the change, I pulled the drunk dog home. Tuuli almost fell asleep walking. We gave Lua a shower with tepid water, we didn't want to frighten him. I had surrendered control to the cocaine and opened another bottle of beer, Felix had unscrewed the flask. The muted television showed dancing women in Afghanistan or Iraq or Silvercup Studios on the river. Then Tuuli emerged freshly showered and naked from the bathroom. She tossed me the purple T-shirt, her naked belly and her breasts flickered in the light of the television. She lay down next to Felix. He laid his hands on her belly as if it belonged to him. Tuuli yawned and repeated that they were not alone but were three. She fell asleep immediately. I remember that at that moment I put down my beer and stood up, that I took Felix's flask and Tuuli's T-shirt, that I shut the door behind me and woke Lua. That I then walked down Lorimer Street and turned the next corner, past Settepani and the cardboard box huts under the BQE, first north, then west, later anywhere, away from Tuuli and Felix in my bed and surrounded by my books.

Now, two weeks later on the Coney Island beach, Kiki Kaufman takes my hand in hers, the hand with the hole in the middle, and under her fingers the throb in the wound disappears. The three of you miscalculated, she says, you're like Borromean rings. Lua's still sleeping, and Kiki takes advantage of his sleeping and his looking away, she strokes me around the eyes as if she were wiping away a tear. A little boy in a bathing suit walks across the beach to the water, dragging an inflated rubber Superman behind him. Kiki holds my wounded hand to her cheek and asks if I want to come along to Fire Island, maybe to Sagaponack, to Great Neck or Port Washington, even better all the way to the end of the island, to Montauk, where there's a lighthouse and a proper view of the Atlantic, the deeper water. For two weeks now she's been taking pictures of rubble, of Lua and me in my bloody T-shirt. Kiki shines in the autumn sun as she talks about her pictures. For two weeks she's basically been a camera, now it's enough. She has recorded how the city's been divided into war and peace, she's photographed the hoisting of flags for and against, and both would have stood equally well in the wind. She has understood that she's always seen things too simply. Kiki sits in the sand and smiles at me. What you could see with your own eyes, what you could touch, she says, never made it onto the television sets. She's been taking pictures to verify her own perception, she has failed.

Kiki wakes Lua and tosses him the last cheeseburger. Her toes dig in the sand and find a bottle cap, they give it to me. Ultimately her camera is only a crutch for her ideas, she says, for her it's about making something new out of the photos and stories, she still has some paint in the car. We should head off. Kiki is right: I've told enough, I've drunk too much and eaten too little, I think, burying my telephone and Tuuli's collected cigarettes in the sand. Kiki is right, I think, we should get out of here. I'll climb into her Honda, drive past the carousels and the shooting galleries, down Surf Avenue, under the F train and along the ocean. A view would be good, I say to Kiki Kaufman, let's go to Montauk.

August 7, 2005
(The deeper water)

It looked like a storm, the clouds were still hanging in the San Gottardo, Svensson said after the Ping-Pong match, fetching a bottle of Lugana from the kitchen, they would be here sometime in the afternoon (north-south weather divide). He didn't usually drink, he said, as he uncorked the bottle. Only today. And when he did drink a glass on special occasions, he didn't move his boat an inch. So I could safely take a sip myself, because I would be staying here (he was still wet from his dip). Svensson simply refused to take me, and at the same time he raised his wine glass as if there were something to celebrate:

Chin-chin!

So I sat with Tuuli, Svensson, and his seventy-seven chairs, and to my own astonishment I took the glass handed to me without hesitation and said "to the storm" (the first cicadas in the oleander). Despite my departure plans, despite my flight booking, and even though my luggage is waiting for me. Maybe tomorrow, Svensson laughed, and I tried not to let any indignation show (my superior and wife is waiting too). Svensson refuses me Ping-Pong victories and answers, then he hands me a glass and wants me to stay (he exploits the full potential of his silence). Chin-chin! The momentary question of why Svensson doesn't want to get rid of me. Tuuli and he don't seem to talk to each other much, I don't seem to be intruding here. There was something to celebrate, Svensson said, and maybe he needs witnesses for this celebration. The three of them paid no further attention to me: Svensson emptied his wine in one gulp and carried a few of the black garbage bags across the property, Tuuli took off her nightshirt and changed into a green bikini as if I weren't there. She lay down on an intact lounge chair in the shade of the oleander and smoked, only occasionally she smiled in my direction. The boy examined the dog with a broken chair leg as if with a stethoscope. I strolled back and forth across the property, I weighed my possibilities, I played with the ring in my pocket, I watched the playing boy, finally I gave up my scheduled plan ("To enable the perception of social life with all the senses, the ethnological method of participant observation is traditionally based on long field stays within the group under investigation"). In the early afternoon I then fell asleep in Svensson's room without another thought about the return flight (maybe I wanted to miss the flight).

Chiarella

I wake up when the bedroom door is shut softly from outside. The pigeons are cooing, now and then chainsaws and the splintering of falling trees, the swallows merely little dots in absolute blue (the afternoon sky completely cloudless over the smooth lake). The small, pretty mother in the green bikini was in my room while I was sleeping. Her scent is still hanging in the air. On the floor next to my head is an open bottle of water (Chiarella) and a glass (Duralex), under them a torn-out page from my notebook with a handwritten note. The passing thought of not reading the note and leaving Svensson's ruin. But I don't know the way, and my plane to Hamburg has already taken off without me (this is your story now, Mandelkern). This evening Elisabeth will close up her office and return to our apartment, but I won't be there. Mandelkern, she'll ask, are you there? Elisabeth will wait and wonder where I am. Mandelkern? Whether I'm going to come back at all. Daniel? Whether I've decided against our marriage.

between the animals

Another note: "Do we want to conduct an immanent analysis of the concept 'relationship' and jettison all contextual references, Prof. Mandelkern?" Elisabeth wrote the message on a promotional postcard for the Brittany tourism agency and put it in my papers, I found it at work in the Museum of Ethnology on Rotherbaumchaussee (my laughter in the witch archive). Back then I divided my time between Elisabeth, my dissertation, and work at *GEO*. Then our first trip together in spring 2003 to the Atlantic, Elisabeth's divorce was on the horizon, but I didn't hear anything about that (she kept all that separate from me). We parked the Renault in the middle of a village square, the restaurant (Le Pélican) was a large room with three long tables and no menus, there were carrots and lobsters for everyone. I had to understand, Elisabeth said, as she opened her lobster claws more skillfully than anyone else at the table, that her first marriage took place at another time and in another place (the sound of the nutcracker in her nimble fingers). Yes, I said, I did understand that. Around us French was being spoken, we drank wine from scratched decanters.

Chin-chin!

said Elisabeth, between the lobsters she shared cigarettes with a retired foreign currency dealer from Paris, I had to dance with his granddaughter. At night we refilled the Renault's cooling water from the fountain and I drove us past fields and stone walls, Elisabeth with her eyes closed in the backseat, she sang *"Der Rote Wedding"* (*Rotfront!* she sang, *Rotfront!*). Then we slept on a wool blanket next to a few menhirs (back then we were the same age).

Petrarch & Simpson

Elisabeth and I made a loop around France (we circled each other). We drove the Renault through Brittany, then along the Spanish border and the Côte d'Azur, we slept in the places that the guidebooks passed over. Every morning I woke up two hours before Elisabeth, read essays, and wrote my notes. She abstained from croissants, I got used to black coffee and observed Elisabeth sleeping in the various pension beds (I failed at sketching her beauty). When she woke up, we immediately set off. She sat in the passenger seat of the Renault and read to me from culinary guides. Two warm meals a day, I got used to Ricard and Pernot and entrails (I still sometimes hated brains and intestines). Elisabeth ordered the red wines, we drank them together. I always got to drive, sometimes she talked on the phone with her husband and I tried not to listen (we learned our rituals). One weekend we visited two of her writer friends in a small village at the foot of Mont Ventoux (Venasque), they spent the summer there with their novels and plays (this is Daniel, said Elisabeth, you're going to have to like him, I love him). After two days of conversations about books and plays and the view of the bare mountain I wanted to move on (Côte Luberon, Côte du Rhône). Elisabeth chose the memorial to the racing cyclist and first doping fatality Tom Simpson (her strange interest in cyclists, the races themselves she never followed). As we finally forced the Renault torturously over the summit, she read to me from Petrarch, *However, the mountains of the province of Lyons could be seen very clearly to the right, and to the left the sea at Marseille and at the distance of several days the one that beats upon Aigues Mortes. The Rhône itself was beneath my eyes.* At the Simpson memorial she placed a full bottle of wine next to dozens of water bottles, flowers, and jerseys. Simpson died of dehydration, she explained, and I took note of her words, he'd ingested only whisky and wine and amphetamines ("put me back on my bike" were his last words, or maybe "go on, go on," they haven't been precisely imparted).

Gulf of Marseille

Change of drivers on top of the windy mountain: Elisabeth's absolutely unambiguous kiss when we came out of the station on the summit. In the writers' small house we'd had to sleep in a walk-through room, the female dramatist's two small children had jumped on our blanket in the morning (sex was unthinkable). I remember that Elisabeth on the hairpin turns on the lower third of the mountain pulled her skirt up and her underpants to the side. I want to come now, she said (she spoke of her bestial lust, I had to concentrate on gorges and sheep). Both of us stared at the narrow, winding road, Elisabeth came with her eyes on inwardly directed emptiness, I concentrated simultaneously on my finger on her pussy and the emergency brake of the Renault. A cyclist overtook us at the decisive moment, Elisabeth had stepped too abruptly on the brake (we laughed, we risked a rear-end collision together). When we reached the beach near Martigues, we parked between the refineries on the left and an industrial port on the right. Artificial palms, fish stalls abandoned in the midday heat, an old man was holding a kite in the air for his grandson (light blue water, light blue sky). Elisabeth and I hopped along the brightly shining stones of the jetty, we bought deep-fried fish and cold soda, we sat in the spraying groundswell. I remember exactly how the rust-red of the refineries was reflected in Elisabeth's sunglasses as she opened a can of soda and told me with a laugh that she wanted to be with me always, I was so wonderfully practical, extraordinarily practical, especially when traveling (I had to laugh at that).

between the books

I lack 3,000 words for Svensson's strangeness. Right now Harnisch must be at the most expensive restaurant in Châtenay-Malabry thinking about morality and urine (his return trip directly after the press conference of the anti-doping laboratory; but no one knows when that will be), Elisabeth will be doing a little more work at home. Where to begin? I look at Svensson's books standing on the desk, I wonder why his shelves are almost empty. Did Svensson throw the books in the garbage bags, is he disposing of his library? Is that where the smoke is coming from? The remaining books are standing there as if they were arranged for me (as if I were supposed to read Svensson's thoughts). For example: Uwe Johnson's *Jahrestage*. In front of me stands only volume 2 of the first edition, in our bedroom in Hamburg a red and black collected edition is lying on the floor, read and flagged, the most famous quote on the spine (the cat called memory). Svensson's books, my books, Elisabeth's books. For example: Max Frisch's *Montauk*. On our honeymoon trip to Kolberg I talked to

Elisabeth about it often enough (and she to me). We had only one weekend in the summer and wanted to get this formality over with. Elisabeth reminded me of Lynn, the Baltic Sea region of Frisch's Long Island. The destination (Kolberg) was her idea, she wanted to bring together her past and her future, she said. I wanted to see her without everything else (without husband, without work, without St. Michaelis in the background, without St. Petri). Continuing along Svensson's thinned-out shelf: Theodore Dreiser's *Sister Carrie* I've never read, Svensson's copy torn and sticky, full of underlined passages and margin notes, on the flyleaf a phone number (646-299-1036 Kiki Kaufman!).

Manteli,

You're still here! This house, these pictures, this garbage. All this is not my fault. Svensson talks melancholy nonsense: he has the world in his rearview mirror, his heart is a book. These old stories, these fictions. This nostalgia! Poppycock! You write all the time, Manteli. I believe: there's nothing true about all this and nothing lasts forever, books, pictures, scribblings. There are more important things. There are things that are worth it. If you stay, I'll show them to you.

   Kauniita unia,
   Tuuli

How do I get out of here?

Tuuli wants to show me things. I'm sitting at the desk and reading the message again and again: things that are worth it? Tuuli was standing next to me in a bikini as I was sleeping, she tore a page out of my notebook and wrote to me. Tuuli seems to know what she's talking about (in that she reminds me of Elisabeth). She must know what the important things are: not words and notes, not the old stories and Svensson's fictions, not pictures. The passing thought that she's not here because of Svensson, not because of the boy and not because of Felix. Maybe Tuuli's here because of me, maybe we were supposed to meet. Maybe all this is about fate (making connections where there are no connections). I remain seated at the desk. What holds me back I don't know. *Kauniita unia* means "sweet dreams," I remember that from my time with the second Carolina. Tomorrow I have to leave, I think, but then: I could stay.

Elisabeth and Daniel

The question of what's worth it and what's special? Elisabeth and I read each other like city maps (we moved into the back courtyards of our city). We exchanged the isolated tables of the Gruner + Jahr cafeteria for late-night bars, we slept together in my apartment (sometimes in hotels). But that's not right. I can't remember whether snow fell in the winter of 2002 and whether it remained on the ground, what was in the newspapers at that time, whether I had a cold. I must have sat in the office all day, leafing through proofs and waiting for evening. Elisabeth was still married, her husband worked for the publishing company too, we should keep that in mind, she said. Sometimes I saw her for days at a time only in a completely official capacity at tables full of journalists (she requested those days). Elisabeth is a pragmatist. But that's not right either: I ignored the thought of her husband. For a few months we actually lived as if it were just the two of us, everything else was of only superficial concern. At her desk with a view of St. Michaelis Elisabeth wrote easily digestible but honest articles (strong women, good-looking men, new movie releases), she called this arrangement a "quite acceptable backdrop against which she could perform her life," I compiled glossaries for *GEOkompakt* ("The Wonder of Humanity") and spent mornings in the Museum of Ethnology. We had no mission outside of ourselves (I found her red hair in the corners of my apartment). From our words and thoughts we designed streets and moved more purposefully, maybe more meaningfully, in them (she showed me the remote map quadrants), we used our bodies (I went beyond my boundaries).

Who exactly is Daniel Mandelkern?

In my head this image remains: Elisabeth and I in bed in the Bismarckstrasse apartment, yogurt jars and red wine bottles, on the floor next to us on the right and left our books, on my side:

The Water-Method Man by John Irving
Montauk by Max Frisch
The Ghost Writer by Philip Roth
A Diary in the Strictest Sense of the Term by Bronislaw Malinowski.

Auberge la Fontaine

I first heard the name Dirk Svensson at dinner with Elisabeth's friends in Venasque (Auberge la Fontaine). Elisabeth and I were again spending a few days in Provence, we were celebrating her thirty-sixth birthday (April 1). We return again and again to our places, we go to the same restaurants and bars, we stay in the same rooms (Brittany, Provence, the Baltic Sea). This time we flew to Marseille and rented a car there (the Renault could no

longer handle long distances, said Elisabeth, even though I'd
love to sit next to you again for days, Daniel). In the middle of
the small restaurant stood a grand piano, around it four tables
and only a few audience members. Before dinner we drank and
listened to Schubert's four-hand military marches, then Poulenc
(we soaked thoughts in wine like plums). The pianist looked
like Woody Allen, his accompanist wore a black evening dress
(her heavy body from behind an upside-down heart). Elisabeth
didn't have to introduce me, her friends knew me: the dramatist,
the writer (we already had a shared story). At the next table an
old woman played along with every single note on the wooden
table. They were here to think, said the dramatist, without all the
networking and the usual milieu. I salted my soup, whereupon
the writer stood up and with an appropriate degree of conspic-
uousness threw the saltshaker out the window into the village
fountain. It was about the genuine gaze, he said, raising his glass:
to the natural beauty of meals and women (Elisabeth's French
laugh)! At some point between foie gras and cheese tasting
(plateau de fromage), he leaned over to me and asked whether I'd
heard of Dirk Svensson, now that was an author a journalist like
me should write an article about. A strange man, Mandelkern!
Elisabeth nodded, I laughed too.

on Elisabeth's side
Unterhaltungen deutscher Ausgewanderten by Johann Wolfgang von
Goethe
Jahrestage by Uwe Johnson
Kinder und Tod by Elisabeth Kübler-Ross
Das Dekameron by Giovanni Boccaccio

Die Hebammensprechstunde by Ingeborg Stadelmann
Die Besteigung des Mont Ventoux by Francesco Petrarca
Who exactly is Elisabeth Edda Emmerich?

the 3-step system

First we speak about visible things. Because the power is still
out (Claasen set a fire, Claasen chopped down trees, Claasen
this, Claasen that), we're sitting in the kitchen and watching and
listening to Svensson (a transistor radio sits silently on a shelf).
Filetto di persico con salvia, he says, taking a heavy pan from a
hook, someone should fetch the sage from the terra-cotta pot in
the garden. The boy has already forgotten his cut and wound,
and Tuuli allows him to pick the sage by himself (he brings back
oleander flowers). From the water we hear the dog coughing. The
boy should also take a look in the chicken coop, says Svensson,
setting three glasses of wine on the table, maybe they laid an egg
this morning. Tuuli is smoking. This is how things look: a late
afternoon with friends, the sun will set, and we'll talk, we'll pass
around Autan (against the mosquitoes), we'll refill one another's
glasses (against the silence). Svensson takes the packet with the
fish from the sink, he praises cooking with gas (the directness of
the manual procedure), he explains the secret to cooking good
fish, the "3-step system," he says (filleting, souring, salting—
dispels odor and refines taste). Svensson praises the boy and
lays out on the table the sage leaves he's now found (he's a real
botanist, says Svensson, a plant expert and biologist). He drops
some butter in the pan and holds up to the light the egg the boy
has brought. He lays the soggy wax paper on the table in front
of Tuuli, she should operate on the fish, he says, that's always

been the task of the doctor in the house. Svensson laughs, and
Tuuli asks whether the fish hasn't been refrigerated all day. Yes,
the power's out, says Svensson, but the fish here on the lake are
almost too fresh to eat. To celebrate the occasion, he says, raising
his glass, to celebrate this special occasion (a watery red trail of
blood on the table).

Elisabeth (red)

Our honeymoon lasted three days and took us to Kolberg. Everything we needed fit in the Renault. The summer of 2003 was a
summer of record-breaking heat (we were wearing a wedding
dress and shorts). At the Eimsbüttel marriage bureau the
throwing of rice was prohibited, and the paternoster elevator tore
a snag in Elisabeth's red dress. All you have to do is stand still,
she said, and it goes continuously up and down. My grandmother
brought lilies (Elisabeth's parents took her between them). After
the wedding we ate lunch in the Four Seasons Hotel and set off
immediately afterward (we hadn't even reserved a table). Maybe
another life is a simpler life. The language of flowers is a foreign
language, Elisabeth said later on the country road. She has been
married, she has lost a child, now she wants to risk it again (her
bulky baggage). I drove and Elisabeth read to me from an old
newspaper, it took us two hours to reach the sea at Lübeck, we'd
left everything behind.

wedding dress (red)

In my head this image remains: Elisabeth and I on a Baltic Sea
beach beyond the Priwall Peninsula, the red wedding dress
spread out under us (sea buckthorn and stunted pines). Elisa-

beth is eating peppered mackerel directly from the wax paper
with her fingers. I fall asleep, and when I wake up storm clouds
have blotted out the sun. Lightning flashes, the beach is empty,
I'm alone (the wax paper and the dress lie crumpled in the beach
grass). No wind, no rain, no thunder. Suddenly Elisabeth surfaces
from the completely smooth water and comes toward me (she has
nothing on). Behind her the Baltic Sea begins to foam, a balloon
wafts over the water (red). When she sits on me, even though she
moves much slower than usual, she comes much too fast (outside
wet gooseflesh and inside unexpectedly warm). I follow suit, then
the thunder, then the rain (as if she were responsible for all this).
Elisabeth says that she loves me and wipes herself clean with the
wedding dress, I'm forbidden to use that against her. Elisabeth
laughs, I laugh too.

our strange preferences

We continued with the red: Elisabeth and I at the balustrade of
the Klütz Mill, the wedding dress folded in the Renault. The sun
was setting (a small detail). Elisabeth was wearing a white T-shirt,
her hair tied back with a rubber band. She ordered plaice with red
wine, I hesitated at the thought. If I may, said the waiter, to go
with the plaice we have an excellent Chateauneuf du Pape. But
it's not about tailoring things to convention, Elisabeth declared,
everyone has his own strange preferences. Isn't that right,
Mandelkern? The sun clear over the fields and flying wheat husks
and swarms of mosquitoes. The same for me, I said (back then I
thought we were forever). Elisabeth laughed, I laughed too.

one-eyed Jack

Tuuli asks for implements and Svensson puts bowls (red plastic) and a knife block on the table. She chooses the smallest and tests the blade with her index finger, then she sharpens it and Svensson refills our wine. The passing thought of asking my questions now without warning into the silent room and waiting for clear answers (the sound of the blade on the stone). I lay my book and pen on the table quite conspicuously, but then I don't ask after all. Instead I watch Tuuli filleting the fish: her fingers trace the creatures' bellies, they open the backs, lay bare the hearts, gills, liver, intestines. Even Svensson stops talking (when no one replies, there's nothing to say). Tuuli is adept, she has no inhibitions, she doesn't hesitate, she first wipes the blood with a towel and then brushes her blonde hair from her face. She shows the dead fish to the boy, Svensson and I follow her explanations. May I have the heart, *Äiti*? asks the boy, but Tuuli throws it in the plastic bowl with the other remains, wipes the blade clean, and lights a cigarette. Hearts are not for people, she says, hearts are for the dog. Besides, Svensson adds, the fried egg is ready (may I serve, sir? one-eyed Jack?). Over the lake the heron is flying slowly, farther out is a steamer with strings of lights. Tuuli says she's going swimming now, it will be dark soon and she doesn't like swimming in the dark, could we manage without her for a little while?

Yes.

Of course.

Minä en pelkää.

She kisses the boy on the forehead and stubs out her cigarette. You smoke too much, says Svensson, serving the boy his dinner. By the time I get cancer, Tuuli replies, we'll have found a cure. Then she leaves (Tuuli believes in the future).

to celebrate the occasion

First the fried egg, later a basket of bread, the bowl of salad, a plate of fruit. Svensson sets the table. The boy stands on his chair and eats with his fingers, we're again or still drinking wine, red and white, Barolo and Lugana, the boy gets apple juice in a wine glass. Svensson stands at the stove like a television cook, he tosses gnocchi in butter and sage, he praises the boy, he cuts his one-eyed Jack into suitable pieces, occasionally he wipes the boy's mouth with his apron (the boy's not afraid).

Interview (Dirk Svensson, television cook)

MANDELKERN: Can I help you, Svensson?

SVENSSON: With the cooking?

M: Yes. Maybe chop something, cut? Anything.

S: You can open another bottle of wine to celebrate the occasion.

M: Where do I find a corkscrew?

S: In my pants pocket. Here.

M: My wife loves Barolo.

S: You're married?

M: For two years.

S: I'm not.

M: But it's not that I regard marriage as the only true life plan.

S: What?

M: Sorry. Do you live completely alone here?

S: I'm not lonely.

M: Did you write and illustrate your book here?

S: The glasses are up there in the cabinet.

M: The pictures in your book, are they . . .

S: Yes?

M: In the seclusion of this house, do you even take notice of the success of your book?

S: I don't read newspapers, Mandelkern, I don't own a television.

M: You live alone with Lua? An unusual constellation for a children's book author.

S: What?

M: I just mean—if I may—that such reclusiveness is somewhat unusual. For a children's book author. What one imagines when one thinks of a children's book author. And Lua is no ordinary dog, if I may say so.

S: Lua and I get along with each other.

M: How old is Lua actually?

S: I don't know, Mandelkern, German shepherds sometimes live to be fifteen years old. Lua is older, Lua is a memory animal.

M: How long have you had him?

S: Lua was already here long before us, Mandelkern. He was Claasen's watchdog, his pack animal, he pulled his children's sled in winter and the wagon in summer, he has barked from San Salvatore and from Monte Cecchi, he has howled at Napoleon's Iron Crown of Lombardy, he has bitten the Habsburgs and peed on Mussolini's leg, he has slept under Klingsor's balcony and brought Herr Geiser over the mountain. But those are other stories.

M: Herr Geiser?

S: Mandelkern! You're supposed to be a cultural journalist!

M: And Lua's leg?

S: I've never seen his leg.

M: But yesterday you said . . .

S: Let's drink, Mandelkern, the wine's been breathing long enough. Chin-chin!

M: To Lua.

S: To Felix Blaumeiser.

To the old days!

he says, but Tuuli doesn't respond. She drinks without looking at Svensson and stubs out her cigarette in the sink (her wet hair combed back). Then the heavy pan and the fragrant fish between us (the eyes now murky), we eat without a word, only the boy asks sporadic questions and gets selective answers. (Why's it called a one-eyed Jack? Do dogs like cold fish?) Tuuli cuts an apple for him, later the boy climbs from his chair onto his mother's lap, lays his head on her chest, and closes his eyes (words fail me). Tuuli enfolds him in her arms and hums the Finnish song that I heard through the wall last night, she removes his shoes and holds his little feet, she herself eats with her left hand (their shared calm, my unexpected emotion). The fish is perfect, the wine a little too warm (Elisabeth would send it back). Svensson and I listen to Tuuli's singing until our plates are empty too, until the boy has fallen asleep, then Svensson gets up and strokes the sleeping child in Tuuli's arms on the cheek. He could teach the boy how to fish, he says, pointing to the yellow fishing rod, which is leaning, still in its plastic, in the corner of the room.

the demotion of the Fiat

Svensson rekindles the light. Tuuli has brought the boy into the room next to mine and left the door wide open, I wash the plates as if I belonged here. Tuuli is watching me as she smokes my cigarettes (Muratti 2000). These candles, says Svensson, are the last light of the day. He speaks with proud enthusiasm of his house, of the chickens and dogs and chairs, of the view of the opposite shore, he tells about Claasen and Claasen's wife and Claasen's sorrow, he talks about the seasons and fishing grounds and plant cycles, about the access road that's been overgrown for years (the extension of the Via San Rocco into nothingness). He laughs about the demotion of the Fiat from small car to a pen for small animals. Svensson is a feverish storyteller, his stories intertwine, his punch lines flare up in unexpected places, our glasses clink (even Tuuli smiles occasionally). I enjoy listening to Svensson, and he seems to have been waiting for listeners. He pours wine into each of our glasses, he speaks of the local birds and trees and water snakes, there are vipers here too, he says, raising his glass with every joke and then at every sad turn (I've given up resistance). If the boy wouldn't wake up, if the candles wouldn't burn down, if the next day wouldn't come, if I didn't have 3,000 words to write, if Tuuli didn't have to sleep too (a gap in her teeth when she laughs)—we could sit here forever, I think, why not? But Tuuli downs her glass in one swig and Svensson gets up. He asks for a cigarette, then he leaves. Tuuli refills the boy's juice glass and pushes it across the table to me (*succo di mele*). Let's conclude the evening by drinking something sensible, *Manteli*, she says, or else tomorrow will be a disaster.

apple juice

With a little patience and spit, said Elisabeth, standing up. The digits of the alarm clock at 2:17 AM, down below on Bismarck-strasse the scrape of a bicycle and a mosquito in the room, the summer settled on the roofs. Elisabeth is not a squeamish woman (at first she'd remained dry). I noticed that I was intensely thirsty and Elisabeth's eventual wetness on my cock was long dry (my own sticky wetness). I first heard the toilet flushing and then the opening and closing of the fridge, Elisabeth was singing "In My Solitude." Then her singing stopped (it felt as if she were dead). When she returned to the mattress, she pushed me back and kissed me with open lips, from her mouth cold apple juice flowed into me (Elisabeth the woman I'd been waiting for).

Interview (anniversary of a death)

MANDELKERN: So are you a doctor?

TUULI: I'm drunk.

M: What kind of doctor?

T: Surgery. In the Charité.

M: I once read that surgeons are the artisans of the field. Is that true?

T: I'm not a psychologist, I amputate.

M: Really?

T: Yes, *Manteli*, Lua's leg was the first body part I cut off. Otherwise Lua wouldn't be alive today, he would have bled to death ten years ago.

M: I thought Lua had always been here on the lake.

T: Poppycock. Did he tell you that?

M: He did.

T: Svensson changes stories the way other people change shirts. He's always done that.

M: You're very young for a doctor.

T: I started early, *Manteli*, I'm old enough. For surgery and cigarettes, for everything.

M: I'm smoking again too.

T: We're all going to die.

M: No one said anything about death.

T: I want to tell you something, *Manteli*: *Tänään on se päivä kun hän kuoli.*

M: Today is the anniversary of a death?

T: Today death is everywhere. Everything here in Svensson's house is stories and death. Just take a good look around. The silverware is old, the pictures are of dead animals, the dog will die soon, the access road is overgrown, the chairs are rotten, the house is a ruin. This lake is a grave, and Svensson is sitting on the edge. I can hardly bear it, *Manteli*. Svensson collects the past so time won't disappear, so each day isn't one more day that Felix Blaumeiser is dead, so life won't go on without him.

M: The anniversary of Felix Blaumeiser's death?

T: Do you speak Finnish, *Manteli*?

a match breaks

Tuuli's hand then suddenly on my chest, our cigarette in her other one. With this beauty rising toward me I miss the sound of the sliding door and the footsteps on the stairs, but Tuuli jumps back decisively just in time and laughs a mocking *"Idiootti"* into the room (she doesn't mean me). Svensson is standing in the doorway, to celebrate the occasion, he repeats, showing us the gin bottle in his hand (a somewhat too-long pause), to celebrate this special occasion,

Bombay Sapphire,

and without asking helps himself to a cigarette from my pack (a match breaks). Tuuli's eyes jump from the bottle to Svensson and back. With the cold cigarette in the corner of his mouth the children's book author suddenly seems heavier and drunker than he did just minutes ago. He reaches into the cabinet and sets three water glasses on the table. Again he pours, but he's already lost his sense of moderation, a good deal of gin drips over the rims and onto the table (Tuuli's lips dashes, Svensson's cigarette an exclamation point). Tuuli covers the glass with her hand, no-no, she'd prefer red wine.

We drink
to the old days (to the good old days, Tuuli, right?)
to New York Oulu Seraverde (all the places we've been, Tuuli!)
to Lua (to the intact Lua, right?)
to Lua's fourth leg (do you remember?)
to the Europa-Park in Rust (the Euromaus, Tuuli!)
to streamers and party hats (to celebrate the occasion, Mandelkern!)
to the holy Mother of God (Nostra Signora)
to the three of us (he doesn't mean me).

Shitty City 2000 (20 x 45, oil on canvas)

The gin gives us the shakes and Tuuli takes a cigarette from the pack (the opposite of laughter). Svensson pours more gin into his glass, I decline, he leans his head back like a wolf (his words are howls). Svensson fills my glass anyway, Tuuli holds her red wine in her hand. I give her a light, we smoke (a certain nausea). When Svensson finally proposes a toast to "the boy and his pretty, because innocent, mother and his father, whoever he may be," Tuuli's glass flies across the table and shatters on the picture behind Svensson (a bloody wine stain on the faces). This night is over. Tuuli has closed the door behind her.

Caesarean Risk

On steady feet back into my room (despite the gin not incoherently drunk). My *Süddeutsche* is still lying on the desk, and instead of describing the wine on the kitchen wall now (heart-shaped, as if it were viscous), I open my notebook again, before my eyes the article and in my head Elisabeth's vertical surgical scar, from which all the bluishness had already faded when I first touched it. First a vertical incision is made, she said, then in the deeper layers of skin a perpendicular one. We lay on the floorboards in my apartment. She'd already given up long before the doctors decided on the caesarean. Elisabeth speaks soberly about her body. The anesthesiologist had read her the consent form and handed it to her to sign (first epidural anesthesia, later even general anesthetic). Due to the heart sounds it had to be done quickly, another doctor on one side and the midwife on the other had pulled open her belly (she said: they tore me open). She hadn't seen anything. At this point she'd already suspected the death of the child, probably her own too, after signing she'd already regarded her own body as cold, as if she had signed it away (as if the anesthesiologist were God). She had provided this signature, said Elisabeth, with a promotional ballpoint pen for Sedotussin cough syrup (she said: provided), she remembered exactly. The scars had healed fast, merely a few weeks of profuse discharge, then she had been herself again. I asked where her husband had been at that time. Elisabeth's reply: it was never fully clear to me how all these things hung together (today she'd want to call that "lucky under the circumstances").

Svensson's books

I rest my feet on Svensson's suitcase and listen to the rattle of the dishwashing in the kitchen (Svensson is cleaning up). Then Frisch again with his Montaigne (THIS BOOK WAS WRITTEN IN GOOD FAITH, READER), then *The Great Encyclopedia of Dog Breeds*, then Johnson's "cat called memory" again (pets, says Elisabeth, are an admission of interpersonal failure and cats unhealthy during pregnancy). *Macumba* is moored to a buoy, the moon is shining over the water, the oleander is wilting, the chairs are waiting. I'm sitting in front of my notebook and have tried to write Elisabeth's and my story in good faith, but my sentences dry up under my fingers. Occasionally my words can hold a candle to the world, for a moment they mean everything,

but that lasts only an instant,

and this thought too is only pilfered. The room smells of damp stone, even though it isn't raining (the roof is cracked). Again the thought of Elisabeth and the assignment she has given me, for a moment I'd like to call her, we have important things to talk about, but my telephone is in my suitcase at the Hotel Lido Seegarten. I'm drunk once again, too drunk for research, I can only speculate. I should put aside my pen, I could break open the suitcase, my questions remain:

—How do I find out who Felix Blaumeiser was?
—Why does Lua have only three legs?
—Tuuli says that Svensson can't paint—who painted those pictures?
—Who exactly is Kiki Kaufman?
—How do I open the suitcase?
—What are the things that Tuuli wants to show me?

Octopus

Between the books on our bedroom floor Elisabeth will now be sleeping with the window open, she'll simply ignore the mosquitoes from the canal. My move into Elisabeth's apartment: I admired her resolution and absence of melancholy. Elisabeth asked for a weekend, and when she called on Monday and asked me to come to the Octopus furniture store on Lehmweg, the first dumpster had already been collected and with it almost all the furniture and all the old decoration ideas. She wanted us to start with a clean slate, Elisabeth said on the telephone, paint buckets and rollers were ready for painting (the echo of her voice in the empty apartment). On the footpath along the Isekanal a sleeping fisherman and an unexpected quiet in the middle of the city. It was Monday and March, I was ready to dispose of my furniture, so to speak, I felt light (Elisabeth doesn't cling to things). Elisabeth in the empty showrooms of the furniture store: how she picked out two tables, a bed, and a sofa. I said "I guess so" and meant "yes," I filled out an order form. We decided on white. At one point Elisabeth spilled paint on her pants and continued to paint half naked. We no longer spoke about her marriage. My marriage, said Elisabeth, has ended up in a dumpster. For weeks I took one box of books each evening to Elisabeth's apartment on my bike, we spoke of "our apartment." At night take-out from the Thai place downstairs, where no one seemed to speak German (you never get what you order). In July we lay between our book piles on the newly delivered bed and drank malt beer. We didn't have to try hard, everything came naturally. At Svensson's desk I notice the inexplicable similarity between Elisabeth and Tuuli (my unfulfilled assignment, my unanswered questions, my many possibilities). But that isn't a question. It's not an answer, either (focus, Mandelkern!).

golden hairpins

The second day on Svensson's lake has passed without hesitation (without concern for my questions). I'm standing in flip-flops in Svensson's dark ruin, I light a cigarette, open the window, and hang my shirt over the window latch (the pane a mirror, in it Mandelkern bare-chested, smoking). The cicadas and crickets can no longer be heard, I see the dog hobbling sluggishly to the shore again, at the dock he falls heavily on his side. Why is Lua waiting for death down there by the water? Svensson is nowhere to be seen. Why am I still here? I don't seem to be bothering Svensson in the least, and Tuuli also seems to want my presence here (my main informant). She brings me water when I'm asleep, she lays her small fingers on my chest (how easily & emptily "beauty" is written, how stupidly this cigarette hangs in the corner of my mouth!). Conjecture: Tuuli and Svensson never touch casually, on the pier in Lugano he grasped her wrist somewhat too forcefully; their relationship has passed its peak, now they're confronting the consequences. Soon it will be midnight, there's no more chance of Svensson unmooring his boat today. Elisabeth will now be standing in front of the fridge in our kitchen and drinking water from the bottle, dehydration is one of her new worries. She'll be thinking about professional and private consequences (I shouldn't still be here). My decision in the light of the last candle: think more about it tomorrow, get to the bottom of things tomorrow, interview Svensson tomorrow about his work and biography in a completely professional manner (were they in love once, is the boy Svensson's son). Tomorrow I should ask for an interview in all soberness, leave, and send 3,000 words to the editorial department. But when I empty my pants pockets, I'm suddenly holding Tuuli's golden hairpin in my hand (I could stay).

journalistic scrupulousness

The moon over everything an appropriate lighting. I've bent Svensson's paper clips and tried his pens, I've searched for the key to the suitcase, I've pulled and tugged. Without success. My kneeling in front of the suitcase, Tuuli's golden hairpin in my hand, the window is wide open: *Macumba* in the water and the lights on the other side of the lake. Do I hear footsteps on the stairs? Do I hear Tuuli singing? Is Svensson still talking? Tuuli's hairpin is slightly curved and rounded on one end, it's sturdy enough to turn in the lock, and Svensson's suitcase (Blaumeiser's suitcase) acquiesces, it opens with a soft click, and that very second all the lights turn on in the room.

That a night can suddenly be so bright.

That a dog can die so loudly.

Quiet, Lua, quiet!

My wincing and springing to my feet and standing paralyzed: I'm frozen in front of the open suitcase in the brightly lit room, the dying dog by the water is coughing and barking at the same time, down below Svensson is emerging from the house (two tinted lights at the end of the dock, a floodlight with a motion detector on the outside of the house). Tuuli follows him and talks relentlessly at him: it was a fuse, *idiootti*, she only had to flip the switch! Not Claasen, not a power outage, not fallen trees, not heroic independence, not rebelliously refused bill payments, not his retreat from this world, *paskapää*, only his morbid collection of old, useless things, his dumb insistence on a corny idea of the ruin, only his inability to deal with the present. Only a damn fuse (a bogus epiphany)! Then Lua is finally quiet.

in the suitcase
Stones (heavy), flowers (dried), finally: a thick packet, brown paper and tight packing string. I put the packet on the desk (that smell of old suitcases), untie the knots very carefully and remove the paper (journalistic scrupulousness). That a night can be so quiet (that paper can rustle so loudly). I find the light switch and turn off the lamps.

Astroland

Observed from the safe darkness of the room: on the way to the lake Svensson takes off his T-shirt, he leaves his shoes in the grass and tosses his pants aside, Tuuli picks them up and throws them at him furiously (can that be explained?). In the light of the motion detector, Svensson finally stands naked on the dock. For a moment he looks across to the opposite shore, then for a few seconds at Tuuli. She's still berating him, but I don't understand what she's saying. Svensson spreads his arms and dives headfirst and perfectly straight into the black lake (reflection of the sky). The water splashes up over him, the surface evens out, Tuuli is standing alone on the dock. On the other side of the lake shines the yellow tower of Santuario di Nostra Signora della Caravina, in the deeper water is the white buoy, above the lake Monte Cecchi, the moon. Svensson has vanished (everyone is waiting). Svensson doesn't reappear. The light over the property goes out, because no one is moving.

Svensson can't lose.

In the unwrapped packing paper in front of me the thick stack of paper:

Capoeira with Heckler & Koch

My bag in the back of the truck, the Antarctica bottles open, and we're off. David at the wheel of the red pickup, Felix in an open shirt and panama hat, me with the twenty-four-hour flight in my bones. We blast through a red light. Between the entrance ramps and concrete pillars the greenery grows rampant, and over everything an airplane thunders in for a landing. Felix reaches for the glove compartment and tears the door off, holy Mother of God, there's nothing there, did you drink it all, he asks. David? And again: David? Felix says "DAVI" with the last *d* silent, as Brazilians do. David with his pitch-black skin drives with tunnel vision down the street, a luminous tube through the sultry night, from the rearview mirror dangles a crucifix. Synthetic lambskin hangs over the seats. At our backs shimmers the Recife airport. Felix raises his bottle, spraying some beer, welcome to the tropics, my Svensson! Felix is wearing multicolored bracelets around his wrists and explains that that's what's done here. I'm out of it, in the glow of the streetlights before my eyes there's a sprinkling of moisture or cigarette smoke. Or is it the light-emitting diodes in the crown of the holy Madonna flashing from the dashboard? Is the driver really wearing the black skull-and-crossbones sweatshirt of FC St. Pauli? I say: The flight from São Paulo was a disaster, they'd unscrewed the seats next to me, there were only two other passengers on board, the propellers were flapping and grating. There was beans-and-rice and nothing to drink, it was hard for me to swallow. Felix and David raise their bottles with a loud clink. Turn on the music, *meu amigo*, says Felix, make it louder, there's something to celebrate, Svensson's here! I say: I guess I am, but where are we actually going?

The pickup roars along the Recife beach promenade, the left rear wheel suspension makes a whistling sound, or maybe it's Felix singing to the music on the radio, "Girl from Mars." Now and then a streetlight, now and then none. On the left the black sea and the white streaks of the waves, on the right beach bars with strings of lights or strings of lights on wooden trellises over the doors or over a few men in open shirts, over beer bottles and card tricks. And the waves crash on the beach. Then steel fences, behind the steel fences high-rises, between them dark green bushes with thick, shiny leaves, Madonnas with low-voltage aureoles, now and then a neon cross, soldiers and armored cars and rifle barrels on the driveways. I ask: Are those Kalashnikovs? No, answers David, all Heckler & Koch, quality workmanship from Germany! Then the pickup leaves Boa Viagem, first come flat buildings made of concrete, then corrugated iron, then plywood, then cardboard. Felix opens another bottle of beer and pushes his hat back, I say: From above the city is a carpet of glowworms and frayed at the edges. Tourist, hails Felix, those are the fires, there are no glowworms here, this here is the favela of Recife, Svensson, you understand? I don't understand anything, but meanwhile I'm holding in my hand my third beer since my arrival in Brazil. David turns the corner and winds through the muddy roads, he avoids the cardboard huts and burning garbage cans, the dark faces between the flames, and they all turn with the pickup like flowers with the sun. I ask again: Where are we actually going? The pickup stops in front of a poorly lit shell of a house, on the second floor a few windows are illuminated, in front of the house a tin garbage can is burning and throwing off sparks. Here, says Felix, to buy weed. I ask: Can't we just get a beer and then go to a hotel? Don't worry, my Svensson, says Felix, jumping out of the truck, this is all great fun.

I ask through the open window: Isn't this dangerous? Felix hunches his shoulders as he walks toward the mossy ruin. I get out and follow him, I ask louder: Isn't this dangerous? Toward the horizon the lights of a tanker or an airplane in descent or the sparks over the garbage can? I say, Felix? But Felix is climbing the dark staircase, stepping over the trash on the staircase, he jumps over a man lying in a watery pool on the concrete, the man is snoring and stinks. Felix? Be quiet, Felix replies, or else they'll hear your fear, and I can't say they're harmless. Up above, light falls through a door into the stink of piss and onto the stains on the walls. Am I breathing too deeply? Can fear be heard? In here, says Felix, and I think: Get out of here! and stay in the stairwell. I hear terse sentences from inside, and someone laughs loudly. I turn around and begin to go carefully down the stairs. Is the man on the landing snoring louder as I step over him? Are the fluorescent lights in the stairwell flickering or am I not seeing straight? Is that piss or liquor or mildew burning in my eyes? Am I sweating going downstairs in the dark? Is that possible? Can all this be true?

I wait in the passenger seat as Felix jumps onto the back of the truck, the air thick with smoke from the garbage cans. Felix with a bulging plastic bag in his hand, printed on it is: *Supermercadinho e Panificadora Bom Jesus*. David turns the key in the ignition back and forth like a screwdriver, the engine sputters and finally starts. We got lucky, says Felix, and I ask: Why lucky? They messed up, says Felix, *meu amigo!* Look at this bag full of weed, he whispers, the idiots made a mistake, *meu amigo,* he cheers, this is at least five hundred grams! And are sparks flying from the garbage cans on the road, or is there even an illegal Heckler & Koch rattling behind us, or are the shadows on the road ducking like flowers in the moonlight? I stare at Felix: Are you serious? David steers the pickup out of the favela, but with my twenty-four-hour flight in my bones I have trouble following. With such curves, with such holes in the ground.

Felix and David show me the area through the truck window. The pickup roars along the sea again and then turns into smaller streets, we drive up a hill and back down, past gardens full of orchids and bougainvillea, past iron fences and shining old buildings. I say: There are palm trees everywhere here! Incredible! Olinda, says Felix, is not a city, Olinda is an attraction. The pickup drives over rivulets and streams, through the window I hear cars honking and beggars singing. Felix passes around an Antarctica, then a Skol, then a Brahma. With Felix you always have to be drinking. The pickup drives past glass facades and gas stations, it turns under bridges, there are mildewed election posters stuck to the bridge piers, Burger King shines in the night. Then the billboards and satellite towns disappear, the pickup leaves the city. David signals to move into the passing lane and steps on the gas, he turns up the cassette player and whistles through his teeth, *Rudi Ratlos heisst der Geiger,* Felix screams to the sky, *der streicht uns grad' 'nen Evergreen!* Half a kilo of weed! And I with the twenty-five hours without sleep in my bones sit next to Felix on the synthetic lambskin and scarcely believe my ears and eyes. I ask: What are we actually doing here? I thought this was alternative service in the rural blight of Seraverde, Pernambuco. David laughs and drinks and throws a Brahma bottle into the stalks and bushes flying by on the roadside, in a way it is. Felix laughs louder, in a way it is! Seraverde, he says, is a town of average size and average beauty between rain forest and desert. Seraverde throws its trash on a piece of fallow land behind the bus station, Rodoviária. The poor live off the trash, they wear old shoes and T-shirts, they drink the oily water, they eat melon rinds and gnaw on chicken bones, they beg for sugarcane liquor. That's why we're here, my Svensson, says Felix, we're building a water tower. We cook them soup, we show them how to use a toothbrush, we pay a doctor, we pull rotten teeth, we teach them the alphabet, we change diapers. The Germans and Italians and French donate money, the Catholic Church pays a padre to hear confessions. We provide salvation, we have a fax machine, we throw condoms on Rua do Lixo. The poor fuck like rabbits, then they get into fights, they stab each other and shoot, they die like flies, and we drive the ambulances, we manage the sutured wounds. Felix turns around to me. Rua do Lixo is the ass crack of Seraverde, the garbage street, you understand? We wipe Seraverde's butt, so it doesn't itch the medium-sized and moderately pretty city. And since this work is a disaster, David laughs and looks at us instead of the road, we got ourselves some weed. Felix cheers and slaps me on the shoulder, *porco dio!* The two of us in Brazil, Svensson! The two of us! Warm night air wafts in through the window, and I'm suddenly so tired that I can't even see straight. I ask: When will we finally get there? Another five hours to Seraverde, says David, then you'll get a hammock and a mosquito net, then you'll get electricity, then you two will have a wall around you and glass shards in concrete. And you? I ask. I'm your night watchman, says David, and takes a Heckler & Koch out of the glove compartment, I guard you. Nothing will happen to you! Felix takes the gun out of his hand and aims into the darkness. Old tires on the median strip, and because David is grinning and the music is clanging so beautifully, I lay my head on the lambskin and close

my eyes. Urinating is good for you, I hear Felix singing, and as the
pickup stops in the middle of the rain forest and Felix pees on a
car wreck, in the din of the crickets, in the howling of the jackals,
with my twenty-seven hours of anxious anticipation in my bones,
I finally fall asleep.

When I wake up, it's bright. The pickup is parked in the floodlight of an armored car. Police, Felix whispers, come on, Svensson,
move your ass! He buries the *Supermercadinho e Panificadora Bom
Jesus* bag under me and the lambskin. I need a few seconds to
get my bearings: Brazil, pickup, lambskin, me, Felix, David the
night watchman. The policemen are hard to see in the glare of the
floodlight, their Heckler & Kochs are shining, the armored car is
blocking the pickup. I slide back and forth on the lambskin and
feel the bulging plastic bag under me. Just arrived, I think, and
immediately thrown in prison. A short policeman approaches
the window between tall policemen, he has a sparse mustache
but is otherwise clean-shaven, he's in shirtsleeves and holds a
pair of leather gloves in his hand. Next to him is a black German
shepherd, it barks deeply and darkly at the pickup. Our night
watchman David puts up his hands, the policeman grins into the
truck and I don't move, at least not visibly. Santos! says Felix. *Oi,
meus amigos alemães*, says the policeman, *tudo bem?* He looks over
the rim of the mirrored sunglasses he's wearing, even though it's
night. Felix nods, so I nod too, as if I understood. The black dog
is waiting next to the policeman like death, his chain rattles, the
muscles under his smooth fur move, his jowls droop, and when
he yawns, I can see his fangs. Get out and put your hands on
the roof, the policeman says politely, so we step out and put our
hands on the hood, one of the tall policemen pulls my passport
out of my back pocket and flips through it. Svensson? *Turista?*
Yes. The pitch-black dog sniffs Felix first, then I feel his wet nose

between my legs. The animal takes his time thinking about what part of this tourist he should bite into first. Just woke up, I think, and already got my balls bitten off. David and the tall policemen seem to know each other, the doors are opened, they take David's Heckler & Koch out of the glove compartment, hold it up to the light and put it back. P10? No, MK23. Permit? In his pants pocket. Santos laughs, David laughs too, but his laugh sounds angry. Can the dog sniff out the weed? He licks my hand, he licks every single finger with his rough tongue, the weed smell reaches this far. I'm trembling, and the pickup's hood fogs up under my damp fingers. Then Santos slaps the dog on the nose with the leather glove and pulls him to the pickup by the chain, *vambora, Lula, vambora!* The dog sticks his nose into the truck and drools on the seat. Does the dapper policeman smell the *Supermercadinho e Panificadora Bom Jesus* bag under the lambskin? Felix reaches into his pocket and presses a few bills into Santos's hand. They both laugh. The policeman twirls his fine mustache and smoothes out the money. He sticks it in his shirt pocket, then steps up the negotiations. Santos stands on tiptoe and takes the panama hat off Felix's head, he turns it and flips it, he puts it on over his thin hair. David holds a forced smile as if he were posing for a painting. If Lula doesn't find anything, says Santos with the panama hat on his head, you'll have to reward him, *Allemaos*. The tall policemen with their Heckler & Kochs in their hands laugh. *Vambora, Lula, vambora!* Of course, says Felix, *meu amigo*, of course! *Compadres*, says Santos, if you still need water for your tower, Lula and I could do a lot for you. All we need is a little favor. *Meu amigo*, Felix says, of course, and he turns to me. Do you have any money? With the black dog Lula breathing down my neck and the lambskin in the corner of my eye, with damp fingers and weak knees, I hand over to Santos all the dollars from my neck pouch. *Beleza, meu irmão,*

Santos shakes Felix's hand and claps me on the shoulder. The tall policemen rub their fingers together, Santos tugs on Lula's chain. He runs a glove across his throat, the floodlight goes out, all of a sudden it's dark. The policemen get in their car and drive slowly toward the city, Lula has to gallop behind the car, we hear the rattle of his chain on the asphalt along with a jubilant song from the radio of the pickup, "Girl from Mars." On the hills in the background the lights of Seraverde. Just arrived, I think, and already robbed. Welcome to Seraverde, says Felix, and David crosses himself and curses, if it were up to him, Santos would drop dead, *safado*, two-faced son of a bitch. Drop dead!

Two months later, the day the new volunteer arrives, everything is at first the same as always. A wall encloses the Fundação Ajuda de Nossa Senhora, on top of it glass shards embedded in concrete and razor wire. When David comes back from his last round at sunrise, Felix and I are already awake in our hammocks and mosquito nets. I make coffee with sugar, and Felix smokes some weed before he goes to the bathroom, he sings, *er ist achtzig, hat zittrige Finger und ist schon ganz weich in den Knien.* David takes off his ski mask and puts the Heckler & Koch in the cabinet, he washes with water from the enamel bowl, he lies down in Felix's hammock. David guards our sleep, he works when we're asleep, he makes his rounds along the walls, he sits cross-legged amid the glass in concrete and smokes, sometimes he shoots a cat with ragged ears, sometimes one of the gray street pigs, and leaves them there until the dogs get them. At first everything is the same as always: at six the gate is opened, in the old people's barracks the residents wake up, at seven the padre says the morning prayer in his purple baseball cap. At seven-thirty comes the soup kitchen cook Cris, at eight the mothers bring the first children, at nine comes the dentist, and I throw the first molars on top of the onion skins and chicken bones. I've learned how to give injections. On the train platforms behind the Fundação Ajuda de Nossa Senhora the railroad children sit with their plastic bags and glue cans, they get orange juice and bread. Felix feeds the chickens, he milks the goats, he gives the smallest children the bottles, he rocks them to sleep. Today he is doing all this for the last time, today the new volunteer is supposed to arrive on the six o'clock bus from Recife, we send one of the railroad children to Rodoviária to pick her up.

Today is a special day, today the water is supposed to come. In the morning I crush ants and spiders underfoot, I sweep the bedrooms and the courtyard, I drink the sugary coffee. I've grown thin, I've already gotten over the vomiting and diarrhea, I've spent nights lying awake next to the toilet. Now I wear friendship bracelets around my wrists like all the Europeans in the Fundação Ajuda, for health, for good luck. At eleven Felix and I drive the pickup into the city. For the last time we buy drinking water in containers, three sacks of concrete and two iron bars for the last steps to the water tower. We buy beer and a bottle of champagne. Felix and I work hand in hand, we saw, plane, nail. In the court-yard the hungry stand barefoot in line, there's *feijoada* and rice, *oi, gringos*, they say to Felix and me. At eleven-thirty the bars are bent into makeshift steps, fourteen metal hooks up to the top, the last two we affix around twelve. We check the struts, we test-run the pump without water. Then the water tower is standing, it took us two months, a large metal tank on four legs, cast in concrete and six meters high. It stands in the middle of Rua do Lixo, against the filth in the area, against the poisonings, against the bacteria, against the dying of children. For two months Felix has driven the pickup into the city every day and bought concrete, pipes, wood and wire mesh with European money. The pipeline runs illegally through the field between Rua do Lixo and Seraverde, four hundred meters of plastic pipes twenty centimeters under the dust, buried by the day laborers at dawn and nightfall, the municipal pipelines tapped only unofficially, officer Santos was willing to turn a blind eye to the construction of the water conduit in exchange for a friendly donation, *meus amigos*. The pump runs on diesel. For a small fee, *compadres*, Santos said, he and his dog Lula wouldn't notice any of this. Everyone helped: David can weld, I learned to mix concrete, Felix can hang in the scaffolding and direct the day laborers, his book in his hand, *Water Supply Systems for Home Farming* by Williams/Steynman, page 27 to 35, everything just roughly tripled.

Today is a decisive day, today Seraverde will become blue or red, today there are elections in all of Pernambuco. The blues and the reds have set up blue and red *trios elétricos* on the city squares, tractor-trailers with stages and speakers, red and blue VW Bugs with megaphones drive through the streets, they announce a red and a blue celebration: free beer and *forró* tonight, drinks tonight! Vote blue! Vote red! On Rio do Lixo too the election is being decided, there's Pitú and promises in exchange for votes: vote for us, *meus amigos*, and there will be two sacks of concrete per head! The district policeman Santos is the reds' district candidate for Rua do Lixo, PT, the Workers' Party, on walls, cars and donkey carts there are pictures of him and his mustache. I ask: Why the policeman of all people? and Felix answers, because everyone knows Santos, everyone has already paid him. Around noon Santos strolls once again down the garbage street, the black dog Lula! Named after the next president of our country, he said, Lula da Silva, remember that name! The black dog is wearing a red-and-white neckerchief, the colors of the Partido dos Trabalhadores. If you vote for me, *compadre*, I'll put a roof on your hut, *compadre*, with the good tiles! Blue and red children play war, their fathers drink sugarcane liquor, *cachaça*. Wanna bet, Svensson? asks Felix, and I wager our souls and twenty dollars on the reds. In the afternoon Felix slaughters two chickens, the steady spinning of the bird in the air and precise chop of the head with the hatchet he learned from David. To celebrate the occasion there's garlic chicken with coriander and pimento, we put halved garlic cloves in each of the seventy-seven knife cuts. At four the mothers fetch the children and the milk powder rations, at five the heavy iron gates are closed. The padre with the cap says his evening prayer, he opens a bottle of water and passes out glasses. Everyone is sitting at the round table in the courtyard, the padre, David, Ailton, Lucinda, Cris, Felix, Svensson, Ivan. Urinating is good for you, the padre says after his third glass of water. Today is a special day, today the radio is playing "Girl from Mars," today merengue and *forró* waft over from the *trios elétricos*, today in the middle of the praying and the clinking of glasses there's a soft knock at the steel door of the Fundação Ajuda de Nossa Senhora. David opens it, and in the dust of Rua do Lixo stands a small, blonde woman with a backpack and without shoes. I'm Tuuli, she says, I'm here as a volunteer.

THE GARBAGE STREET IS seething. It's dark, on the equator night always falls like a curtain. On the left desert, over us the sky, on the green hills in the east the city, where the rich people live, their streetlamps, the lights of their cars. On a pulley hang a bucket of beer bottles and a bowl of cold chicken leftovers. Tuuli passes out the glasses like someone from here. Everyone has left, David is patrolling along the walls, only Felix, Tuuli, and I remain. Speeches about Rua do Lixo are now wafting from the city, Santos promises order and progress, *ordem e progresso,* for Rua do

Lixo, along with a bottle of Pitú for every vote. Merengue steams through the air, the music gets louder, the speeches, the roar. The smoke of a hundred fires hangs over the huts, burning plastic and earth. On the empty field between the garbage dump and the bus station, which the people here call the murderers' field, wild dogs are yowling, people are singing and cursing. Over the past few months, three men have been shot here and four stabbed. The reds shoot the blues, the blues stab the reds, the poor kill each other. Two weeks ago someone shot at Felix when he was sitting and smoking in a blue T-shirt in the scaffolding, but this someone only hit the metal bucket next to him. The blues are giving out meat and beer, we hear, but the reds have better music. Occasionally rockets shoot into the night sky, red on the left, blue on the right. Champagne for everyone, says Felix, opening a beer. The water tower is standing, there's room for three people on the wooden top. David is still patrolling along the walls, we can hear him whistling down there. Tuuli is sitting between Felix and me, her legs dangling over the garbage street, she eats garlic chicken and licks her fingers and lips. Felix and I watch her as she rolls cigarettes and drinks, we look at her fingers, her wrists without multicolored bracelets, her hair tied back, we listen to her Finnish German, we watch her drink and laugh and sing, we fall in love voluntarily.

IF NO WATER COMES, Felix shouts from below over the noise of the motor, it looks bad. Is anything coming? Tuuli and I are lying on the water tower for cover, Tuuli rolls another cigarette. I shout: No! Nothing! *Safados!* An hour ago the music on the squares died away. Felix and I take turns getting beer, and we start the diesel pump as a trial run. The speeches are over, the poor return to the filth satiated and drunk, cheering, screaming, fighting. Red! Santos! Blue! Gonçalves Meirinho! They lie down in the dark recesses of the garbage street and sleep. Behind the garbage dump the desert dogs are howling, occasionally a shot rings out, sometimes a salute, sometimes a signal. On the horizon a fine line indicates the cardinal direction, in an hour the sun will rise. Tuuli hides the burning tip in her small hands so no one will see it. The pipe doesn't even drip. Nothing, she shouts, nothing! Felix hoists up more beer. Macumba is the Brazilian form of voodoo, he says, as his head appears over the edge, we now turn to magic! In his hand Felix is holding an election poster of Santos and his mustache. The name José Santos Tourão Splitter is photocopied on it, Partido dos Trabalhadores. Does anyone have a light? Tuuli reaches into her pants pocket. Felix stands on the wooden cover of the water tower and holds the lighter to Santos's name, then to his face. The poster catches fire and hangs ablaze in Felix's outstretched hand. Macumba! Felix shouts, burning his fingers. If we had water, he laughs, that wouldn't have happened, *compadre*!

DAVID! DAVID! Someone is pounding on the iron door of the Fundação Ajuda de Nossa Senhora and screaming for David. I wake up. Tuuli is lying with her head on Felix's chest and her legs on my belly. Dawn is breaking. David, someone yells outside the wall of the Fundação Ajuda de Nossa Senhora, "DAVI" without the last *d*, then we hear the clip-clop of hooves and the wheels of a departing donkey cart in the gravelly dust. I wake the other two, in the courtyard we hear David's keys and the dark bark of a dog, then David's sudden command, hurry! Hurry! Felix and I almost fall off the water tower, because David is very close to shouting, we've never heard him shout before. Tuuli follows us. We run across the freshly swept courtyard, I trip over a goat and cut my knee. David is standing in the open doorway, his Heckler & Koch

in his hand. Outside the door lies a man. Blood everywhere: on
the steps, on the wall, on the iron door. The man has pissed all
over himself, he's not saying anything and isn't screaming, he's
groaning softly, on his sleeves dust and dark blood, from a frayed
hole in the middle of his belly lighter blood. The red party jersey is
torn open and soaked through. His chest hairs are stuck together
like gulls' feathers in oil. He's lying in his blood and looking at
Felix and me with glassy eyes. Someone has shot off the man's
abdominal wall and left him on the doorstep of the Fundação
Ajuda de Nossa Senhora, the tracks of the donkey cart can still
be seen. Next to him stands a big black dog, he licks the sweat off
the man's face. The dog is wearing a red neckerchief, his chain
is lying in the dirt behind him, his fur is blood-spattered, blood-
smeared. Holy Mother of God, says David, it's Santos! Shit, says
Felix, hurry! Hurry and do what? asks Tuuli. I say: the truck. My
fear like ice-cold water. We have to go to the hospital!

Just a second, says Felix.

What?

He's not going to make it anyway, is he? He's already dead,
isn't he?

He's breathing, see?

It's Santos.

Who gives a damn who it is?

Santos is a corrupt asshole.

You want to let him bleed to death?

He makes everyone's life hell here. He's preventing us from
getting water, think about it, they don't want to bump him off
for nothing.

What? Get the pickup, David, hurry!

Yeah. He's got enemies here. Give me the gun, David.

Are you crazy? You want to play avenger of the poor?

Santos is an asshole and has been shot, we have to put him out of his misery.

The man has to go to the hospital!

I'm going to shoot him now. An act of mercy.

Felix, cut the crap.

Step aside.

Felix!

I'm going to shoot him now.

FELIX RAISED THE GUN and aimed it at the policeman's head, I grabbed his arm. We wrestled. The Heckler & Koch went off. It was only a joke, man! I kneeled in the dirt, Felix stood next to me, a fine mist wafted from the Heckler & Koch: Felix missed Santos and hit the dog instead. That was supposed to be a joke, Svensson! Idiot! The shot sobered us up. On the way to the state hospital on Avenida Osvaldo Cruz, the pickup now weaves around the huts and the holes, avoiding the sleeping bodies and the waking dogs. David honks, David yells, David slams on the gas so hard that the stones spray. In the back of the truck Tuuli is holding Santos's head in her hands, the corrupt district policeman and local candidate of the Workers' Party has closed his eyes and is breathing shallowly and rapidly. Lula is lying with his head close to Santos and moves only when the pickup jolts over the speed bumps. Felix and I heaved the dog onto the back of the truck too, with the lambskin from the seats as a cushion. Lambskin and dog and candidate are blood-soaked. Felix and I have a healthy respect for big dogs, Felix keeps the weapon pointed at the wounded animal to be safe. Tuuli with her finger on the candidate's neck looks at me and smiles, I smile back and wonder why I'm smiling. We have a severely wounded police officer in the back of the truck, a Heckler

& Koch in hand, a half-dead dog on the lambskin. I'm worrying
about fingerprints and gunshot residues. The crack of the shot is
still ringing in our ears. When we opened our eyes three minutes
ago, the candidate was still lying in his pool of blood, his eyes
closed and his lips pressed together as if he were waiting for death.
I let go of Felix's arm with David's Heckler & Koch and stood up,
we stopped our wrestling. Felix tried to explain his joke: he hadn't
wanted to shoot the man, of course not! A joke, Svensson, a joke!
The shot had simply gone off, Felix explained, under no circumstances had he really wanted to shoot. You have to know when
the fun stops, Tuuli finally said. Lula was lying in the dust, his left
foreleg split open or broken off over the joint. The policeman's
heavy dog tried without orientation or control to get back on his
feet, without making a sound, not a bark, not a yelp, nothing. With
each attempt to stand up he sooner or later put his left foreleg on
the ground, but the bone gave way again and again, his leg was
attached to the rest of his body only by fur and sinews. The candidate's dog fell again and again on his side and finally stayed down.
The animal blood mingled with the human blood, in the dust
they were the same color. Help me, Tuuli said, laying her hand
on Lula's heavy head. She grabbed the dangling foreleg and tied it
off with the dog's neckerchief. Meanwhile Santos refused to stop
breathing, he clung to life, to the dog and maybe even to Tuuli.

The man is dying, Tuuli says with her finger on the candidate's pulse, faster! We're driving along the main street of
Seraverde, the bars are closing or are opening again, red and blue
paper is wafting down the side streets and getting caught in the
trees, there are shards everywhere, everywhere there are dogs
rooting around in the garbage, the street sweepers sweep, a pig
is strolling about. It's taking us too long. David honks the horn
and disregards the right of way, between the streetlamps hang

red garlands and blue paper flower chains. The yellow light over everything is fading when we reach the hospital, a bungalow under fluorescent lights. David stops next to the emergency room and shouts, *oi! Edson!* The nurses know the pickup, it brings the emergency cases from the garbage street, the problem births, burn victims, gunshot victims. They know Felix and David, they pay with money from donations, they always pay immediately. A nurse wheels a metal stretcher out the door, *oi, David, meu irmão! Oi, gringos!* Behind a glass pane a female doctor wearing rubber gloves is talking on the phone, she's smoking. The four of us lift Santos onto the stretcher, he's no longer groaning. The doctor is a volunteer from Birmingham and shines a flashlight in Santos's eyes. He was lying outside the door, says David, someone shot him and left him on the doorstep, *safado.* The doctor stamps out her cigarette, today all hell has broken loose, she says, today the knives are dancing. It's Santos, says Felix. Yes, says the doctor, pressing her stethoscope to an unbloodied spot on Santos's neck. We have ten stretchers, she says, as she closes the glassy eyes of the district policeman and PT candidate, we can't work wonders for everyone.

WE REPORTED ALMOST everything to the police, David translated. We didn't say anything about the dog and the gunshot, the Heckler & Koch is in the glove compartment of the pickup. Tuuli smoked a cigarette with the doctor, we signed our statements and were permitted to go. We'll clear up the rest tomorrow, *gringos*, the police said, we'll come by. The decision on Rua do Lixo has been made. Red is dead, says Felix, long live blue! On the murderers' field the blue *trio elétrico* is playing merengue and *forró* again. I with the twenty-four hours of red and blue in my bones scarcely believe my eyes and ears. The garbage street

wakes up as if nothing happened. Are the children yelling just
as loudly as yesterday? Are the chickens clucking and the goats
bleating? Are the men raising their hands in greeting? *Oi, gringos?*
Are they raising their bottles? The bell of the church shack in
time to all this? Are we supposed to believe in Macumba? And
are those vultures up there in the sky? Lula is still lying in the
back of the truck, and I with my first dead man in my bones sit
next to the animal and swallow my tears. David parks the truck
outside the door, we lift the heavy dog off the truck and onto the
dried lambskin in the middle of the courtyard. Lula has closed his
eyes, he isn't barking or growling, his leg has stopped bleeding.
I can't go on. I wonder whether Lula will survive, I wonder how
to wash off the blood without running water. I wonder whether
the police will think we're the murderers when the investigations
continue tomorrow, when they discover the water conduit, when
they remember our Heckler & Koch, when they find the great
policeman Santos's dog with us. I take the chain off Lula's neck
and hope that he goes away, but Lula can't go away.

Flies circle the policeman's dog and the bloody lambskin.
Welcome to Seraverde, says Felix, and Tuuli replies, we should
save the dog, two deaths on the first day are too much for me.
Amputation? Felix asks with a laugh, right? Tuuli knows what to
do, she studies medicine. She sends me to the goats, David to the
liquor shacks and Felix to the truck. In the sickroom next to the
kitchen she finds isopropyl alcohol and an old scalpel, in the office
a roll of packing string. Felix gets the bolt cutter from the pickup,
I milk a goat. David gets liquor at one of the shacks, he mixes it
with my goat milk. Tuuli pulls Lula's dried jowls to the side and
pours the spiked milk between his teeth. Lula doesn't resist, he
swallows half a bowlful, then he lays his head on the ground. Tuuli
rolls a cigarette and takes a sip herself, we pass around the enamel

bowl. We tear the Sunday tablecloth of the Fundação Ajuda de Nossa Senhora into fine strips. Then Tuuli stamps out her cigarette and asks for the belt from Felix's pants, she fastens the drunk dog's snout shut. Hold tight, she says. So we hold tight: Felix the hind legs, David straddles the animal and clasps the intact foreleg. I hold Lula's head in one hand and the injured leg in the other, I can see the white bones in the wound. Tuuli now ties off the leg above the knee, come on, she says, as she tightens the tourniquet with all her might, come on, and Lula opens his eyes. Only a little bit more blood comes out. Lula doesn't move. He doesn't move when Tuuli cuts into the healthy fur over the wound and opens the flesh. He doesn't move when she severs the sinews and the bones lie bare. Lula doesn't flinch when she waves away the flies and disinfects the bolt cutter. He doesn't tremble like David and he doesn't clench his teeth like Felix when Tuuli clamps through the bones with two cracking movements. Lula and I don't look away, his eyes are wide and glassy. With Lula's head in my hands my vision blurs. The tears I managed to swallow before are dripping on the dog, into his face, into his eyes. Tuuli pours isopropyl alcohol into the wound and binds the flaps of skin with packing string, she bandages the stump with the tablecloth strips. Then it's over, half of Lula's left foreleg is lying on the ground. Let go, says Tuuli, standing up. Lula still doesn't move. My first amputation, says Tuuli, and now she smiles. Then Felix throws up in the enamel bowl, which she holds out to him.

It's already noon when I start the pump again. We washed Lula with drinking water, the lambskin we threw into the fire, followed by our bloody T-shirts and pants, then Lula's leg. Tuuli is sitting next to the dog and smoking. At one point she changes the bandage. Lula is sleeping, Felix and David are lying in their hammocks. The stink of the diesel pump mingles with the smoldering lambskin and the blood. I'm waiting for the padre with his cap. Today is Sunday, and on Sunday the padre takes off his cap and reads three consecutive Masses, first on Rua do Lixo, then in Majada, lastly for the glue-sniffing children of Mimoso. Any minute now his Peugeot will pull up in front of the Fundação Ajuda de Nossa Senhora and honk, any minute he'll want to eat with them, but no one has cooked. I'm sitting next to Tuuli and waiting for the police. We've burned what was left of the weed, but our fear remains. Why, I don't know, and of what, I only suspect. I said everything I could say, I told them everything I understood, but still the fear is stuck in my bones. The motor is running, the pump pumps, and just as I'm about to turn off the motor, there's a soft burble. I take Tuuli's hand and point to the sound. Then comes more and more. The tower is still standing, the tower doesn't even creak alarmingly, we hear the water gurgling into the tank. The pipes seem to be watertight. I run into the bedroom and wake Felix and David. The water, I say, the water! Felix gets the Heckler & Koch out of the drawer and fires into the sky, as if he wanted to shoot the fear dead from behind. Peace to the huts! he sings, war to the palaces! To the tower of Seraverde! he cheers. On the decisive Sunday in Seraverde, the day of district policeman José Santos Tourão Splitter's death, the day of Lula's greatest pain, the day of Tuuli's first amputation, the day of her arrival in the lives of Dirk Svensson and Felix Blau-meiser, the diesel motor pumps the first water into the garbage street. We test the water fountain in the courtyard, we let the faucet run, we pour water on our faces, we try the shower and the shower works, we bathe in the first water of Rua do Lixo, we stand in the midday sun, we rinse the sleep out of our eyes and the fear out of our bones, we wash the blood off the doorstep and off the iron door, we give Lula a drink.

August 8, 2005
(Bar del Porto)

Mandelkern! Svensson's loud knocking wakes me too early and much too fast, I must have slept less than an hour. Mandelkern? I become aware only slowly that I'm in Svensson's house, on his lake: Svensson's desk under the window, his books and pictures (the suitcase under the desk). I'm dizzy from not enough sleep and too much gin. Yes? I ask, and Svensson is immediately standing in the room and holding out one of his shirts to me, his voice too loud and too firm for the early morning:

Take your notebooks, Mandelkern, and come with me!

My first thought: the *Astroland* manuscript. Last night I opened the suitcase with Tuuli's hairpin and unwrapped the packet, in it almost three hundred typed manuscript pages, the title page a photo of Astroland covered with scrawls. At first I turned the pages drunkenly, then I sobered up over the course of Svensson's story. After the first third I could concentrate better and read until the candle had burned down, then read on in the moonlight, it didn't rain all night. I read *Astroland* through from beginning to end like a child under the blanket. I couldn't stop, even though I was tired, even though the manuscript isn't intended for my eyes (forbidden time, forbidden book). *Astroland* tells a love-triangle story, two men, a woman and a dog: Svensson, Tuuli and Felix. The dog is named Lua or Lula. Svensson has apparently tried to find words for the past years (1993-2003). His life story has turned for him into a sort of novel, maybe a roman à clef (I used Tuuli's hairpin). The story takes place in Europe, North and South America, Svensson's characters have endless possibilities and no obligations, they're always on the move, tourists in search of a home, like those "nostalgia tourists" journeying back to their roots abroad (Elisabeth and me in 2003). Svensson's story should have ended on the Italian side of Lake Lugano. That is, here.

Astroland

Svensson and I in white shirts and flip-flops, he holds the door for me, I carry my red plastic bag with the notebooks out of his room (headache). My second thought, as I pass Svensson on my way out the door: I won't be able to take the manuscript with me if he's bringing me to Lugano now. I should leave with the hidden stories, but the stack of paper is in Svensson's old suitcase (*Astroland* is the reason I'm here). After you, Mandelkern, says Svensson, closing the door behind me, after you (as if nothing happened). I wrapped up the stack of paper again and put it back in the suitcase when the roosters began to crow (my journalistic thoroughness).

Tuuli

On the stairs, passing the pictures of black, dying animals, I'm struck by the question of why Svensson wants to get my departure over with today and so early in the morning, of all times, even though yesterday my presence still seemed to be pleasant to him (we ate his fish, drank his wine, his gin). Tuuli and I offered each other cigarettes by the pack. I smoked what I could smoke, my night was short (now I'm paying for it). Then in the kitchen the emptied ashtray, the sorted empty bottles, the clean plates (the glass shards in the middle of the table). Svensson hurries ahead, and I follow him like a dog (my sudden nausea, the spring in his step). My third thought: I got too close to Tuuli. We sleep in adjacent rooms, I could have knocked on her door. She seems to still be asleep, she and the boy are nowhere to be seen (her Finnish-plumed singing on the other side of the wall while I was reading). I won't meet her again, I think, as Svensson and I walk side by side to the water, I don't even know her last name. I wonder what I've done wrong, why Svensson wants to get rid of me. Could he be more than just strange? 288 meters. The air over the lake is slightly hazy this morning, distant chainsaws, the sun is still waiting behind the mountains. Svensson is bigger than I, the borrowed shirt flutters around my body, the sleeves too long, I have to roll them up (his shoulders and strides, as if he made a decision).

Lua's Spot

A yellow swan stretches its neck. It stretches it up along the wooden side of the boat and toward Svensson, he feeds it seeds from his pants pocket and mimics the animal (the forward and back of both heads). When I reach out my hand, the swan hisses, as if I came too close to it. *Cygnus olor*, says Svensson, directing me to the bench in the bow, the mute swan. I feel like I'm going to throw up, Svensson has jumped onto the boat and is observing me from the stern as I clumsily climb on (he doesn't help me). Lua is still lying motionlessly by the water, he doesn't even lift his head when Svensson revs up the outboard motor (Evinrude 25). Lua doesn't look up when the motor starts only on the

seventh try, when Svensson laughs and curses, when the swan
thrusts out its head and hisses (the multihued gas on the water,
in its feathers). The mute swan, says Svensson, commits for life.
Above all during mating season the males are very aggressive
and defend their territory against people too. They hiss and with
a well-aimed blow of the wingtip can break human bones. Then
he turns his wrist, *Macumba* rises steeply and moves out onto
the lake in a wide curve (for a few seconds I'm looking down at
Svensson). House and dog quickly grow smaller, the swan soars
from the water with three or four heavy strokes of its wings and
follows the boat. He likes these birds, says Svensson, they have
their memories and their freedom. That's enough for them. But
that freedom doesn't last forever either. Memories disappear
too, if one doesn't do anything to stop it. Svensson observes the
swan. Of course animals can't tell their stories. He looks at me.
Of course not, I say, because I now have to say something (the
pollen on the water's surface like souls). Just as none of us can
tell our own stories. As an author of children's books he must be
acquainted with this dilemma, I say, but also as a novelist

(I break off)

Then my fast talking about myself as an ethnologist and my notes,
as if I could take back my remark (the remaining color drains
from our faces). Svensson suddenly smiles at me, he rolls up his
sleeves once more, showing me his upper arms. Then he revs up
the motor somewhat and steers *Macumba* in a straight line into the
middle of the lake. The passing thought: the suitcase, his manuscript, Svensson has noticed my spying. Now he wants to get rid
of me. You look at surfaces, says Svensson, and make your articles
out of them. What do you know about writing, Mandelkern?

Interview (nausea)

SVENSSON: You look so pale all of a sudden, Mandelkern, are you nauseous?

MANDELKERN: A little. The gin.

S: That was good gin. The cigarettes?

M: Maybe the fish.

S: The fish was fine, Mandelkern.

M: Can you drive somewhat slower?

S: You mentioned your questions, Mandelkern, now would be the right time.

M: Isn't Lugano in the other direction?

S: Lugano?

M: Yes?

S: Yes.

M: Okay.

S: Is that all you wanted to know?

M: Well. The fact that you live in solitude here. For example.

S: Yes?

M: I mean: why do you live here of all places? Why not in America?

S: America?

M: Or Berlin, if you prefer.

S: Go stand over the water and look out at the lake, Mandelkern, the mountains sleeping animals, ships with the speed of glaciers, below the surface the fish, over the lake the clouds and the whizzing of the swallows overhead. Swallows turn gracefully, have you ever noticed that? Tourists come here only with the ferry. When any come at all. The overland route isn't interesting enough, the road clings to concrete piers just over the water. There's nothing here. A rundown campground, three

or four rusty garages, a quarry without orders. Back there. You
see? Nothing else. Even the curves are not as sharp as on the
other side of the lake. Over there. Now and then the seasons.
The sage grows and lemons and kumquats. I wake up and go
to sleep, and all this would go on exactly the same way without
me. Every day the church tower clocks make their odd music.
I could work anywhere, but here I'm not so important. This
house stands at the edge of time. Here the dog has his peace.

M: How's the dog doing?

S: How are you doing, Mandelkern? You look bad.

M: You obviously have a higher tolerance for alcohol than I.

S: Come on. That was only one glass of good gin.

M: A water glass.

S: And I trust the fish seller here. We all ate fish.

M: Fish seller?

S: We don't have much time. Keep asking your questions, if you
can.

M: Is it going to be just the one children's book? Or are you already
working on the next one?

S: I'm trying to give memory time.

M: Your book is based on memories?

S: I think people can only write about themselves. And fail at it.

M: But the themes of loss and compensation have significance for
many people.

S: Good observation.

M: Can you explain your work method?

S: I wake up and feed the chickens. Then I see what needs to be
done. I build a cistern. I renovate. This and that.

M: I mean: Are you primarily an author or an illustrator?

S: The pictures are not by me. The pictures are by Kiki
Kaufman.

M: I see. And where did you get the idea?

S: Death dictated the story to me. Yesterday was the anniversary of a death, Mandelkern.

M: I heard.

S: What did you hear?

M: Felix Blaumeiser has been dead for three years.

S: I wonder whether you should use this information at all. It's not that simple, of course. Maybe our interview is unusable.

M: Any information is helpful.

S: Felix Blaumeiser drank himself to death, and yesterday we toasted to that.

M: With Bombay Sapphire?

S: The lake swallows everything that is given to it, all joy, all sorrow. The lake isn't that particular. You can throw up overboard, Mandelkern. Don't make such a big deal out of it.

Macumba & my decision

Svensson asks if I can swim as I take his advice and surrender the gin, wine, and fish to the lake. Svensson says I shouldn't lean out too far, one shouldn't lean out all too far anyway (little fish feed on the vomit on the surface of the lake). It must have been the cigarettes, I think, I smoked almost the whole pack (eventually smokers' sperm give up). I haven't slept. Svensson revs up the motor again and turns the gas lever. He's sorry, he says, in situations like this it's necessary to maintain the stability of swaying boats, he says, it's like riding a bicycle, you can't just stand still (Svensson revs up his voice). The boats of the Guardia di Finanza have a fairly strong wake, so he'd better bring me ashore now. Svensson steers *Macumba* in a wide and scarcely perceptible curve back toward the shore, and by the time I can finally stand up again, we've almost reached the small port (my pants wet at the knees from the water in the boat). I could wait for him on solid ground and in the fresh air, says Svensson, he has some errands to run, I should watch the fishermen. I could also take the ferry to Lugano and leave. Whatever you like, he says and steers the boat carefully to the ferry dock of the small village on the other side of the rock shelf,

You decide, Mandelkern,

and then Svensson's friendliness catches me completely off guard as I cling to the steel ladder on the quay of Osteno (as if he were pursuing a strategy). With his hand he keeps *Macumba* away from the concrete piers, and declares what a pleasure this has been for him. I hope I was some help to you, he says, your questions are questions I sometimes ask myself! He'd like to continue our conversation, out here there's not much chance to talk. With Kiki Kaufman, for example, he speaks exclusively English, and Lua too has grown taciturn (he says: in another language one is another person). Tuuli refuses to remember anything, says Svensson, shifting the outboard into first gear, Tuuli only thinks about tomorrow, the boy is ultimately a mystery to him anyway (Svensson is now talking as if he wanted to tell me these things). Then he revs up the motor and *Macumba* stirs the green water. Feel better, Mandelkern, Svensson shouts as he departs, leaving me behind on the dock (Macumba is a sort of voodoo among Brazilian peasants, that much I learned last night). On the dock a ferry timetable (Società Navigazione Lago di Lugano).

Piazza G. Matteotti, Osteno, 8:30 AM

It will get better soon, I think, a short stroll through the village will dispel the nausea, the fresh air the burning from the tobacco, a coffee the fatigue (solid ground underfoot). Osteno a deserted place without a real restaurant, without a supermarket and with only one café, early in the morning the two plazas are empty (Piazza Ugo Ricci, Piazza G. Matteotti). In the morning fog a black eagle with outspread wings commemorates the local dead (World War I + II). The only store in the village is closed, a paint and lacquer shop (Colorificio). On the wall of the village hall a poster announcing a fair in Porlezza for the summer of 2002 (Luna Park), there are also the recent deaths in the village. I follow the serpentine Via Val d'Intelvi up the mountain, in the cemetery overlooking the village an old woman in an army raincoat is kneeling in front of a gravestone. To avoid intruding, I wait among the urn compartments at the other end. I wait for the wretched nausea to go away (she nods at me before she leaves). On the small gravel grave a tiny brass bicycle and a wooden model of a boat, behind the gravestone a beer glass for watering flowers (Aronne Gobbi, 1937–2002). Felix Blaumeiser must have died the same year, if I am to believe Svensson, but his *Astroland* manuscript breaks off at that decisive point. I should ask my main informant. In the whole cemetery there are no living plants, on the Via Mulino behind it only stinging nettles (I throw up into the weeds).

How do I get out of here?

Porlezza 13:05

Osteno 13:20

San Mamete 13:28

Oria 13:35
Gandria Confine 13:40
Gandria 13:45
Castagnola 13:58
Paradiso 14:08
Lugano Giardino 14:15

What would I like,

asks the maybe forty-year-old waitress in the only bar in the
village, first in too-fast Italian and then in somewhat antiquated
German. I need a coffee, or else I'll fall asleep before the ferry or
Svensson picks me up. The bar is a flat shed, the only bungalow
in a row of whitewashed, multistory harbor houses. At the red
plastic tables in front of the bar, four men are playing cards
(coffee cups & *Tuttosport*). An old man with white hair and the
yellow and black armband of the blind is sitting off to the side
and drinking Prosecco, even though it's only nine o'clock in the
morning. Here too sparrows on the tables. I order: espresso for
the fatigue, mineral water for the headache. The waitress's reply:
immediatamente, Signore. The old man with the Prosecco glass
hears my whispered German and extends his arm in a Nazi salute,
the waitress goes over to him and pushes down his outstretched
hand with a smile. Sorry, she says, looking at me, are you unwell?
Sembra pallido (my Italian is doing miserably). And because all
words and reasons for the answer fail me, I alternately nod and
shake my head (headache).

BAR del PORTO/Caffè Manzoni

I wait for recovery. Plastic seats under pruned lakeside lindens, on the sidewalk orange-red umbrellas (Algida), the gold-green paint is flaking off the window frames. Linden leaves, a toy vending machine full of blue, pink, green capsules (the ferry back doesn't leave for three hours). Two days ago I fell out of time. I've been here since Saturday, two days without a word to Elisabeth (two days outside my life). Two days ago I bought the *Süddeutsche Zeitung* at the Hamburg Airport: caesaerean risk and air running out in a sunken mini-submarine in the Black Sea, along with three notebooks. *Un altro espresso?* asks the waitress behind the bar, as I slowly slink back from the bathroom. Even with my finger in my throat there was nothing left but thready saliva and useless coughing (Lua). I can't get rid of last night. *Sì,* I say, and flop down on the plastic chair next to the entrance. Elisabeth and I didn't make an arrangement as to when to give notification of my absence (the absence of my article). By now she will have called several times, sober on my cell phone, insistent with Lufthansa, indignant with the hotel (her singing-resistance-to-pieces frequency). Tomorrow evening the next issue will go to print. Mandelkern is the perfect man for this story, Elisabeth said. I should have refused the assignment outright. The nausea isn't subsiding, the ferry isn't coming. I notice that I've forgotten my Svensson file on Svensson's desk, along with the *Süddeutsche Zeitung* and my shirt with the red wine stains (Svensson won't find out anything new about himself). This morning too the mini-submarine with the eight confined crew members will still be on the bottom of the sea. They'll calculate their oxygen, as Svensson calculated his oxygen on September eleventh (my coughing after all the cigarettes). The blind man with the white hair has extended his arm again and is babbling German and Italian commands to himself. I would have liked to reread the article about the risks of caesareans, I would have been interested in the report on the mobile lifestyle (Elisabeth and me). When the waitress sets another coffee in front of me and my notebook, it becomes clear to me that I should call, but there's chewing gum stuck to the pay phone of the Bar del Porto.

the deeper water

I go to the bathroom two more times, I lean on the scrawl-covered tiles and order water when I return (the change accumulates next to the notebook). Between retches I search for words for my next decisions. I'm a journalist, I say to the waitress, I'm researching a story. I should leave, I could stay, I could examine Svensson's manuscript, possibly his attempted autobiography, maybe his *Speculations about Felix*. I would sleep with Tuuli (I would have decided). I observe a fisherman on the shore and, later, *Ceresio*, the name of the ferryboat that travels between Lugano and Porlezza. A couple disembarks, the man is carrying a backpack, the woman is holding a child. A few boxes and cartons are thrown onto the metal dock (the mail). The flags along the shore are hanging, the blind Prosecco drinker's white hair is lying straight (the age of the people on the quay). My body isn't calming down. The lakes of Ticino, Elisabeth said on Friday on the way back from the restaurant, are deep, in winter the snow never stays there, and in summer they keep their shores pleasantly cool. Lake Lugano is a stable body of water. Not all that back and forth like the Atlantic, not all that burbling like the Baltic Sea. It can be relied on, Mandelkern. In the early afternoon *Ceresio* could take me back to Lugano, but I remain seated (I myself can't rely on myself).

*"The Master of Chickens
(Profile of Dirk Svensson/about 270 words)"*

On the pier it's almost windless. Scattered clouds hang around the
peaks of the Ticino mountains on the shore of Lago di Lugano.
Under the lindens and palms of the lakeside promenade walk
extraordinarily well-dressed women and men, radiant with world-
liness, they drink Campari under cypresses. Lugano is beautiful,
and the Ticino city knows it too. It was not for nothing that the
grandmasters of German literature strolled here. Hermann Hesse
wrote for fourteen years in Montagnola in the hills overlooking
the city and painted his famous watercolors, and Thomas Mann
was particularly fond of drinking his Sunday tea in the cafés of the
Piazza della Riforma. Two generations of writers and one world
war later, this city remains a hub for rich, beautiful, and smart
people. And then, true to style, Dirk Svensson appears for the
interview with his boat—as might be expected from a successful
author. His first children's book struck the nerve of the times: *The
Story of Leo and the Notmuch* has already sold 100,000 copies, and
sales are projected to more than double. But of course the first
impression is deceptive: instead of the expected light summer
suit, Svensson is wearing an old T-shirt, his boat is a wooden tub
with an outboard. In the stern sits a black, ugly dog, a kind of
German shepherd with a gray spot on his chest and only three
legs. Dirk Svensson is a woodcutter in a fishing trawler, exactly as
I imagined a media-shy children's book author. "Climb aboard,"
says Svensson, "come along!" The small wooden boat named
Macumba rocks alarmingly as I . . .

It can't go on like this, Mandelkern!

About Osteno? I'm not writing about Osteno, I explain to the waitress, the story only takes place here, it's a profile of a children's book author residing here. Residing? The waitress doesn't know the word. Yes, I say, Dirk Svensson. *Si*, she says, Svensson and Kiki are the only foreigners who stay well into autumn. I feel nauseous again, suddenly the waitress's sentences contain incomprehensible words and names. They're artists, she says, and so only half tourists, the other half belongs here. They're famous in some way, that much she knows, the only celebrities on this end of the lake (*lo scrittore*, she says, *l'artista*). Despite that, the two of them have stayed normal, says the waitress, as she prepares the coffee and refills the card players' glasses with Prosecco, welcome guests, thank God (the roar of the espresso machine grates off a layer of my composure). The waitress points behind her. On the wall: a framed mirror (image: the intact New York skyline in black and pink), a signed poster of Valentino Rossi in front of a motorcycle (signature printed on). Between them a picture that also must have been painted by Kiki (Lua and a dark-haired toddler sleeping between red chair legs). That's Lua, says the waitress, *il buon samaritano a tre gambe*. The dog is faithful, she says, how do you say? Faithful until death? *Obbedienza cieca*? Last summer Lua could still walk, and the three of them came here for coffee every day. The waitress imitates Lua's bark (she only manages his cough, she smokes too much). Isabella was born in Lugano too, sweet little Isabella (I don't ask who Isabella is).

False assumption: the Italians here don't want Svensson.

The waitress lights a cigarette, pulls out a photograph from under the counter and asks: is your book a sad story? Take this, she says and hands me the photo, a souvenir. My reply: I'm writing for a newspaper, for a book you need years and a real story. In the photo: Osteno in deep snow, two children playing under the small but already pruned lindens along the shore, the bar in a real house: "Caffè del Porto, Osteno, Invierno 1939/40." The waitress points to the bar furniture, to the pictures on the wall, to the tacky sofa, to the pinball machine, to the toy vending machine, to the card-playing men, out the window, to the red chairs, to the lake, to the opposite shore. Newspaper or book, she says, Osteno is a good place for sad stories.

What I've found out:

Elisabeth wants a profile of the children's book author Dirk Svensson, so I flew to Milan. Svensson's dog Lua really does have only three legs, he's old and will soon die. Felix Blaumeiser is already dead. Svensson didn't draw the pictures in his children's book himself, he's not an illustrator, all the pictures are by Kiki Kaufman. Kiki Kaufman is not here on the lake. Svensson seems to have been expecting Tuuli and the boy. Svensson's reclusiveness is his concentration. Svensson is a man of rituals. He cultivates his own vegetables, he breeds chickens, sometimes he takes the boat to the supermarket, otherwise he doesn't go anywhere. Under his desk is Blaumeiser's suitcase, in it is Svensson's *Astroland* manuscript. I'm a slow reader, but I devoured it in a night. I'm piecing together Svensson from what I see and hear and read, but the manuscript is lying unfinished in the suitcase (Svensson is a memory animal). *The Story of Leo and the Notmuch* is taken from his life as much as *Astroland* (this line of thought is naïve biographism, Elisabeth would say, you yourself should know that with your literary studies minor, art and life are two completely different things). I take Svensson's stories at face value, even though I should be more careful (my considerations are based on the interpretive principle of the critic Louis Simpson: "my rule has been to give these matters as much importance as he himself gave them"). Now I want to get to the bottom of his strangeness after all. Svensson is no stranger than I am. I should investigate Tuuli's divided love (either Blaumeiser is the boy's father or Svensson is), Felix Blaumeiser's drinking habits, his carelessness, his death, finally Svensson's tendency to flee.

write or leave?

In the early afternoon I'm still sitting in the Bar del Porto in Osteno (on the brink of vomiting for the fourth time). Another attempt to decide, another attempt to fulfill my assignment and write the profile as planned (another attempt to go back to Elisabeth). I could take an early train home and start the profile from scratch on the way. I would write the last lines as the train went through the Free Port of Hamburg, past the wholesale fruit market, the warehouse district, the Deichtorhallen galleries. I should could would, but my stomach wants to wring itself out, my body wants to stay. On the table in front of me lie the notebooks and the change, the clock in the Bar del Porto shows 1:15 PM (the smell of toast and cigarettes). In a few minutes the ferry will dock, pick up passengers and cast off again. I have to decide. The coins would be enough for a phone call, I think, I could ask Elisabeth for another day (I would only have to scrape the chewing gum off the pay phone).

phone call (straightening things out)

INTERN: Culture pages, Elisabeth Emmerich's office, what can I do for you?

MANDELKERN: Mandelkern. I'd like to speak to my wife.

I: Who's calling, please?

M: It's Mandelkern.

I: Who?

M: My wife, please. Frau Emmerich?

I: Sorry, but I can barely understand you, Frau Emmerich is in a meeting at the moment. Could you try again?

M: No! DA-NI-EL MAN-DEL-KERN? Hello?

I: I really can barely understand you.

M: It's urgent!

I: Herr Mandelkern? Where are you?

M: I'm still here.

I: Where exactly is here?

M: I'm sitting here in a café at the end of the world and have to throw up every five minutes. I have fish poisoning. Please tell that to my wife.

I: Frau Emmerich wants me to tell you that we've been worried. It's been raining for days.

M: Who? We?

I: We thought you'd drowned. Frau Emmerich wants me to ask you what you're thinking. Your phone is turned off, you're not in the hotel. That's fucked up, those are Frau Emmerich's exact words. To drown without a word.

M: I ate fish. Filetto di persico. And now I'm throwing up. Tell that to my wife.

I: What's going on with the profile?

M: There really is a story here. Several, even. Svensson has written something like an autobiography. I'm in the middle of it. I've taken a lot of notes. I need some more time.

I: Frau Emmerich wants me to ask you whether ethnology is getting in your way again.

M: What? No.—Maybe.

I: Herr Mandelkern?

M: I'm on death's trail.

I: Now I can't hear you again. The line is really bad.

M: Why did I have to be the one to come here? It's not that simple, tell that to my wife!

I: —

M: I'm going to stay longer, do you hear me? Your research was terrible, by the way! Do you hear me?

I: —

M: Elisabeth?

plastic cups & imagination

It's the creeping professionalization of our love that I can't bear, its purposefulness. Elisabeth is a goal-directed woman, her voice sings resistance to pieces (Elisabeth and I are slipping away from each other). She took over the editorship of the culture pages, she's 38 years old. I'd like to have your problems, Mandelkern, she said, maybe there's a good story there. That's what she wants (now she wants a child).

Ceresio 13:20

I'm watching the ship depart. The swallows high in the sky, the fog has dispersed. I already missed my return flight yesterday, the 13:20 ferry has just cast off with a loud blast of its horn and is crossing the lake (I can no longer leave this place today, not even if I wanted to). I will stay. My body will recover, I remember that "the ethnologist should physically work and dance, but also suffer. Stoller stresses the importance of experiences of illness and temporary paralysis" (here Spittler is referring to Stoller, *The Taste of Ethnographic Things: The Senses in Anthropology*). I've already filled the first notebook (Semikolon, blue), the second and red notebook is lying in front of me and waiting.

How can someone really tell his own story?

I follow the waitress's recommendation and don't drink any more coffee (the gray chewing gum under my fingernails after I scraped it off the coin slot). She asks if I'd like Prosecco instead. *Grazie*, I say, *grazie* (everyone wants decisions). I pay. Svensson still hasn't returned, I can no longer wait for him and *Macumba* (I have to finally sleep). The waitress takes my money and points along the shore to the end of the Via San Rocco and farther into the woods (the extension into nothingness). Then another kilometer. She'll tell Svensson that I've already left, she says, and points to a stack of letters behind the bar, he comes every afternoon for the mail anyway. *Arrivederci, scrittore*, she says (apparently she means me).

with his back to the wall

High above the village, at the end of the Via San Rocco, there's a thrown-together park bench between two dumpsters: two blocks of stone, two screwed-on planks (civilization reaches to this point). The road peters out in a gravelly dead end. Next to the dumpsters lie the same black plastic bags as on Svensson's property. From up here Osteno is indistinguishable from the other villages on the lake (wood, stones, and ferryboats are the same color in this region, a weathered red or orange). Svensson's ruin is somewhere down there on the water to the north, wedged between the green lake and the wooded cliff wall of Monte Cecchi. It can be reached only by a narrow road that must have been drivable at some point years ago (now Svensson's chickens live in the Fiat, the ivy creeps over the mossy windows). Here the trees don't have it easy, I think, but trees grow on the steepest slopes (Svensson lives with his back to the wall).

Ficus elastica

On a Sunday morning during our first summer Elisabeth and I ended up at the Hamburg fish market, the market vendors cried their wares, we ordered coffee and bratwurst, we didn't want to stay long. Away from the stalls we fed two ducks in the oily harbor water. Our few mutual friends we'd forgotten in the Pudel Club (the red of her hair between the strings of lights). Elisabeth dispelled my caution, I peed in the entrance to a warehouse. On the Elbe a single pilot boat. When I returned, Elisabeth had bought a rubber plant (*Ficus elastica*). For us, she said, taking the flowerpot off the quay wall: now we should get out of here (the rust on the bollards). Later, in the taxi heading toward Hoheluft, she said that starting now I had to really touch her, she wasn't made of cotton candy (Elisabeth's tangibility).

Let's push things forward

In the late summer Elisabeth and I grew together. When it got dark we smoked barely dried weed from our neighbor's window box, we walked through cobblestone streets, our footsteps resounded between the buildings (Elisabeth was the only woman in the city). When the bars chained up their chairs, we lay down by the Eimsbüttel canals or next to the rose beds in the Planten un Blomen park. Elisabeth said that she wanted to see me always, and I fell asleep early in the morning only so as to wake up next to her again around noon. We bought ice cream at the twenty-four-hour gas station (Langnese, Aral), we listened to British pop music, we waited for the *Hamburger Morgenpost*. Most of the time we awoke in my apartment on Marthastrasse, sometimes at her place too. Once I got up and said I had to go now, sometimes it was too much. Yes, said Elisabeth, but it's never enough (we were both right).

Are Svensson's stories made up?

Over the lake in front of Osteno a gray haze has replaced the fog. Claasen is his own crematorium, Svensson said yesterday, but the smoke isn't coming from the woods above Svensson's house (Claasen's direction). The cloud is spreading over the lake from beyond the village. This morning Svensson mentioned a quarry in Osteno, its lack of orders (Svensson makes up his stories as he pleases; I shouldn't believe him). At the path's entrance a sign: *Attenti al Cane/Warnung vor dem Hund/Beware of the Dog.*

What exactly do you actually want, Elisabeth?

Elisabeth and I on a Thursday evening in autumn on the way to the Literaturhaus on the Outer Alster Lake, we were supposed to meet her still-husband. I'd like to introduce Mandelkern to you, Elisabeth had said on the phone, Mandelkern makes my everyday life easier (I stood next to her and felt like a teenager). Elisabeth had already been living alone for years, she was still married only on paper. There was still some time and it was a clear evening, so we got out of the taxi on Schöne Aussicht, we wanted to walk the last stretch. When I asked why this meeting was necessary, Elisabeth pulled me into a rhododendron by the Wolfgang Borchert memorial. We're reasonable people, said Elisabeth, clamping my head in her hands (vise). Take your finger, Mandelkern, she said, I want you to mark my pussy (words fail me). But she showed consideration for the people out for a stroll and came only softly or not at all, *We are the generation without ties and without depth* was engraved on the Borchert stone, a large dog crawled to us in the undergrowth and was whistled back (different generation, different abyss). Elisabeth believed in clear boundaries and was about to set one. Wash your finger, said Elisabeth, he doesn't have to smell us right away. What exactly do you actually want? I asked. Elisabeth's reply: I want to sense where I belong (we once belonged to each other, I remember). Later we were sitting at one of the back tables in the large hall of the Literaturhaus Café, when Elisabeth's husband canceled our meeting. Not much later he went into retirement, the divorce they settled the next spring, I never met him.

Attenti al Cane!

I'm sitting at the end of the Via San Rocco in front of my last bile and my inability to leave (coffee and soul), when Tuuli is suddenly standing next to me. The boy behind her seems intimidated by the sight of the helpless man (Mandelkern). She's holding a black garbage bag in her hand. My body's acting crazy, I say to Tuuli between two retches, an influenzal infection maybe. We would definitely detect a fever, I say, but then I can't go on talking because I have to gag (one has a high temperature when the body is fighting something, says Elisabeth). When not even bile is coming up anymore, Tuuli tosses the garbage bag into the heap and hands me a handkerchief:

It'll be over soon, *Manteli*

she says, I already thought you'd left without a word. No, I say, wishing I weren't sitting in front of my own vomit. The boy observes me and his mother (her hand on the back of my head). Of course I would have said good-bye, I say, if I'd left, for me politeness is a cardinal virtue (where am I now getting such words?). Tuuli laughs, the boy doesn't. Bile, says Tuuli, is produced in the duodenum, *Manteli* (such facts, such details). Then she lays her hand on my back. I will stay. I have to take a closer look at Tuuli, I think, I want to see behind Svensson's stories, I have to ask her.

Samy! Antakaa hänelle vesipullo!

says Tuuli with her small hand on the nape of my neck. The boy holds a bottle of water out to me, and I rinse the sourness out of my mouth. We slowly walk deeper into the woods, back to Svens-

son's house, back to his pictures, his animals, his stories (sometimes people find themselves on a journey together: we arrived
together, we could leave together).

my curiosity

Back in my room Tuuli holds the thermometer up to the light
(her gap-toothed smile). She says, 36.7° might seem slightly low,
but it's completely normal for an adult body, even in this heat. Do
you usually smoke as much as you did yesterday, *Manteli*? No? I'm
lying on my back in Svensson's room, Tuuli puts the boy's thermometer back in the light blue plastic case (Thermex for Kids).
There are no viruses involved, *Manteli*, she says, it's not an infection and nothing bacterial. Tuuli gets up and leaves my room, it
must be your curiosity, *Karvasmanteli*.

William Wordsworth vs. Robby Naish

I TURN THE RADIO DIAL AND SAY TO THE PADRE: FOR DAYS THEY'VE been playing nothing but *forró* here. Urinating is good for you, the padre replies, stopping the car. He leaves the engine running, gets out and pisses on a horse corpse on the roadside, his piss drums on the swollen belly like rain on a car roof. But for days it hasn't rained, for days Tuuli and I haven't understood a word, for days there's been no sign of Felix. Tuuli is lying on the back-seat and sleeping, sometimes I turn around and observe Tuuli and her sleep, curled up and her mouth slightly open. I wonder whether Felix was arrested, I wonder how the Seraverde prison smells, I wonder how we can get him out of there. And whether we can at all. For days I've been seeing Felix in every cactus on the roadside, in every desert dog, in every palm tree. Felix speaks my language, Felix understands me. Get away from here and recover, he said, and sat us in the padre's Peugeot on Sunday afternoon, you guys go along on the donation tour, then things will look different before long, you'll get to know the country and people, don't forget your passports! I'll stay here, I'll deal with the police and the dog, we'll meet on Sunday in Tupanatinga on the BR-232, Pousada Majestic. Then we'll see the country, desert and rain forest and sea, the *seleção* and cockfighting. So for days I've been sitting in the passenger seat of the Peugeot 405 and counting cacti, 517, 518. Sometimes Tuuli wakes up and rolls a cigarette, sometimes she tells stories from Finland, sometimes she touches me with all due caution. For days we've been listening to *forró* and watching the padre drink, for days the padre has been buying gas and a cooler full of water in the morning at some gas station. I drink with him, because without Felix I'm not touching a sip of alcohol. The padre takes off his cap, crosses himself and puts the cap back on. We drive through the steppe, sertão, until dusk, we stop every afternoon and every evening in a different village, Itaporanga, Sera Bonita, Guanumbi. I've forgotten the days of the week. I stand next to the padre and piss on the corpse too.

I paint my world in the darkest colors. The black horse, I think, the second corpse. For days I've been seeing the dark blood of the district policeman and city council candidate oozing. For days I've been explaining to the padre what happened. Santos was lying outside the door, I say, his abdominal wall shot off, blood everywhere, on the steps, on the wall, on the iron door. But the padre with his right hand on the priestly cock isn't listening, he's rolling his hips as if he were dancing the limbo. He's trying to hit the flies on the horse's milky eyes, with his left hand he adjusts his cap. José Santos Tourão Splitter had pissed all over himself, I say, from a frayed hole in the middle of his belly flowed light blood. José Santos Tourão Splitter? asks the padre, Partido dos Trabalhadores? I haven't drunk enough water to keep up with the padre, he shakes his cock. *Safado*, says the padre, buttoning his pants. His chest hairs were stuck together, I recount, like gulls' feathers in oil. Santos was lying in his blood and looking at us, someone had left him on the doorstep, the tracks of the donkey cart could still be seen. The padre takes a cold chicken leg from yesterday out of the cooler and strolls around the Peugeot. We lifted him onto the pickup, I say, following the padre, we drove him to the hospital, we got there too late, the man was dead! His dog was injured too, we don't know whether he's pulled through. We amputated his leg with the bolt cutter. We don't know how the Seraverde vote was decided, who has won the elections and who has survived. We don't know anything! The padre climbs into the Peugeot and gnaws at the chicken leg. Do you know Lula? I ask the padre. The padre smiles, Tuuli's still sleeping. I thought this was peace service in deprived areas of Latin America, I say to the padre, and the padre says, urinating is good for you.

The horse corpse is shining, the car is parked on the roadside in the middle of the desert, then the padre engages a gear and things go on as they have been for days, on the right and left cacti, now and then a rocky hill, then hours of steppe, occasionally an intersection, occasionally an armadillo, occasionally a road sign. The names mean nothing to me, I don't know where I am or where we're going. Tuuli has even less of a clue, she just closes her eyes and sleeps, her hands folded into a pillow. The padre throws the chicken leg out the window, the car lurches to the left and lurches to the right, in the rearview mirror the black horse is lying on the roadside, and I take another bottle of water out of the cooler. Where are we actually going, I ask the padre, and are you even listening to me? *Sim*, says the padre, shaking his head. He takes his hands off the steering wheel and nods toward the backseat, he traces a curvy silhouette of a woman in the air and winks at me. The church doesn't understand me, I think. Is Santos really dead? Felix asked the doctor in the state hospital. Election night here is Sodom and Gomorrah, she replied, stubbing out her cigarette, we can't save everyone. So I ask the padre whether salvation exists, and the padre points to the horizon, Tupanatinga, he replies. For days the padre starts talking and singing around noon, Tuuli and I can't follow his song and talk. He never gets tired, the padre might be saying, he can always drive straight through the desert. In two hours it's lunchtime in Tupanatinga,

we believe we understand, he has to sleep there, and the mayor is
a friend. In every town the padre has a friend, in Sera Bonita the
chicken grills are fired up, in Itaporanga the beans are cooking, in
Macarimba the donation managers are waiting. *Saúde!* the padre
laughs, throwing a water bottle out the window, *mais uma água!*
I turn the radio back on. Still *forró*. The sun shows three o'clock,
Tuuli talks to me only at night. Five hundred twenty cacti are a
lot of cacti, I say to the padre, next to the horse corpse there were
three tall, thin, flowerless ones.

We really do arrive in Tupanatinga. The town hall is a brick
hut with a coat of arms over the door, a rearing black horse. Large
and small pigs run across the marketplace, they root around in
the dust and in the garbage bags. In front of the town hall the
mayor of the town turns a bottle upside-down and the beer spills
on a small brown pig, it drips in the dust, and the pig shakes itself
off like a dog. Celina, cries the mayor, *cerveja!* and the mayor
of Tupanatinga's wife sets two bottles of Antarctica in a styrofoam cooler on the table. The padre only drinks water. Celina
has served meat on a skewer, feijoada, bean stew and rice, fried
cheese and onions. *Saúde!* cries the padre, *saúde!* cries the mayor,
kicking at the small pig, it evades the mayor's shoe and escapes
under the Peugeot. Tuuli pushes her plate away from her and
rolls a cigarette, she throws a few potatoes under the car for the
small pig. The mayor eats, the padre drinks, they've taken care
of business, they seem content. The padre has opened the door
of the Peugeot, the radio is now playing international hits. The
mayor of Tupanatinga loves Sinatra: I got you, he sings, under
my skin. The mayor loves Celina: he kisses her painted lips, he
kisses her hair, he kisses her golden cross in her impressive décol-
letage. Celina runs her fingers through his chest hair in time to
Sinatra. The hairs like gulls' feathers in oil, I think, the hole in

the middle of the belly, I remember, the lighter blood. I'll switch to beer now after all, I decide, even though I usually drink only with Felix. Celina fills my and Tuuli's glasses. The mayor cheers in the eternal summer of the Pernambuco desert and grabs his head in his hands. Fat from the chicken with garlic and coriander drips on his blue uniform shirt. New York, New York, he sings softly, scratching his beard, his laughter resounds over the noon emptiness of the marketplace. The padre too takes off his Los Angeles Lakers cap in all the enthusiasm, he tosses it into the air. Tuuli smokes and smiles. I say: I don't understand anything that's happening here. You? Suddenly Tuuli leans toward me and kisses my ear. Me neither, she says, but I understand you. I feel the first beer in my head and Tuuli's left hand on the nape of my neck, her right hand feeds the small pig under the Peugeot bread. Its squealing sounds like happiness. I wonder where the Pousada Majestic is, here there's no hotel or inn to be seen. I wonder whether Felix is waiting there, I wonder whether Felix will show up there at all.

On we go! The padre pounds on the table and stands up, on we go! and I think, where are we even going? The padre reaches for the water and takes a sip from the pitcher. On we go! We're waiting here for Felix as planned, Tuuli whispers in my ear, in Tupanatinga on the BR-232, she murmurs, just the two of us. Let's go! says the padre, taking the key from the table, but Tuuli says no. I remain seated. Celina presses her pink lips on the priestly cheek, the mayor of Tupanatinga presents to the padre a packet of meat, *Obrigado, padre*, he says. I'm astonished by Tuuli's lips on my ear, by the pink on Celina's mouth. The padre blesses the house, he flings his arms around Celina's neck and throws himself at the mayor's feet. With his eyes closed he draws a pig in the visitors' book of Tupanatinga, and I kiss Tuuli. I kiss Tuuli, and the padre jumps into the Peugeot, he turns the key in the ignition. Tuuli kisses me as the engine whines and the bells toll. The mayor of Tupanatinga and Celina stand arm in arm in front of the town hall and wave goodbye to the Peugeot, the dust wafts from the desert and toward the desert. The padre jiggles the gear-shift, finds the right gear and slams on the gas. The stones spray, the pigs flee, the dust swallows up the view. The Peugeot bumps where there are no bumps at all, then it drives straight across the marketplace toward the church, toward the road, then it vanishes, honking, between the houses. The padre has forgotten his cap. Tuuli leans her head on my shoulder, and as the cloud of dust and diesel subsides, Celina is kneeling over the small pig, moaning and wringing her hands. Blood in the dust yet again, I think, blood yet again. The black horse, I say to Tuuli, the red candidate. The small pig, she says, the small pig.

IS TODAY SATURDAY? I ask, stroking Tuuli's rib cage, her belly, her small breasts. Tuuli and I have found the Pousada Majestic, on a side street behind the marketplace. We're lying in room 219 under the fan, I'm drinking water. I've slept the beer out of my head, I've showered for the first time in days. Now I'm lying on my back next to Tuuli and reading the only English book in room 219: William Wordsworth's *Selected Poems*. The inn is a colonial building with high ceilings and window shutters, our pants and shirts flutter freshly washed in the back courtyard. Outside the window an empty plaza, the Praça de São Geraldo, a turned-off fountain and dry palm leaves, yellow streetlamp light and here too street pigs and dogs, over everything the smell of desert and fire. Tuuli wakes up and pulls my head to her lips. She seems not to know the answer. I don't want to tell the days of the week apart anymore, she says. Tuuli and I are lying in room 219 of the only and therefore best hotel in Tupanatinga, in the middle of the *sertão*. We've stopped counting the days of the week. We could inquire at the reception desk, but we don't ask. Instead Tuuli leans first over my mouth and then over my body. The padre has left the village and forgotten us without the supervision of the Catholic Church in a room with wooden shutters and high ceilings, we drink water with ice from each other's mouths, our lips tell who we are and our fingers report how we look. I've told Tuuli about myself as a child, about the Ruhr area, across the gap between the beds she reached for my hand and described Helsinki to me, the snow and her parents' snail farm. And so on, Tuuli said. For example, I replied. Each morning the squawks of the parrots in the lobby wake us, we start again from the top and stop only to order abacaxi, pineapple, water, and coffee. Tuuli asks about Felix, and I tell her about my oldest friend. I say: Felix will find us. I say: We're where we're supposed to be. The sun and the days of the week, the desert dogs and the tolling of the bells, the small pigs and black horses vanish beyond the corners of the Praça de São Geraldo.

A few days later I'm woken up by a honk and shouting under our window. It's evening, on the plaza an accordion is playing, the parrot in the lobby is squawking to itself. Tuuli is asleep. I fling open the shutters of 219. In the moonlight or in the street-lamp light the pickup is parked next to the fountain. Felix in a panama hat is kneeling in the back of the truck and ruffling the fur of the district policeman's heavy dog, David is leaning on the hood and smoking. *Oi, Svensson!* he shouts, come down, we're late! The dog barks, and Felix laughs. For the first time in days I have to go outside, for the first time in weeks Felix and I clap each other on the shoulders. Not missing, Svensson? Not in jail, Felix? Not dead, dog? We have a table and chairs put out on the Praça de São Geraldo of Tupanatinga, Felix gesticulates for Antarctica and small glasses, and the innkeeper sets a bottle in front of him. David fills the glasses, the dog gets a bowl with beer, and Felix summarizes: no one got thrown in jail, as you can see of course, the pipelines are now officially approved, the Fundação Ajuda de Nossa Senhora has fresh water. Rua do Lixo didn't vote, the decision was postponed, but there are no longer any candidates, the blue candidate Gonçalves Meirinho deeply regrets the death of the red Santos, under such circumstances he cannot enter the city council, *porco dio!* Maybe later. The reports in the Seraverde newspapers came fast and furious. Toward morning Santos had been strolling all in red across the blues' square, he laughed at blue drunks, pointed to the blue *trio elétrico*, he'd wrapped his dog Lula in the red flag of the PT and was pulling him along behind him on the chain. The blue musicians were long since in bed, only the last remnants of the blue celebration were still sitting there under the blue garlands or lying under the benches. Of course they mocked and laughed at Santos as much as he had them, Felix says, they told him off in the most un-Christian manner. But then a shot rang out, and the red candidate was suddenly lying on the ground and in his own blood, in front of the silent *trio elétrico* and amid the last guests of the blue celebration. From one second to the next the square emptied out, no one had seen anything, they'd heard nothing but the shot. No one called the police, the fire department or an ambulance. Santos must have been lying there for several minutes among the drunks and sleepers and waiting for his death, says Felix. He raises his glass to clink, and David nods. But then, and this the police have since verified, a street sweeper passed by in his donkey cart and immediately thought of us and the Fundação's pickup. With the cart he never could have reached the hospital on Avenida Osvaldo Cruz in time. He didn't want any trouble either, and therefore didn't inform the police. Santos left the blue celebration square and the political stage on, of all things, the donkey cart of a garbage collector, Felix recounts, he was left outside the door on Rua do Lixo so we would save him. We, of all people! Felix and David's laughter comes fast and furious and resounds on the empty plaza in front of the Pousada Majestic, the bandaged Lula is lying at their side. Felix has forgotten the blood on the door, the gulls' feathers in oil, the crack of Lula's bones, Lula's eyes and his own vomit, I think, and toss back another glass. I waste too much time on memory. The hotel's shutters are still closed, Tuuli must still be asleep, I'll tell her this story later, but Felix interrupts my thoughts. There's fresh water on the garbage street now! Santos was shot, okay, it was in a certain sense a political murder, okay, in his own way he provoked this end himself. The dog sat next to Santos and licked his face, police dogs are faithful souls, but he couldn't prevent the shots, he couldn't get help. The doctor on Avenida Osvaldo Cruz phrased it right, it was Sodom and Gomorrah, you can't save everyone. Still, the dog is a good dog, the stump has healed, the doctor ministered to him movingly, the dog didn't slobber or bite, he simply lay still for a whole week and waited to heal. And then he healed. He stood up and was a completely different dog, Felix says, and pets this completely different dog, sweet and friendly. On the night of the full moon a few days ago they then came up with the idea of giving this new dog a new name too. The dog is lying on the cobblestones and looking at me, without batting an eyelash. I notice Lula's clear eyes, I notice the bandages on his stump, I sense the healing itch under those bandages. The sharp police dog and corrupt PT candidate's four-legged mutt Lula has become the three-legged Lua, purified and named after the moon, four letters have become three. Felix laughs and pets the dog's head. To Lua's health! he says, refilling the dog's bowl. Lua's accident, says Felix, if he may call the incident with the Heckler & Koch that, should be understood as a catharsis, the corruption has literally been shot out of the reds' bones. Lua is calmness itself. Even Felix's own guilty conscience has sort of gone up in gun smoke. I ask: Sort of? Sort of, says Felix, and at the same time the wooden shutters open on the third floor of the Pousada Majestic. Tuuli looks down at us from above. We're doing fine, says the black dog Lula or Lua, don't worry, he barks up to Tuuli.

Tuuli and I pack our things and leave our room 219 over the Praça de São Geraldo, she steals an ashtray, I take along the Wordsworth poems. The bill for the Pousada Majestic we pay in *reais* and dollars one to one, our American money is enough for the days and nights we spent waiting for Felix. We fell out of time and can afford it, we tip well. David throws our luggage in the back of the truck, and Lua marks the turned-off fountain of the Praça de São Geraldo of Tupanatinga with lifted hind leg. The three-legged dog jumps without help onto the back of the truck and we leave the town. Away we go, I think, on we go! David drives, Tuuli sits next to him and rolls a cigarette, I with my two thousand eight hundred eighty-three hours of peace service in my bones wonder whether all this can be true. Everything is the same as always, we buy cans of beer in various villages and stop on the roadside. We do as the padre does: Urinating is good for you, we say, and laugh. Felix and I hit each other on the shoulders and remind each other that we really exist, in the middle of Brazil, in the middle of the desert, in the middle of the jungle, on the way to the sea. We drive through the sertão and bathe in a river full of piranhas, we sleep in the monastery of the Holy Mary, we stroll in orchid gardens. We drive to Pedra, and climb up the black stone, and Felix declares with hands raised to the sky that the world belongs to us. Tuuli looks out the window for hours, we talk, she sings, we laugh. We drive past bananas and sugarcane, past green hills and herds of cattle, we dance in Caruaru and sleep on the bank of the Rio Ipojuca. Lua sings "Girl from Mars." Felix wins a hundred *reais* at dice in Fortaleza, he loses a hundred *reais* on the international game Brazil versus the Netherlands, in a café in Macarana he bets on Oranje, everyone thinks his blond hair is Dutch. The game ends 2–2. You can't win them all, says Felix, patting Lua's head. Tuuli sees the ocean first, Lua sees the ocean for the first time. We sleep a few nights in the sand. Tuuli removes the bandage from Lua's stump. In Natal we take off his chain, Lua hesitates. When he then runs along the water, you can almost no longer tell that his leg is missing. Felix borrows a surfboard, I'm Robby Naish! he cheers, and Tuuli applauds. In the morning she wears my purple Los Angeles Lakers cap and in the evening Felix's panama hat. David leaves the Heckler & Koch in the glove compartment. I read and lie on my back, sometimes I take notes. On the white beach of Jericoacoara we collect the roundest and palest stones. Tuuli, Felix and I throw the pebbles far out into the Atlantic. No one wins, no one loses. It's a tie, says Tuuli, and never wants to let us go. Lua asserts that this is happiness. David talks on the phone with the padre, everything is all right in the Fundação Ajuda de Nossa Senhora. The water is running. Felix and I learn capoeira, we fight and dance at the same time, we walk barefoot, we never hit each other intentionally. Lua orders chicken hearts for breakfast. On the large dune overlooking the village Tuuli kisses first me, then Felix, then me again. Peace service in deprived areas of Latin America, says Felix, crazy, aaah!

On my last night David stops at the beach of Olinda next to the largest wooden shack. Here there are Volkswagens and Chryslers, here there are Chevrolets and Hondas. We get out, behind us a taxi is honking. Olinda, says Felix, from the Portuguese *ó linda*, "how beautiful!" On the horizon two tankers in full regalia, shining cranes and cabins, floodlights on the monastery on the hill too, over all this planes in descent. The sun has already disappeared, my time in Brazil has expired, tomorrow I'm flying back. I've finished reading Wordsworth's *Selected Poems*. I'm using the return ticket for Varig Airlines as a bookmark and stick the book in my bag, Recife-São Paulo-Frankfurt. The others are heading back to Seraverde, Tuuli will stay for a while in the Fundação. She takes my hand. Your last night, she says, so let's go! So let's go? I think, and before my eyes I see Tuuli and Felix sitting on the water tower, her head on his chest. They're smoking without me. So let's go, says Felix, so let's go, says Lua.

OI, COMPADRE, David says to the guard at the door. The two of them know each other. He makes sure the police aren't coming, Felix explains to us, cockfighting is prohibited. Lua has to go back on the chain, but we're allowed in. No photos! I with my three thousand two hundred sixty-four hours of Brazil in my bones have never seen anything like this: the guests are sitting at small tables around a dance floor made of clay. We get a table in the second row. A waist-high barrier made of light blue wood stands between us and the dance floor. Old men in shirts, young men in suits, occasionally a woman with dyed blonde hair and high-laced breasts holding a bottle of Guaraná. Men and boys lean on the bar in shirts and pants of the same color, red, yellow, green, blue, black, white. At the bar there's no drinking, at the bar the teams talk shop, says David, the cock breeders and handlers. Under strings of lights people play poker and dice and pass money back and forth. An old man is playing the berimbau, another is smoking the stub of a joint until it's completely gone, black with oil, the lighter close to his calloused lips. To celebrate the occasion we have grilled red mullet with lemon and black beans, to celebrate the occasion David pours one beer bottle after another into Lua's bowl. Lua is lying under the table and drinking. Tuuli asserts that I look tired. Tired or awake, Felix laughs, this is your last night, my Svensson! Now let's have a beer! Tuuli is sitting between Felix and me, she's laughing, she's holding our hands. We bet! Felix indicates to the server the size of a bottle with both hands, *mais uma cerveja*, we raise our glasses into the light, my dear Svensson, our last night!

Around ten the cocks are brought in. The dice and card games stop, the berimbau keeps playing, the guests turn to the dance floor on which no one is dancing. A man with a bell asks for quiet. We have to stand up to see anything. Money is pulled out of pants pockets, shirt pockets, leather wallets and embroidered purses. The cock handlers have disappeared, instead men and women in shorts and shirts crowd all around us, the air is thick with smoke. I observe Tuuli. Lua is sleeping, and when Lua is sleeping, all is well, says Felix, and kisses the nape of Tuuli's neck. He pulls a few bills out of his pants pocket. The birds arrive, the conversations cease, the fights begin. The first handlers step into the ring through a small gate: grandfather, father and son with the same mustache and same jerseys, their hands press the cocks' wings against their bodies. The birds' heads jerk back and forth, their combs shake. David translates: the animals' names, their ages, their wins and losses. The shack nods and murmurs. One after another, all the handlers present their birds. There are roosters of all colors, white and brown and black, some are one color, some speckled, they're named Desert Storm and Senna de Vila Desterro IV and Sharkinho Noventa. I can't remember the names, I want to take notes and I get muddled. On the animals' legs shimmer the spurs, made of metal or horn, some look like they're made of glass. Sharp as razor blades, says Felix, they'll cut off your finger if they get you. In the shack there's a soft buzz, for several roosters it rises to an excited murmur, for others it peters out with boredom. When a brown and white speckled rooster with long feathers and metal spurs is displayed, the spectators cheer. That's the champion, David translates, 43 fights undefeated. I take note of this brown and white rooster, 43 fights and not a single loss. A moment later follows the snow-white challenger, and David explains that this bird has gone undefeated in seven duels, he hasn't had to fight that much, he's been well trained, he's supposed to be the best in Pernambuco.

What are the stakes, Svensson? asks Felix. When the first preliminary fight is announced, the spectators begin to gesticulate, they pass money through the room, there's shouting at the bar, coins jingle. The hall goes silent, and two roosters are brought in. As in a boxing match, the handlers stand in the corners, they give their birds a light shake, they pull at their roosters' heads and bodies as they talk relentlessly at them. The men are now wearing small bags around their bellies, in them Vaseline and bandages, needle and thread. They put the birds in the ring, they hold the scratching roosters tight for another few seconds, then comes the signal, and the audience begins to scream. The cocks flutter toward each other, they assail each other, they peck and kick, they want to tear each other to shreds. The spurs cut deep wounds in their wings and bodies, their beaks peck at the eyes. After a few seconds the first cock is lying and flailing on its side, its belly is covered in blood, on its neck an open cut is gaping. The handlers take their animals out of the ring, the loser draws a knife and puts his dying rooster out of its misery with a single slash, the winner gets the executed rooster. For honor, says David, for soup.

One bird after another is put in the ring, sometimes it goes fast, sometimes it takes the cocks several rounds. During the short breaks, their handlers tape up their wounds, they blow air into their lungs and pry open their encrusted eyes, sometimes they pray. If both animals are injured, the rule is: whoever moves last is the winner. A brown cock flies over the barrier, and the audience immediately jumps out of the way. Fear of the spurs splits the crowd, I think, and see Tuuli laughing as she clings to Felix. When the cock notices the absence of his adversary, he turns, and immediately his owner is there, the spectators yell and whistle. I can't tell who here is betting against whom and how much. David bets a few *reais* on a speckled cock named Iguaçú and wins, Felix bets everything and loses everything to a man with a pink tie. Tuuli gives all the roosters her own names: Nightingale and Orchid of Olinda and Moby Dick. In the second-to-last fight of the evening, Tuuli says with an announcer's voice, Don Quixote finishes off a rooster named Sancho Panza in three tragic rounds. Both birds are lying in the bloody dirt, the owners shake hands, they cut off their animals' heads.

The clay floor is saturated with the blood of the animals, the audience is getting nervous, at the tables in the first row the bets are increasing. Now comes the main fight, David shouts. I register the iron smell in the air, the cigarettes, the sweat of the gamblers. The owners of the champion rooster have taken their position in the left corner of the ring, the champion is fed chili seeds, the handler whispers something in his ear and makes the sign of the cross three times over his comb. Forty-three fights, I remember, not a single loss. The challenger is the whitest rooster I've ever seen, says David, look at the spurs! Black as hell! In the other corner the snow-white cock is being prepared for the fight. That one's mine! shouts Felix, I'm betting on the white cock! Is that wood? I ask. Exactly, says David, jacarandá, rosewood, filed sharp a hundred times. Tuuli's hair is fragrant as Felix and I bend down to ask her for the names of the roosters. We've drunk and gambled away our money, I'm the only one who still has a few *reais* for a last round. I say: Everything on the champion! Our former police dog is lying under the table and snoring, the heat and the squawking of the cocks can't wake him. How Tuuli's foot caresses Lua's flank, I think, following every word from her mouth. Shall we bet? asks Felix, and I answer, yeah, let's bet! Tuuli smiles. And? asks Felix. And? I ask. The names of the next combatants, says Tuuli, are William Wordsworth in the left corner and Robby Naish in the right. Your bet, please! Sodom versus Gomorrah, David laughs, Sodom versus Gomorrah. Tuuli is the top prize, says Felix.

When the left corner puts Wordsworth on the ground and lets him feel the clay under his claws, Lua wakes up. The shack holds its breath, the berimbau player stops plucking and beating, Lua's chain rattles softly. The bettors are staring at the cocks and their handlers, the strings of lights, the blood. They're waiting for the timekeeper and his signal, they throw the last bills into the pot, stack the last coins. I look at Tuuli, her eyes shift between me and Felix, they shift between the animals and the people. The second the bell rings and the cocks are released, I suspect the worst. I suspect that the fun stops this instant, I suspect that Wordsworth will lose his forty-fourth fight, I suspect the winnings of the victors and the losses of the defeated, I suspect the knife for the loser, I suspect Wordsworth's blood-spatters on Naish's rosewood spurs, I suspect Tuuli and Felix in Seraverde and myself alone on an airplane over the Atlantic, *jacarandá*, I suspect, *jacarandá*.

The fight lasts less than a minute. When their handlers release them, the two cocks stay where they are on the blood-soaked

floor. No frantic fluttering, no squawking rage, and no flashing
blades. Wordsworth opens his wings and closes them again,
Naish just stands there and crows. The handlers shout their
commands, *vambora! Vambora!* the spectators fold their hands,
vambora! Vambora! they make their signs of the cross, they yell
and whisper, the air in the shack is burning. And then the champion flies the first attack. Wordsworth half flies, half charges at
the challenger, he slams with all his might into Naish's side, and
even though the white cock jumps up and strikes out around him,
I already see the first steel-spur cut on his body. Now the audience is screaming, the roosters' owners are screaming, the birds
are screaming, the first white feathers are falling to the ground.
Wordsworth is suddenly a blur of beak-pecking, spur-kicking,
and wing-storm, he drives the challenger against the light blue
wooden wall, he pecks at the snow-white rooster's head, he deals
him another two or three blows, then Naish manages to break
free. He jumps over Wordsworth, he beats his wings wildly and
almost touches the ceiling of the shack. The spectators back away,
but Naish doesn't end up over the barrier, he turns above their
heads and then swoops down on Wordsworth. With both claws
and both rosewood spurs, he lands on the champion and digs
into his back. Now Naish is pecking insistently at the champion.
I notice the first plucked spots on William Wordsworth's neck,
his first wounds, the first blood. The spectators are holding their
breath, I see the red in the colored plumage, his torn and shredded
feathers, his down in the air over the ring. But then Naish pushes
himself off Wordsworth's speckled back and flutters through the
arena, he dances around his wounded adversary, he grazes the
battlefield only rarely. Wordsworth has to stay on the ground and
react, he turns in a circle and follows Naish with bloody eyes.
Naish attacks Wordsworth from above, he doesn't let up, he pene-

trates the colored birds' defenses, he seems to be proceeding tacti-
cally and playing with Wordsworth, he moves with the lightness
of the sure winner. Float like a butterfly, says Felix, grabbing the
nape of my neck, sting like a bee! I bet on Wordsworth, and Felix's
rooster seems to be winning. Tuuli isn't laughing anymore, she's
observing the fight with her mouth open. She just watches us, I
think, as we gamble her away. When Naish flies another airstrike,
Wordsworth falls to the side, and this time he manages to drive
his claws into Naish and hold on to him. Naish can't get back in
the air, and they roll in each other's embrace through the dust of
the arena, a cloud of feathers and blades and blood, the noise in the
shack is deafening. The cock handlers pull the birds apart, Naish's
beak is caught in Wordsworth's eye. The roosters are again put
head to head in the middle of the ring, both can neither fly nor
walk, they crawl toward each other and again go directly at each
other. The shack roars the real fighting names of the animals,
which I don't understand, the names of the owners, the names of
their colors. Lua looks at me with drunken eyes. The pecking gets
slower and ceases, the cocks lie twitching on top each other, then
Wordsworth's head flops to the side and stays there. The bird is
dead. The handler in the right corner lifts Naish over his head,
Felix and Tuuli are embracing. I've lost the bet. Without saying a
word I get up, take my cap, and go outside, I lie down in the back
of the pickup. On the horizon an illuminated tanker, on the shore
the fishermen's boats, over me airplanes or stars. With the return
ticket in my bag I wait for Tuuli, I wait for the morning of my
departure, eventually I fall asleep next to Lua.

August 8, 2005
(The screams of the animals)

In the afternoon the lake is smooth like oil. Tuuli's prescription for me was to stay. My headache has gone away, I drank Tuuli's Chiarella with all due caution (tepid water is good for the stomach). From the window: an oddly flat tourist steamer, its foghorn can't be heard until a few seconds after a white cloud comes out of it (time can be seen). I'm sitting in front of my notebook again, I'm observing the steamer on its way across the lake toward Lugano. Svensson is no stranger than I am (we both write ourselves). He looks to the past, Tuuli looks to the future, I look at the ships. Everything that's more than a hundred meters away exists in a different time (Elisabeth).

Profiles & Strangeness
In the autumn of 2004 I temporarily broke off my dissertation, because Elisabeth's editorial department could use me (I wanted to be with her). In editorial meetings my wife thinks of me as Mandelkern, the freelance cultural journalist. My dissertation has been shelved, I haven't added a word for months (the abortive ethnologist). Elisabeth and I have confused our life with our work. Participant observation is the reflexive gaze upon others and therefore upon oneself (Bronislaw Malinowski was nonetheless a ladykiller). I'm Mandelkern when I write my articles, my profiles, my reviews of strangeness. From time to time I'm paid

reasonably for my work. Elisabeth is a woman with history and a future. She calls me Daniel when I don't talk back to her. Why don't you go ahead and do something with actual consequences sometime, she said, you need to be somewhat more decisive for this world (Elisabeth's voice).

Are Svensson's stories made up?

I put aside the notebook and pick up the binoculars (a mixture of conscience and anticipation). By the water: Tuuli and the boy are feeding the swan, Svensson is chopping wood with an ax, Lua is still breathing. Svensson keeps carrying new wood from the open shed, he stands amid logs and tinder (Svensson is building a pyre). As long as I hear the splintering, I can open Blaumeiser's suitcase again. It takes me less than two seconds, the lock and Tuuli's hairpin click into place. Next to all sorts of stones (flat, light, dark, angular, small, large) and a map of Brazil (little crosses at places with interesting-sounding names) lies Svensson's stack of paper.

Salvation and Insight

Stories don't help, Svensson has noted down. He wanted to write his story out of his bones, but didn't finish it. New York, for example: I've read Svensson's September eleventh, about Tuuli, Svensson, and Felix on the roof, stiff with uncertainty or fear. I've read about Kiki Kaufman and her camera, about Svensson's escape attempts: he left Felix and Tuuli and escaped with Kiki Kaufman to Coney Island. I've seen the television footage of the World Trade Center countless times (there's no getting around those images), but Svensson has written those days differently, he has sketched his New York as he wanted to see it. In the margin he noted in red handwriting: Kiki Kaufman—salvation and insight. What remain are a PricewaterhouseCoopers T-shirt and the photo in a green plastic frame, taken on a roof in Williamsburg, Tuuli pregnant, Blaumeiser laughing. What remain are words: Dreiser's *Sister Carrie* and Frisch's *Montauk*, Svensson's manuscript in the suitcase.

Horrifying! Horrific!

From September 11, 2001, this image remains: my lathered face in the bathroom mirror of the apartment in Berkeley, when the telephone rings and the department secretary informs me that the Third World War is imminent (World War Three around the corner, she says, you better turn on the TV, Daniel, it's horrifying! Horrific!). I'd been a doctoral student of anthropology at UC Berkeley for just under a year, my girlfriend, Anne, and I were sharing a small apartment. We'd thought we understood things: that our world was a barely comprehensible and yet somehow structured chaos of television and books and movies and newspapers and music. That this chaos of art, media, and bodies touched, of wounds dealt, would ultimately coalesce into a complete picture. Sorry, I said, I'm all covered in shaving cream (the dried foam on my face, the blood from the little cuts). Don't, said the secretary, the beard looks good on you. My conference lecture was canceled half an hour later:

9/11/2001, 11:15 AM, Kroeber Hall, Authenticity in Documentary Film (D. Mandelkern, Hamburg/GER)

Later I sat half-shaven on the edge of the bed, my lecture scattered on the floor, the images of the collapsing towers before my eyes

for the very first time. Anne came home from the university and
shook me. She wanted to immediately pack our things and go
back to Europe. In *Astroland* at this time Dirk Svensson and Felix
Blaumeiser are worrying about Tuuli. They've smelled the smoke
I watched on television. Here in Svensson's house on the lake the
unplastered walls and Kiki Kaufman's pictures of ruins and the
cameras in front of them. Anne took one of the first flights back
to Zurich, I stayed another few months and sat alternately in front
of the television and my dissertation (so much for the authenticity of images). I didn't write another word and learned almost
my whole manuscript by heart. I flipped through magazines and
books and didn't have a wet shave again until I met Elisabeth. Not
out of superstition or trauma, but because she finds it more direct
(it is actually more pleasant).

Svensson unpacks

Svensson was in the supermarket. As the mute swan flies in for
a landing, there's a slight breeze, the oleander sheds its flowers.
The dog is still lying motionlessly by the water. Tuuli is sitting on
the stone bench under the oleander, she's smoking and observing
her son and Svensson. Now and then a flower falls on the table
or in her hair, now and then she says something and the boy
turns around to her. Svensson puts his Los Angeles Lakers cap on
Samy's head (he adjusts it to the boy's size). He lugs a few cartons
ashore, vegetables, several boxes of bottles. The boy helps him
unload, he gets a small, pink box with a light blue bow and puts
it down next to Tuuli in the oleander flowers (pastry shop). The
ailing dog lifts his head once again when Svensson kneels down
next to him in the grass and buries his face in the fur on the back
of his neck.

Stories people tell themselves about themselves

The *Astroland* manuscript is lying in front of me. Elisabeth is right: there's a story here (Svensson's colorful Third World, the story of the dog, the cockfight). I wonder whether something fishy's going on. I'm an ethnologist, and Svensson writes a story about cock-fighting, of all things? I remember Clifford Geertz's "Deep Play": "The cockfight's function, if you want to call it that, is interpretive: it is a Balinese reading of Balinese experience; a story they tell themselves about themselves." I can stay as long as Tuuli the doctor prescribes, she has diagnosed my curiosity. What's still missing: Felix Blaumeiser's death, the story of this last and most important death in Svensson's stack of paper (Svensson's guilt and Tuuli's contribution). Decision: save from Svensson's stories what I can. Copying it down is out of the question, I won't have enough time. I'll have to steal.

interference with the research plan

The blows of the ax on the shore break off. When I look out the window, Tuuli kisses the boy on his forehead and points up to my window. The boy nods, takes the pink box, which is waiting in the grass, kneels down next to Lua in the oleander flowers, and whispers something in his ear. Are they sending the boy to me, are they putting him in my care? Since I've been here, I haven't seen Tuuli and Svensson talk with each other (why is Tuuli here?). I hurriedly close the suitcase (from my dissertation: "Communication and interaction with members of the ethnos under investigation can occasionally interfere with the original research plan; occasionally they bring it to a complete standstill. Therefore participant observation always entails balancing one's own research objective with the conditions of the investigation and modifying it if necessary."). By the time I'm back at the window, the boy is running toward the house with the box in his hand.

Interview (Samuli)

MANDELKERN: Hello, Samuli. Samy.

SAMULI: —

M: Come in, don't be afraid. I'm just sitting here and writing.

S: —

M: Did you climb up here all by yourself?

S: —

M: Not bad, my friend. What have you got there? Did you get a gift?

S: —

M: For me?

S: —

M: Cake! That's really nice of you, Samuli, thank you very much. Do you want some too?

S: —

M: Red or blue? Would you rather have strawberry or this here? I'll take the blue piece. It's blueberry, I think.

S: —

M: Strawberry's better, right? Here.

S: —

M: Do you like it?

S: —

M: Can you draw? I mean: do you want to draw? There are a few crayons here. I'll keep writing while you draw?

S: —

M: Here. Blue for the sky. Yellow for the sun. Green for the water snake. Red for the flowers.

S: —

M: What's that? A grocery receipt? You want to draw on a grocery receipt?

S: I'm writing a prescription, *Manteli*.

M: You're a little doctor, right? Like your mother. You've come just in time, because I have a stomachache.

S: I'm drawing a prescription for Lua.

M: Great.

S: Lua shouldn't die sad.

between Christmas and New Year's Day

On a blue winter Sunday between Christmas and New Year's Day Elisabeth began, at first without discernible cause, to tell a story. We were lying on the bed and had been reading to each other, we'd been laughing. Both of them had been against the fashions of the moment, Elisabeth said suddenly, her husband had preferred something biblical, she something moderately Nordic (something imperishable: Jonas, Lasse, Joakim). But the child never got the name she'd had in mind, she said, he died before she and her husband could agree. Elisabeth emptied her cup of yogurt, I closed the book (the clink of her spoon). When she regained consciousness after the anesthesia, her husband already knew about the child's death. He sat at the table next to several bunches of ten tulips and looked at the muted television. At that moment their marriage was over (the tragedy of wrapped flowers). In hindsight she would remember her husband's facial expression as old and resigned. Even in retrospect she couldn't really believe that he'd bought flowers after the boy's death, as if there were something to celebrate.

Johannes Emmerich

She had seen the boy only for a few minutes. Elisabeth was lying stretched out stiffly next to me on the bed and looking at the ceiling, down on the street a bus drove by (the hiss of the hydraulic doors). Her husband had taken on the washing of the child, the measurements and weighing, finally the filling out of the documents for the registry office. She had still been almost completely anesthetized. Her husband had to register the birth, said Elisabeth, even though the death certificate was already lying on the table next to him. That's how the child ended up with his name (Johannes). When she finally awoke from her half-conscious state, she and her husband were silent for a few minutes. *He* was silent, she said, she herself, due to the intubation and repeated vomiting, that is, due to the acid and minimal injuries to her pharynx, couldn't speak at all. Then her husband grasped her left hand and began to speak (in her right hand the tube for saline solution and painkiller). For a long time she couldn't cry or react appropriately, she was numb (lifeless, she said). I remained lying and hesitated, I didn't know what to do with my hands, I felt like I was too young. The child, wrapped in a towel, had been brought from the postmortem unit for the good-bye, around noon her parents and the designated godparents had relieved her husband in short shifts. Elisabeth was lying motionlessly next to me (I would only have to turn my head). The clinic had scheduled the autopsy for the days to follow and summoned a mortician. Usually the clinic psychologist arrived immediately in such cases, but it was the 1996 New Year and there was a lot to do, she explained. Christmas and New Year's Day are the preferred dates for suicide attempts. I didn't say anything (words failed me). I should still touch her, said Elisabeth, she wasn't made of cotton candy. But when I then brushed her hair aside, she bit her upper lip bloody. Pro forma the police had to be informed, the autopsy was compulsory due to the initially unknown cause of death. A few weeks before the birth all they'd been able to detect with ultrasound was a narrowing of the unborn child's small intestine (duodenal stenosis), which had not indicated a risk for the birth, all that had been discussed was a later surgical widening. Elisabeth got up and opened the window, then closed it again a moment later. It had actually been duodenal atresia. Under the stress of the prolonged birth the child had to vomit (Elisabeth in the middle of the room alone, not even the furniture, not even I). That wouldn't have been an unusual occurrence either, but the bile had been unable to flow downward because the small intestine was obstructed. It had therefore been forced to escape upward from the duodenum. When the child had ultimately inhaled the vomited bile as he gasped for his first air, the strong acid had irreparably corroded the upper layer of the lungs, as a result the child could apparently no longer receive artificial respiration (he must have struggled for air, she supposed). Because the death was an internal clinic matter, Elisabeth explained to me, the police investigations had already been concluded before they even commenced (she had never been alone with the boy). She lay back down on the bed, and I finally tried to hug her. But when Elisabeth then saw that I had tears in my eyes, she ran her fingers over my face as if she had to console me.

coarse granite

They'd hesitated, said Elisabeth, as we later walked along the frozen Elbe beach. She and her husband hadn't separated immediately. The sun was shining, the beach full of strollers and frolicking dogs. The child's death had been a break in the perspective of their relationship (from that point on they'd had increasing differences). It was several years before she was able to part from her husband, Elisabeth explained, they'd first had to become friends in order to get out of each other's way (she had already stopped saying "my husband" when we met, she called him by his first name). The child was buried in the Niendorf cemetery, they still met for visits to the grave at irregular intervals. At that time her husband had supported Elisabeth's desire to focus for a while on her studies and afterward on her work. Back then they'd still occasionally been of one mind. During her last year and a half at the university, she'd already worked her way up in various editorial departments of Gruner + Jahr (he had supported her in that to the best of his ability). Elisabeth looked across to the cranes and dry docks. She felt for my hand. She'd meanwhile grown accustomed to the boy's name on the gravestone (blackened steel on coarse granite). Her husband, though, would never go to the grave alone. It astonishes me, Elisabeth then said, turning to me, that it gets visibly harder for him. She seemed to want to laugh. Though he was now in Hamburg only occasionally, the lost possibility plagued him (he's getting more melancholy, said Elisabeth, almost even pathologically so). He had two adult children from his first marriage, but he was focusing more and more on the missed opportunities of his life. Elisabeth leaned her head on my chest. She, on the other hand, had the past, the future, and me (I have you, Daniel).

Is that so, Elisabeth?

The screams startle me, but the boy is unruffled. He's still kneeling on the floor of Svensson's study and drawing pictures only he comprehends (I can't interpret children's pictures). The sun, he says, holding the green crayon in his fist. Lua, he laughs, scribbling a bright red on the white wall below the window. *Äiti*, he whispers, decorating the sun. The screaming by the water doesn't stop. The screaming gets louder. Svensson is standing bare-chested by the water, holding a brown rooster in the air by its feet (William Wordsworth). He's standing on the dock, he's spinning the animal in circles like a swing carousel, he's spinning the orientation out of its head (his arm a swing). Lua lifts his head. The dog rolls heavily from one flank onto the other, he puts his remaining foreleg into this roll, his hind legs he braces in the flowers, then he gets to his feet, lurches a bit to the side, and is standing. Tuuli is waiting off to the side and watching Svensson (the panicked fluttering of the other rooster behind the windshield of the Fiat 128 Sport L). Svensson with the dazed rooster in his hand approaches the firewood block on which he was just chopping wood and picks up the ax. William Wordsworth slowly opens a wing and closes it again, then Svensson chops off his head. He holds the bird like a wet umbrella, its blood drips on the ground and the dock. He hangs the empty animal on a chair and gets Robby Naish from the Fiat. Svensson has to spin the white rooster much longer, he doesn't get the neck until the third blow into the bloody fluttering (it surprises me that the dead bodies remain completely motionless, I was expecting a headless escape). Then everything is the same as always: the pigeons are cooing, the cicadas are making their shrill noise, Daisy Duck, the hen, is clucking on the roof of the blue Fiat. Lua is lying heavy and black on his side in the sea of oleander flowers, in the hiss of the mute swan. Svensson steps over the blood on the planks and jumps in the lake. Tuuli takes the animals' heads and bodies and walks toward the house. Far beyond the white buoy Svensson resurfaces and waves (Lua is too old to lift his head again).

bikini (green)

As the roosters were dying, the boy disappeared, I hear his small footsteps on the stairs. He took the stuffed mouse in its blue overalls with him. His crayons are lying scattered in the room, he drew on the paper, the grocery receipt, the walls, and the floor too. The window is open, in the vine and the ivy wasps are buzzing, occasionally one flies in and lands on the dark wood (my headache gives way to fatigue). Svensson far out in the water a tiny dot, he's swimming back and forth. Tuuli in a green bikini comes out of the house, she's moving as if no one could see her. My fingers are slow as I make a note of "Tuuli in a green bikini," as I write "the blood on the planks." She sets her sunglasses on the dock and takes off the bikini, first the bottom, then the top (her small breasts in the afternoon light). Her left foot is standing in the middle of the roosters' blood, she leaves three dark footprints on the way to the water. Without any hesitation Tuuli dives head-first into the lake (I at the window like James Stewart).

the little doctor

Samy is standing next to the black dog and listening to his chest with the chair-leg stethoscope (the animal twice as heavy as the child). Lua has stopped coughing, what is happening and being said down by the water now remains soundless in the drone of the wasps. Samy moves closer and closer to the dog. He carefully lifts one of the animal's ears and looks inside, he feels Lua's missing foreleg with his fingers, he touches his scar. Through the binoculars I can't discern any movement of the flanks. The dog lets the little doctor do as he likes, maybe he's already dead. Eventually the boy puts down the chair leg. He's no longer afraid of the dog and lays his ear on his chest, directly on the light spot. With both arms he reaches around the animal's neck, he plunges his face into the dark fur, as Svensson did before (Lua is a perishing animal). Svensson sits down next to Samy in the grass. They lift Lua's ears, examine his paws and his speckled fur, they pull Lua's jowls to the side, Samy examines his teeth (face to face). He seems to be explaining something to Svensson, who then takes the cap off the boy's head and strokes his blond hair. He lays his hand on Samy's shoulder and gestures to the small church on the opposite shore, in the setting sun its yellow turns into a glow. Svensson talks and gestures to the sleeping mountain over Cima, he points to the boat in front of him moored to the dock, he points to himself, he points to the house and maybe to Tuuli out in the lake. Svensson points to the blood-smeared planks of the dock (he must be telling the child the truth). Svensson's world is a more beautiful place than I expected. The swallows high up above the lake, in the evening sun only two water-skiers very far out (practicing at a standstill). For two days they've been predicting rain, for two days the view has remained clear, for two days Lugano has stood in the distance like an admonition, at night the city twinkles like a home. Svensson gets his mail at the Bar del Porto, he turned his real life into a fictitious story and sold more than 100,000 copies. He has pigeons and swallows, crickets and cicadas. He slaughters his chickens when he pleases, he erases his characters. Svensson apparently doesn't live alone here (Kiki Kaufman: salvation and insight).

palimpsest

Between the crayons and papers: the grocery receipt with the boy's picture on it. When I view it more closely, the momentary question of why Svensson bought so much wine (Barolo), so much beer (Heineken), so much meat. He brought groceries ashore by the box. Samy's picture consists of a few lines, astonishingly clear for such a small child. I should eat something, I think, I should finally sleep. But when I turn the receipt sideways, the child's picture becomes the little doctor's prescription (I'm drawing a prescription for Lua, the boy said, Lua shouldn't die sad). The grocery receipt shows a syringe and the letters L U A. With my feet on Svensson's suitcase of stories I realize: the little doctor is prescribing Lua a gentle death, the boy is helping Lua out of the world (Lua becomes history).

	EURO
PIRROVANO TREBBIANO R	1,50
PIRROVANO TREBBIANO	1,50
BIRRA FELD.	7,00
S.PELLLEGRINO FRIZZ	3,06
CORVO ROSSO	3,20
CORVO ROSSO	3,20
BAROLO	14,37
BAROLO	14,37
BAROLO	14,37
BAROLO	14,37
BAROLO	14,37
BAROLO	14,37
BAROLO	14,37
APEROL SODA	3,94
HEINEKEN LATTINA	0,65
HEINEKEN LATTINA	0,65
HEINEKEN LATTINA	0,65
HEINEKEN LATTINA	0,65
HEINEKEN LATTINA	0,65
PRIMIA OLIVE VERDI G	1,31
CARNINI LATTE BOTT	1,38
CARNINI LATTE INTERO	1,41
BIRRA PERONI CL.33x6	3,30
VIPITENO CILIEGLIA	1,10
MULINO B. CANESTRINI	1,55
ESPLOS.ART.KIT	
COTOLETTE DI MAIALE	12,83
SALSICETTA	2,52
N. ARTICOLI	
ESPLOS.ART.KIT	
PEPERONI	1,81
MELONI	2,56
REPARTO FRUTTA VERD	2,17
CIPOLLE GIALLE	0,74
INSALATA RICCIA	0,58

Auberge la Fontaine

Elisabeth and I a few months ago in a guestroom above the restaurant in Venasque where we'd celebrated her birthday that evening, her friends' laughter had died away around midnight on the Rue de l'Hôpital. Elisabeth sat backwards on me and arched her back, then she told me for the first time that she wanted a child. Not at some point, not from anyone, but now and from me (from you, Daniel, she said). She sensed that her body was driving her thoughts in this direction. In my head this image remains: her body from behind bright in the almost complete darkness of the room, her face turned in the orange glow of the streetlights (her back a distinct exclamation point).

now she wants a child

Lying on the examination table in the urology unit of the University Medical Center Hamburg-Eppendorf in May (birds chirping and sirens on the clinic premises). Elisabeth had changed her gynecologist, a recent and thorough examination yielded no cause for concern. Now it was my turn, she said, just to make sure. Her gynecologist had recommended a urologist, Dr. Thankri Sitar, and in answer to my perhaps somewhat too-nervous question as to whether he had anything to do with the instrument of the same name, he told me completely humorlessly to hold my penis a little bit higher, please, he couldn't see anything. At which point I caught myself for a moment in the suspicion that there might be something to see (the cold ultrasound gel). He gave me a cup and an instruction: sperm sample for the fertility test.

Use your imagination, Mandelkern!

This time everything has to work, Elisabeth apologized afterward in the park at the medical center. We sat on the steps of
the central medical library next to our chained-up bicycles. It felt
absurd, just a moment ago to have jerked off into a plastic cup
and now to be sitting next to her. This is my last try, Daniel (she
didn't even sound silly).

my central medical library

My hesitation in the face of doctor visits surprises Elisabeth. She's
a pragmatic woman, she observes her body, she notices something, she gets treatment (I get things sorted out, she says). It
must be her age that has made her so sober. I write and read my
own records, I consult reference books. Daniel Mandelkern, born
07/12/1973, height: 1.85 meters, weight: 79 kilograms. Circum-
cision in 1975 due to foreskin nonretractability (phimosis),
1981 greenstick fracture of the left forearm after fall from a
swing (radius, ulna, humerus), no predisposition to wisdom
teeth (dentes serotini), 1983–1985 orthodontic treatment of gap
between teeth (diastema), 1985–1987 regression of same. Child-
hood illnesses: chickenpox (varicella), mumps (epidemic paro-
titis, epidemic salivitis), as well as a prepubescent series of scarlet
fevers overcome probably without permanent damage (infertility
would be possible). In 1985, on the occasion of the delivery of a
mail order catalogue with skin-colored corsetry, first self-grati-
fication under the reproachful poster look of the Pet Shop Boys,
subsequent irrational crises of conscience (sex makes you weak,
pale, and unsuccessful) and development of compulsive neuroses
focused on gaining strength, a healthy complexion, and success
(push-ups, vegetarianism, tanning salon). From 1983 to 1993,

anxious anticipation of hair loss (matrilineally inherited, I know
that from photo albums), 1991 torn ligament in the left ankle,
1994–1995 hair loss and embarrassing gel hairstyle. In 1995, final
visit to the haircutter, and purchase of electric hair trimmer
(Grundig). Then, as of 2001, joint pain in the knees, increasing
weight and accelerated aging (the precision of my diagnoses).
Last self-diagnostic discovery: eczema on the ring finger of the
left hand, an incredible symbol, I've never heard of an allergy to
precious metals (it must be psychosomatic). Now I've been given
an official medical opinion. It's not an infection, says Tuuli, it
must be your curiosity.

my decisiveness

I'm extremely tired, but Svensson thinks I'm sick, he'll leave my
care to the small, pretty doctor (he won't discover my spying).
At twilight and on my knees in front of the suitcase I unwrap
the *Astroland* manuscript from the packing paper. Tomorrow I'll
continue searching: in the kitchen, in the bathroom, on the boat,
in the hallway, on the shelves, in the cabinets (I'll talk). I'll find
out the whole story. Svensson and Tuuli know how Blaumeiser
died (it's their story). I take my notebook and *Astroland*, I take
Svensson's books, and lie down on the mattress.

my books, his books

I leaf through Svensson's thinned-out library (books are a takeoff
into another life over the course of pages, a suspension of one's
own body for a few minutes). I reread *The Story of Leo and the
Notmuch*, I flip through Svensson's encyclopedias, I skip around in
Max Frisch's *Montauk*. I skip around in my notes and keep finding

sentences that pretend to be only my own thoughts and feelings. At times I understand things as someone else has understood them. On Svensson's mattress in his library on Lake Lugano I'm writing, but I'm making use of nothing but read words, lists, and parentheses. I'm surprised by the speed with which I forget these connections and the amazement when I then rediscover them. That's not new, scarcely anything is new (title page *Astroland: hardly art, hardly garbage*).

Craze for the Mobile Lifestyle

is printed on the front page of the *Süddeutsche* from my plastic bag. I speak German, English, French, and miserable Italian. I learned a smattering of Finnish from Carolina (I could brush up on it here). I'm lying between books and people, between words and bodies. My language is of no use for decisions, each word is only true for a few seconds, then it dries and turns to paper (for Mandelkern decisions as such are suspect). It would be good to be able to set clear boundaries, Hamburg would be Hamburg, a life with Elisabeth would be a life with Elisabeth (a life with Tuuli would remain an unlived life). Svensson has decided on things: he lives in a ruin, now he chops the old wood, he jumps in the clear, reliable water. Is that how one should live (is that how I should live)? Svensson has told his version of the story, he has wrapped it in paper and locked it in the suitcase, Svensson does push-ups, he plants kumquats and potatoes, he catches his own fish (Svensson has put words behind him).

PricewaterhouseCoopers

Tuuli is suddenly standing in the middle of the room. She opened
the door without a sound. She's wearing Svensson's T-shirt (I
know it from the *Astroland* manuscript: the much too large and
bright purple PricewaterhouseCoopers promotional T-shirt). I'm
lying between Svensson's manuscript and my notebooks, I can no
longer hide my curiosity, but Tuuli seems to want to disregard
my notetaking (she knows the symptoms). The T-shirt actually
reaches down to her knees, under it she's still wearing green, she
has knotted the bikini top behind her neck (her bare feet). My
small, pretty main informant has a soup bowl in one hand and a
spoon in the other. Chicken soup for the soul? she asks, and smiles
as if she just came up with this herself. For someone who's sick
with the flu you look quite fresh, *Manteli*. She takes the pen from
my fingers and hands me the bowl. Yes, I say, I'm already feeling
better. Tuuli remains seated next to me on the mattress and waits
for me to take a spoonful of the chicken soup (Wordsworth &
Naish). Only when I say it's good does she take the first page she
happens to grab from the mattress and hold it up to the light.
What is this anyway? she asks and reads aloud without waiting
for my answer:

"Shitty City 2000? What you don't hold on to disappears. A hotel
room on the second floor, a clock was ticking. I lay between Felix
and Tuuli and smelled the darkness yawning. A double bed and
Tuuli's hand on my neck, her smell in my ear and Felix's leg over
mine. It's bitterly cold in Oulu, I thought, and the darkness is a
black dog. We lay under blankets and jackets, the heat vent was
breathing dryly and uselessly, at midnight the champagne in the
glasses was frozen. The darkness rose and sank calmly, through

the closed blinds fell the red remains of the neon sign next door: *Ravintola*, firecrackers exploded on the street. The darkness lay at our feet. Felix: in this cold having your own fur doesn't help anymore. So he put his blue parka on Lua and tied the left sleeve in a knot. Lua lay there like a disabled veteran. In this cold only liquor and other bodies help?"

Where will the small, pretty mother sleep?

Tuuli is reading and laughing, she looks straight into my face (I'm at her mercy). *Astroland?* she asks. She gets up and closes the door. Where'd you get this, *Manteli?* Have you been rummaging around in Svensson's things? Is it possible you've gone a step too far there, *Manteli?* She's smiling. What would Svensson say about the fact that you've been snooping instead of asking your questions directly? Tuuli takes Svensson's manuscript from the mattress and lies down next to me (her smell like warm milk). Move over a bit, *Manteli*, she says, without even waiting for my reaction. Tuuli begins to read, as I empty the soup bowl in focused soundlessness (the clink of my spoon). She leafs through Svensson's stories and laughs, she adjusts her bikini under her T-shirt. Then she reads on. This doesn't have much to do with me, *Manteli*, she murmurs. I haven't eaten anything yet today, I haven't slept today, I could simply close my eyes. As I put the bowl down softly on the floor, she turns to me and kisses me briefly on the mouth (she forgives me). Sleep well and don't worry, *Karvasmanteli*, Tuuli whispers, *nuku hyvin älä pelkää.*

I'll read, you sleep.

And in fact I don't wake up until I hear the boy crying from the next room, then Tuuli's soft singing, *minä tulen sinne, rakkain terveisin*. In my room the light is out, the moonlight is falling through the window onto the floor (the cicadas now turned up loud, waves soft on the shore). In the spot where Tuuli was lying, the bed is still warm. I'm lying among Svensson's papers, without a blanket and with a sleep erection. Did Tuuli notice it? I wonder whether she'll come back. The chapter that Tuuli read to me before I fell asleep takes place on the night of New Year's Eve in a rundown hotel room in Oulu. Felix, Tuuli, Svensson have spent Christmas with Tuuli's father in Lapland, now they're waiting for their car to be repaired. Outside it's bitterly cold, the three of them crawl under blankets and hide themselves away from the world. In this story Svensson tells of a perfect moment of love, no more, no less. I wonder whether Tuuli will sleep with me, between the pages of a book in which she appears (the story doesn't have much to do with me, she says). The momentary awareness of the improbability of this situation. The *Astroland* manuscript is lying read on its belly, only the last page is open in front of me. I reread the part where Svensson's manuscript breaks off:

Lua & the Third Death.

Lua and the Third Death

I SEE SAMULI FOR THE FIRST TIME IN A BURGER KING ON THE
A5. There's something to celebrate, Felix said on the telephone.
What's to celebrate is his secret, and I packed my bag without a
great deal of thought. You two meet in Frankfurt in two weeks,
then drive down to Lake Lugano. I'll be waiting for you. This
morning Lua and I took the train from Berlin Ostbahnhof to
Frankfurt, Kiki is coming later on the night train, she has things
to do. I haven't seen or spoken to Tuuli and Felix for months, the
last time Felix said that the boy was born: Samuli, almost two
months early, but everything was all right. Then came a year of
silence. Now Felix is waiting at his parents' house in Italy, Tuuli
is leaning on Felix's blue Fiat and smoking outside the west exit
of Frankfurt Hauptbahnhof, as Lua and I emerge from the train
station. Tuuli has short hair. Samuli is still less than a year old, I'm
amazed that his feet reach his mouth, I'm amazed that Tuuli is
smoking again. Svensson, she says, stroking Lua's head, how are
you? Good, I say, throwing my bag in the Fiat. Lua jumps into the
footwell as always, and we set off heading south, Felix's secret is
waiting for us.

The boy is hungry when Tuuli parks the Fiat in a Burger King
lot on the A5 beyond Heidelberg. Samuli has to eat, Tuuli says, I
don't have enough milk. In the parking lot a giant foam rubber
mouse in overalls is walking around between the parked cars
and sticking advertising leaflets under the windshield wipers: I'm

the Euromaus, she sings, from the Europa-Park in Rust! Thrills galore, she shouts, and gives Tuuli a flyer, the sensational Silver Star roller coaster! Tuuli reads and hands me the boy, I touch him for the first time, his hair color is hidden under the blue cap. We have a bottle of milk warmed up in the microwave, Lua gets a Whopper. We sit outside the Burger King in the sun with our milkshakes, and I give the boy the bottle. Tuuli talks about the past year without me and how it has come to this, she tells me about life in Hamburg and this and that. I nod, Samuli drinks. Tuuli has stamped out her cigarette and is petting Lua, then she leans her head on my shoulder, for the first time in months I can smell her hair and her smoke. What's this secret Felix mentioned? I ask, even though I know what it is. No idea, she answers, it's not that important. For a few seconds in the parking lot of the Burger King at exit 57 on the autobahn, Tuuli, the boy, and I are a family, then the foam rubber mouse in overalls interrupts us: the Silver Star—breathtaking fun! No thanks, I say, but Tuuli takes another leaflet and says that we ~~are now going to ride the roller coaster, there really is something to celebrate.~~

August 9, 2005

(The pretty mothers)

Down by the water: Lua motionless, then Svensson steps onto the dock from the right. A few minutes ago I woke up with a stubborn erection and between manuscript pages (the empty soup bowl on the floor). For the first time in days I'm not tired or drunk. The door is ajar, the window open. It comes back to me: last night Tuuli was lying next to me on the mattress and reading. I fell asleep, even though she now and then touched my shoulder (her occasional laughter in my half-sleep). I gather up the manuscript pages and put them in the suitcase with the stones. I sit down at the desk as if nothing happened, I open my blue notebook (my rapid recovery). Down below on the dock Svensson scoops lake water into a light blue cleaning bucket and pours it on the dried chicken blood. As they do every morning, the two fishermen glide along the shore, the blood-scrubbing Svensson on the dock raises his brush and shouts something Italian. The fishermen laugh. Svensson scrubs and scours and rinses the blood into the light green lake. Then he bends down to Lua and watches the boat (Pike Machine). Svensson is kneeling there and looking across the lake to the opposite shore, to the glowing yellow of the church. I gaze at the villa below it in the morning sun. That villa belongs to Blaumeiser's family, Tuuli said. Blaumeiser drowned. Svensson's hints come back to me (Tuuli's reproaches). He's standing on the shore like the sad Jay Gatsby, I'm observing as unreliably as Nick Carraway. Svensson has come up against a limit, he hasn't finished writing his autobiography (his stories don't extend into the present). I'm waiting for my cock to give way, but the thought of Tuuli remains. This morning the swallows are sailing their sharp turns just over the water's surface on a wind I can't feel yet, they're avoiding the storm that's supposed to come soon (Svensson's been talking for days about a storm caught in the St. Gotthard Pass). The sycamore is shedding its leaves due to dryness, the oleander is spitting its flowers at our feet (the question of whether this storm will come).

The Story of Leo and the Notmuch

In the next room Tuuli is reading softly to the boy from the children's book, Samy is reciting along. The two research folders still on the desk. "*The Story of Leo and the Notmuch* doesn't downplay anything," writes the *Frankfurter Allgemeine*, "it's more than another illustrated trivialization. It explains death to children as what it is: loss." And "against loss it is above all memory that helps" (literary supplement of the 2005 Leipzig Book Fair). The *Neue Zürcher Zeitung* speaks of "potent images that create a palpable grief and then dissolve this in imagination and memory." *The Story of Leo and the Notmuch* tells a story of loss because Felix Blaumeiser is dead (naïve biographism, Elisabeth would call that; but she sent me here). Svensson is a collector, he wants to retain memories in stones, chairs, pictures. He wrote the *Astroland* manuscript. Lua has almost always been there, the dog has seen and heard most of it. I'm sitting by the window and surmising: The Blaumeiser family's house is in Cima di Porlezza on the other side of the lake, so Svensson lives directly opposite. The blue Fiat once belonged to Felix, that's why Svensson has parked the car probably forever in his yard. At the cockfight in Olinda they bet on Wordsworth and Naish, so Svensson gave two roosters those names (I can't tell the ages of animals). Tuuli and Svensson were in the Fiat on the way to Felix on Lake Lugano. There was something to celebrate, Blaumeiser apparently said. His death remains a mystery. Tuuli and the boy can no longer be heard (my main informant must know the solution).

chicken blood

I'm lying on the mattress again, my erection won't go away on its own. Under the white sheets my fingers summon the memory of Elisabeth's dried blood (my wife's blood), my nose smells Tuuli's tobacco and milk, I think about last night (the missed opportunity). I could consider myself lucky that Tuuli didn't come closer to me last night. I've fallen out of time, I haven't been able to wash myself, I haven't brushed my teeth for days. The bed bears her smell, her golden hairpin is no longer lying where it was still lying last night. A line of thought: if Tuuli doesn't open the suitcase for me now, it will remain locked, and I won't be able to save Svensson's story. Without the story I need not even go back to Hamburg at all. I could jump in the lake to get rid of Elisabeth's blood, I could jump in the lake to wash off my wife. Down below on the dock Svensson is scrubbing the animals' blood from the planks, in his study I want to expel my strategies, my fingers work on the usual mechanics, in my pants pocket I search for and find the necessary handkerchief. Tuuli's singing and Svensson's footsteps are nowhere to be heard, only a single pigeon is sitting silently on the windowsill, and I help myself to the images in my head, Elisabeth and Mandelkern, suddenly

I and you

in the white of our bed like a single body, we'd been reading to each other (*Das Dekameron*). When I eventually fell asleep in the sun and woke up again, Boccaccio was lying open between us. You were sitting next to me with open mouth and open legs (your eyes fixed on my face, your right hand between your legs). It won't take much longer, you said, you were almost there (you had to concentrate on those words). My cock had already anticipated you in sleep. Then you actually came, before I could help your fingers, there was enough time only for our open mouths. It was of no consequence who came how and when (we talked about our orgasms).

I just wanna fuck you right here

And now this mattress (another awakening). With my cock in my left hand the realization that I'm not going to write a 3,000-word profile of Svensson in this room. I would tell about Tuuli, her somewhat too-tired eyes and her blonde hair, how she was suddenly standing in the room yesterday, in a purple T-shirt, a bowl of chicken soup in her hand, her note from the day before still on the floor: Tuuli wants to show me things that are worth it. I jerk off the way I write (I mingle past and present, Tuuli Elisabeth, Elisabeth Tuuli, etc.). I mix Elisabeth's image with Tuuli's smell on the sheets around me, I help my thoughts to Elisabeth's heavy breasts and Tuuli's small ones, also briefly to the first and the second Carolina, to their open mouths, to Svensson's stories ("I just wanna fuck you right here"). Suddenly the shouting of the boy penetrates through the window to me from the water (under the chestnuts in Hamburg: bicycle bells and children's noise). And then the suitcase comes into my view, and the situation. I'm still on the mattress, unwashed and alone, the research folders on the desk (the blood still on me).

I break off,

because the boy's voice suddenly seems to enter the house downstairs, and in this house, too, doors are opened suddenly and without knocking. I won't get myself caught. I remember Elisabeth and me, purely professional and businesslike: in the spring of 2002 in the Renault on the way back from the Côte d'Azur. I drove and Elisabeth read me articles from the culture pages of *Die Zeit* (her still-husband had just gone into retirement). Then she switched to the road map. The Renault had already been sputtering for a few days and burning more gas than usual. After an eight-hour drive on coastal roads and toll highways we reached the Lyon city highway around midnight (we were looking for the Hotel Imperial, which her writer friends had recommended to us). Through a tunnel, said Elisabeth, then down and two lefts (her freckled feet next to the dashboard gearshift). The engine conked out. Because there was no shoulder, I steered the Renault on its last legs onto an emergency strip in front of the entrance to the tunnel. While honking French people passed on the right and left, we let the engine cool down and drank warm mineral water (we spoke about marriage as a possibility). The telephone interrupted us, and Elisabeth's husband mentioned a position he'd heard about on the culture staff of the weekly newspaper (they had meanwhile become friends). Starting when? asked Elisabeth, and he answered, starting now.

Lyon Garage

In my head this image remains: Elisabeth and I on a whitewashed boundary stone in front of a Renault-authorized garage on the outskirts of Lyon, she was sitting on my thigh. In the garage two burly Frenchmen were working with gum in their mouths and disparaging looks in their eyes, they were repairing the engine. Elisabeth had briefly negotiated the prompt repair and an appropriate payment, now she was taking pictures of us (the euphoria of her imminent promotion). She photographed us in the windows of the office (in the garage yard, white pebbles and a tall linden). The first photos of us as a couple, in the background three new cars and an agricultural utility vehicle. Would it be okay with her if I remained a penniless academic, I asked, and Elisabeth took my head in her hands. Not for long, Daniel, she said, and photographed our kissing tongues, you could write for me! The mechanics didn't take their eyes off us (they'd never seen anyone like Elisabeth before).

Barbaresco

Elisabeth speaks fluent French and Italian, a smattering of Polish. Nothing's going to get in our way, she'd decided, and I'd agreed (the feeling of knowing the other). A few days after my first day of work in her editorial department we traveled to Berlin for some British writer's book launch, Elisabeth was supposed to moderate and lead the discussion to follow. The Literaturhaus in Wilmersdorf was sold out, it was Elisabeth's first appearance of this sort and magnitude, she nonetheless seemed not the least bit nervous. Not even when she was told that the simultaneous interpreter was stuck at Tegel Airport. She stepped onto the stage before the author, I was sitting in the second row and drinking Barbaresco (at Elisabeth's recommendation). I was sure that I knew my wife and her history, but when she opened the event and invited the author onto the stage, I choked on the wine. I was flabbergasted by her perfect British accent. I'd never heard her speak English before.

things that are worth it

It's my indecisiveness that I become aware of as I lie on Svensson's mattress and listen to the footsteps on the stairs. I hesitate because a decision makes every other path impossible (we've never had to make final decisions). I came here to write an article about Svensson, instead I'm thinking about other things: Tuuli is a mystery, Elisabeth is my wife, Svensson has committed himself to things. I, too, should exchange my thoughts for something concrete: find out the recipe for the chicken soup, touch the dog, gather the wilting oleander flowers, renovate a ruin. I should pull myself together, I should be more precise. I should reflect on my work approach (my pitiful methods).

—What exactly are Borromean rings?
—Is another life a better life?

his shirts

Is anyone here? On the top landing the oil-covered gull in the pictures is first dead, then awakens laggingly and gradually to life as I descend the stairs. Next to those are pictures of the heavy, black dog: Lua with bandaged stump on a Brazilian beach, a cliff with a hole through its base in the background, Lua wearing a hood on a hotel bed, Lua on cracked concrete slabs, in the background Manhattan and the column of smoke (we'd discussed the Thomas Hoepker image and its supposed actuality in the editorial department). Finally the framed pictures of garbage: blue and black sacks, burst-open plastic bags, overturned cans, knocked-over dumpsters, shattered bottles, soaked-through paper bags, beer cans and plastic bottles, cardboard boxes, a naked doll without arms, lamps, armchairs, solitary shoes. But then there's the kitchen, cleaned up, sun on the tiles, flowers on the table. From the fridge Tuuli and Blaumeiser are smiling at me (death is everywhere).

Svensson? Is anyone here?

Another look at Svensson's white room: in the small mirror on the wardrobe my shirt and I look equally rumpled. I'll jump in the lake and iron myself out, I think, and take a white shirt from the wardrobe. Svensson will notice (I don't care). I take a towel from a wooden shelf, it smells like laundry detergent, on it is a disintegrating piece of embroidery, white on a white background (Hotel Turisti).

the animals and us

Lua doesn't move. I take off the creased shirt and imitate Svensson, I have only enough strength for seven push-ups and seventeen sit-ups. Then I lie on the dock breathing heavily (no trace of the animals' blood). It must be eleven o'clock, the sun is burning on my shoulders and my head (lizards on the stones). A thin water snake between the stones, a school of tiny fish (a mosaic of escape). I kneel down next to Lua in the oleander flowers. What I couldn't

make out through the binoculars: his fur is dull with scattered
gray, the longer hairs on his chest are matted and pale. Lua is
lying on his side, his eyes half closed. His mouth is hanging open,
his jowls are blotchy and dry (Lua smells putrid). From up close
the dog is much thinner than expected. In the shallow rhythm of
his breaths his ribs stick out, the fur on his belly hangs down in
tangles (an old and ill-fitting suit). His strangely thin neck seems
no longer capable of holding his head. I examine Lua's stump. The
leg wasn't amputated with clean cuts and cleanly sutured flaps
of skin, but rather severed close to the body. What remains is a
rough and crudely healed web of scars (Svensson wrote of a bolt
cutter, and Tuuli speaks of her first amputation). Lua's left ear is
flopping open, here too lighter skin, scabby and mottled (a small
white spider slowly crawls inside).

I need your help, Mandelkern.

Suddenly Svensson is kneeling next to me and putting his hand
under Lua's bony head. His eyes are bluer than usual, almost
watery. Lua hasn't eaten anything for days, he says, I have to bring
him to the vet in the village (the soft clucking of the widowed
hen). When I look around, Tuuli and the boy are also standing
behind me, though I didn't hear them coming. This morning Tuuli
is wearing a bright green short-sleeved dress that I haven't seen on
her yet. In it she doesn't have the laxness of our first encounter,
she looks more deliberate and older (as I look up: the heron far
out over the lake). Tuuli spreads a wool blanket on the ground.
The boy is waiting for the departure with the yellow fishing rod
in his hands, he's wearing a children's life vest and Svensson's
Lakers cap. By the time I'm nodding at his request, Svensson has
already jumped in the water and is swimming to the boat moored

to buoy 1477. He hoists himself over *Macumba*'s railing and starts the motor. Svensson overlooked his freshly ironed shirt and his towel in my hand. You should help him with the dog, *Manteli*, says Tuuli, and as Svensson maneuvers the boat with a quiet motor to the dock, I catch the rope as I did on the Lugano pier. Tuuli kisses the boy on his forehead, *älä pelkää*, Samy. *Minä en pelkää, Äiti*, whispers the boy, he's not afraid. Then he climbs into Svensson's outstretched arms. Tuuli and I roll Lua onto the wool blanket, and the three of us lift him onto the bow, the swan hisses. Once the disconcertingly light dog is finally lying in his spot and the boy with his fishing rod is sitting next to him, Svensson nods to us, Tuuli should take a seat in the stern with him, I in the bow (the sluggish movement of the remaining legs). But Tuuli shakes her head:

Manteli and I are staying here!

He should make the best decision for Lua on his own. Svensson hesitates and looks first at Tuuli, then at me. Svensson nods, he seems to have more important things on his mind, his eyes tear. He turns the gas lever, the screw stirs the water. He steers *Macumba* in the same wide curve as yesterday around the rock shelf (he knows his lake). The swan takes a running start and soars into the air after ten, maybe twenty slapping steps on the water's surface. The bird's squawks and the noise of the motor can still be heard when the boat itself has long been out of sight. What remains are: the cicadas, the pigeon droppings, Tuuli and I.

buoy 1477

The water splashes up over me. I open my eyes and see green. I plunge and count the breaths, 27, 28, below me the dark green, above me the light. At 29 my air is running out. I manage another six or seven increasingly rapid strokes, then comes the dizziness, then I have to surface. When I turn toward the shore, the ruined house is reflected in the smooth water. The midday sun flings itself over the green of the sycamores and palms, over the rampant vines on the walls (the oleander is shining). Tuuli is nowhere to be seen, she must have gone inside after Svensson's departure, and the cypresses are blocking my view of the door. I want to swim to the white buoy, I want to catch my breath. But as I'm about to reach for the metal ring, the water between buoy 1477 and me breaks apart, a watery spraying and slapping, a bright thrashing, I paddle backward and kick around me, I don't hit anything. Then it's over. Only a few bubbles on the surface and several seconds of complete silence. I hold on to the mossy buoy, I rub the water out of my eyes (around buoy 1477 dance mosquitoes). The fish down there are white and insanely beautiful, Svensson said, and I think I see a bright shadow plunging away below me. The passing thought of calling for help, but no one would hear me (I'm alone with the monster of Lago Ceresio, I think). But then there's a soft splash, and behind me Tuuli says,

You almost got me, *Manteli!*

Her hand grasps my shoulder before I can even turn my head. Tuuli holds on to me and buoy 1477, I paddle with my legs. We're alone, she says, *Karvasmanteli.* I'm sorry, I say, I didn't mean to hit you (her skin underwater, the fabric of her green bikini is missing). That's fate, says Tuuli, you hit what you're supposed to hit.

Interview (1477)

MANDELKERN: I thought you were Moby Dick.

TUULI: That's a strange mix-up.

M: I thought a fish was attacking me.

T: You were almost about to kill me.

M: I would have caught you and then thrown you back. You're far below the permissible catch weight.

T: Is this a fishing lesson, *Manteli*?

M: We're clinging to the buoy here side by side, I would only have to turn around.

T: So turn around.

M: The water is much warmer than I expected.

T: Only on the surface. What's your wife's name, *Manteli*?

M: Elisabeth.

T: Why don't you wear a ring?

M: The ring is upstairs on the desk. We're swimming around here. I could lose it.

T: It's a ring, *Manteli*. You're getting almost as dramatic as Svensson.

M: It's a lake. And apparently it's deep.

T: Shall we swim back, *Manteli*?

Oscar and Corner Store Oscar

Tuuli and I still side by side holding on to buoy 1477, we don't swim back. The wind is getting stronger. When I try to change the subject and ask about the vet, about Lua, his leg and his faith-

fulness, Tuuli answers that she once knew someone, his name was
Corner Store Oscar, in the last days of the Vietnam War he had to
be retrained as a medic. The guy from Svensson's manuscript? I
ask, and Tuuli laughs at me and my curiosity. Yes, from Lorimer
Street, she says, Corner Store Oscar really liked Lua (our Lua,
she says). Instead of a theoretical training each of the candidates
had to go out one afternoon and shoot a dog in the street. The
soldiers waited next to a garbage dump on the outskirts of Hanoi
for the hungry street mutts. The animals weren't allowed to die,
each soldier had only one shot. The medics were supposed to
aim for the extremities or the underside, typical wounds compa-
rable to those of people. After the shot the shooter had to rush
immediately to do first aid on the most severely wounded animal.
The others could take this opportunity to perform a simulation
of covering fire. Each animal was given the name of its shooter,
each shooter ministered to and took care of his victim from that
point on. The surviving dogs quickly befriended the medics.
Shortly before the dogs recovered, the medics had to tear open
their wounds again, rub salt, shards and latrine contents in the leg
and stomach wounds so they got infected. Then these infections
were themselves treated for training purposes, in further training
steps came fevers, gangrene and emergency amputations. But
meanwhile the animals' faithfulness grew, they no longer left
their medics' sides, they followed their torturers wherever they
went. Dogs stay with the people who hurt them the most. That's
why the camp was full of medics and dogs of the same name with
compresses, casts and splinted legs, Fred Smith and Freddy, Jack
White and Jack Black, Corner Store Oscar and Oscar, says Tuuli,
and we laugh, our heads half underwater, half above the surface.
In the end there was often a tacit euthanasia, that is, the stepping up of the symptoms until death. There were also soldiers,

Tuuli recounts, who simply opened their animals' veins, even though that was punishable by several days' arrest. Corner Store Oscar ultimately killed Oscar out of pity with a shot in the head, declared his training finished, and the next day was immediately sent back to the front, where his lower jaw was accidentally shot off on the second morning by a soldier of his own unit (friendly fire, says Tuuli). But that dog follows Corner Store Oscar to this day, you see, Oscar the dog remains faithful to Oscar the man beyond the grave. Lua, she says, is exactly the same way. I ask whether those were really tears in Svensson's eyes before, as we were lifting the dog onto the boat. No, says Tuuli, rubbing the water out of her eyes, no, no, she says, no. Then she lets go of the buoy and plunges under me toward the shore, I swim after her (I can't do the crawl).

William Wordsworth & Robby Naish (2005–2005)

In front of Tuuli lies the plucked and gutted rooster. This is Words-worth, she says, taking the biggest knife from the knife block and the whetstone from the hook, Naish has been in the soup since yesterday. Did you hear the screams, *Manteli?* Yes, I did. We came directly into the kitchen, Tuuli's standing in her puddle of lake water, I in mine (both wrapped in towels). It was loud enough, I say, and the soup was good, it was just what I needed in my condition. Tuuli sharpens the knife, which is almost as long and wide as her delicate forearm. Svensson didn't hit Naish's neck precisely, she explains, that happens to him often, that he doesn't hit things precisely and thus causes pain, instead of—for example, when slaughtering the white rooster Robby Naish—dealing with things as quickly and as painlessly as possible for all concerned parties. Tuuli checks the blade, then she continues to sharpen

it and looks me directly in the eyes (her fingertip on the bare
metal). Once the knife is sharp enough, she pulls open Wordsworth's wings and lays bare the rooster's belly and breast. Hold
tight, she commands, and because I've already marveled at her
nimble fingers when she was filleting the fish, I press the cold
wings down on the tabletop. Tuuli holds the knife between her
teeth and takes a water glass out of the cabinet. Svensson must
have gotten the bottle of vodka at the supermarket yesterday, and
since the fuse has been reset, there are ice cubes again. Tuuli puts
the glass between me and the rooster. She asks whether I've read
all of *Astroland*, whether I believe such stories? Not all of it, I say,
but the part with the vodka. At that Tuuli taps lightly on the glass
with the blade.

You're weird, *Manteli*,

she says with a loud laugh (she's quoting Svensson's New York
escape attempt). I raise the glass, we take turns draining the
vodka, the ice clinks. With the cold vodka in my mouth I kiss
Tuuli, but her thin lips remain closed. She smiles, Wordsworth on
the table draws his wings very slowly to his body (he has ceased
his defense). Tuuli points with the blade at the bird, I press it
down on the table again. The knife slowly pierces his soft breast,
first carefully, the second time already more forcefully. Again
and again Tuuli stabs into the bird (she will have given Lua the
heart).

Elisabeth's Musical Streak
By the fountain near the gate
There stands a linden tree

I dreamed in its shade
Many a sweet dream.
I carved in its bark
Many a dear word,
In joy and in sorrow
I was drawn to it always

Brazilian garlic chicken

On the table there's a list of things to cook. The rooster we
stuff with pimento, coriander, and half a clove of garlic in each
knife cut. Tuuli ties the legs together with poultry string, I chop
onions and shallots, we add pepper and salt and oil, then Tuuli
puts Wordsworth back in the fridge. We've stopped talking. She
takes flour and sugar out of the cabinets, we peel apples and soak
raisins in rum, we melt butter, I clean radicchio and Tuuli dices
tomatoes, she removes the seeds from red peppers, I from yellow
ones (Daisy Duck laid two eggs). I wonder why we're preparing
such massive amounts of food. We wash strawberries, we roast
pine nuts, we rinse fava beans. Tuuli and I circle each other, since
the kiss we haven't touched. We chop flat-leaf parsley, sage, basil,
green olives, black olives, garlic, capers, we squeeze lemons and
oranges, we scrape out vanilla pods, we beat aioli, I with the
whisk, she pours in olive oil from a small canister. Out of flour
and oil we knead pizza dough. Potatoes and tomato sauce are
cooking on the stove, apple pie is baking in the oven. We drink
another vodka, and Tuuli smokes a cigarette (I say no thanks).

Interview (main informant)

MANDELKERN: Why are we actually cooking all this stuff?

TUULI: Lua's dying, *Manteli*, he hasn't eaten anything for days.

M: And now all this at once? But that's not healthy.

T: The food is for the guests.

M: I had no idea that guests were coming.

T: Well, you were rummaging around in Svensson's things instead of asking questions.

M: I was sick.

T: Cigarette?

M: Did Svensson really collect cigarettes?

T: I'm only one of the characters from *Astroland*.

M: Maybe even the most important one.

T: So no cigarettes today?

M: I don't actually smoke.

T: The stories are one-third truth, one-third fiction and one-third the attempt to glue the other two together with words.

M: You were really together in New York?

T: In New York, in Seraverde, in Oulu.

M: Is the boy an American?

T: He has several passports.

M: And who's the father, if I may ask? Svensson writes at least ten times that you were not alone but were three.

T: Are you familiar with the Borromean rings, *Manteli*?

M: No. But that Kiki mentioned them.

T: Then look it up and ask me about Lua instead.

M: What?

T: Ask me: was Lua really once named Lula?

M: What about Blaumeiser's death?

T: Felix was too careless. He was waiting for us, he drank more

than you and Svensson together. He lived himself to death.
But one thing at a time. Ask me about Lua and Svensson about
the rest.

M: Okay.—So was Lua really once named Lula?

T: Yes. Lula da Silva was the watchdog of a policeman named
Santos.

M: Did Felix really shoot off Lula's leg?

T: Yes. And then I sawed off Lua's leg with a saw from the carpenter's workshop, and sewed together the flaps of skin with
sewing thread.

M: Svensson writes of a bolt cutter.

T: He writes *like* a bolt cutter. Or do you think Wordsworth and
Naish really existed? It sounds good, but it's not the truth.

M: How long do chickens live?

T: Here chickens don't live to be one year old, *Manteli*, Svensson
always gives his animals the same names. He keeps his eyes
fixed on the past with sentimental tricks. And he collects the
dead, because the living are too much in motion for him. Things
pass away, but Svensson imagines that his stories remain.

M: Isn't that why we tell stories? Writers glue fiction and truth
together, they preserve the world otherwise than it is. That's
why that Kiki paints pictures and photographs animals and
garbage. Isn't it?

T: Is it? I'm not a psychologist, *Manteli*, I amputate. It would be
best for you to ask Kiki herself.

M: Are we cooking for Kiki?

T: I'm here only because of Samy. I face forward.

M: Svensson is Samuli's father?

T: I face forward, and you're standing in front of me. Even if you
are strange, *Manteli*.

Drink with me!

says Tuuli, *juo minun janssani!* What I say: Cheers! What she replies: *kippis!* What I think: that I'm going to kiss her again, once we've emptied this glass, in her green bikini, her thin body will be lighter than Elisabeth's, her breasts smaller. I will compare, as Svensson compared, I will touch the possibility of another life, this kiss will be the attempt to take two paths (where does that bring me?). We drink. Tuuli takes the Polaroid off the fridge and holds it next to the red-wine-stained picture on the kitchen wall. Shitty City, she reads, and tells me about Oulu and the Hotel Turisti. We drink. Tuuli talks about the cold of the Finnish winter, about her father in the Arctic Circle and about the Borromean rings. The rings were just like them, Blaumeiser, Svensson, and Tuuli herself. We keep an eye on the pie in the oven. When I finally do put my hand on Tuuli's back so as to bend down again toward her mouth, so as not to let this opportunity pass, she says that I touch her as if I never touched a woman before, as if she were made of cotton candy.

Nice to see you

Now I'm sitting at Svensson's desk again in front of my notebook, out of breath and ambushed for the second time this afternoon by the arrival of a woman. I kissed Tuuli, she bathed my mouth in coriander and icy cold, the hair on the back of her neck still damp from the lake water (*suutele minua!*). I could observe us as we kissed, her fingers, my hands between her shoulder blades. After a few seconds, the squeak of the sliding door stabbed Tuuli's and my ears, in my head the thought of Svensson and the death of the dog, in Tuuli's eyes the fright at her fatherless son in the doorway of the kitchen, my thought of Elisabeth in Hamburg, in Tuuli's face maybe the possibility of a first self-caught fish in Samy's small hands (in me Elisabeth's red hair, her red dress, her green eyes). But then a woman's voice from below, speaking English: Where the fuck are you, Svensson? Tuuli and I jumped apart like two teenagers, we fell away from each other, we looked at each other, she put her index finger to my mouth and her other hand on my chest, I brushed a wet strand of hair behind her ear (her smile, my smile). I took a hairpin out of her hair, and when the sound of women's heels on the stone steps approached, I pushed myself off Tuuli as I had off buoy 1477, and disappeared into Svensson's study (I swam ashore). Where is everybody? the woman's voice asked on the steps, what's going on here? A few seconds later I heard the English-speaking voice in the kitchen say "look at that!" and finally, after a brief pause and a few footsteps through Svensson's kitchen, the name I've often read in the past few days and have been finding everywhere in Svensson's house: Tuuli Kovero, this voice declares, nice to see you again! Tuuli's reply: Kiki!

August 9, 2005

(Lua leaves)

Suddenly wide awake: I'm standing barefoot in front of Svensson's desk, the fresh imprint of Tuuli's lips on mine, the warmth of the vodka in my belly. As it does every day at this time, the smell of something burning hangs in the air, over the lake lies the stone smoke (Claasen is torching again). I can hear the two women's voices in the kitchen, then footsteps on the stairs. Tuuli Kovero, I think, because Tuuli's last name has eluded me until now. Kiki Kaufman knocks on the door of Svensson's study, comes in, a cardboard box in her hand and a small child on her hip: Hi, I'm Kiki. Daniel Mandelkern, I say. The two of them seem not the least bit surprised. And this is Bella, says Kiki Kaufman, say hello to Daniel, but the child only looks at me motionlessly and sucks on an orange pacifier (younger than Samy, maybe one and a half, dark curls and eyes). Kiki Kaufman is a tall woman with huge eyes, which beam despite their darkness. She's wearing a red dress and yellow flip-flops, I notice her freckles and the gray strands in her hair, the paint on her strong fingers. Switching to German, she says that it's nice to meet me, Svensson already told her about me on the phone yesterday (Bar del Porto). It's good to have visitors, Bella should see other people now and then besides just father and mother and dog (he told me you're feeling better, she says in English, are you?). Bella has the same large eyes as her mother, she has her warmhearted mouth, she has Svensson's broad nose. I'm taken aback as I stand opposite her and the girl, I imagined her differently while reading *Astroland*, thinner and more reserved. Downstairs in the kitchen Tuuli is busy with kitchen things (the taste of her lips). Kiki hands me the box and puts the girl down on the floor of the study. Bella strolls through the room, she rattles the airplane mobile still hanging from the ceiling (Mandelkern can't tell children's toys from dog toys, incredible!). She and Bella have just returned from Rome, her first exhibition in Italy, a group show, but still (*quattro*, she says, then in English: all pictures of the dog, how fitting, he's so sick). Bella has come to the bookshelves, she laughs, her little teeth shine. Kiki follows her daughter, she briefly runs her finger over the boards, she straightens one of the pictures (*gut, gut*, she says). She's sorry that I have to stay in this empty and dreary room, Svensson and she are currently renovating this house. I must have already noticed the preparations for renovation. This room first, the books in the shed, the junk out of here, the chairs and loungers, the things left by Blaumeiser's family. Did I need anything, something to drink maybe, I should make myself completely at home. Yes, I say. Kiki jumps between her languages, she falls from one into the other (*und so weiter* and so forth). Without books, she says, the room immediately looks much drearier and bigger, but now it can be turned into something completely new. Apparently someone has already begun beautifying the room. Have you been drawing here, Daniel? Kiki laughs (I thought of Svensson as lonely). Would I agree with her that the view from this window is gorgeous, she loves sitting here in the morning (the American ease with which she uses the word *Liebe*). The lizards, the wasps, the swallows. She talks and laughs, I nod. Finally she takes the box and removes the tape, she pulls out a PowerBook, styrofoam and plastic she throws back in the box. The old computer was so old, she says, after a while you couldn't read a word, and when it came to photoshopping, it froze every time I started to work, so I threw it out. I'm glad to be back for the party, she then says, looking at me. You're not much of a talker, Daniel, she says, switching back to English, are you? I'm just somewhat surprised, I say, sorry. She asks why exactly I'm here. I'm a journalist. My superior sent me, I say, but Kiki doesn't understand the German word, so I speak English: My wife is my boss, I explain to her and myself, and as I hear myself speaking, I think that that's precisely what could change. I blundered into this situation, I say, I was supposed to conduct an interview in a café in Lugano, but then I suddenly found myself on the boat, and now I'm still sitting here. My wife wants a profile for the news-paper, I say, but only a tiny bit of what I've learned so far is usable, a lot of it isn't suited to a newspaper article, which can only feel its way along the surface. Kiki lifts up Bella again, the child squeals, the two of them laugh. We're barely gone for a few days, she says, and Svensson invites over his listeners. Kiki is standing by the door holding the box and the child, Bella throws her pacifier on the floor. I pick it up. Do you have kids, Daniel? asks Kiki, looking at me. Not yet, I say.

the ethnological phenomenon of the informant switch

I've misjudged the weather conditions. As Tuuli's imprint on me slowly disappears and the smoke disperses, I sit down at the desk, my feet on Svensson's suitcase. My wedding ring is still lying on the two black folders. I've gotten into a situation that I wasn't expecting. I didn't resist (vodka and the possibility of another life). Nonetheless, everything remains as always: the pigeon drop-pings, and the swallows are flying again, higher than they were earlier this morning. I hear the rubberized closing of the refrig-erator door, Bella's squealing, the two women's English. Svensson

has gone to the village with the boy and the dog. I'm an ethnologist and literary scholar, I've learned to distinguish between text
and life (I've forgotten what I learned). I should write that I don't
know these people, but I've stumbled into Svensson's manuscript,
I've kissed one of his characters and have just shook another one's
hand. From the kitchen Bella's noise and the smell of onions in
butter (ethnology increasingly differentiates itself from neigh-
boring disciplines through the method of participant observation
rather than through its focus on the so-called "culturally alien" as
its object of investigation, Spittler 2001, if I remember correctly).
I wonder:

—Have I lost scientific distance toward the object of the
investigation?
—What does all this have to do with me?

the limits of the text

What is not in Svensson's manuscript: whether Svensson and
Kiki ever reached Montauk. What drove them back to Europe.
When they decided to step out of time. How old Lua is. Whether
Svensson has stepped out of time at all. Felix Blaumeiser is dead,
I've been able to find that out, but not where he's buried. Why
Tuuli works in Berlin but was sitting, of all places, in my airport
bus at the Hamburg Airport, why our journeys then led to the
same destination (her lips on mine, my lips on hers).

onions in butter

Elisabeth's and my honeymoon ended in a Polish hotel in the
Kolberg (Kołobrzeg) Old City, the rooms in the back facing the

courtyard, below the bedroom window a single sheep. The town house that had belonged to Elisabeth's grandparents was on the other side of the street, in the garden hung a Polish flag on a rickety pole. The plaster was flaking off the walls, the old windows had been replaced by thermal panes in plastic frames, behind a curtain in a small bay window stood a child, observing us. This is where they lived, said Elisabeth, number 17, in the back of the house was my grandfather's practice. Elisabeth and I walked up and down the bank of the Persante (Parsęta), we ate dinner at an inn, herring in oil, potatoes and beer. We could have lived here, I said, if it hadn't been for the war, for example, if not for this and if not for that, and Elisabeth smiled and kissed me. That, she declared, is nonsense, though charming. You couldn't escape the past, that was obvious, but we shouldn't forget the future on account of that. Crossroads were crossroads, and decisions were decisions, Elisabeth took my hand: she had decided on me and on now. After the third beer she kissed me again and longer (the taste of onions in butter). The Poles at the bar saw in us nostalgia tourists of the third generation, not honeymooners, the food was mediocre, and the men's eyes were hostile, they hadn't reckoned with Elisabeth's beauty. The next morning she rolled up the red wedding dress, we brushed our teeth, the water tasted like metal. Heading back westward, we drove over cobblestones, across the border of the voivodeship, later through the tree-lined streets of Mecklenburg, we picked apples and bought cider in plastic bottles on the road-side. As we rolled onto the Priwall ferry, Elisabeth took her phone out of the glove compartment, turned it on and declared our future open (that's how she expressed herself). Now I'm sitting in Svensson's house at Svensson's desk, but nonetheless hear Elisabeth bustling about in the kitchen, the sound of uncorked red wine bottles in our possible kitchens in Hamburg, Kolberg or

Saint-Malo, in Venasque or Sausset-les-Pins, in New York as far
as I'm concerned, maybe Lugano, in one of our possible lives. I
hear the sound of my name from her mouth (Daniel Daniel), her
precise, earnest laughter, I see her hair and her scars, the light skin
of her body, easy to imagine as the body of a mother, her thin and
nonetheless strong arms, her hair pulled back, Elisabeth always
ties and pins her hair off her neck, the vein on her forehead, now
her lips on mine (our bodies did fit after all), and from the kitchen
a woman calls my name,

Manteli, Manteli,

but I don't move, I don't allow myself to be interrupted. Shh,
replies Kiki's voice in English, let him sleep (even though I'm not
sleeping), and Bella's sounds mingle with the hiss of the gas stove
and the sizzling fat, with the clacking of the knife and the stirring
of the spoons, with the onion and butter vapors, with Wordsworth in the oven and Naish in the soup, with the outboards on
the lake and the pigeons on the roof, with the soft and ever softer
voices of the two women in Svensson's house, in Svensson's book,
in Svensson's life.

our professionalism

Elisabeth and I had arranged to meet in the late afternoon at Café
Paris near the Hamburg city hall marketplace, it must have been
in the autumn of 2004. There was something to celebrate, she'd
said on the phone. We ordered Ricard and *merguez frites*, then
she informed me that I could begin in the editorial department,
though I'd have to be more readily available than I'd been up to
that point (Elisabeth doesn't hesitate). In the winter of 2003 I'd

offered a feature and two profiles to Elisabeth's department, all
three had been bought and printed ("Michael Moore and Peter
Krieg: Didactic Montage in Documentary Film" the editors
turned into "Michael Moore's Krieg"). That isn't going to work,
I said, pouring water into Elisabeth's anise liqueur, Professor
Jansen is demanding the exact same thing for my dissertation,
on top of that there's the work in the witch archive and at *GEO*.
The waiter placed the *merguez* between us. Here too Elisabeth
pinned a strand of her hair back from her forehead, this might
be the chance of your life, Daniel. She had even been able to
negotiate a steady salary. As an ethnologist, after all, I couldn't
necessarily expect always to earn enough money to afford life in
Central Europe. Elisabeth laughed, I knocked back the Ricard. Or
did I want to go to Tanzania to do field research like Hornberg?
Elisabeth licked the grease off her slender fingers and ordered
more wine, we ate, I reflected, we drank. And here was the best
part, she added: she herself would be my direct superior, wouldn't
that just be crazy, Mandelkern? The momentary reflex to have
to reject her offer (the crumpled-up napkin on Elisabeth's plate
a mushroom cloud). I have only the last third of my dissertation
left to write and can definitely imagine staying at the university,
I said (Jansen had already hinted at the possibility several times).
Elisabeth said that I could always imagine lots of things, she'd
relieve me of the decision for now. You can't eat possibilities,
Mandelkern, eventualities aren't enough to fill us up! The way
she imagined our working together, we could connect work and
private life, our marriage could be a symbiosis.

my dissertation

Elisabeth and I came to an agreement that same night on my regular freelance position in her department (we always come to an agreement). Not without a twinge of melancholy I quit my glossarist job, I cleared my desk in the witch archive, and explained the new situation to Professor Jansen. The main thing, he urged me in his office in the Museum of Ethnology, is that you don't hesitate too long, Daniel. In 2006 I'm retiring, and by then we should have put your project behind us. Immediately after the conversation I rode my bike to Elisabeth's office and from there took the train directly to Munich and Berlin and back to Hamburg, jumping right into writing a story about suicides in opera houses and theaters. During the first months I read my ethnological essays in train compartments, cafés, and airport waiting areas and worked on my dissertation on weekends. When Jansen asked me about new pages at our occasional lunches together, I strung him along (he read my articles in the newspaper and knew that my explanations were excuses). Then I wrote him a letter by hand and requested a break, the balancing act between journalistic and academic writing had temporarily become an unproductive situation. In the everyday routine of newspaper reporting, though, there were always new opportunities for shorter field studies, I wrote, so I would by no means lose sight of ethnology and my topic. Therefore, I would ask him not to write me off. I read the letter to Elisabeth before I sent it. Strangeness, she laughed, really is your specialty, Mandelkern.

obbedienza cieca

It's the swan's singing that finally makes me look up from the notebook (it follows *Macumba* like a memory). The boy is kneeling in his life vest in the stern, Svensson is steering the boat with one hand. Lua only comes into view when *Macumba* has already almost arrived at the dock, he's lying stretched out on the bench, the blanket under his head and another under his body. When Tuuli emerges from the house, the two of them have disembarked and the boy runs to her from the dock, the yellow fishing rod in his hands. Lua is lying on the bench as if in a deep sleep. Svensson puts the light blue bucket down on the dock and rolls up his shirt-sleeves. He reaches into the bucket, suddenly there's spraying and wriggling. Samy jumps up and hides behind Tuuli's legs. When Svensson extracts his arms, he's holding a fish in his outstretched arms, Tuuli claps her hands and hugs Samy. Svensson holds the animal in the air by its tail and pats Samy on the shoulder. Kiki! he calls. Mandelkern! And Tuuli, too, turns toward the house, she waves and points to the fish. *Manteli*, she calls, filetto di persico! Svensson rocks the motionless fish in his arms like a baby. For a brief moment the three of them are a family coming home (father, mother, child, and dog). But then Svensson jumps back onto the boat to Lua, the three-legged, the miserable, the faithful dog (*obbedienza cieca*, the waitress in the Bar del Porto called his faithfulness). I close the notebook and climb down the rickety outside staircase (I will stay one more night).

The Story of Leo and the Notmuch

Lua is lying in his spot again, he's lying on the blanket in the grass as if he were asleep. Svensson and Kiki on one side, Tuuli and I on the other, we lifted the dog's body, the blue blanket between us a jumping-sheet. Tuuli is smoking absently and watching the dog breathe, but even from up close the rising and sinking can only be surmised (she doesn't touch me). Why does Lua have to die? asks the boy, and begins to cry just as suddenly as he broke out in cheers a short while ago. Svensson just barely manages to deter the little doctor from another examination with the chair-leg stethoscope, he puts him promptly on his shoulders (Svensson fears the diagnosis). Tuuli carries the bucket with the fish into the house. There's still a lot to do, says Kiki, at eight it will be time (it looks like a good-bye, it looks like tears). Svensson takes a stroll around the property with the boy on his shoulders, I follow them. We feed the hen, we pick a few tomatoes and some sage, we look for eggs in the footwell of the Fiat. Svensson asks the boy whether he knows the story of Leo and Fips and the Notmuch. Yes, says the boy, do you want to read to me? All right, says Svensson, all right. Is *Manteli* coming too? Of course he's coming, says Svensson, slapping me on the shoulder. After all, that story is the reason you're here, right? He slams the doors of the Fiat (to protect against the fox). We walk through the high grass and the flowers and leaves toward the house. The women will have gutted the fish already, I think, they'll still want to spare the boy (everything is passing away: the dog, the fish, the oleander).

Elisabeth and I

In my head this image remains: on a Monday morning in May Elisabeth and I are standing in the hallway of the Bismarckstrasse apartment when the telephone rings (the early stripes of sunlight on the floor). We're about to set off for work, I'm standing next to her with my shoulder bag and a sack of empty bottles. She says her name, then doesn't say anything for a long time, finally she says thank you and hangs up (the soft and incomprehensible voice from the receiver). She leans her head on my neck and closes her eyes, everything's all right, she says, that was the gynecologist's office. Elisabeth and I in the white frame of the mirror (for a few seconds the possibility of a family). We have to go now, Mandelkern, she then says, or else we'll be late, or else I'll have to reprimand you.

So why a children's book?

As I follow Svensson and the boy on his shoulders into the large room on the ground floor, into the smell of sage and mint, of garlic and onions, of tomato sauce with red wine and capers, I notice my hunger and my thirst. Kiki is standing in the entrance to the kitchen, she's wearing an apron, holding the crying Bella. When I ask if I can help, Kiki hands me the girl (don't worry, says Kiki, she's tired anyway). She disappears into the kitchen and comes back with two glasses of wine, one for Svensson, one for me. So there will be drinking again today. Svensson kisses his daughter on the nose (in doing so, he comes closer to me than ever before). Bella reaches for my ear, then she leans her head on my shoulder, she has her mother's hair (children are heavier than I thought). Start! shouts Samy, start! We raise our glasses. *The Story of Leo and the Notmuch*, Svensson starts with the boy on his shoulders, begins like this.

The Story of Leo and the Notmuch

SVENSSON: Our Leo is a cheeky little boy, just like you, / and best of all: . . .

SAMY: . . . his friend Fips is with him too.

SVENSSON: Fips and Leo are the best / friends in the whole town, / Fips and Leo are so funny . . .

SAMY: . . .

SVENSSON: . . . that . . .

SAMY: . . . there are always laughs when they're around.

SVENSSON: Exactly. This here is Leo and this here is Fips, with the yellow hair, you see? The two of them are the best of friends.

SAMY: Yeah. Keep going.

SVENSSON: Okay. What comes next?

SAMY: Fips and Leo do all sorts of things . . .

SVENSSON: . . . no one here has ever seen before . . .

SAMY: . . . and the fat neighbor Wuth gets scared . . .

Leo and Fips

We carry the children from picture to picture. I follow Svensson and bounce my knees up and down slightly to soothe the girl, but she's already asleep at the first picture (down by the water the dog sees death coming). Svensson and Samy take turns, both of them can recite the text. Leo and Fips are two boys in colorful T-shirts and shorts, Fips with yellow hair, Leo with brown. The pictures are hanging in front of us on the wall (a picture of the two of them in a lion costume, they scare a man with a watch chain and hat, the fat neighbor Wuth; Svensson and Samy in chorus: ". . . when they jump out as a lion with a mighty roar"). Fips and Leo play pranks, they drive the control-obsessed landlady crazy and free the chickens of the sinister butcher Mussolini, they steal and take revenge like Robin Hood, they turn the world into a fun and exciting place. Kiki's pictures are colorful and friendly and full of

little details (Samy points and points and points). Svensson and I
make our way around the large dining room as we drink wine,
we climb the steps toward the kitchen, we rock the children to
the beat of our footsteps. The boy cheers and pulls at Svensson's
hair, the author seems surprised (I'm amazed by how much text
the boy retains).

the picture with the cookies

Ms. Evernasty from the bakery
grumpily stops the cookie sales,
'cause Fips and Leo were too fast for her
and all they left were cookie crumb trails.

Leo and the Notmuch

Tuuli is cubing meat, Kiki is peeling potatoes, Bella is sleeping
on my arm (the women fall silent when we enter the kitchen).
Svensson and Samy ignore the filled bowls and pots, they're
absorbed in the story on the walls, they throw the words to each
other and finish each other's sentences. Leo and Fips have meanwhile saved a dog from the evil butcher and educated the baker
to be a better person. Fips, the daring, wild boy with the straw-
yellow hair, has taught Leo that you should be brave, just, and
honest. Over the stove in Svensson's kitchen hangs a picture of
Leo, lying on his back on a railroad embankment, a blade of grass
in his mouth and a hat on his head. Fips has gone off to steal
apples on the other side of the railroad tracks, because apples are
the two boys' favorite food. Leo is explaining to a cricket how
unique a friend like Fips is. The boy sits on Svensson's shoulders
and repeats the last line, he almost sings it:

. . . stay together through thick and thin!

The boy laughs, but when Svensson again points to the picture,
to the cricket and the blade of grass, when he then turns away
and walks across the kitchen, Tuuli lowers the knife onto the
tabletop, she stubs out her cigarette in the wax paper on the table,
her eyes are moist. Up to here, she says, for the rest he's still too
little (at what point do children understand death?). Kiki too has
stopped peeling and is observing the three of them. The next
picture they approach is the book's first darker picture, about a
third of the way in. The colors are now menacing and dark (Fips
is never coming back). Svensson carries the boy slowly through
the kitchen toward the canvas. A train races powerfully through
the picture, in the background a storm is gathering, the hat is
blown off little Leo's head (Samy on Svensson's shoulders first
covers his ears, then his eyes). Up to here he knows it, repeats
Tuuli, no further! In the file that I read in preparation an eternity
ago, a review speaks of the "palpable grief" created by Svensson's
illustrations (the fact that the illustrations are not by Svensson I'll
keep to myself, it might be the only relevant detail I've gleaned).
But in spite of Tuuli's admonition Svensson continues toward the
train picture,

As evening suddenly fell
and the sun went down
the sky grew ever darker
because . . .

Svensson reads, and then breaks off after all (everyone breaks
off). I put my wine glass down as softly as possible on the table

and rock Bella on my arm, Kiki seeks and finds my eyes. The boy is hiding his face in his small hands, he suspects what's coming. Finally Tuuli goes to her son to console him (pictures are worse than words). Samy cowers on Svensson's shoulders, his mother tries to reach him, but then she too hangs on Svensson's words, suddenly real tears can be seen in her eyes (the book was never a children's story). The children's book author seems almost surprised by his own story, he doesn't read on, he only whispers,

Fips isn't coming back,

and the missing rhyme hangs awkwardly and hollowly in the room. Kiki carefully pushes me with her daughter on my arm out of the kitchen (the children's book picks up where *Astroland* leaves off). Tears run down the boy's cheeks, he's not only grieving for Fips, he's crying about the sudden silence in the kitchen, he's crying about his mother's tears. I'm just hoping they'll finish the story, says Kiki, as she pushes me down the steps, out of the house and down to the water. Given the circumstances the story turns out well. Give me a hand, says Kiki, and despite my clumsy help she ties Bella to her back with a baby sling. Now comes the better part of the *Story of Leo and the Notmuch*, which is the story of the Notmuch: how to deal with things as terrifying as that, now come the pictures that are hanging in the stairwell on the way to the bedroom (I've seen those pictures: the colors brighten, the details return). The lake still low and lurking, as if it were waiting for something, farther out the wind roughens the water. Lua is lying in front of the bowl of beer Kiki has given him. He doesn't drink, and she ignores the yellowish slime under his snout. She rolls up the blanket anew and pets Lua's head and belly. Lua loves beer, she says, pouring the bowl down the slope, wait a second. Kiki goes back to the house. I touch Lua carefully, first on the head, then on the skin over the ribs. With my hand on his flank I can feel the last remains of his heartbeat, fast and weak and stumbling (an anxious child). I read the book on the plane, Leo is despondent without Fips, he hides away in his room. His mother gets worried and asks how he's doing and what he's up to in there. Not much, answers Leo, not much. He lies on the bed and grieves for Fips (a childlike depression). Then Leo begins to create a friend in his mind, a cheeky, brave, and honest friend like Fips. Leo dubs this "good monster" the Notmuch (a childlike mania). Now the two of them play, they're cheeky and brave together, Leo now answers his mother: Notmuch. The Notmuch is half memory of Fips, the other half is imagination, the two halves together enable Leo to overcome grief (*Astroland* works the same way, I notice, the house on the lake works the same way). How to deal with things, says Kiki, as she returns to the dock, Svensson at least has been waiting for this moment for months (everyone is waiting). In her hand she's holding one of Bella's clear plastic baby bottles (beer). It's time to finish reading this story, says Kiki. The boy will recover from the shock, says Kiki, and then switches to English: It's time to close this book ("It is the subcutaneous melancholy of regained courage," wrote the *Frankfurter Rundschau*, "that makes this book astonishing. It doesn't deny it, it deals with it."). Kiki pulls Lua's jowl to the side, she sticks the bottle between the dying dog's teeth, and Lua drinks (your last beer you drink from baby bottles: life is a circle, not a straight line). It starts in an hour, says Kiki, once Lua has finished drinking, we should get the things from the car.

Interview (main informant two)

MANDELKERN: Why isn't your name actually on the book? You
  did draw the pictures, after all.

KIKI: I turned Svensson's story into pictures, Daniel, that's something else entirely. They're still his stories.

M: And the other pictures here? So when is a picture your
  picture?

K: I listen to people and make something out of their words. Only
  when something from myself ends up on the canvas, from my
  own colors, does the canvas become my picture. Most of the
  pictures here are mine, just not the ones from Svensson's book.
  And then my name is on the bottom too. Have you seen the
  Astroland pictures?

M: In the study?

K: Nursery. The *Astroland* pictures are my own. Mine alone.
  I'm the sole creator of those pictures, they're nothing but my
  perspective. For those pictures I listened to myself. Svensson
  wouldn't see himself like that, above all he wouldn't describe
  the situation like that, on the slide and without any pants on.
  But Svensson's book is his. He sat next to me and dictated his
  story directly into my brush.

M: So it's a commissioned work.

K: I would call it artistic symbiosis, you know, *Zusammenarbeit*,
  collaboration.

M: Can you explain that to me?

K: The Polaroid on the fridge, have you seen it? Three people:
  Felix, Tuuli, and Svensson, plus the dog. I've never been to
  Finland, Daniel, but Svensson has told me the story, the story
  of that New Year's Day in Finland. That they were in love and
  were certain it would stay that way. But it didn't, you know?

The picture is called "Shitty City." The three of them were Borromean rings, though they didn't know it yet at that time. When I began to paint the book, I knew it. That's why Svensson's not laughing anymore in the picture. Tuuli's not laughing, because she made the wrong decision, but that's my personal opinion, don't tell her I said so. I've seen what has become of the people in this picture. Felix isn't laughing in the picture, because he died. The work of art knows the past, the present and the future.

M: Did you know Felix Blaumeiser?

K: No. But we found him, over there at the yellow house, right there below the church. At his parents' house on the other side. I was at his funeral, and I live with Dirk Svensson. Believe me, Daniel, Svensson has told me about Felix, many, many times.

M: I thought you were a photographer. All the pictures of the gulls and Lua, for example.

K: Photos never show what you want to see. For that you need your own paints and your own brush.

What exactly are Borromean rings?

On the narrow road through the woods toward Osteno: I'm carrying two garbage bags, Kiki one. The road must have been drivable once, but the woods have reclaimed it, we step over nettles and vines, dried branches, twice there are tree trunks lying across the path. Kiki knows the fauna and flora of Lombardy, she points to the plants on the path, she explains to me the cypresses and crickets, she gestures to an orange tree on the steep slope above us and an African fan palm in the ravine. Walking ahead of me Kiki points to a waterfall I missed the first time, Bella's asleep on her back. I ask about the Borromean rings and how they work,

but Kiki says that I should first take a look at the swallows. She
explains to me the birds' behavior before the approaching storm,
which Svensson's been talking about for days, she explains to me
the subtropical underbrush. Last time I was on this road I had to
throw up twice, I think, and that it's simpler now following Kiki
and Bella, the honest chaos of her languages, her brown curls
with gray strands in them, her pointing finger (she shares Svensson's gestures, she shares his life). This time my stomach growls
with hunger. When we arrive at the end of the road, we throw
the plastic bags into the heap. The garbage has been lying here
for days, flies are circling the cans (plastic bottles, paper, yogurt
cups, fish heads, orange peels, etc.). The fox, says Kiki, pointing
to the torn-open bags and the kitchen scraps. The garbage gets
collected only on Wednesdays, she explains, there are raccoons
here too. The makeshift bench is impossible to use (fish smell,
rotten fruit). There's a red Volkswagen family car with an Italian
license plate parked on the gravel, Kiki pulls the key out of the
pocket of her green dress and opens the back (MIT1-4737). In the
trunk are paint tubes and plastic bottles, a chewed-up baseball,
a wool blanket and dog hair. On the backseat a child safety seat,
next to it a few canvases, wrapped in spattered sheets. Here, says
Kiki, two cases of beer, can you give me a hand, I'll take the bags.
As I lift the beer out of the trunk, I ask again about the Borromean
rings. Nothing special, says Kiki, she always compares Svensson
and Tuuli and Blaumeiser with these rings. Three linked hoops,
one of those mind-fucks, but if one of them is removed, the other
two aren't linked anymore either, get it? Two of them don't work
without the third. I don't understand: could she draw it for me?
Natürlich, says Kiki, in the house sometime (I remember a quote
from Nigel Barley's *The Innocent Anthropologist: Notes from a Mud*

Hut: "I was quietly convinced that I would return having learned and understood nothing").

master of chairs, master of lights

Now two more boats are moored to the dock in front of Svensson's ruin (Pike Machine and Valsolda), torches are shining on the way to the shore, they stand in a row on the dock, candles on the stone tables, clouds of mosquitoes and moths around the light. Svensson has broken his rickety chairs into firewood and thrown it on the pyre he built yesterday (the screams of the animals). A multicolored string of lights is hanging in the oleander. Kiki leads me around: this is the journalist Daniel, *ciao* Andrea, *buona sera* Signora Gobbi. Nice to see you, she says in English again and again, she kisses and hugs and shakes hands. This is Daniel, says Kiki, this is Francesca (the waitress from the Bar del Porto). We've met, says Francesca. Yes, I say, and shake hands and get kissed and pulled along. The blind Prosecco drinker with the long ears, who greeted me like Hitler the day before yesterday in the Bar del Porto, is named Mussolini and is Francesca's father. *Forza Roma*, he says, he's the village butcher. That's not his name, says Kiki as we walk on, though he's just as old. The paint-and-lacquer man Carlo Materazzi is playing Ping-Pong with the carpenter Luigi Gobbi, they shout, they gesticulate, and Luigi's mother opens beer bottles (I saw her in the cemetery). The guests drink and chatter and argue. Kiki and I walk around the tables, I try to remember the names: the veterinarian Pompeo Castelfranco, Donata Buti from the dry cleaner's, the lawyer Pelegrino Rossi. The official from the Guardia di Finanza is in civilian clothing today, he drinks and drinks and gives a thumbs-up when Kiki refills his glass (his outstretched thumb, the bow wave of his boat on the day of my arrival). A bald guy is actually playing mandolin, Kiki explains that he's Andrea, the shipbuilder, it must have been twenty years ago that he built *Macumba*, back then the sailboat was named *Giulia*, after Felix Blaumeiser's mother. The bonfire is burning, the fishermen Marco and Alessandro are grilling fish, the cypresses over them paper cuttings against the dark blue sky (the glow of the yellow church on the other side). Lua is lying in the aroma of the good meat and in the warm looks of the guests and isn't coughing anymore, he has closed his eyes. Samy is kneeling next to him and smoothing the speckled fur with Kiki's brush, he's giving Lua beer from the plastic bottle (Lua will be drunk for the last time). What's the occasion, I ask, and Kiki says *nichts*. There doesn't have to be a reason for everything. Tuuli is sitting next to the two of them, smoking and observing her son, she's observing the people under the oleander, she's observing me. This is Daniel Mandelkern, says Kiki yet again, and a suntanned man in a linen suit stands up from his rusty metal chair, tips his straw hat, and shakes my hand. It's a pleasure, he says, Claasen is my name.

Claasen talks

Am I from Hamburg too? Someone hands plates to Claasen and me (chicken, fish, tomatoes). Then our evening here is officially an exile meeting. I work on Speersort? Yes, I say. He himself was a magazine man from day one, *Der Spiegel*. Claasen names names, I nod. I name names, Claasen nods. He lives on the slope over Osteno, he always came here with his children and his wife, they spent every summer since 1964 here, his children practically grew up here, such a beautiful place! I agree with him. He took projects with him, even under the old vacation provisions there were always four weeks. Now he writes only occasionally. Claasen bites into a chicken thigh. He values the seclusion, the climate too, the food. Does he occasionally burn things, I ask Claasen, but he doesn't understand: he has a fireplace, of course, but he spends the winters in Hamburg anyway. Claasen says that he doesn't know Elisabeth, he's heard of her ex-husband, yes, but he's never met him in person. I sit next to him and observe Svensson, the creator of stories, stoking the bonfire. Claasen's wife has been dead since 1989, his children now have children themselves, and he's a grandfather. His grandchildren come visit him in the summer, he never thought things would go this far. Claasen laughs. Svensson's world is a web of reasons and references. A world in which every gesture, every word, every thing has a meaning that I can only suspect (the understanding of cultural systems). It sounds mundane, says Claasen, but I'm a satisfied man.

Lua leaves

Svensson is sitting next to Samy and feeling the dog's pulse. When the candles have almost burned down and the fire is only glowing darkly, he stands up and taps a wine glass with a spoon (laughter and chatter). Tuuli takes the bottle from the boy, because Lua doesn't want to drink anymore, and Svensson climbs onto the bench with the lion heads. Claasen and I halt our conversation, the other conversations die away too, all the guests raise their glasses. Svensson climbs onto the lion bench in front of the oleander and looks at Kiki. When he begins to talk, the cicadas cease their screaming, the water black and quiet between the mountains, the large birds are resting. The death of pets and livestock, says Svensson, isn't usually assigned excessive importance in this region. He will now explain why that's different in Lua's case. The guests are sitting on Svensson's chairs like churchgoers. Svensson is a good speaker, he tells the stories of events I've already read about, he varies his themes, he alternates between languages, he talks Italian, German, English, and everyone understands what he's saying. Svensson tells anecdotes and stories, he makes the guests laugh, he pauses at the right points, the guests are glowing with emotion and affection and candlelight. Svensson praises Lua's life, his connoisseurship of women and international beer brands, his courage and his political development. Svensson gives the saddest speech of his life, a eulogy for the barely breathing dog, the guard and herding dog of the highest quality, the former police dog of Seraverde, for the good soul of Astroland, Coney Island. As Svensson raises his glass to the best dog in the world, the guests too stand up one after another, they murmur prayers and wishes, they laugh and praise Lua, they pull handkerchiefs from pants pockets and skirts and handbags, they pet his forehead the way people pet dying dogs' foreheads (animals, the hearts of people, Svensson wrote). Then the talking and Ping-Pong playing resume, the wine and beer, the rattling of plates, the celebrating, the dying of the dog, the chatter and laughter. Around midnight Claasen tips his hat. The guests pat Svensson on the shoulder and kiss Kiki on the cheeks, they tousle Samy's hair, they nod to Tuuli and me. Then one after another they board the boats at the dock. Today is a special day, today is a sad day. And when the rudders can no longer be heard in the water, when Claasen too has ultimately disappeared into the woods, Svensson kneels down next to Lua and lays his hand on his chest. Grief falls over the lake. Kiki buries her face in her hands, and even Tuuli forgets to smoke (I know how Elisabeth cries). Lua opens his eyes and closes them again, and even in the screaming of the cicadas I can hear the dog's voice: *Ciao ragazzi*, says Lua, *e arrivederci*. Svensson runs his fingers carefully over the dog's face, then he stands up and nods to us. Kiki doesn't bother to wipe away her tears anymore, now they're running unimpeded down her cheeks, and then Tuuli, too, starts to cry, for the second time today. Samy has fallen asleep with his head on the dying dog's chest (Lua, the heart of his fathers). I don't know what to do, so I go back to the house (anything else would be too personal now). Lua isn't breathing, I hear Svensson say, Lua isn't breathing anymore.

Knowledge Forwards and Backwards

Svensson came back to the room that I've been calling the study up to this point (without knocking, without a word). I stood up from my notes and his desk, and Svensson pulled out Blaumeiser's suitcase from under the desk. He said that he needed the suitcase now. Could I help, I asked, and he smiled at me with a strange friendliness: no. I stay behind and have to surmise, because I can't make out anything clearly (for the field researcher wait time is synonymous with work time, his presence is his work).

Why am I still here?

I summarize, because summaries facilitate understanding: Lua is dead. Felix Blaumeiser already died three years ago, he drowned on the other side of the lake. Svensson has struggled as everyone struggles, he's conceded his defeats. He's not a player, but he has lost nonetheless. Svensson is no stranger than the rest of us. At some point he decided to stop playing the game, and turned to the tangible things: Svensson and the painter Kiki Kaufman have a daughter named Bella. Bella has two teeth (the research intern did a terrible job). Svensson and Kiki are turning a ruin into a house, they're turning a study into a nursery, they plant and harvest and breed animals and slaughter and cook. They cry for Lua. Svensson carried the heavy piece of luggage effortlessly down the stairs, but then I could hear his curses through the window (his bulky baggage). I wonder why Svensson has taken the suitcase out of the room this evening, I wonder what's going to happen with the *Astroland* manuscript. Svensson is carrying his story out of the house, what remain are Tuuli's golden hair-pins, along with Svensson's books and my ring. The torches have burned down, the motion detector is off, even with the binoculars I can't make out the dead dog by the water (the moonlight isn't enough). Kiki and Svensson collect stories and paint pictures, they hang these pictures on their walls ("Knowledge Forwards and Backwards," Kiki calls it, they want to make their past inhabitable). I wonder what's done with dead animals here. I wonder where Tuuli is at the moment.

things in the dark

I wonder what Elisabeth would say about these things (I should talk to her). I've spent four days taking notes and haven't completed Elisabeth's assignment, I've asked simple questions and gotten complicated answers. I've stayed on the lake instead of leaving. I've washed off Elisabeth's blood in the water, I've kissed Tuuli. I turn out the light (maybe things will be discernible in the dark).

Bella & Samy

The crack of light from the hallway illuminates their way, Kiki and the children are standing next to me. Kiki says that she's now superfluous, as she lays her sleeping daughter down on the mattress. Samy is clinging to the hem of her dress and rubbing his eyes, she lays him down next to Bella and covers the two of them with my blanket, after all, she says, someone has to look after the children. Then she sits down on the floor under the window. She nods. This is now between Tuuli and Svensson and the dog, she says, smiling wearily and seriously at me, she doesn't necessarily have to watch. I have no idea where to begin, I begin, but Kiki's whisper interrupts me in English, you said you're married, Daniel? Yes, I say. No response, we're sitting in semidarkness: Kiki in the wedge of light, I at the desk. After four days I take the ring from the desk and put it on the proper finger (E. E. E.). Switching back to German, Kiki says that I probably know that everyone has his skeletons in the closet—or, for that matter, in a suitcase. She assumes so, anyway. What do skeletons have to do with my being married, I ask, what does she mean by that (I know what she means). Instead of answering, Kiki asks for a pencil and paper, all her supplies are temporarily stored in the shed. There's nothing to answer, I give her the hotel bill from the desk and tear a page out of my notebook, I hand her the crayons with which Samy made out his prescription. *Danke*, Daniel, says Kiki. Lua shouldn't die sad, the little *Dottore* said (Lua didn't die sad).

We're sad, you know?

Kiki is drawing, I'm taking notes. The sound of the nocturnal water, the soft breathing of the children, the waxy scratching of the crayons on the paper (Kiki Kaufman and I are practicing our professions). When Kiki finally puts aside her implements, it must be one o'clock. I ask Kiki whether she and Svensson are married, even though she's now leaning against the wall with her eyes closed. *Nein*, she says, *nein*. Why not? No reason. Are these questions too personal? No, Kiki is still whispering, not at all (she doesn't even open her eyes). The passing thought that Svensson must have felt just as calm with her as I do now (Kiki Kaufman: salvation and insight, he wrote). Svensson and she met by chance, says Kiki, in New York in 2001, those were unambiguous times, either good or evil, and in the middle of all that they crossed paths. Kiki laughs softly and opens her eyes. Of course they could have just gotten married to avoid visa problems, but by the time they became aware of this possibility, they were already sitting in a taxi on the way to Chicago's O'Hare Airport. She asks me whether I'm interested in things like this. Yes, I say, I still have a lot of questions—for example, what's going to happen with the dog. Kiki stands up and says, I'm drunk. Svensson will bury him under the oleander, she says, nodding toward the window, you want some coffee?

Who exactly was Felix Blaumeiser?

When Kiki brings the coffee, the property is again bathed in cold floodlight beams (against the fox). Tuuli and Svensson are sitting on the dock, the suitcase full of stones and paper between them, the dead dog still on his blanket. The floodlight flashes on when Svensson throws a stone into the water, the light reaches it in midair (the white plunge into the black lake). We're standing by the window and drinking coffee, Svensson's stone breaks through the surface and makes ripples, after a few seconds the light goes

out (a silent theater). The motion detector is working again, I say.
Chickens and rats don't set off the light, says Kiki, large movements are necessary for that. Lua's death is actually such a movement, and the next time the light flashes on, Svensson has flung a
stone out of the light (we don't see the bright splash). Even from
up here I can see *Astroland* lying in the suitcase. Svensson and
Felix knew each other since they were kids, Kiki now says more
to herself than to me, Lua entered their lives the same night as
Tuuli, he's been with them almost ten years. Kiki seems astonished by her words:

Lua is dead now.

Down by the water Tuuli and Svensson are lifting the dog from
his blanket and laying him down in the suitcase (Lua doesn't
fit). They grasp his hind legs and push them carefully toward
Lua's body, the lone foreleg Svensson likewise bends into place
(they're curling Lua up like a baby). The floodlight is staying on
now, because Tuuli is running back and forth between oleander
and suitcase, she's picking oleander flowers and scattering them
handful after handful over the dog in the suitcase. Svensson bends
down over the dog and lays his ear on the dog's chest (he wants to
be sure). Kiki is standing in the pale reflection of the floodlight.
Do things like that make no difference to her, I ask Kiki, and she
looks at me in surprise. This really is sad, she says, brushing the
sleeping boy's hair from his forehead. Lua has always been with
Svensson, just as Tuuli and Felix and Samy have always been with
him (*hier und hier*, she says, pointing to her chest and her forehead). After Felix's death the rings just weren't linked anymore,
she says, you can see that from a distance (can't you, Daniel?). By
the shore Svensson and Tuuli are now closing the suitcase, they're

pushing and pressing, then the heavy lock catches. On the night of New Year's Eve between 2000 and 2001 they reached the ideal state, on the coldest night of the year, says Kiki, Svensson has told her that over and over again. She asks whether I can visualize the picture in the kitchen. Yes, I say, Shitty City 2000, right? I remember that early chapter from *Astroland*: the hotel room, the breakfast, the dog wearing a hood (this isn't the first time Kiki has told this story, I think, she really is drunk). Svensson puts the suitcase in Lua's favorite spot on the boat (bulky baggage). The momentary idea that I've met Svensson only in the stories that might now become Lua's funerary object. The man by the lake has remained hidden from me. Exactly, says Kiki, interrupting my memory. After those days everything slowly came apart. Tuuli and Svensson walk across the meadow toward the house. Kiki takes Bella from the mattress as she brushes her brown curls behind her ear. At the thought of Elisabeth in this exact position, bent over her desk as far as I'm concerned, holding her red hair away from her face, over a child as far as I'm concerned, I'm overcome by an unannounced wave of emotion. Good night, Kiki says before she leaves, and I swallow my tears in the dark. I look at the piece of paper she was drawing on while we were talking: the wilting oleander, the dying Lua, the Borromean rings. Kiki has forgotten Samuli. Good night, I say, and remain standing at the window (the last spectator).

the fox

The opening and closing of the bathroom door, then the night. The yellow church on the other side of the lake has long since ceased to glow. It's dark, the coffee was too much. Shitty City is the name of the Polaroid, and Shitty City is the name of Kiki's

painting in the kitchen (her signature is missing). Shitty City is the
Astroland chapter that Tuuli read to me. The story of the turn of a
year in Finland. I'm lying on my back and listening to a nocturnal
motorboat far out on the lake, I gaze at the mobile in the dark,
Samuli, for a while I was still hearing sounds from the kitchen,
voices and glasses. I'm waiting for sleep. I think about Elisabeth,
about the unwritten profile, about my own story. Tuuli hasn't
come yet to get the boy, the door is wide open (I haven't heard
her singing). I'm lying awake and thinking about a series of New
Year's Eves, early New Year's Eves and fondue with my mother,
later with Hornberg and Eva at the Port of Hamburg, 2001 alone
in Berkeley, the first New Year's Eve with Elisabeth, but then my
thoughts find their way back to the supposedly perfect moment
in *Astroland*, the story told by Svensson and Tuuli and Kiki. But
Svensson's manuscript is now lying in Blaumeiser's suitcase and
waiting to be buried (Lua's coffin). The new computer is on the
desk (inner emptiness). I wonder whether Svensson has a copy
of *Astroland*. Kiki seems not to have read it, but she destroyed
the computer. Tuuli and I might be the only people who know
Astroland (I would be the one who didn't save it). I turn Tuuli's
hairpin in my fingers. The suitcase is on the boat, in it the perfect
moment and Tuuli's prophesy of its passing. The house is asleep,
so I get up. On the desk in front of me the two research folders:
I open them and take out the photocopied material. With super-
ficially researched information on Svensson I came here, I will
leave with his story. My journalistic precision: I will exchange
page by page (Svensson won't notice). I creep out of the house,
past Tuuli's open door, past Kiki and Svensson and Bella's room,
then through the kitchen and the large room on the ground floor.
Nothing. I slide open the glass door and walk barefoot through
the damp grass. I notice my fear of Lua, the dead watchdog, of his

bark, of his teeth. I walk on nonetheless, and only stop when the floodlight on the house suddenly again illuminates the property as bright as day. Everyone will be able to see me, I think, and once my eyes have adjusted to the brightness, I notice the fox next to the Fiat, stiff as I, frightened as I (the brownish red fur shaggy, its eyes are glowing in the floodlight).

Shitty Paradise City

As fast as the light came, the fox is gone again (we stared into each other's eyes). I walk to the edge of the property and wait for the darkness. When the floodlight goes out, I decide to take the risk (I have to be fast to avoid notice). I inhale and run to the dock. With a slight delay the light flashes on, I jump into the boat and duck as low as possible. The suitcase is now lying in Lua's spot in the stern. After a few seconds the light disappears, and because I approach the suitcase in slow motion, it stays dark. I take Tuuli's hairpin out of my pants pocket, I exhale, I turn it in the suitcase's lock and feel the slight resistance of the metal (I've been practicing the movement for days). I keep turning, the lock opens with a soft click (even in the moonlight "Felix Blaumeiser" can be read on the tag). *Macumba* is rocking, I balance out the automatic light. In the shallow water near the shore, the swan is sleeping, its head under its wings. I open the suitcase. Only a single cicada is louder than my research. Wrapped in the blanket, Lua is lying stiff and strangely bent between oleander flowers and paper and is pretending to be asleep (*Astroland* under his head a pillow, stuffed with memory). I have to lift up his bony head briefly so as to be able to pull away the manuscript under him. In the moonlight Lua seems to nod, his fur has grown cold (the ethnologist as grave robber). Despite the darkness, I find the chapters I'm looking for, and replace them page by page with photocopied book plugs, reviews, brief bios. Then I wrap up the manuscript again and push it under the black dog's head. I'm careful not to bend his ears, I stroke his snout, I wish the brave Lua a good night. *Älä pelkää*, Lua, I say, sleep well, you've earned it.

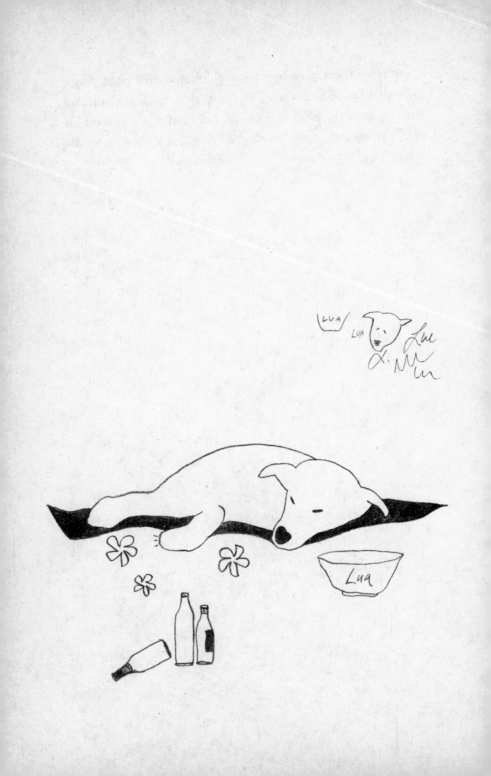

Shitty City 2000

WHAT YOU DON'T HOLD ON TO DISAPPEARS. A HOTEL ROOM ON the second floor, a clock was ticking. I lay between Felix and Tuuli and smelled the darkness yawning. A double bed and Tuuli's hand on my neck, her smell in my ear and Felix's leg over mine. It's bitterly cold in Oulu, I thought, and the darkness is a black dog. We lay under blankets and jackets, the heat vent was breathing dryly and uselessly, at midnight the champagne in the glasses was frozen. The darkness rose and sank calmly, through the closed blinds fell the red remains of the neon sign next door: *Ravintola*, firecrackers exploded on the street. The darkness lay at our feet. Felix: in this cold having your own fur doesn't help anymore. So he put his blue parka on Lua and tied the left sleeve in a knot. Lua lay there like a disabled veteran. In this cold only liquor and other bodies help, said Felix, at which point Lua yawned and I could smell his yawn, it must have been morning now, even if I couldn't see the clock, the morning of the first day of the new year, and I asked into the dark, is anyone hungry? and Tuuli said, breakfast for three.

The bright light downstairs in the lobby: three anti-depression lamps over the buffet. In the constant night of the train station hotel Turisti there was only a Japanese man in a Santa Claus costume sitting at a table and drinking his Crazy Reindeer as he'd been doing last night. He blew a streamer toward me. At reception a woman with a fur cap and a cigarette was mopping the remnants of New Year's Eve off the floor, the cleaning bucket was boiling, the water was steaming on the linoleum. Outside the window someone had spray-painted black letters on the wall across from the hotel: *Paska kaupunki*. I loaded up a tray. Breakfast for three, Tuuli had said, so I took toast for three and cranberry marmalade and butter and milk, corn flakes and coffee and packaged cheese on a stick. Lua liked Lapin Kulta beer, so I took a few cans, Tuuli loved apples, I took a Braeburn. Then: two vodkas in little plastic bottles and orange juice, because Felix chased liquor with juice. I took the last three mandarin oranges and juggled, then one fell on the floor and rolled to the feet of the cleaning woman with the cap. The Japanese man was waiting in the Finnish night and humming in the empty lobby, he was waiting for the air guitar world championships of Oulu and for the next morning sometime in March, he was sitting in the antidepressant light of the hotel lobby and plucking Guns n' Roses on his invisible instrument. Breakfast wasn't included here, I paid at reception and got permission to take the toaster with me. Shitty city, said the woman with the cap, when I asked about the writing on the wall, *paska kaupunki* means shitty city.

At least this: Felix with the Polaroid camera. In the room the breakfast was waiting on the floor, I was standing by the window and observing the frost patterns on the glass. The snow on the train station plaza was glowing orange, we could still hear individual firecrackers exploding and shards clinking. Behind me Tuuli and Felix lay intertwined in the blankets and jackets. Our car was parked under the streetlamp, freezing. We'd come from Rovaniemi, we were on the way to Helsinki, now we were stuck in Oulu, because the car couldn't go on at thirty-nine degrees below zero. The coldest day of the year. In Rovaniemi Tuuli's father had a snail farm, and in the winter he sold the deep-frozen animals in the shopping mall, eat, eat, he said on Christmas, please eat! Breakfast! I said now, opening a can of Lapin Kulta for the dog, please eat! Lua woke up and rolled off the bed, under Felix's hood he looked like a monk. Tuuli reached out her hand to me, and I poured the beer in Lua's plastic bowl. The monk drank beer, the disabled veteran greedily emptied the bowl, my thermal underwear struck sparks into the darkness as I took off my ski pants and Tuuli's hand followed into her cave of blankets and jackets. Tuuli's smell might have condensed, she bit into the apple, and Felix said: stay still! The coffee's getting cold, I said to Tuuli's mouth, and her warm tongue made the word "cold" melt. I drank the apple taste from her mouth. Felix put aside the camera, his hand moved between Tuuli's legs, our breath hung over us in the cold like a cloud, Lua drank his New Year's beer, firecrackers exploded, we wore our caps. We are here, said the dog, lying down in front of his bowl, we are here where we belong.

We leaned our heads together, and Felix held up one picture after another over us. Santa Claus is waiting down in the lobby, I said. Once, whispered Tuuli, Santa Claus wore a white coat and shone in the sky like the brightest star with the longest tail. Tuuli took Felix's right hand and my left in her small fingers, I could smell Felix's liquor breath and Tuuli like hot lemonade on his fingers. Santa Claus rode on his noblest elk, whispered Tuuli, the most faithful animal with fur like snow and a heart of gold, it carried him everywhere and always brought him back home. But one day they ended up in the worst snowstorm since the beginning of time. Tuuli's fingers trembled. It was so terribly cold that the lakes froze to the bottom and the air cracked. Santa Claus and his faithful friend were buried in the high snow of Rovaniemi and looked death in the eye, his red beard turned to ice, and his heart froze. If we warm each other, master, said the elk, then we'll live.

But Santa Claus grabbed an icicle and stabbed the elk with his fur like snow and his heart of gold, he opened the soft belly with a sharp shard, he buried himself inside the animal, he soaked his white coat in warm blood, he slept between the stomach and the heart of his faithful friend and so survived the cold and the storm. On the street someone was shooting flares, and we read the colors on the walls of the room. Nothing, said Tuuli, nothing is true and nothing lasts forever. We're not alone, said Felix, clasping our hands, we're three. *Paska kaupunki*, said Lua on the floor. Felix threw aside the blanket and got up, take me down to the paradise city. The cold crept between our bodies. A good year, said Tuuli, kissing me on the forehead and Felix on the neck, happy New Year, you two. My loves, she said.

Hotel Stella D'Italia

Ubicazione Esercizio - Luogo conservazione documenti fiscali

S. MAMETE - VALSOLDA (CO) - P.zza Roma, 1 - ✆ 0344 / 68139

GESTIONI ALBERGHIERE S.R.L.

S. MAMETE - VALSOLDA (CO) - Piazza Roma, 1

C. F. - P. IVA 02286510132

Cap. Soc. € 10.329,14 i.v. - Reg. Imprese CCIAA Como n. 10576 del 03/02/97

☒ RICEVUTA FISCALE	*Feb* ☒ N.	31
☐ FATTURA (ricevuta fiscale)		

20 MIL 13.X1.1979 2.7.1980 - 15.1.1981 - 28.1.1981 LEGGE 30.12.1991 n. 413

XAAA   32368 / **..**   Data *18/08/2004*

CLIENTE (Ditta, residenza o domicilio)

Codice Fiscale - Partita I.V.A.

QUANTITÀ	NATURA E QUALITÀ DEI BENI O DEI SERVIZI	IMPORTO
	Per N. _____ pasti completi	
	Thuli	*Jonsson*
	Per N. _____ giorni di pensione mezza / intera	
	Per N. _____ pernottamenti	
2)	Pane - coperto	1.80
1	Vino	6.00
1	Acqua	25.00
2)	Antipasto	
	1° Piatto	37.50
2	2° Piatto	
	Contorno	*blue top*
	Formaggio	
	Frutta	*red middle*
	Dessert	*yellow*
	Liquori	*bottom*
	Caffè	

DETTAGLIO IVA			Corrispettivo pagato	84,50
ALIQUOTA	IMPONIBILE	IMPOSTA		
ALIQUOTA	IMPONIBILE	IMPOSTA	Corrispettivo non pagato	
			Totale documento	84,50
Totale				

Tip. GRAPHIC 3 s n.c. di Abbate Francesco e C. - Mezzegra (Co) - Via degli Artigiani, 8 - CF/P. IVA 01286730130

Autorizzazione Ministero Finanze N. 352046 del 7/6/1982

August 10, 2005

(Funeral for a dog)

Wednesday. Today I'm leaving. I've put my shirt with the red wine stains back on and folded the shirt I borrowed from Svensson. Packed the cigarettes back in the plastic bag, the *Süddeutsche Zeitung* of August 6–7, 2005, the grocery receipt and Kiki's sketches, *Astroland* (hidden in the black research folders). Looked up the departure times of the ferry to Lugano: Porlezza 13:05, Osteno 13:20. The last notebook is lying on the desk in front of me, next to it six postcards:

1. *Hamburg Volkspark Stadium*, aerial view, 1999
2. *Monte Brè at Evening*, poster by Daniele Buzzi, 1950
3. *Vaccatione en Svizzera*, illustrator unknown, 1925
4. *Ticino Village Scene*, poster by Daniele Buzzi, 1943
5. *Caffè del Porto*, b/w photograph, "Invierno 1939/40"
6. *Monte Brè at Morning*, poster by Daniele Buzzi, 1950

Meanwhile I'm listening to Kiki in the kitchen clearing away yesterday evening. Tuuli must have come to get Samy at some point without waking me. The door is closed. Svensson has written down his love for Tuuli and Blaumeiser, he has frozen it: the morning of the coldest night of the year at a train station hotel in the Finnish city of Oulu, liquor for breakfast, coffee and apples (I calculate: Samy will have been conceived shortly thereafter). I've gone over Svensson's story in my head, instead of Dirk Svensson his manuscript answered my questions (several things unresolved). By the shore Kiki is gathering the empty bottles from the tables. Our lives consist of chance occurrences and possibilities. I, too, could have lived in Oulu, Seraverde, or New York, met Tuuli in Hamburg, maybe Kiki in New York, Lua, Samy, and Bella (I could have been Svensson). Probably Svensson has at some point asked himself the same questions I'm asking myself now: when to leave, when to stay? What to remember, what to write down? I've made a note: Svensson and I struggle as everyone struggles, I've taken down: Svensson is no stranger than I am (our dwindling possibilities, our paths not taken). Svensson has ended up in this house on the lake. He has written himself, in what he regards as the right way (*Astroland*), he has simplified what would be too sad.

Svensson is renovating his ruin.

Over the lake the heron again and its extremely slow flight, its wings paddle and stir in the air. Lua is dead, time refuses and doesn't stand still. Every decision is a step toward the end, I think (I've marked down the grief over that). I observe my fingers, how they write my own words in my own notebook. Daniel Mandelkern is Daniel Mandelkern, I write

Elisabeth
Elisabeth
Elisabeth

even though I can't help finding that melodramatic. My new courage for pathos: Svensson's desk, the lake outside the window, the empty shelves, wasps, swallows, pigeon droppings, the swan.

The dusty border around the spot where the suitcase was (Lua and I are departing). I close my notebook, do a few push-ups, I take my plastic bag and carefully close the door to Svensson's room so I don't wake anyone (the door to another life).

Franz Schubert, *sings Elisabeth*

In the kitchen the radio is playing softly, piano, in the intervals Italian-language news. Tuuli is still asleep, says Kiki, without looking at me and my plastic bag, the kids too, only Svensson is already on the way to Porlezza, he needs his run. Kiki is wearing men's pajamas and ballerina flats, she presses a dish towel into my hand, in front of us lie plates and bowls and glasses from the party. I dry the first plate that Kiki holds out to me (white porcelain, red flowers). I'm leaving, I say, I've already been here too long. Kiki shakes her head and laughs, stay, she says, no problem (it doesn't seem to strike her as strange to have a journalist in the house). So when is the profile going to appear? she asks, handing me the next plate from the sudsy water (blue earthenware). I take it, hold it for a few seconds in my hands, and while my head is trying to formulate a journalistic answer (date and length and potential visual material), my mouth utters a different certainty:

I'm not going to write the profile.

And even though Kiki's "I thought so" surprises me, I stand in front of her on the warm kitchen tiles as I stood next to Tuuli a few days ago and listen to my reasons: I mention the ruin and the calm of the lake, I describe my scientific eye in general and my ethnological gaze in particular, I describe the presence of the children, the water, and the mountains, I mention Tuuli and the notes I've compiled so far, which are not really ethnological, but not journalistic either. I explain that I've stumbled into the personal (Mandelkern's ethnological dilemma). As I talk and stack the dishes neatly in the cabinets, I believe myself (arguments and household effects). I want to go back to Hamburg, I explain in Kiki's kitchen, I have to inform my wife that the article isn't going to appear, I have to call Professor Jansen (she doesn't know who Professor Jansen is). Speaking of my wife: I hint at Elisabeth and the child she wants from me, I talk about the mixing of work and private life. The music on the radio suddenly sounds like Schubert. I go to the radio and turn up the volume: not "The Linden Tree," but one of Elisabeth's songs (her voice in me sings the lyrics to it). Kiki listens to my chatter, Schubert sounds like Elisabeth. I actually talk about love. Suddenly the desire to finally return to her, on any ship, bus, train, or airplane whatsoever (every song sounds like her). I stand still and observe Kiki's hands in the dishwater, the paint on her fingers doesn't come off even in warm water. What's going to happen now with the dog? I finally ask, so as to turn the conversation away from me, the suitcase is still down by the water. Kiki gives me the next plate as if I were staying. What's going to happen now with the dog? I repeat into our dishwashing, but Kiki points to the kettle on the stove, which begins to whistle now, of all times. She takes the fresh dishwater from the stove and resumes our conversation of yesterday:

Dirk Svensson and Felix Blaumeiser

were opposites, Kiki tells me, she says so even though she never saw Blaumeiser alive and even his corpse she saw for only a few minutes. Kiki squirts German dishwashing soap into Italian water. Even in a white shirt and the dark coffin, despite the unconcealable head injury, Blaumeiser appeared reckless and carefree, a joyful drinker, a blond surfer, a stoner, a blue-eyed daredevil, as far as I'm concerned, says Kiki (a popular kid). Svensson has told her their twenty-year history (in detail, let me tell you). Svensson's family isn't rich, but Blaumeiser's is. Kiki nods out the window, Felix's parents still spend the late summer over there in Cima di Porlezza, Kiki says, even though their son died there. In any case, Svensson and she got this boathouse here rent-free. That's how the Blaumeiser family is, she explains with her hands in the dishwater, no melancholy, completely unsentimental. Felix was the exact same way, she says (the Svensson family is the exact opposite). Kiki rinses and rinses, I dry the dishes from the dinner that turned into a farewell party. Blaumeiser died of a head injury? I ask, taking another plate from Kiki's hands. You want the whole story? she replies, and I say, yes, very much (my new main informant).

Well, then:

Svensson and she were finished with New York and Chicago, they'd just come to Berlin, when Svensson got a phone call from Felix. At that point they'd thought of Berlin as their city, Svensson was working at night in a hotel on Potsdamer Platz and writing during the day, she applied to the Academy of Fine Arts. *The Story of Leo and the Notmuch*? No, Kiki smiles, he was working on his stories (the first draft of his book). And the phone call? Kiki takes her hands out of the water, dries her fingers on her pajama pants, and points to the house below the yellow church: the phone call was an invitation to come here to Lake Lugano, to Felix's parents' house. Svensson heard from Felix and Tuuli for the first time since September 2001 in New York. By telephone, as if nothing had happened. There was something to celebrate, Felix said: he was going to marry Tuuli. She didn't know anything about it yet, but he'd prepared everything. Felix was apparently a person, says Kiki, who was confident he could always turn things to good account. Because everything always effortlessly sorted itself out for him. On the phone he spoke about a few days on the lake, about his joy and Samy, about Hamburg, where Tuuli and he were living at the time. She was studying again, Felix said, he was taking photographs again. He was calling because he needed a best man! And who would be a more suitable choice than Svensson, Felix asked, no one! Svensson, of all people! She herself was curious, of course, says Kiki in her kitchen, she knew only the difficult constellation of the three, and now there was going to be a wedding (the Borromean rings, for Christ's sake). Felix threw in that Svensson should of course bring along whomever he was currently living with (that would be me, says Kiki). Two weeks later Svensson took the first train to Frankfurt, where he was meeting Tuuli. She remembers the exact date, August 6, 2002. In Frankfurt Svensson was supposed to meet Tuuli and drive with her to the lake as a diversion from the surprise. That too was Felix's idea. Kiki smiles. She herself preferred to travel to Lugano at night and by train, to stay out of the way of conciliatory words between the two of them (everyone has to clean up his own mess). During the first days of August, as the day of the trip approached, she could sense Svensson's impatience more distinctly each day. He worked day and night on his book and was nervous when he and Lua boarded the train to Frankfurt at the Ostbahnhof early in the morning, the manuscript in his bag and the end of the story already in sight (he had planned a happy ending, says Kiki, but never finished the book, I guess). Svensson spoke of the feeling of a homecoming.

On the sixth of August she stood at the Ostbahnhof and waved to Svensson and Lua, though only with a napkin from the Viennese pastry shop. She wasn't worried at all. Kiki unscrews the espresso pot and asks whether I'd like some coffee. Yes, please. Then Svensson called her from Frankfurt, later from a rest area on the A5 near Ringsheim. Their conversation felt artificial, says Kiki in the kitchen with a laugh, almost unreal. To meet Tuuli and the boy was simpler than expected, Svensson reported on the phone, both were healthy, their conversations were pleasant, and Tuuli didn't have the slightest suspicion of Felix's wedding plan. Then he whispered: the question of who the father was hadn't come up yet (well, then, does he look like you, idiot? she asked him, does he seem like your son to you?). Felix and Tuuli had a new car, by the way, he then said at a normal volume again over the roar of the autobahn in the background, a blue Fiat 128 L (the chicken coop outside). Svensson had never been interested in cars and vehicles. In the late afternoon he called again, this time from an amusement park just a few kilometers from the rest area. He seemed in high spirits to her, says Kiki, he said that Tuuli and he were now going to ride the roller coaster. Since she's known him, Svensson has had a weakness for roller coasters and amusement parks (I've read about that). Wasn't Felix waiting for them on the lake? she asked, but instead of answering, Svensson described to her the foam rubber mascot at the entrance to the amusement park, a giant mouse. The Europa-Park in Rust was a permanent carnival like Astroland in Coney Island, he said, only German and without the ocean. Very close to the phone she heard Samy crying, along with a barrel organ and screaming children (roller-coaster screams from summers past, Kiki says in English). Svensson kept coming back to that mouse (*Astroland* breaks off here). Jealousy isn't her thing, says Kiki, and tries to pour the coffee into two clean cups, but the coffee spills out the side of the metal pot and over her fingers. Holy fuck! Kiki jumps up and holds her fingers under the cold water. She tries to smile, holy fuck! (That crappy mouse, she smiles, that Euromouse.) She still had a few things to do before her own train's departure and so didn't give it any thought later when Svensson's telephone was turned off. When she boarded the night train to Lugano, she tried again. Svensson's voice sounded distinctly softer, but content: she shouldn't worry, they'd eaten cotton candy, they'd taken turns riding the roller coaster and watching the boy. Eventually they couldn't bear any more loop-the-loops and talked instead until the park closed. They'd straightened everything out. To recover from all the loops and words they were now in a hotel room at the amusement park, Tuuli had insisted: she needed sleep. On his arm the child hadn't cried a single tear yet, Svensson reported. He was sitting in the bathroom to avoid disturbing her. Yes, Tuuli had kissed him, Svensson then whispered, and he'd only belatedly resisted, but with this kiss he'd meant Kiki. Kiki wraps her hand in a wet dish towel (as long as they didn't stay in fucking room 219, she says, Svensson has a knack for symbols). They were going to get back on the road immediately to meet her toward morning in Lugano. This decision he'd made in the exact second of the kiss. I believe him, says Kiki (I must have meant Elisabeth when I kissed Tuuli).

the lake awakens

Outside on the water a single Jet Ski, a wasp lands on the kitchen table, finds nothing, and flies away again. On the radio there's talk of rainfall in central Switzerland, but on Lago di Lugano the sun is shining as it has been for days. The leaves of the sycamore rustle, then the bells toll in Osteno, and seconds later on the opposite shore in Cima or San Mamete (in the distance the clocks run differently). I finish the dishwashing and fill the cups with milk and coffee. Lua is going to be buried today. I'll leave Svensson and the dog alone, in the Hotel Lido Seegarten I'll pick up my baggage, toward evening I'll be in Hamburg. I hear Kiki and Bella in their bedroom, their footsteps on the stairs, then mother and daughter are standing in the doorway, Bella on Kiki's hip. It's not so bad, she says, as I look at her bandaged finger. Kiki takes a sip of her coffee and nods when I ask about the end of the story.

Interview (the whole story)

KIKI: You won't write about this, right?

MANDELKERN: No.

K: Good. When I got off the train early in the morning at the Lugano train station, Svensson was standing on the platform with a stuffed animal, the Euromaus. He seemed tired, but somehow cheerful, he said he was happy. Tuuli was waiting outside in the parking lot, the Fiat was much too small for three adults, a child, and a dog. I had to squeeze in between the child safety seat and bags, stupid Italian cars! Tuuli greeted me, reservedly but not impolitely. We drove down the mountain to the lake, along the lakeside promenade and then beyond Castagnola up the serpentine roads to Monte Brè. Samy and Lua were sleeping like stones, the rest of us admired the sun and the cypresses, the white gates of the villas, the shimmering lake. The air felt clean, crisp, like it does after a storm. What really happened that night in the hotel room at the Europa-Park in Rust, why the two of them decided to eat cotton candy and keep Felix waiting with his surprise, is between them, you see? They don't know themselves, I guess. Tuuli and Svensson can't agree on the reason for the delay. Svensson says that on the long drive Tuuli was anxious to take a break so they could talk in peace, and Tuuli claims that Svensson was anxious to ride the carousel, which seems reasonable. Both blame the other, probably they're both right and wrong. In any case I was lying in the night train to Lugano and couldn't sleep. To make a long story short: what was said or straightened out or done that night is at least the reason the blue Fiat arrived twelve hours late in Lugano, early in the morning on August 7. We then drove through this sixties-style residential area above Castagnola, when Tuuli suddenly said into the lake view that she couldn't reach Felix, not on his cell phone, not in the house either. He must be worried, she said. Svensson laughed, Felix Blaumeiser never worries! When we arrived at the road's highest point, we could see to the end of the lake for the first time. We were like birds, Daniel! On the way down to the shore, through the tunnels, Tuuli then drove much too fast. All of a sudden there was a disconcertingly cheerful tension in the air, a weird lightheartedness. We crossed the Italian border without being stopped, the border guards winked at Tuuli and waved. *Buon giorno la bionda!* For the narrow village roads and the sharp curves the Fiat was perfect, Svensson rolled down the window and Tuuli honked like an Italian. We drove past the small ports, Albogasio and San Mamete, Castello above us on the mountain. At the Stella D'Italia we noticed a runover cat, right by the hospital, Croce Rossa Italiana, just before the Chinese restaurant. Svensson told jokes, and the closer we came to the end of the lake, the louder Tuuli laughed, you could tell they were hoping to be happy. I let myself be carried away by all this, everything struck me as more genuine than in the travel brochures, the mountains, the lake, the old villages.

Then Tuuli stopped suddenly at a large yellow villa, Lua and Samy woke up. Svensson turned around and grinned at me. I remember perfectly the crunch of the tires on the white gravel, I was surprised by the size of the house. The billowing curtains in the open windows! Lua jumped out of the car and immediately ran down to the water. The terrace doors stood open, the car doors too, oleander in the terra-cotta pots along the path, red and white. On the white pebbles there was a colorful trail of confetti leading from the house down to the shore. I was completely overwhelmed by so much storybook Europe, Lua's barking by the water sounded like he was barking into a bucket, hollow and artificial. Holding Samy, Tuuli walked across the veranda and followed Lua to the water. She sang Felix's name, her voice like dripping water. When there was no reply to this singing, her shouting for Svensson finally came loudly and clearly. I entered the house after Svensson through the terrace door, Tuuli was following the confetti trail to the water, half walking, half running. On the set table, among confetti, streamers, and burned-down candles, there was a piece of paper. Next to it two party hats. The table completely bedecked with expensive dishes and cut glass along with a decoration kit from the supermarket, corny, Daniel, you wouldn't believe it. No rings, Felix's penchant for symbolism didn't extend to that. It was as if the marriage proposal were supposed to be made ironically, Felix must have been absolutely confident. Almost as if he found these industrially manufactured and plastic-wrapped gestures more appropriate than a serious one. Almost as if a few party hats would be enough to turn things to good account. Felix wanted merely to sketch this big step. So between expensive dishes and cheap decorations there was a note.

M: From Blaumeiser?

K: His handwriting wasn't proficient, blue ballpoint-pen ink on thin, lined paper. I didn't read the note, but Svensson's fingers on my back trembled as he read. The air smelled of candle wax and standing lake water, I remember that perfectly, deck chairs and cigarettes. That we didn't put on or even touch the party hats on the kitchen table, one blue, the other pink. An absolute silence despite the occasional cars and birds. Then: Tuuli's abrupt and brief scream, but that's not the right word, she howled. A horrible sound! Svensson and I ran after the scream and Lua's barking, following the confetti trail, all over the garden furniture streamers and candles and lamps along the path. Even though the sun was shining, just like right now, Daniel, just like today.

Milk?

At this moment Samy is standing in the room and rubbing his eyes. Kiki and I didn't hear his footsteps. She interrupts her story, gets up and bends down to the boy. Milk? she asks, and Samy nods. Kiki puts a glass on the table, she gets crayons and paper, she sits the boy on my knee and says

Lua is dead,

but he wasn't sad and fell asleep peacefully, because everyone was with him. The boy takes a sip of his milk. Did he want to make the dog a farewell gift? She heard he could already draw, says Kiki, and Samy nods absently (so early in the morning he can't understand death). Kiki gets up.

Interview (main informant Kiki Kaufman)

KIKI: Felix Blaumeiser was lying next to *Macumba* on his belly in the shallow water, his left leg twisted, his shoelaces caught in the the oarlock, navy blue Converse like two pigeons. On the floor of the boat bottles were banging together, Samy was screaming, little children always cry with their mothers. Tuuli and Svensson were kneeling on the slippery concrete of the boat ramp, she was holding Felix's head, and he was feeling around frantically on Felix with his fingers, the learned procedures couldn't bring Felix back. Svensson tried again and again to detach his shoelaces from the boat. Pale streamers were wrapped around Felix's neck, he was wearing a sodden party hat with an elastic band and his white polo shirt had turned pink and yellow and blue, the bottles were banging and rattling and clinking, two bottles of Veuve Clicquot and one wine bottle, all empty. Above Felix's right eye was a bump, the water had already washed off or diluted the blood. The bluish shards of a bottle of Bombay Sapphire were shimmering in the water.

MANDELKERN: An accident?

K: Svensson called the police and the ambulance, yes, he used the words "accident" and "*Unfall*" when he did so. The swan hissed, Lua barked. The sirens along the shore got closer and closer, Samy was hungry and cried, a bizzare peace hung over everything, as if something had occurred that everyone had long been expecting. The emergency doctor put his finger on Felix Blaumeiser's neck and declared him dead, but it was Tuuli who closed his eyes. I was standing next to them with Samy, but I didn't get what was going on, we were paralyzed. The forensic specialists in Como handled the case, and the police investigations didn't last long either. Felix's blood alcohol content was high, but not deadly. His shoelaces had gotten caught, he must have fallen and hit his head on the concrete, but his skull hadn't been fractured. Felix didn't die of an injury. He simply lay unconscious in the water and drowned. An accident, yes.

M: And then?

K: The next afternoon the police briefly questioned us again, this time with three interpreters from Lugano. Tuuli, Svensson, and I gave statements about our versions of the day in our native languages, we didn't exactly understand one another in the process. When a policeman inquired what it was that was actually supposed to be celebrated here, Tuuli still didn't know the answer to this question, but Svensson mentioned the surprise: engagement. Tuuli suddenly realized that she'd been eating cotton candy with Svensson instead of getting a marriage proposal from Felix. The paralysis turned into a brief and fierce quarrel, Tuuli stood on the terrace and screamed. Svensson had never been able to be as spontaneous and carefree as Felix, and now, of all times, he'd wanted to ride the roller coaster, a fatal roller coaster. He'd wanted to talk about their love! He'd kissed her! He'd wanted to prevent this marriage! Because of him they'd kept Felix waiting, he'd indirectly killed him! And so on. Svensson shouted back that she'd turned off both their phones, that she'd had to explain to him on the way to Felix's, of all times, that they were three and not alone. Still! Felix and Kiki were waiting, he'd said. Then he hadn't kissed her, but she him. In confusion he'd bought beer and cotton candy, and when he could no longer drive, she'd refused. Even though they'd run out of words and there was nothing more to explain besides the end of the past and the beginning of the future. But that was impossible after Felix's death, because without him they could neither finish nor start anew. Tuuli screamed and howled, she called Felix and Svensson accomplices, she blamed both of them for her sorrow. She would have said yes, I assume. Then she lay down in Felix's room and slept for two days. It was a tragic accident, the two of them have been grappling with the consquences to this day. I have no idea who's right, not the slightest idea, Daniel. Svensson took care of Samy during those days, he sat down next to the baby carriage on the dock and filled up page after page of a whole notepad. Then he crumpled every single page and threw them into the lake. For two days I waited for the arrival of Felix's parents and the release of the corpse. I tried to sort all that out, eventually gave up and cleaned up the house. I just believe him. The parents decided very pragmatically on cremation. Not without discussions, Svensson was for a burial. At the cremation an Italian priest spoke Italian and Latin, I understood only snatches. We were allowed to see the corpse, Tuuli surpassed Svensson in staring, he pressed his forehead to Felix's forehead and remained like that for a few moments, it felt like forever. Felix was wearing a white shirt, the coffin was some sort of expensive tropical wood. The ashes were then scattered one or two days later at the deepest point in the lake, illegally, of course. No one will notice, said Felix's father, the fine is affordable, the lake will keep it a secret. Tuuli left with Samy directly after the ceremony, she seemed sobered and was anxious to put affairs in order in Germany. Svensson and I stayed awhile longer. He mowed the lawn and trimmed the hedges, I took pictures, he refurbished the boat and repaired the motor, we climbed the Monte dei Pizzoni with Lua. Svensson wanted to work with his hands rather than with his head. Blaumeiser's parents then offered us the unused house here. Nobody ever used it but Felix, you know. Our last night on the lake, two weeks after Felix's death, Svensson translated the note for me, I know it by heart: "My dearest bride, dear best man," he said, "I am celebrating our engagement today and since you are late, idiots, I will have to drink everything by myself. In case you should arrive, come down to the water, chin-chin & much love, Felix."

garbage bags and oleander

We put away the remaining dishes in the cabinets, we mop the floor, we help Samy with his farewell gift, we wait for Svensson. Kiki has told me everything. We move on to simple subjects, foreign languages and boats and baby food. Around noon Tuuli's singing from upstairs, her cigarette-lighting in the kitchen and her forehead-kissing (smoking, she kisses first the boy, then me on the forehead!). On the lake a pleasure steamer is chugging, Samy explains his picture: Lua in his spot on the boat, his flowers, a can of his favorite beer (I drew the oleander). Suddenly Svensson is standing in a sweaty basketball jersey in the doorway to the kitchen: could someone help him with the dog? Sit down first, says Kiki, Tuuli nods in her green nightshirt (the sun at her bare feet). Svensson sits down at the table, he drinks the glass of milk that Kiki hands to him, he buries his face briefly in his hands. Then he looks up and gazes at the boy and his picture. He looks tired. For the first time I understand that Svensson strikes me as much older than he is (the years cling to him). I sit on my chair and observe these people, how they're still sitting barefoot around a table and drinking coffee, in the smoke of the past years, with sleep-creased faces and unbrushed teeth. On the fridge hangs Felix Blaumeiser's smile, on the picture on the wall the red wine

has dried, down by the water waits the suitcase with the dead
dog, and Svensson in the kitchen pours Tuuli coffee, because he
knows how she likes it: with milk and no sugar. She takes the
cup without a word. Kiki sets plates on the table in front of us,
Svensson gets knives from the drawer, Tuuli wipes pap off Bella's
chin. Life goes on, between pictures and children, between plates
and cups and animals, between chairs and oleander, between the
dead and ghosts and stories. I want to go back to mine. I take the
pack of cigarettes out of the plastic bag and put it on the table in
front of Tuuli.

I have to go!

I say into the kitchen and point first to my dirty shirt, then to the
plastic bag: I'm four days late. The people look up from their life.
Svensson doesn't contradict me, and Kiki puts the milk in the
fridge. *Manteli?* Tuuli asks with her mouth full, pointing to the
cigarettes. I don't actually smoke, I say. She takes a crayon and
pulls the newspaper out of my bag, she writes two phone numbers
on the front page. "Air in Sunken Mini-Submarine Running Out,"
I read, and wonder whether the air will have lasted long enough
for the eight Russian crew members, I'll be able to find out. I
read "Caesarean Risk," before my eyes the sticky Renault under
the trees of Bismarckstrasse, Elisabeth, the linden blood on the
windows, the green of the chestnut trees. Tuuli folds the newspaper and pushes it back into the bag, from up close I smell sleep
and smoke and milk. Call me if you're in Berlin, she says, the first
number is my cell phone, the second the office number in the
Charité. She takes Samy from my knee, I stand up and reach for
the bag. It would be my pleasure! Thank you, I say, and then Tuuli
stretches herself toward me and kisses me a bit too clearly on the

mouth, as if the others weren't there. Kiki's voice interrupts us: are you taking Lua to the vet? she asks, and Svensson answers, yes, and says I could accompany him, half an hour won't make a difference at this point. Right, Mandelkern?

288 meters

Svensson pushes *Macumba* off the dock and pulls at the motor's cord. Now he's wearing a white shirt and gray pants as in the picture of him that people know (the picture of him that I had). The suitcase is now lying in the water on the floor of the boat. Tuuli didn't touch it, Kiki ran her fingers several times over the cracked leather. No one opened it. Samy's wearing the life vest again, he's holding his farewell gift in one hand and his fishing rod in the other as I hand him to Svensson on board (does he know about Lua in the suitcase?). The motor starts, and Svensson turns it as far as it will go, the screw whisks the green water, *Macumba* leans. The two women stand by the water and wave as they grow smaller (the dark green of the woods, the light green of the water). I'm sitting next to the child on the bench,

the small, pretty possibility on the shore

is the first to lower her hand, and I memorize the dark of her eyes, the green of her nightshirt and her Converse, next to her Kiki's bright dress. The mountain grows ever mightier and larger over the women as we move farther away from the shore (the possibilities are put in a different pespective). Samy is silent in the face of the wind and spray and gesticulating, with each wave Lua's suitcase slides closer to Svensson. The old man in the white shirt steers *Macumba* directly into the middle of the lake, past a few rocking sport boats in the late morning sun. I look for the heron and can't find it, but the houses on the opposite shore can be made out better than they could four days ago: the church of Cima, below it Blaumeiser's parents' house (how things acquire a story). In the wooden beat of the waves under the bottom of the boat, for the first time in weeks the feeling of heading in the right direction, but just as I'm about to ask where Svensson is going to bring me, he turns off the motor at full speed. *Macumba* glides another few meters, then we're standing still in the middle of the lake. The owners of the sport boats, tan and in too-skimpy bathing suits, seem to be trying to ignore us. During the ride Samy was clutching a handhold and trying to protect his picture from the lake water (he's forgotten the dead dog). Out here the water is a deep green, under us are more than two hundred meters of darkness. Samy seems to remember this position of the boat and moves closer to me. Now we can only vaguely perceive the women on the shore. *Macumba* drifts sideways into the waves, and Svensson has trouble keeping his balance. He kneels in the water on the floor, takes a small key out of his pocket and unlocks the suitcase. Are you afraid too, *Manteli*? asks Samy, and I answer, speaking more to myself than to him: we don't actually have to be afraid. When Svensson opens the suitcase, wilted oleander flowers fall on the floor of the boat. Svensson turns the suitcase so that Samy can't see Lua, and the dog's wrapped body remains hidden from me too (I know that his head is lying on *Astroland*, I see Svensson's watery eyes). We can now smell death. Can you give me the farewell gift? Svensson asks the boy, but Samy wants to explain his picture: this is the mountain, this is the lake, and this is Lua. He holds the paper out to Svensson, Svensson balances as he walks across the boat toward us and takes the picture from his hand: lots of blue, lots of green, lots of red (he doesn't have a black crayon).

When Samy asks about the dog, about his fear and his dying and where they will bury him, Svensson doesn't answer. The lake, the mountain, repeats the boy. Lua's happy with the picture, Svensson then says, Lua loves water (the paper a white flag in his hand). He bends down over the sodden suitcase, throws the blanket aside and presses his forehead to the dead animal's forehead (he wants to be sure that Lua existed). Svensson puts the picture in the suitcase, and Samy suddenly seems to understand that Svensson is not going to bury Lua like a normal pet (I suspected it).

Is Lua in there?

he asks. Yes, Svensson answers, and suddenly reaches again into Blaumeiser's well-traveled suitcase. He holds out the stack of paper *Astroland* to me. At one corner the paper is soaked, the water has already gotten into the suitcase. Can you hold this for a moment? he asks. Svensson is speaking with a calm voice, but his eyes are tearing. *Astroland*, he says, wiping his face with the back of his hand. Have you ever been to New York, Mandelkern? Yes, I say after a brief hesitation, I know the city (I could say that I know his story, that I've been with his characters in Seraverde, in Oulu and Coney Island). I've been there, I should have played Shoot the Freak, but only the can toss booth was open. Svensson laughs. I take the aborted manuscript from his hand, the words and sentences with which he has invented the past ten years of his life, I hold Svensson's story in one hand and my notebooks in the other (*Macumba* is rocking on Blaumeiser's grave). Svensson now smiles with tears in his eyes at Samy, and I understand that we aren't going to bring Lua to Porlezza: Svensson is not going to leave anything to the veterinarian as he promised Kiki, Lua will not be buried in a field behind Porlezza, he will not be cremated.

Svensson abruptly closes the suitcase over Lua. I think of the photocopied pages in his manuscript, the stolen pages in the research folders. Svensson now stares into my face and spits into the water. I wonder for a brief moment whether I would make it to the shore swimming, but Svensson takes *Astroland* from my hand, again opens the suitcase a crack and shakes his head. He puts his story in with Lua, snaps the suitcase shut once and for all, and locks it. Okay, Svensson says with a smile, okay then. He grabs the heavy suitcase and heaves it first onto the bench, then onto the railing. Svensson pauses one, maybe two seconds, then he lets go. *Macumba* sways. The boy seems surprised as the suitcase hits the water's surface with a thud and floats. Rocking, the black dog's coffin slowly recedes from Svensson's boat, leans slightly to one side and sinks so suddenly and swiftly that the dark shadow in the green water is only briefly visible. The stones pull Lua down, the oleander flowers sink with the black dog, the manuscript disappears at the deepest point in the lake. We're alone with the mountains and the water, the swan swims around the boat at an appropriate distance and Svensson finally wipes away Samy's tears (a few air bubbles still tell of Lua's life).

August 10, 2005

(Ceresio, 2,092 Words)

"Imbarcadero" is written on the sign above me (I'm leaving). Svensson and the boy drop me and my plastic bag off in Osteno. We're heading on to Porlezza now, says Svensson, to buy chickens. Right, Samy? Yes. The boy has stopped crying. We're buying two chickens, he repeats, and then we're going to catch fish! One fish or a hundred! I sit down on a bench on the quay and watch the two of them as they leave the port of Osteno (children's tears don't last long). I see the bright orange of the life vest and Svensson's white disappear, behind me a garbage truck and the hiss of its hydraulics. I'm again sitting on a bench under lindens and adding what there is to add. The garbage is getting picked up today, the black plastic bags of the Via San Rocco. Lua is dead, *Astroland* is buried. I've saved what I wanted to (what I consider decisive). In my pocket my ring and Tuuli's hairpin. We didn't say another word about my article (take care, Mandelkern).

Ceresio

At 13:20 my ship leaves. The bald captain greets me, I buy a ticket (18.60 Swiss francs for the way back). Besides me there are no passengers on board. *Ceresio* casts off and crosses the lake with a softly humming motor, the pleasure boats are still lying at anchor, even pedal boats. I sit down at a scratched-up wooden table on the foredeck in the sun and search the lake for *Macumba*. Nothing.

Svensson's house is lying in shadow as we pass the steep slopes of Monte Cecchi, it's scarcely distinguishable from the woods and the cliffs (Tuuli will be able to see the ship). I remember things, as I've learned from Svensson: the dock, the desk, the pigeon droppings, the pictures, the sycamore, Santuario di Nostra Signora della Caravina.

San Mamete 13:28

In the middle of the lake the hoarse horn. We're approaching San Mamete, the old plastic seats are shining in the sun and blinding me (life preservers and turned-off strings of lights). The captain throttles the motor and announces the old village, then he steers the ferry to the pier in back of Hotel Stella D'Italia (the bill in my bag). No one disembarks. The hotel guests on the terrace raise wine glasses to us, a few tourists board, two Americans, a senior hiking group, thermal shirts and blouses, the pale colors and empty mineral water cases in back of the houses (the inhabited side of the world is waiting for me). I turn back and can no longer make out Svensson's house. *Ceresio* passes the point where we just laid Lua to rest, as if nothing happened (on larger ships you don't feel the waves). Svensson sank his past, Kiki knows his secrets, Felix was scattered here (Samy is wearing a bright orange life vest). I wonder what death does to those who remain. Some want to forget, others inhabit the ruins. I think of Elisabeth's scar and her bloody-bitten lips as she told me about the child's death, about his gravestone and her husband (the fine cut on my lip has healed). Elisabeth and Tuuli are not similar, not their appearance, not their pragmatism, not their breasts, not their lips (golden pins for Tuuli's hair, Elisabeth's red, maybe copper). Elisabeth doesn't want to forget, she doesn't want to conceal anything, she doesn't want to consist of only memory. The hotel guests take photos of the few tourists, the few tourists take photos of the hotel guests. I've started the return journey into my life. I wonder what Elisabeth will say about all this.

Oria 13:35

In Oria the same ritual: the foghorn and its echo off the backs of the houses, this time a church directly on the water, a cemetery with urn compartments, in the church garden a fisherman. Old men in undershirts on plastic chairs, their feet in the water, cigarettes in their fingers (I don't smoke). As we dock on the pier, I notice a poster in the window of a dilapidated house:

Vendesi!
031 869 767
Telefono e Fax

and wonder whether I could pay the price for a life on the lake. But I admonish myself: I'm on the way back into the existence of an abortive ethnologist (real estate in Oria is not what I should be thinking about). Elisabeth's intern wanted to know whether ethnology was getting in my way. On the foredeck of *Ceresio* I wonder what I've actually been doing during the four days at Svensson's house on the lake. I didn't maintain distance, I should have answered the intern, I got closer to the ethnos. From my dissertation: "Ultimately the ethnologist always remains himself and thus a stranger, every ethnography remains subjective and more or less empathic, every image is selected and every word invented. It is always his own experience that the ethnologist brings with him: he himself is the object of every investigation, he is at once ethnographer of himself and recorder." And so on. I've stolen and kissed, I remember Geertz: "There are enormous difficulties in such an enterprise, methodological pitfalls to make a Freudian quake and some moral perplexities as well." In Oria more tourists board the ferry than at all the previous stations, the plastic seats around me fill up, a French couple wearing Breitling caps sits down in front of me and takes pictures with a digital camera. I've observed and participated, now I'm departing (the ethnologist is leaving the group under investigation). When *Ceresio* casts off again, the children on the pier wave, they jump into the water behind us (they're swimming in unknown memory).

Gandria Confine 13:40

We cross the Swiss border, the flags flutter, the stern of the boat full of seniors and families, hiking backpacks and ice cream cones, laughter and cameras. On the slope above us snakes the road Tuuli must have driven down too fast a few years ago. The border: a few hundred meters of underbrush and debris on a steep slope, mossy concrete buildings and moored boats of the Guardia di Finanza (no security check). In the enclosed part of the boat a Swiss woman is selling drinks, I buy a can of Diet Coke. On the red fake leather seats there are still a few empty spots, with the notebook on my knees I record: Writing by itself can't give meaning to one's experience. Writing is not true the way a can of Coke is true (my belch covered by my hand). When one compares one's life with what has been written, there remains a mere residue of similarity, not much. Dirk Svensson files things away, Daniel Mandelkern considers his possibilities, our words don't halt time (secretaries of disappearing).

Gandria 13:45

In Gandria boxes of empty bottles and shabby paper garlands over a wilted pergola (Ristorante Milago, Ristorante Antico, Ristorante Roccabella). Lugano is only a few stations away, Monte San Salvatore is directly in front of us (postcard stands, balloons, street musicians). This morning *Ceresio* dropped off the tourists on the way here. They've looked around and now want to be taken away again (in this they're no different than I). The midday sun vertical over the water, even in the shade it's very hot. Tuuli and Kiki will be sitting under the oleander and waiting for Svensson, Samy, and his freshly caught fish. (Tuuli will be smoking my cigarettes.) Svensson and I addressed each other by our last names, Lua has reached the bottom of the lake (take care, Mandelkern!). I will disembark in Lugano. On the pier of Gandria a boy, maybe three years old, is holding two balloons on red ribbons in his hands. When his mother tries to tie the red balloon to his wrist, the child is distracted for a brief moment: the other, green balloon slips out of his fingers and blows away over the tiled roofs of the village (barrel organ music). *Ceresio* takes leave of the village with a coughing horn and heads for Lugano. On the battered fake leather seats, between Americans and French people and Germans, I decide to switch to "you":

I'm not going to work for you anymore, Elisabeth.

I'm tired of newspaper pages, Elisabeth! Our life is not a brief article; it's a spiral, not a line. I've been taking notes for four days. I'm an ethnologist, Elisabeth, I'm not a journalist (I've observed and participated). I'm tired of editorial meetings, Elisabeth, I want a wife without word limits!

Castagnola 13:58

On the dock the cameras click for the young stoners and cliff divers. In front of the expensive villas on the slope cypresses stand in a row, behind them loiter oleanders, magnolias, and ginkgos, flights of steps and piano rooms. Here almost no one gets on or off, we're approaching the city (the Frenchwoman in front of me points her finger: *c'est Castagnola, il y a beaucoup de riches*). The teenagers plunge off the cliffs into the air, the passengers applaud. What I've learned: that I don't have to make such a big deal out of everything. That I misjudged Svensson. That I don't smoke. That time passes and doesn't come back. That I've found words for myself that I can't muster when I'm sitting opposite you (your green eyes). That it's not about 3,000 words. That I want to be understood by you. That I'm a back and forth, an either/or, a perhaps. That I will finally get to the bottom of myself. That I want to stay with you, Elisabeth. That I'm not afraid of children, Elisabeth. That I can decide when I have to (I can commit myself to things). That I miss your body, Elisabeth, that my body misses you.

Paradiso 14:08

Ceresio crosses the Gulf of Lugano, on the right the large hotels and yacht harbors, promenades and apartment buildings, the Hotel Eden and its over-the-top fountain. In Paradiso I disembark because Paradiso is an appropriate place to disembark. I buy another postcard and ask the salesman about the Hotel Lido Seegarten (image: Porlezza, 2001). On the other end of the city. This time I walk, past construction sites and gravelly lakeside paths, past dredges and rusty pedal boats. A few children are playing with empty Coke cans and ask for change for the binoculars. I stroll past Louis Vuitton, McDonald's, and H&M posters, past the Piazza della Riforma, past the lindens and benches of the Riva Albertolli, past tennis courts and a Migros supermarket. Then I'm standing in front of the Hotel Lido Seegarten (back in the world).

my own story

On the terrace of the Lido Seegarten: I've changed my shirt, brushed my teeth, and showered. The sun is setting, the strings of lights are turning on. Your reservation has expired, Elisabeth, but my luggage was waiting for me in a back room. The receptionist asked whether I wanted to stay nonetheless, and I said, if there's a room with a lake view: yes. Over the water there's now a slight haze, the sailboats are rolling gently toward the port. I don't call, I've asked for a large envelope, along with a bottle of Barbaresco. In the water behind the hotel there's a floating dock with green Astroturf, but no one is swimming here this evening, and the pool, too, is deserted. A rat is waiting next to a pot of flowers, in the water a few black plastic ducks are drifting. The Hotel Lido Seegarten really is beautiful, Elisabeth, but it's decaying, as all beautiful things decay (roses, geraniums, plastic deck chairs). Next to me there's a freezer on the cracked tiles, the cord yanked out (here Algida is called Pierrot Lusso, in Hamburg Langnese). I'm alone. He was expecting rain, the sweaty waiter said, as he set the bottle of wine and a scratched silver bowl of nuts on the table in front of me. I remain seated. I ask whether they have the *Süddeutsche Zeitung* here, all of this past week's editions, I have some catching up to do, and the waiter asks, all the editions, Signore Mandelkern? Yes, I say, feeding nuts to the rat. The heron lands very slowly on the floating dock, the beats of its wings calmly stir the air (I've learned to observe such things again). I read my notes, page by page, I sort Svensson's stories between my own pages. I will send you this stack of paper, Elisabeth, I hope you understand me. You wanted a decision. On the table in front of me lie this story and seven postcards.

Acknowledgments

My immense gratitude
Katharina Adler for always being there; Adler & Söhne for every
seventh sentence; Ross Benjamin for his meticulousness and
friendly persistence; Christine Bredenkamp; Erin Edmison for
getting me started in the first place; my thesis advisor Bettina
Friedl for her leniency; Daniela Greven; Josef Haslinger; Patrick
Hutsch; Thomas Janiszewski; Laura Kovero; Benjamin Laut-
erbach; Johann Christoph Maass; Timo Meisel; Mika Jasper
Petersenn; Olaf Petersenn; Jens Pfeifer for his anthropology; my
parents Winfried & Elisabeth Pletzinger for everything; Char-
lotte Roos; Carol Houck Smith for seeing this project through in
the most miraculous ways; Saša Stanišić for his glowing enthusiasm, his assurance, and his stories; Gerald Stern for his poetry
and encouragement; Dieter Wellershoff; Juli Zeh; and finally
and most of all my wife Bine Nordmeyer for her immeasurable
patience (this book is hers).

The work on *Funeral for a Dog* was supported by Kulturstiftung
des Freistaates Sachsen, Sparkassen-Kulturstiftung Rheinland,
and the Max-Kade-Foundation. The translation of this book was
generously supported by the Goethe-Institut's Helen and Kurt
Wolff Translation Grant program.

About the Author

Thomas Pletzinger was born in 1975 and grew up in Germany's industrial area Ruhrgebiet. He holds an MA from Hamburg University and an MFA from the German Literature Institute Leipzig. He has worked for publishers and a literary scouting agency in New York and participated in the University of Iowa's International Writing Program. In 2009, he was Writer-in-Residence at Deutsches Haus at New York University, and in the spring of 2010 he taught at Grinnell College in Iowa. Pletzinger lives in Berlin where he works as a novelist, screenwriter, and translator. He has received various literary awards and fellowships, among them the Uwe-Johnson Prize in 2009 and the NRW Prize for Young Artists. *Funeral for a Dog* is his first novel.

www.thomaspletzinger.com

About the Translator

Ross Benjamin is a writer and translator living in Nyack, New York. He was awarded the 2010 Helen and Kurt Wolff Translator's Prize for his translation of Michael Maar's *Speak, Nabokov* (Verso Books). His other translations include Friedrich Hölderlin's *Hyperion* (Archipelago Books), Kevin Vennemann's *Close to Jedenew* (Melville House), and Joseph Roth's *Job* (Archipelago).

www.rossmbenjamin.com